MW01243710

HIVE QUEEN

Trinity of the Hive (Book Two)

by

Grayson Sinclair

License Notes

Hive Queen (Trinity of the Hive: Book Two)

A Starlit Publishing Book
Published by Starlit Publishing
69 Teslin Rd
Whitehorse, YT
Y1A 3M5
Canada

www.starlitpublishing.com

Ebook ISBN: 9781989994368
Paperback ISBN: 9781989994351
Hardcover ISBN: 9781989994375

Contents

Dedicated to TJ Reynolds

For being the best friend I never knew I needed. Thanks for barging into my life and not giving me a say in being friends.

From where you're kneeling, it must seem like an 18-carat run of bad luck.
Truth is…the game was rigged from the start.
—Benny

CHAPTER 1 - THE CRACKS APPEAR

Sampson

The dead woman in front of me wore a light smirk as I tried and failed to rationalize her resurrection. She was dead, had been dead for centuries, yet here she was, standing in the darkened throne room of the man I considered my enemy.

What the hell is going on? My mind ran through all the possible explanations and came up empty. She walked over to Magnus, her black dress swaying at her ankles, the cracks of her footsteps on the gray stone tile shattered my nerves and sent abject fear coursing through my veins.

"How are you alive?" I stammered.

She refused an answer; instead, she kept her chilling gaze on me as she climbed the obsidian steps, mischievousness sparking from her insectoid eyes. Black and yellow like the stripes on a bee. She stood next to Magnus and draped her arm onto his shoulder. Magnus brushed her fingers affectionately, and only then did she acknowledge me, with an ice-cold smile poised on her pink, cupid's bow lips.

Silence hung in the air as the moonlight cast colorful shadows across the floor from the stained-glass windows above us. I just stared them down until Magnus spoke.

"Aliria, do you plan on enlightening the boy?"

Aliria? So that's her name. But before the words even left her lips, I knew her answer. Her eyes told me she had no intention of illuminating me.

She smiled sweetly at me. "Why would I do that? His utter confusion is so delicious."

Magnus chuckled softly, while I stared dumbstruck at the dead woman.

"Well, Duran, it's not exactly my story to tell. So if it's her wish to keep you in the dark, I shall respect it."

"Yeah, great. Sure. It's not that big of a deal," I said, my voice biting.

Sarcasm was my go-to defense, as if I didn't make light of the situation, I'd likely to run screaming from the room. Aliria was alive, even though I watched her die in the Mnemosyne; she was standing before me. Allied with Magnus, the man who'd brought an army to my home.

"Can someone explain what's going on…please?"

He stayed silent, a bemused grin lifting the corners of his tanned mouth as he watched my meltdown. His shamrock eyes lit the darkness.

"You weren't brought here to listen to a story you haven't earned the right to, you were brought here because I wanted to meet the man who has my daughter so enraptured."

Aliria rose and crossed the room toward me. Her gait was playful and predatory; she was a tiger toying with her meal before she devoured it, and I was the meal.

Despite her devious visage, she was an undeniably beautiful creature, though the resemblance to Eris was enough that it made my heart ache. Her golden hair was much longer than her daughter's and fell past her shoulder blades, though lighter in color and much finer.

Her hair wasn't the only separating distinction. *Eris would never have such cold and callous eyes.* Hers were enchanting, while her mother's terrified me. I'd compared them to a bumblebee's stripes, but that was naïve of me. The woman in front of me was no playful bee; she was a wasp. Angry and mean— and wouldn't hesitate to fuck up my day.

Aliria stopped a foot from me, gazing at me as if she were staring through my very soul. She stood a few inches short of me, which put her almost a foot taller than Eris.

"Caution, knight. This queen is dangerous."

Before I could respond to the Aspect, Aliria reached out and laid a finger on my chest. Right over my heart.

The pain was so sudden, it caught my breath and floored me. I dropped to the floor as torment crawled through my veins and ice stabbed through my brain. The duality of magics flowing through me turned to magma in my veins. I fought for a single breath, just so I could scream.

Then she removed her hand from me, and the pain vanished as swiftly as it arrived.

I gasped for air and rejoiced in the pure bliss of the act. My sweat-stained copper hair fell in my face as blood dripped from my torn lip. I'd accidentally bitten it, and salted iron ran over my tongue.

The stone, cool against my bare fingers, grounded me in the moment. I worked to get myself under control and stumbled up for the floor, glaring murder at Aliria.

"What in the nine hells was that?"

She narrowed her eyes and furrowed her brow, humming to herself under her breath in a low, guttural tone.

I was deathly afraid of her, and it wasn't just my personal fear. The Aspect recoiled from her presence and retreated to the confines of my heart, leaving me alone in a den of wolves.

Aliria spoke, smiling. "Such a waste of a knight. Abominations like you should never be allowed to exist," she said, her voice held delight as she savored each word levied at me.

What? I took a step forward, wanting, needing to understand what she'd said. "Tell me what that means!"

"I don't think so, not yet." Aliria laughed and turned from me, walking back to Magnus.

I didn't let her take another step before I took one of my own and clamped my hand on her shoulder; her sleek black dress balled in my fist as I turned her around to face me. A flash of annoyance marred her face before being replaced by quiet amusement.

"Can I help you, knight?" her voice sweet, a bastardization of Eris's.

"Answer me!"

Her eyes flashed at my outburst, filling with excitement. She moved closer to me, her breath heated as her tongue rolled out, giving me a quick look at her duel sets of elongated canines. Aliria licked her lips with anticipation. And she looked hungry.

"If you wanted to play, you should have just said so!"

She pinned my arms to my sides with enough force that I couldn't attempt to break free. Even with my Strength maxed, I could do nothing as she opened her mouth far too wide and latched onto my neck. Her teeth ripped a chunk from my flesh as she gorged on my blood.

Her saliva mixed with my blood and numbed my skin as she fed. Her tongue lapped up every spilled drop that fled from my body. I fought against her and tried to pry myself free, but it was pointless. I wasn't going anywhere.

I succumbed to the inevitable and let her drink her fill. Magnus watched the scene with fierce interest, leaning forward in his throne with his chin propped under his arms. My voice broke and wheezed as I attempted to speak, so I asked him with my eyes to intervene, but he just continued staring.

My vision grew hazy, and fog filled my thoughts as the blood loss took hold. My skin tingled, and by the time she'd finished, I was barely conscious. Aliria released me, and I slumped to the ground, the stone cold against my feverish cheek. I attempted to stand, but I was weak. Through sheer force of will and indignation, I rose to my feet.

I clenched my teeth, splitting my torn lip even wider as I bared my teeth in rage. *She has no right to my blood, to my memories!*

Magnus frowned at Aliria, a reproachful gaze, which she shrugged off. I knew that she would go unpunished for her vile intrusion, and fire roiled in my chest. *Let's see how you like it. Show me what you refuse to tell!*

I initiated *Dance of the Immortal,* and the world slowed to a standstill. Magnus sat on his throne, staring at Aliria as she froze mid-step, her foot an inch from the floor. I raced for her, my teeth bared to sink into her ivory skin.

The snap of fingers stopped me in my tracks.

The hell? I couldn't move my body from the neck down. I turned back to the throne. Magnus was no longer staring at Aliria, he was looking dead at me.

He smiled at me and rose from his throne, taking his time down the steps. Before he landed on the final step, he held his hand aloft and from nowhere, an ivory cane appeared in his hands as he stepped off the last stygian step. I'd seen the cane before; it was the same one Liam wielded when we fought.

"*Dance of the Immortal.* A neat parlor trick," he said as he reached me.

Magnus leaned against his cane, his eyes flicking up and down, taking me in. He held up his left arm and tapped a phantom wristwatch. "Five, four, three, two, one." He counted down the seconds till *Dance* timed out, but as he reached one, *Dance of the Immortal* stayed active.

He let his arm fall and titled his head back to me. "I understand your anger, Duran. I do. Aliria was out of line, and that's my fault. I let her have her way far too often. Still, you are a guest in my castle, and it was incredibly rude for her to behave that way.

"So I'm going to overlook your attempt to harm her, though I strongly caution you not to try it again if I were you."

With a nod, the paralysis on my body vanished, and I could move again, though the world was still awash with gray. *How is this possible? Dance should've timed long ago.*

"How are you doing this?"

He shrugged and turned, walking back to his throne, the dark mantling of his cloak slapping against his emerald tunic. As he sat back down, he snapped his fingers and *Dance* shattered.

My battle fatigue rose to nearly max, and exhaustion sunk into my muscles, robbing my already-fading strength. I sank to my knee as sweat ran in rivulets down my forehead, dripping into my eyes.

Aliria glanced back at me with delight in her eyes. "I guess you were about to try something foolish."

"He was, though you deserve a bit of foolishness. Try to refrain from harming our guest going forward." Magnus glanced down at me, nearly collapsed from blood loss and fatigue. "Ah, let me ease your discomfort."

Another snap, and my exhaustion vanished in an instant. Strength returned to my limbs, and my battle fatigue dropped to zero. I was back in perfect condition, and I had no idea how it was possible.

"There, good as new," Magnus said with a wry grin. "Now that our little drama has ended, I'd like to invite you to dinner."

"It's midnight."

"I'll see you in an hour, then."

Without another word, he stood and strolled out of the throne room, Aliria nipping at his heels. As the door to the throne room opened, the maid who'd led me here was waiting patiently outside the door, her russet hair covering the side of her face.

Aliria looked at me with a dark grin. "If you need anything before dinner, just ask Jasmine. She's programmed to receive."

Then she was gone, and I was left standing in the hallway of a strange place, and my only company was a maid. *Yeah, that's about par for the course with my life lately.*

"Follow me."

Jasmine escorted me back through the maze of identical hallways to my room, and even I had to admit, it was the nicest prison cell I'd ever been in. Expensive wooden furniture and a bed big enough to fit half a dozen full-grown men. *Magnus hasn't said it, hasn't even come close to saying it, but I'm a prisoner here.* I was held here against my will, by his mere presence, for I could do little else.

I walked over to the bed and sat down, sinking deep into its luxurious softness. The dark comforter was like lying on a cloud, and I hated it. The bed was far too comfortable. *I'll never be able to get any sleep on it.* But it was only half because of the bed.

Gods, I miss Eris. We didn't get to spend hardly any time together on the road, and now this. Seems like months since I've seen her.

Out of habit, I checked our connection. *She's sound asleep, dreaming deeply.* It wasn't much, but the fact she was safe and sleeping comfortably was a huge relief. Muscles I didn't even know were tense uncoiled themselves, and relief eased my troubled mind.

Now that my guard was lowered, I took note of my body—namely, my stomach. It screamed in protest, probably thinking my throat had been cut.

I tried to put my hunger out of mind and went to wash up. The only other door in the room led to a bathroom, and I just stared in amazement. *If I thought the bathroom I'd built was large before, I'll need to reevaluate.* To call it a bath was laughable, as it was the size of a swimming pool and sank deep into the floor.

Whereas my bathroom was all stone, Magnus had a flair for the ostentatious, floor to ceiling wood, vibrant hues of chestnut through mahogany. The warm air hit me as I stepped through the door.

Magnus knows how to impress; I'll give him that. The steam rising off the water in the bath was tantalizing, too much for me to resist. Even if I was clean, the hot water would help ease my apprehension.

I stripped out of my extravagant clothes, tossed them aside and walked down the steps to bask in the heat that licked my skin with the perfect amount of warmth.

I'm surprised Magnus had the foresight to set the temperature ahead of time, but with Aliria around, he's probably well-versed in entomancer body heat.

"Shit." *Eris isn't going to take the news of her mother being alive very well.*

From what she told me, Eris and her mother hadn't had the easiest relationship. Her family had caused so much pain in her life, but never again.

She's a threat, and I don't care that she's Eris's mother. I'll kill Aliria if it means protecting Eris.

Assuming I even can.

I waded through the chest-high water to reach a shelf on the far wall. It was laden down with all manner of soaps and wash rags. I picked one at random and set about scrubbing myself clean. I ran soap through my hair and looked around for a brush to help detangle a few knots that had accrued. I searched in vain. *My brush is with the rest of my supplies back at Gloom-Harbor. I'm defenseless here. Well, almost.* Even if I didn't have my gear, I still had my class Abilities.

I pulled up my character page.

Character Name: Durandahl
Level: 51
Exp: 4100/5100
Race: Hybrid (Hive)
Class: Hive Knight
Reputation: Wanted Criminal
Bounty: 1300 Gold

Stats (-)
Strength: 100 (80)
Sub-Stats (-)
Attack Damage: 30
Constitution: 100 (80)
Sub-Stats (-)
Health: 25
Health Regen: 25
Durability: 15

Endurance: 75 (50)

Sub-Stats (-)

Battle Fatigue: 10

Battle Fatigue Regen: 10

Agility: 50 (30)

Sub-Stats (-)

Attack Speed: 15

Movement Speed: 10

Wisdom: 25 (5)

Sub-Stats (-)

Mana: 20

Luck: 0 (10)

Charisma: 0 (0)

Proximity to Hive Queen greater than 100 meters

Penalty Active (-20 to all Main Stats)

No wonder I was so weak against Aliria! I forgot about the penalty when I'm not close by Eris. Damn, this puts me at a heavy disadvantage, though none of my sub-stats were affected. That's some good news.

The soap suds in my hair slid down my face and stung my eyes. I dunked my head under the water and rinsed them from my strands. When I came back up from the water and brushed my sopping hair from my face. I wasn't alone in the bath any longer.

Jasmine had slunk into the room without my notice, betraying either her level of talent or my ability to be completely oblivious to my surroundings. I was betting on the former.

She stood at around my chin, which would put her at around an inch or two over five and a half feet. Her auburn hair stopped just below her chin, barely licking at her throat. She stared at me with large, honey brown eyes that darkened in the steam.

And to top it all off, she was naked as the day she was born.

Her body was slender, yet toned, her rich, tawny skin complex. Pale hues of brown beaded with sweat as steam drifted past. Her breasts were larger than average and ever so slightly uneven. Her dark nipples stiffened, despite the heat. I dropped my gaze quickly, only to see a neatly trimmed patch of brown hair just below her waist.

She stood under my gaze with calm indifference, as if she didn't care that she was baring herself to a complete stranger and lowered into the bath.

"Jasmine, what do you think you're doing?"

Her voice was soft and warm, yet robotic. "I was ordered to tend to your every want and desire, as commanded by Mistress Aliria."

"Did she tell you to undress yourself?"

"Of course."

I sighed. *I should've figured she'd try something like this. Testing the new boyfriend as it were.*

I backed away from the young woman, as pretty as she was, she was nothing to me, and she didn't even register.

"Well, please dress yourself. Your services aren't required."

Jasmine nodded to me and exited the bath to my relief. My libido notwithstanding, I didn't have any desire to feed into whatever game Aliria was playing.

I finished cleaning myself and dried off with the fluffiest towel I'd ever seen, before tying it around my waist. I made my way over to the nightstand and withdrew several of the outfits, trying to find the one I wanted to wear.

Not that my attire mattered much, but taking a few extra moments to dress properly wouldn't be the worst idea. *Not when Magnus is playing gatekeeper.*

I chose an ivory tunic with a matching set of pants. The white soothed me. I tended to stay away from white clothing as I found myself in far too many fights for me to have any hope of keeping them clean. The white looked nice, and I reasoned I couldn't get into much trouble at dinner. As I dressed, they clung to my frame perfectly.

I tied my still damp hair back and moved to open the door. Jasmine was waiting outside. Although having been in the bath with me not ten minutes ago, she was dressed immaculately in her maid uniform, not a hair out of place.

She curtsied politely upon seeing me. "Is there anything you require, My Lord?"

"Could you not call me Lord for starters?"

"No, My Lord."

Of course she'd be difficult.

I sighed, leaning against the door frame. Jasmine blocked the door, preventing me from exiting without pushing past her. A prospect I considered for a brief moment before reconsidering—there was something about the young girl that unsettled me. I had a feeling there was more to her than appeared, and I might bite off more than I could chew by resorting to violence.

Look how well your first attempt went. What is with the people here? Is everyone in this damn castle a badass?

Regardless of any of that, she may have been just a maid, but she was still a woman and had offered me no reason to be untoward to her.

"Is dinner ready yet?" I asked, my stomach rumbling.

Jasmine shook her head. "Not just yet, My Lord. However, I do believe Magnus is having a drink in the dining hall. If you'd like to join him, I can escort you."

It beats standing in this doorway, twiddling my thumbs. I inclined my head to her. "Be my guest."

Without another word, she turned on her heels and proceeded to walk down the hallway. We walked in silence through the identical halls. I tried again to keep track, but they all looked the same. The same gray stone, even the same number of doors and torches along the walls. It was maddening.

To break up the silence, I tried small talk, which I hated, but I still tried to make some attempt at conversation.

"How old are you, Jasmine?"

"Eighteen."

"Have you been here long?"

"All of my life."

"Do you have any hobbies?"

"No."

Well, I tried. After that, I stopped attempting to befriend the strange girl. It seemed a pointless waste of breath, and these weren't the questions I really wanted answered. Magnus was the one I needed answers from.

It took us around five minutes of walking through the twisting halls before we reached another unmarked door. How Jasmine was able to tell the doors apart from one another in a place this massive was beyond me, but if she had spent her entire life here, I guess she had ample time.

She opened the door, and with a bow, she bade me to enter.

"Thank you, Jasmine."

"Of course, My Lord."

Jasmine shut the door behind me, and I went alone to face Magnus.

The dining hall was comparably muted to the rest of the extravagance in the castle. An equal mixture of dark stone and wood filled the room. Stone floor and ceilings, with wooden support beams along the walls that formed rows of archways. Wide-open windows let in soft cool light along with a gentle warm breeze. From a glance as I passed by the window, I spied the deep sand dunes of the Badlands in the distance.

That puts this castle on the furthest edge of the Isle of Nexus, past the ruins of Machine City and into some truly dangerous territory.

I was distracted from gazing out the window by the clink of glass on wood. I turned to find Magnus drinking alone at the head of a large banquet table. Two long rows of chairs sat unoccupied. Magnus had just finished a large drink and spoke to another one of his maid staff. It wasn't Jasmine, but it could've been her mother. She had the same skin tone and hair color, if longer and pulled back out of her face.

As I approached, Magnus stopped whatever he had been saying to the woman and acknowledged my presence.

"Ah, Duran, would you like a drink before dinner?"

"Sure."

He nodded. "Magnolia, please uncork another bottle of wine if you don't mind, and whatever our esteemed guest would like."

"Of course, Master. Another bottle of the surilie?"

"Please."

Magnolia turned her attention from Magnus to me. Her darkened eyes were waiting. When I didn't immediately respond, she cleared her throat and spoke. "And for you, My Lord?"

"Oh, uh, ale," I said.

"Any particular?"

"Surprise me."

Magnolia nodded and exited the dining hall. Leaving us alone with each other. I just stood there in front of the table, not so sure of what to do with myself. Magnus took note of this and chuckled. "Come now, Duran, I won't bite. Sit down and share a drink with me; it might surprise you to learn I don't get to do this very often."

I find that hard to believe. As much power as you wield, I imagine there isn't much you couldn't do. I kept my thoughts to myself, but raised an eyebrow, a frown formed as I stared at him.

He grinned wide at my expression. The tanned skin of his face only brought out the sharp white of his teeth.

"I imagine you could get anyone you wanted to have a drink with you," I said.

Magnus threw back his head and laughed. The much-needed sound broke the tension in the air. I chuckled myself; his laugh was infectious. I pulled out one of the heavy oak chairs and sat down next to him.

He spoke through his laughter. "Much as you might be right about that, it's rare that I have anyone other than my servants or Aliria to drink with me, certainly not someone I could treat as an equal."

I scoffed. "Equals, not hardly."

He just laughed harder at my words, thumping his empty wine glass on the table in the process. "Ah, dear boy, maybe not in terms of wealth or power, but those are trivial matters. You have tenacity and strength of spirit. Things neither money nor power can purchase."

I didn't get a chance to respond to his words, as the door to the hall was thrust open. Aliria strode through, followed by Magnolia carrying our drinks.

"Ah, I figured I would find you here…and Duran is here too, lovely."

Well, it was a nice evening while it lasted.

I inclined my head to our new arrival. To which she just smiled at me. A wicked grin that showcased her prominent sets of canines. "How was your bath?" Aliria asked.

"Not as quiet as I'd have liked, but I made do."

What the hell is your game, Aliria?

She frowned at my words. "Did you not like my present?"

"It was unnecessary."

Magnolia came and poured Magnus another glass of wine, and a rich aroma spilled out of the bottle. She filled his glass to the brim, to which Magnus drank deeply. She then set down a large mug of ale in front of me.

It was a perfect golden brown and had a good head to it. I took a long pull, savoring the richness on my tongue. The sweetness of the malt was accented perfectly by the hint of bitterness on the back of my tongue. It was a full-bodied drink, and it went down far too smoothly.

Magnolia noted my appreciation for the booze with the hint of a smile. "Would you like another, My Lord?"

"If it wouldn't be too much trouble," I told her.

Magnus, who has been occupied with his wine, finished off his glass and joined the conversation. "Aliria...what did you do to the poor boy?"

Aliria laughed at Magnus's reproachful tone. "Nothing much, I just sent Jasmine to entertain our guest."

Magnolia accidentally knocked over my empty glass as she attempted to pick it up. "Sorry, My Lord," she apologized.

"Don't worry about it."

Magnus's humor fled as he gave Aliria a withering glare. "Jasmine is far too young for such things."

"Morrigan's feathers, you should stop treating her like a child. She's older than I was when I was bonded, you know."

"And look how well that turned out." I turned to Magnolia. "So that you know, I didn't lay a finger on her. My heart belongs to another."

Magnolia unclenched her fingers from the mug and gave me an appreciative smile. It smoothed the lines in her forehead and under her eyes, making her look years younger.

Aliria just rolled her eyes at my words. "I'll never understand you humans and your desire to shackle yourself to a single person. It's unnatural."

"Says the woman who murdered her own husband."

"I had my reasons."

Because you enjoyed it, you sick monster. The memories of the Mnemosyne were vivid, and I had witnessed up close the delight and the bloodlust on Aliria's face as she brutalized her husband. He'd been a bastard, scum who treated his family like objects and bargaining chips. I'd have killed him in a heartbeat and slept soundly, but I wouldn't have enjoyed his death. I wouldn't have reveled it as she had.

I slammed my fist down on the table. "Bullshit! I saw what you did to him. You took pleasure in killing him; you ripped him to pieces!"

Aliria's eyes widened, for the first time since I'd met her, she looked shocked. Something had surprised her. Her surprise twisted into a black grin. The yellow of her eyes lit up with dark delight.

She relaxed her shoulders and glided towards me, and she moved to pull out the chair next to Magnus and me. "Well, well, well. Someone has been a naughty boy. Your memories didn't show me that. If you've experienced that particular memory, that means you've tasted of my little Eris. Tsk, tsk."

Shame and heat flushed through my face. I couldn't deny it, I had drunk of Eris, had tasted of her flesh and blood. The mere memory of it sent waves of revulsion through me. I'd scarred her. Even if I'd never meant to hurt her.

The heat of my face was plain as day. Aliria laughed at my reaction.

17

"Oh, wipe that look off your face. I'm not judging you. It's quite all right. It's natural for entomancers to partake of our bonded."

I wanted to say something, but she'd left me with nothing to say. She didn't seem to care about the fact I'd drunk her daughter's blood. She just wanted to watch me squirm. *She hasn't even mentioned Eris except as a jab at me, hasn't once asked after her daughter's well-being. She's one cold bitch.*

My retort to her was put on hold as Magnolia entered back into the dining hall, carrying a tray laden down with drinks. Magnolia wasn't alone, as several more men and women swept into the room. From the style of dress, I assumed it was the cook and their staff.

They brought carts heaped with platters of food. Almost every kind of food I could've imagined wheeled out. Plates piled high with chicken, fish, roasted pig, and steaks. Along with steamed vegetables and potatoes. Several soups and salads, as well as a tray of different loaves of bread and jars of butter. It was an extravagant feast, and the sound my stomach made was audible to the whole of the hall.

They arranged the carts in front of us, and the staff served us a little bit of everything. I was eying the boar steak like a thief eyes a noble's purse, but I held back from snatching at the food like a savage. I could wait a few moments more and dine like a gentleman.

Magnolia set down another ale in front of me. As she placed it on the table, she leaned down and, so quiet I almost missed it, whispered. "Thank you."

Then she stood up as if nothing had happened and continued to serve our table their drinks. Magnus gleefully accepted more wine; from the slight flush of his cheeks, I'd say he was tipsy. Magnolia sat down the decanter, filled with the strange liquid, next to Aliria, who was looking at the container with anticipation. My curiosity got the better of me, and I had to ask.

"What is that?"

Aliria licked her lips, her long tongue dancing across her teeth. She picked up the decanter and poured a generous measure of the drink into a wine glass next to her and brought the glass to her lips, taking a long drink before looking at me and answering my question. "It's bloodwine. Would you like some?"

"Too strong for my taste. I prefer hard liquor."

"Hmm, you don't know what you're missing—or perhaps you've just developed a taste for my daughter's blood instead, is that it?"

Her words sent rage and disgust rolling through me. In the back of my mind, I knew she was just goading me, looking to get a rise out of me, but I couldn't take the callous disregard of Eris any longer. I bolted out of my chair to jab my finger at Aliria. "You don't know what the fuck you're talking about!"

Magnus looked up from the bottom of his wineglass at the hostility in the room. He didn't look upset; instead, he wore a grin on his face and spoke up as Magnolia poured him yet another glass of wine. "Now look what you've done, Aliria. Did you have to provoke him like that?"

Aliria smiled wide. "Of course I did. He's bonded to my daughter, after all. I must see what the little abomination is made of."

Magnus nodded his head and returned to his drinking with a murmur. "Well, I won't interfere with a family dispute; just don't make me break up a fight."

Before his words, I'd been ready to stab Aliria, and my hand gripped the handle of my steak knife so tight, my knuckles stretched white over the skin. *Calm yourself. This is what she wants, and besides that, I can't take both of them, maybe not even one of them. Not to mention my lack of weapons. This isn't the time to lose control.*

I brought the calm and collected logic to soothe the coals of my rage. While not dousing them completely, my rage had subsided into mere embers rather than the raging inferno. I turned to Aliria. "That's the second time you've called me that. I'll bite. Why am I an abomination?"

Aliria cocked her head to the side, a gesture so like Eris, it hurt. She reached out with her hand and pointed at my chest. "Do you not feel the magic within you?"

"Of course."

I couldn't not, even now. It writhed and swirled in the ruins of where my once human heart had been. The Aspect never rested; it pulsed constant in my veins.

"You shouldn't exist. My careless daughter, through her ignorance, created you, a creature that the previous generations of Hive would have killed on sight."

"I don't understand?"

She sighed. "Let me put it another way. Why do you think I killed my bondmate?"

"Because you're a cold-hearted bitch?"

Magnus spit out his wine and devolved into a fit of raucous laughter. He giggled to himself and tried to drink more wine, which sloshed around in the glass from his shaking hand. "He has you on that one."

"Are you not supposed to be on my side?"

"Oh, I am, darling, but even you have to admit: it's true."

Aliria growled, knocked back the rest of her bloodwine, and motioned to Magnolia to pour her another. "Be as that may, that's not the point I was trying to make.

"All entomancers, and the other races to a lesser degree, have access to the Hive magic. They are only scratching at the surface, and only a few can handle the process to connect to the Hive on a deeper level. Namely, the Hive Monarch and their knights."

"Me?"

"Yes, you. The first human Hive Knight in existence."

Ah, I'm just a filthy human, not worthy of being with her daughter. I jabbed my fork at Aliria. "So that's why you're calling me an abomination, because I'm not one of your precious Hive?"

Her eyes flickered with surprised amusement, and she let out a quiet laugh as sharp as her cheekbones.

"Oh, little one, I couldn't care less about you being human. I never had conflict with your species. No, that's not what makes you an abomination."

By the nine kings of hell, quit dancing around the question and spit it out already!

I'd had enough of her antics. "Answer the question!"

Aliria sighed, a deep, disappointed sigh, signaling I was ruining her game. *Too bad.*

"You're no fun at all, but fine, I'll tell you," she said, taking another drink of wine. "The Hive magic inside you isn't what make you different, but when you freed my daughter from her prison, she was bound to you through black magic. That sliver of magic is what makes you an abomination, as the two were never supposed to coexist."

Her words troubled me, but beyond that, I didn't know what to make of them. I took my time pondering the implications as I ate. The boar steak, my favorite food, cooked to absolute perfection, crumbled to ash in my mouth. I chewed through it anyway; if nothing else, to give me time to think. I swallowed a few mouthfuls of the meat and washed it down with another gulp of ale, which, thank the gods, still tasted sweet.

I remembered the pain I was forced to endure, the agony of my heart being ripped to shreds by the war of the two magics, and when Eris told me of the Aspect, she had mentioned it was acting unusual, so her words made sense. But beyond that, I think I knew all along. *Ever since I became the Hive Knight, the Aspect's had a hold on me, twisting me into something dark.*

Aliria smiled. "But you've known, haven't you? You can feel the Aspect inside your mind, driving you, pushing your anger and rage."

"How did you know that?"

"Because I was once like you."

"I don't understand?" I replied.

"You wouldn't know this, but the black magic that cursed my daughter to her prison and bound the two of you together is a much stronger version of the bonding magic the Hive used to bind our partners together. Though, because of the nature of the spell, you have it far worse than I did."

Son of a bitch. I understood the meaning of her words now. All this roundabout speak was leading me to the only conclusion available. I drained the rest of my ale, though it too was losing its flavor. My stomach was in knots. Magnolia was there to hand me another mug of ale, but I held off.

Eris told me once that the females were considered the property of the males, but what Aliria was saying was much worse than that. If they used a form of black magic to bind them, then the females were literally slaves. Eris and I were bound through the black magic, and then we'd bound ourselves together through the bonding ritual.

Not to mention Ouroboros's influence, turning me into the Hive Knight. Yeah, after all that and the Aspect, I'd consider myself an abomination too. So that explains Aliria's behavior in the Mnemosyne.

"You killed your husband to remove the magic that bound you together."

Aliria smiled and laughed, a true laugh that held none of her earlier bitterness. It was throatier, but her sing-song musical laugh was very much the same as Eris's. She kept up her laugh and looked at me in a new light. "You're not as inept as I first thought."

Magnus let out a disjointed bark that I took to be laughter. His eyes glazed over, and he swayed in his chair, which looked ready to topple to the floor at any moment. "See, A-Aliria…told you he was c-c-lever."

Least I have the drunk's vote of confidence. At the sight of Magnus deep in his cups, Aliria scowled, which, strangely, fit her face better than if she were laughing. I could handle it better than her friendly laughter. "Dear, I think you've had enough to drink this evening."

"Psh, no, you're…you're ridiculous." He turned to me and breathed heavily as he tried to speak, his wine-soaked breath pungent even from where I was sitting. "Hey, Duran, you tell her I'm still good to go!"

"Sorry, Magnus, but you're trashed."

At this, Magnus stopped. He had been reaching for the next bottle of wine on the table, but hearing my words, he put down the bottle and seemed to consider what I'd said. He looked down at himself for a moment. "Hmm, it seems you are both correct. I am quite…how did you put it? Oh, yes. Trashed."

I laughed a bit, and the heavy tension between Aliria and me seemed to abate for the time, as we both had to deal with a drunk Magnus. "It's okay. Happens to the best of us. All you need is a little time to sober up."

Magnus's eyes glinted—something I said was funny to him. "You're quite right about that; I just need to sober up is all." He raised his hand and snapped his fingers. It cracked through the hall, echoing around before sinking into the heavy stone walls.

What the actual hell? In the span of half a second, Magnus had rid himself of his drunken stupor. Before, stood a sloppy drunk with glazed eyes and a bright red face. Now stood the man I had met in the throne room. His sandy hair swept out of his eyes, which stared at me, alert and with intent.

"How?" I asked.

He smiled wide at me, a knowing grin, but one that wouldn't let slip his secrets easily. "It's bad form to ask a player about their class, and besides, that would be telling."

He had me on that one, but still. "Oh, come on, you're doing things that should be impossible. I don't think game etiquette really applies here!"

Aliria interrupted me. "I'd save your breath; he wouldn't tell me either. I had to figure it out myself, though if you guess right, he'll tell you."

I sighed as a headache crept in. *Dealing with these two will drive me up the wall.* "With how infuriating you both are, you guys are made for each other."

At that, both Aliria and Magnus smiled at each other, a gesture so different than what I'd come to expect from them, it put me off. It was a look of affection between two lovers, two people who cared dearly for one another. A look I knew well.

Aliria's hardened features softened as she spoke. "Well, we've had plenty of time to get used to each other." She reached across the table and took hold of Magnus's hand, to which he responded with an affectionate squeeze. "That we have, love. That we have. A hundred years, and its flown by so fast."

Their clear adoration for each other only made my longing worse. It hurt to be away from Eris, and to see such love only drove it home.

I was so lost in thought that what Magnus said hadn't really registered. And then it crashed into me as my brain caught up to what he had said. *A hundred years? Has Magnus lost it?*

"Hey, Magnus, you might want to check your math. We haven't been here thirty years yet, let alone a hundred," I said.

Magnus shifted his gaze from Aliria to me, and his eyes went from lovelorn to filled with sorrow in an instant. They held an emotion I couldn't place, sadness and regret perhaps. It, more than anything else Magnus had done, frightened me.

"Oh, dear boy, you don't know, do you?"

"Know what?"

He sighed deeply; it sank my heart to hear, and the heartbeat between his sigh and his words stretched on forever. After a lifetime, he spoke again.

"We haven't been in the Ouroboros Project for twenty-nine years, Duran. We've been here for over a thousand."

Chapter 2 - Alone

Eris

The early morning light hit my eyes and woke me. I groaned, not wanting to get up, but I was cold and hungry, and I really needed to pee. I blinked my eyes, but they were heavy and didn't want to cooperate with me. After I wiped the sleep from them, I rolled over.

The stone ceiling above me wasn't the same as the one in Sam's room, which confused me for a moment before I remembered. I was in the guest bedroom. I sat up from the comfy pillows I'd been lying on and noticed Tegen and Cheira huddled together against my side, their fine brown hair a chaotic mess.

They'd clung to me ever since Sam saved them from the slavers. *I know they're still frightened about being near humans, but I do hope they'll come out of their shells a bit more. They'll be scared of humans forever at this rate.*

Though, those two weren't the only ones who needed to be open-minded. *Sam's kept his distance from the spiderlings. I know he's afraid of spiders, but he's an adult. He can afford to be more open.*

Thinking about Sam brought a smile to my lips. I hadn't spent much time alone with him in the last few days. *Which is my own fault.* I'd spent the entire trip back to Gloom-Harbor with the little ones. Neither of them liked being alone and were so wary of Sam and the rabbitmen that they'd refused to talk to anyone but me.

"We'll just have to change that. All right, time to get up and start the day!"

I sat up off the comfy bed reached over to shake the children. Tegen's eyes jumped open at my touch, but he smiled when he saw it was me. "Time to get up, Tegen," I said.

"It's too early, just a few more minutes," he mumbled.

"You don't want to sleep the day away, do you now? Come on, wake up your sister, and let's go get breakfast!"

Tegen just rolled over and cuddled up with Cheira. I smiled at his back. *I guess it won't hurt anything to let them sleep in, and there isn't anything important to do today anyway.*

That and it would give me plenty of time to bathe and get myself ready. I didn't have any of my clothes in the room with me, but Sam had cleared a bunch of space in his wardrobe for me, which I appreciated. It was kind of him to turn his bedroom into our room.

I opened the heavy oak door that led out into the hallway, the guest room was located on the top floor of the castle with everyone else's bedrooms, but it was also the furthest from Sam's room. I shut the door as quietly as I could; the spiderlings would sleep through a thunderstorm, but I didn't want to wake any of the guild if I could help it.

They've all been very gracious to accept me into their home. I know Sam's the leader, but everyone's been very welcoming. I made my way through the hall as quiet as I could, though the thick red rug that lined the entire hallway made it very easy. My bare feet enjoyed the plush carpet under them.

I reached the door to the room and was just about to go inside when footsteps rose from the stairwell. They were light and padded, muffled by the stone walls. Almost as soon as I heard the steps, I wrinkled my nose. The rough stench of water, moss, and fungus tinged my nostrils. It was the smell of Lake Gloom. *Strange, who'd be at the lake at this hour?*

A second later, a thin man with long shaggy brown hair walked up the stairs. His hair was so thick and unruly that I couldn't even see his eyes, though he could see me. He smiled when he noticed me, waving.

"Ah, good morning, Eris. I hope fortune finds you well, and may your skies never darken."

"Good morning to you too, Markos. How are you today?" I asked. I didn't really understand his words, but they were meant with sincerity, and that was good enough for me.

"The Fates have found me in fine health this morning, is Duran up yet? Miguel and his crew just finished unloading our profits and picked up their shipment of mushrooms. Duran told me to tell him when the *Delilah* arrived."

Ah, that explains the smell. I shook my head. "I'm not sure if he's up yet, I was just going to see him and get a bath. Would you like me to get him for you?"

Markos shook his head, "Oh, no, it's not that important. He can deal with the coin at his leisure today or tomorrow, though I'm sure Wilson would insist it being today."

I pressed down the brass handle and kept my voice low. "I'll let him know, I promise."

"Thank you. May the light always find you smiling."

"The same to you." Markos was a strange man, but he was an easy person to like. I nodded my goodbye to him and stepped inside.

Sam wasn't in bed. His bed was unmade, and the pillows were strewn all over it. His fluffy crimson blanket was halfway off the bed.

I chuckled at the sight. *Sam never makes his bed. I'll have to try and break that bad habit.* A bed should always be made properly each morning. Well, I could at least make the bed for him in the meantime. It wouldn't take long. I busied myself with the task. *The sheets are dirty and will need to be washed before we leave for the Silvanus Darkwoods.*

My heart swelled at the prospect. *There are still some Hive left.* I couldn't fight the wide smile that tore at the corners of my mouth, and I hummed while I worked.

I'm not alone anymore! I tried to keep up a brave face for Sam, but some nights I could still hear the call of the void, and I knew it would never truly leave me.

Sam was the only reason I hadn't succumbed to my misery, but the fact that there were others of the Hive sent my head spinning. I went to head into the bathroom when I noticed the door to his balcony was open. *Is he outside?*

I walked onto the balcony to find it empty. There was nothing out here but a large crystal bottle, half-filled with amber liquid. I picked it up and took a sniff. The sharp medicinal scent burned my nose and made me want to sneeze. *Why would Sam leave his liquor lying on the floor? He's lucky it didn't break.* I didn't know what to make of it. Sam was usually a neat person; he wouldn't just leave something lying around to get damaged or lost.

Well, he's not in bed, and he's not on the balcony, maybe he's bathing? That thought brought a smile to my face. We hadn't shared much intimacy with the children around, and while I had to take care of them first. I missed Sam's touch. I crept to the door and opened it as slowly as I could, wanting to surprise him.

As I opened the door, I was met with silence. The clear absence of the room told me Sam wasn't here either. I couldn't stop the smile from falling from my face. I wanted to spend some alone time with him. *I don't know why, but I'm starting to feel uneasy.* But I was being ridiculous; Sam was just downstairs getting breakfast.

I could've used our bond to check on him, but Sam valued his privacy. He wouldn't say it, but I know he didn't like it when I abused our connection.

Even if I can't share it with him, I still need to bathe. We could always take one together later, after all. I stepped over to the edge of the bath and stripped out of my shirt. I sat down on the lip and stuck my feet in the water. The heat was wondrous. Sam had increased the temperature of the water, and steam rose off it to swirl about in the air. It floated towards me and was blown away when I breathed out.

I stayed there for a few more minutes, staring off into space and daydreaming, the shimmer of the water along the walls made getting lost in thought easy here. I had to quit when my stomach growled with hunger.

I lowered down into the bath, the water came up almost to my neck. The bath was built for Sam, who was a bit taller than me. At least it didn't swallow me completely, though if I were any shorter, it would. I proceeded to wash myself clean. As the soap ran over my pale skin, hints of vanilla, lavender, and cherry stuck to me. It smelled like Sam, which sent my heart fluttering.

I washed the sweat from the night before from my skin and let the water carry the suds away. *I wonder how the bath stays clean?* Sam said he had help from Adam in building it, but I hadn't the first clue how it worked. Sam told me Adam was a genius with building things, but I couldn't begin to understand how he did it.

When my hair was clean, I grabbed the washrag floating in the water and cleaned my ears. They needed extra attention, and I would need to see if Sam had any oil I could rub on them. They dried out and flaked easily if I didn't take care of them.

I looked through the rack, but there was nothing there. I didn't expect there to be, but Sam was very hygienic and kept himself clean, so I was hoping. *I guess I could ask Makenna or Evelyn if they have any. Yumiko also takes good care of herself, but I'd rather not ask her.*

I wouldn't bother the vampire unless I didn't have a choice. *Maybe Sam isn't the only one who needs to get past his prejudices?* I had a strong distaste of the nocturnals, but I could do with being more tolerant of them. Or Yumiko, at least.

My rumbling stomach screamed for attention, and so I unwillingly climbed out of the bath. My hair was still soaking wet, and it kept getting in my face. *I wonder if Sam keeps an extra hair tie around somewhere?*

I padded over to the washbasin next to the bath. The gray stone was cool to the touch. It was nice after the heat from the bath. The steam made me lightheaded. The mirror had fogged over, so I wiped it clear with my hand. My reflection stared back at me. The pale skin of my face was red with the heat of the bath.

My dark blonde hair even darker and heavy with water, it streamed down my face to drip onto the floor. My black eyes stared back at me. I'd always hated them because they were so different than the others. Everyone else got pretty rainbow colors, and I got stuck with the ugly black ones. Father hated them and would insult them whenever he could. But that was then.

I don't mind them so much anymore; they have a depth to them that the others of my kind didn't have.

It took time, but I was coming to accept and even enjoy the previous aspects about myself that I once hated. Though as I stared down at my breasts, I still wished they were a bit bigger, even if Sam liked them. I grabbed a towel and dried and brushed my hair. There wasn't a hair tie on the basin, just more soap and Sam's razor. With the towel wrapped around me, I left the bathroom and went to get dressed.

I placed the towel in the wicker hamper by the bathroom door and went searching for a hair tie. The first place I searched was the wardrobe, but I didn't have any luck. There were several sets of armor and my chestplate in the top, along with our casual clothes in the bottom drawers, but no hair ties. Since I was over here, I picked out what clothes I wanted to wear.

Sam bought me plenty of outfits to wear, as well as several matching skirts, I didn't really see the need to wear them, but Sam was adamant about it. At least he didn't make me wear shoes. I hated shoes with a passion. Nothing but cramped, sweaty toe prisons, and I'd had enough of prison to last several lifetimes.

I picked up one of my newest shirts. It was a deep burgundy color with a high collar that clasped around my throat. *I might just leave it unbuttoned, though.* I slid it on and tried to find a matching skirt. I had several ones that would work, and I decided on a black one that stopped mid-thigh. I had a longer skirt, but I preferred the short one.

"If I'm forced to wear one, I'm going to wear the one that covers me as much as absolutely necessary and not an inch more."

When I was dressed, I checked the last place I could find a hair tie, the nightstand. I opened the top drawer to find it dominated by pieces of wood in disarray, along with a set of knives and odd instruments. There was a rather large piece of wood that looked to be in the process of being carved. I picked it up and turned it over.

I gasped in surprise. It was me. A tiny, incredibly detailed statue of me, down to my eyes and ears. It was carved with loving detail and could only be from someone who loved the subject. I couldn't stop the few tears that fell from my eyes, nor from my heart straining against my ribcage like it was going to burst from my chest. *It's beautiful, Sam. Thank you.*

I set the sculpture back in the drawer carefully as not to damage it in the slightest. I didn't want him to know that I'd seen it; I would have to act surprised when he showed it to me. Just thinking about it brought more emotion welling up, so I doubted it would be too difficult.

As I shut the top drawer and opened the second one, I found it was filled with Sam's underwear neatly organized by color, mostly hues of black and gray with some dark reds sprinkled in. A quick glance told me what I was looking for wasn't here. I shut the drawer and opened the last one to find it mostly empty, barring two small chests. I opened one to find it filled with gold coins, nearly to the top—thousands of them, but no hair ties.

With the first one having no luck, I closed it and opened the second one. It was a makeshift jewelry box. Separate compartments for rings, necklaces, and bracelets. All made with the highest level of detail, some with gemstones set into the metal. *Why would Sam have these? I've never seen him wear jewelry, except for his wedding ring.*

The matching band around my own finger. I played with it as I searched. *Spin, spin, spin.* There were plenty of beautiful pieces here, but no tie. I was about to close it when one item caught my eye. It was a silver hair clip, masculine in its structure, but it was so pretty with its emerald stone set in silver. It was otherwise unadorned and plain. It suited Sam, and I would have preferred something more feminine, but it would work, and it was still pretty.

I picked it up and held it with my teeth while I pulled my hair back and used the hair clip to keep my hair in place. With my outfit and hair problem solved, my ravenous stomach demanded attention. *The children have been sleeping long enough. Time to get them up and go eat.*

Closing the drawers, I left our room and headed back to wake Tegen and Cheira. The hallway was clear and silent as I made my way to the guest room. The torches had been lit and cast ample light. I reached the door and entered. The children were right where I'd left them. Tegen was still cuddled into Cheira. I went over to the far side of the bed and shook Cheira; she awoke slowly and yawned, showing her rows of sharp teeth.

"What is it, Aunt Eris?"

"Time to get up, sweetie. Breakfast."

Her rumbling stomach was her reply, and I giggled at hearing it. "C'mon, get your lazy brother up and let's feast."

Cheira sat up and rubbed her brown, human eyes. Even though both of them were in safe company, they preferred to use their *Camouflage* to conceal their true natures. I wished they wouldn't, but I understood why.

Cheira turned and started poking Tegen, not gently either, with a heavy voice. "Hey, get up, Tegen. I'm hungry."

He just scooted away from Cheira and waved her off, which made her frown. She grumbled to herself before grinning like a madman. A devious idea played around in her head. She leaned over her brother and whispered to him, "Wake up, or Misumena will eat you."

Tegen bolted out of bed as if it were on fire. "I'm up, I'm up! I swear!"

Cheira rolled on the bad, clutching her sides as she shook with laughter. It went on for a half a minute before she calmed down and climbed out of bed, tears streaming down her face.

She wiped them, still chuckling to herself. "Gets him every time."

Meanwhile, Tegen glared daggers at his sister for pulling her prank. He was upset, and there were a few tears in his eyes, though for different reasons. I went over to him and knelt to wrap him in my arms. "There, there. It will be all right, little one."

Tegen was prone to tears easily, and Cheira knew it, too. For her to be younger than Tegen, she acted like the big sister. The mean tomboy big sister.

"Cheira, apologize to your brother."

She huffed but apologized. She knew she had gone too far. As soon as the words left her mouth, Tegen stopped crying and went and hugged his sister. *Much as they fight and bicker, they love each other to death and would do anything for each other.* It was a wonderful sight to see, and it made me hopeful for the remaining members of the Hive. With both of the spiderlings up and my belly crying from lack of food, we all headed for the kitchen.

I held both of the children's hands as we left the room and walked down the many stairs to reach the first floor. The top floor bedrooms were deserted, but the second floor was bustling with half a dozen of the maids that kept the castle clean. I hadn't explored the second floor much; it was filled with training rooms and workshops. Things I didn't have any business with, so I stayed away.

We descended even more steps till we reached the first floor. Even though we were still a good distance away from the dining hall, hints of food being cooked wafted our way: baking bread and the heavier scent of cooking meat. Bacon, if my nose was telling me straight. The curious sniffs from the children told me they could smell the food too.

I smiled down at them. "Let's hurry!"

We quickened our pace and, in a minute or two, had reached the heavy door to the dining hall. Before I even opened the door, several people talking at once and boisterous laughter slipped through the crack under the door. I tugged on the door and just managed to pull it open. I held the door for the children and squeezed in just as the door shut with a thud.

If the scents of food were strong in the hallway, in here, they were nearly overbearing. A dozen different smells swirled around me, from the soothing scent of fresh milk to the sharp tang of peppers cooking. Too many different kinds of scents sent my poor nose into overwork, but I tried to ignore it as best I could. It was all heavenly, but thick and heavy.

The dining hall was built with the same stone as everywhere else in the castle but had over half a dozen windows that were open to let in a cool breeze which swept some of the heaviest scents out. The morning sun shimmered off Lake Gloom in the distance. The water looked inviting but would have to wait, as I desperately needed food.

From a quick glance, it looked like most of the Gloom Knights were here eating. There were several huge wooden banquet tables in the room, but everyone sat around the largest one that sat closest to the giant stone fireplace, which had a raging fire going. I searched the faces of everyone, looking for Sam, but he wasn't here.

Odd, I wonder where he could be? I'll ask the others after we eat. Most of them were busy with the food on their plates, but Gil, Wilson, and Evelyn glanced up as we entered. Both Evelyn and Wilson returned to their food, but Gil welcomed me with a broad smile that showed his shining teeth that only served to stand out next to his chocolate skin.

"Good morning, Eris. I was wondering when you and the lug-head would crawl out of bed," Gil boomed, his voice deep and rumbling like thunder as he spoke.

His serious voice didn't match his friendly attitude at all. Gil was the big brother I'd never had, and I couldn't help but grin at the giant.

"Good morning, Gil!" I beamed at him.

I sat down across from him, and the children sat on either side of me. The children were frightened of so many humans around, and they huddled into me, refusing to look at anyone but each other and myself. I stroked both of their heads in an attempt to get them to open up.

Gil just watched the exchange with quiet bemusement on his face. Though his words finally registered past my hunger.

"Have you not seen Sa—Duran this morning?" I said. *Whoops, that was a close one.*

Gil picked up his mug and gulped what smelled like ale and wiped the foam from his mouth before speaking.

"No, least I don't think I've seen him today. We talked for a bit last night, but that's it. Why? Wasn't he with you all night?"

Grayson Sinclair

I shook my head and was about to answer when one of the maids tapped me on the shoulder. She was cute, with dark brown hair that stopped at her chin and curled. Her brown hair and freckles gave her a mousy appearance.

"What can I get for you, Miss?" she asked.

"Oh, uh…"

I'd completely forgotten about food, but as soon as it crossed my mind, I couldn't notice anything else. I looked down at the children and asked them what they wanted, and I wasn't picky, so I let them decide.

"Meat!" they said in unison, and I couldn't help but laugh. I turned back to the maid with a chuckle. "Well, you heard them."

The maid blinked. Squishing her eyebrows together as her eyes darted from the children and me to Gil.

"Um, am I missing something?" I asked Gil.

He looked like he was trying so hard to hold in a laugh, his cheeks were red, and he was trying not to smile. He pointed to the children. "We can't understand them."

I nearly slapped myself. *How could I forget such a simple thing?* "Oh…right, I forgot that."

Gil couldn't hold back his laughter anymore and nearly doubled over from his giggling. I had to smile at my own idiocy. I forgot that no one else could speak Rachnaran. Through all this, the maid was still waiting patiently for our order.

"I'm sorry about that; I completely forgot that little fact. Um, could we have a bunch of meat? No other preference beyond that."

The maid nodded at me. "Right away, Miss, and what to drink?"

"Milk will be perfect."

She nodded once more and turned to head back to the kitchen. I wasn't brave enough to drink ale first thing in the morning, and from what Sam had said, I was a lightweight, whatever that meant.

Gil was still chuckling softly to himself. *I wonder if anyone else has seen Sam?*

I looked over to where Evelyn was eating. Her pale skin and silver hair were perfect, not a strand out of place. She was picking her way through a plate of eggs and bacon, though she was hardly touching the food; instead, she was buried in a conversation with her brother.

I hated to interrupt them, but my need to ask about Sam outweighed my reticence. "Um...Evelyn, could I ask you something?"

She looked up in a flash, her golden eyes ringed with fury. It sent a wave of chills down my spine, but as soon as she noticed it was me who had spoken, her fiery gaze softened considerably.

"Oh, it's you, little queen. What can I do for you?"

I was suddenly less sure of asking her questions, I hadn't truly believed Sam when he had told me Evelyn was dangerous, but the darkness in her eyes was unmistakable. I sat with my hands in my lap, running my fingers over each other while I worked up the courage to speak.

"H—Have you seen D today?"

With the drop in temperature from her eyes came quizzical humor. "The guild leader? I haven't seen him since yesterday. Why? I thought you and he shared a bed. Trouble in paradise?"

"Of course not, but Tegen and Cheira didn't want to sleep alone, so I slept in the guest room."

Evelyn picked up a piece of bacon. The smell sent even more waves of hunger through me. She took a deliberate bite and chewed thoroughly. Her eyes never left mine, but there wasn't a trace of her earlier hostility. Her eyes were smiling at me, but I hadn't the first clue why.

"Right, the spiderlings."

She nudged Adam with her elbow; he jumped and looked up from the book he was reading. "What?"

"Have you seen the guild leader today?"

"D? No, not since yesterday. Why?"

I frowned. *This is getting strange.* "Surely, someone has seen him today?"

Adam returned to his book and picked up a strawberry from his plate and popped it into his mouth. "I'm sure he's fine," he mumbled, already engrossed with reading.

I was about to ask Makenna and Harper, who were sitting a few seats away, but the maid returned with our food, and my stomach forced me to put Sam out of mind while I focused on quieting my pangs of hunger. She set the plate down along with three mugs of milk. Tegen and Chiera's eyes lit up at the sight of so much food. The dish was piled high with bacon, sausages, and ham along with a half a loaf of bread and some spicy smelling pork in a brown sauce. All were nearly spilling over the plate.

I let the children dig in, but there was more than enough food for all of us. I picked up a piece of bacon and nibbled on it, but it was overcooked— well, overcooked to me. So I let the children devour the rest of it. I tried one of the sausages, and the hot juice and spice flowed into my mouth when I broke it open.

I savored the flavor. It was indeed quite spicy, but I enjoyed the heat as it brushed my tongue. Tegen enjoyed the bacon, but Cheira didn't much care for it. She, like me, stuck to the spicier meats. They didn't touch the bread, so I tore it apart and dipped it into the brown sauce. Which turned out to be spicy gravy. It was delicious, and I mopped up every last drop, and when the spice became too much for my mouth, I washed it away with the milk. It was cold and tasted fresh, which was strange, as I hadn't seen any cows in the castle. *Where did the fresh food come from?*

I was going to ask, but the children were eating their weight in food, and there wasn't much left, so I picked at whatever they didn't like until I was stuffed. From the looks of content on the children's faces, they'd eaten their fill. They simultaneously took hold of their milk and drained it to the last drop. It was adorable.

With my hunger satisfied, my thoughts immediately turned back to Sam. I knew he wouldn't like it, but I was getting worried, so I trailed a tendril of thought through our bond. It was just enough to crack open the door to his psyche. It was also enough to tell me everything I needed to know.

Sam was gone, far away from me, and he was afraid.

A pit of despair rose up in me, and there was nothing to stem the tide of grief that overtook me.

Sam was far away, so very, very far. It was like a punch to my stomach, and for a second, I forgot how to breathe. I choked and nearly spit up my milk, but I fought back the bile and the sadness that rose in me.

My heart was about to crack at the terror radiating from my bonded. My lungs wouldn't work anymore, and I let a few tears escape while I fought to keep from sobbing.

CHAPTER 3 - THE CRACKS DEEPEN

Sampson

"What are you saying?"

I understood Magnus's words, but they refused to make sense. My mind didn't want to comprehend what I'd heard.

A thousand years? That's impossible!

I stood from the chair so fast, it tipped over, clacking heavily against the stone floor. *It can't be true. It can't be. There was a plan, right? A plan for going back to Earth after the ghouls had been dealt with. They wouldn't just leave us here!*

But my thoughts rang false. We were nothing but lab rats, to be discarded when we'd served our purpose. I'd known that from the moment that man placed the barrel of his pistol against my head. We were completely disposable.

I grabbed the mug of ale in front of me and downed it. The sweetness did nothing to ease the turmoil running through my head. I looked around for Magnolia and motioned her over. She came to me immediately.

"What can I get for you, My Lord?"

"Whiskey," I managed to stammer out.

She left without a word, and I stared down at my hands for a minute or two, trying to process things.

While sweet, the ale had some effect as inebriation kicked in. Rapturous bliss brought heaviness to my thoughts, removing my inhibitions and, by some miracle, it let me think around the world-shattering revelation Magnus dropped on me.

What am I freaking out about? So what if we're stuck here? There was nothing left for me to return to anyways. Mom, Dad, Micah. They're gone. Sophia's gone. I've been dead for a very long time. My body is probably dust by now. There is nothing left in that world for me. This is my home now.

By some miracle of the gods, Magnolia returned quickly and set down a rather large bottle of liquor and a glass.

I didn't even bother to read the label, it'd probably cost a fortune. *I don't give a fuck what it is at this moment, could be paint thinner for all I care.* I poured the whiskey in the glass and chugged it, barely paying attention to the sickening burn and nausea as I filled my throat to the brim with forgetfulness.

All right, so we've all been here a hell of a lot longer than any of us realized, so what? Doesn't change anything. Doesn't change the life I've built.

I poured one more glass of the top-shelf whiskey, not nearly as full as the others, and knocked it back. The drink was already starting to hit me. A soft fuzziness slipped in from the edge of my vision.

I poured one more and drank it slow. After nearly three glasses of liquor, I was finally ready to face Magnus.

He hadn't moved from his seat. Both he and Aliria watched me devolve in silence. Magnus still held his look of sadness like he'd accidentally kicked my puppy, rather than shoved a stick of dynamite in my skull and lit it.

Regardless of the turmoil I was going through. All I had to do was ignore it and keep pushing on. *Easier said.*

I put the thoughts out of mind and focused on Magnus. "Okay, so we've been here for a thousand years. How? Why?"

Magnus sighed and leaned back in his chair as he worked through his thoughts. "Are you sure you want to know? It won't change anything. You can leave, you know, go back to your castle and live the rest of your days in peace."

"After all this, all I've gone through these past weeks, just pack up and leave?"

"Of course. You weren't supposed to be involved in the first place. A mistake on my part for handling the situation poorly, but nevertheless, you can wash your hands of this, go home and spend time with your wife."

His words were tempting, enticing even. I fiddled with the ring on my hand, considering his offer. Just leave Magnus to his own devices and go back to running the guild and spending time with Eris. It was my dream goal. The goal I'd been trying to find for so many years—a life I was content with.

Magnus was a bad man, yes, who kept company with some of the worst scum I'd ever come across here, but who was I to cast stones? With the things I'd done, I had no room to judge anyone, and he was right, after all.

This wasn't my problem. I liked his offer, and I was going to take it. Walk away from all this, go home, and spend a week in bed with Eris.

I told this to Magnus, but what I said wasn't what I meant to say. My words twisted, and what I spoke wasn't what I'd said.

"Regardless of any of that, I'm here now, so tell me."

Godsdamn it, Ouroboros!

This was the second time it'd taken over my words. Whatever purpose it wanted me for was here, with Magnus, and I knew too well the pain that awaited me if I tried to fight it.

I growled under my breath. *Fine. I know you're listening to me, so hear this. I'll cooperate, for now, but don't you think for a second I won't settle accounts when this is all said and done with.*

He rose from his chair, along with Aliria. "Well, if you want to know the truth, then come with me."

I finished the last of my drink, slammed the glass down on the table, and stood, walking with them out of the dining hall.

Magnus led us through the hallways. The sameness of it all made me think I was being led in circles. *I doubt I could find my way out of this place if my life depended on it, holy hells.* Magnus knew right where to go, and before long, we'd arrived at another plain unmarked door. Without a word, the door opened for Magnus, and he strolled inside.

It was a study, well-furnished with extravagant decor, lit by a chandelier that hung above our heads and by several other candles that hung on the walls or in holders around the room. A desk sat in the corner with a plush leather chair pushed against it.

The center of the room was dominated by a scale model of the Isle of Nexus. Crafted with such incredible detail that buildings and towns were recreated almost exactly. Near the center of the map was a model of Castle Gloom-Harbor nestled against Lake Gloom. To the west of my home were the Compass Kingdom and the outlying villages.

I just stared at the detail for a long moment; it was incredible. I could even pick out the capital of the elves, Yllsaria, nestled deep in the Emerald Ocean.

As I continued to gaze at the map, I noticed a few things — places on the map that I'd never seen before. Far in the Northern Mountains, Magnus had mapped the location of the home of the rabbitmen, the Pale Everlands. Which I'd never been to before, but I'd heard it was located on one of the four great mountains. If this map was to be believed, the Everlands were situated on the smallest of the four.

How does he know all this? This is more detail than I've ever seen before.

"What is this, Magnus?"

He grinned at me. "The work of dozens of years and far more gold than I expected."

I leaned over the table, still taking everything in. "For what purpose, though?"

He ignored my question for the time being, instead he was busy showing off his map, rambling about its construction and the time it'd taken. It was a little disconcerting to see the most powerful man I'd ever met nerd out over his creation. At this moment, he reminded me so much of Adam that it was almost funny.

He pointed down at the Rolling Hills that were located next to Castle Gloom-Harbor. I'd traversed across most of them at one point or another, but there was something there that shouldn't be.

"The hell is that?"

"Crystal Court," Magnus replied, nonchalantly.

I whistled. *By the nine kings of hell, that's close to home, far too close.* "Does The Alice know?"

"Of course she does."

The queen of the fae usually doesn't take kindly to interlopers into her domain. Wonder how he managed that?

Magnus scratched at his beard. His eyes were someplace else, lost in thought. *He probably won't tell me, but I've got to know.*

"How'd you manage to glean the location of the home of the faeries?"

"I bargained."

At that, Magnus pursed his lips, making it clear he had said all he was going to on the matter. I relented; I probably didn't want to know anyway. I left the gods of this world to their own devices. But in showing me all this, there had to be some point. As amazing as it was, Magnus didn't strike me as the type who showed off on principle. I was here for a reason.

"So why don't you tell me why we're here?"

Aliria spoke from the doorway. "How much are you going to reveal to the boy?"

His eyes flicked to Aliria, and a warning flashed in them. A tint of anger that was gone as soon as it came. So quick, if I hadn't been looking, I'd have missed it.

"As much as he is willing to listen. My payment for the burden I've caused him." He turned to me. "Are you sure you want to know? I owe you a debt, but this is a poor payment. I can send you home with enough money to live in luxury for the next seventy years, if that would be preferable."

Hell yes, that would be preferable, but I don't get a choice in this. "Tell me."

Magnus let out a breath, long and slow through his nostrils. Not the answer he was expecting, but he would honor my wish even if it wasn't my godsdamn wish at all.

He moved back to the table, stretching his arm over it. Fingers splayed out in all directions as he conjured magic from out of nowhere. In an instant, a spell formed in his hand. No Script circle or incantation, Magnus bypassed the laws of magic and just willed his spell into existence.

I don't get how he's doing it, but worry about that another time. The better question is what the hell is that spell he cast?

It wasn't a spell I was familiar with, and I'd seen most of them. A shimmering wave appeared over the map, like the heat that rose off buildings on a hot summer day. It drifted over the table and condensed into a small circle the size of a dinner plate made of pure glass. I peered over to get a better look at it.

Magnus noticed my interest and decided to demonstrate the function of the spell. He brought the glass lower over the map. Right over Castle Gloom-Harbor. From within the circle, every single detail of my castle was clear, as if I were standing directly in front of it. Magnus manipulated the spell to circle around the castle, showing it from all angles. Light and movement on the ramparts of the castle drew my attention. Several men-at-arms were patrolling around the castle, torches in hand. *Was this in real-time?*

I shot my head up to stare at Magnus; he was already looking at me with a wide smile on his face. He had anticipated my question and had the answer at the ready.

"Yes, you are seeing your home as it is right now."

Not possible...illusion magic or some other explanation.

"There's no spell that can do that!"

With a flick of his wrist, Magnus canceled the spell. It fizzled out with a pop, and he backed away from the table, walking over to his desk and pulled out a large roll of parchment. He rolled it out and beckoned me over.

"For you and the rest of the players, you'd be correct. It's a little creation of mine."

"You can't create—" I shut my mouth. I was getting really tired of Magnus shattering my worldview.

Magnus kept doing things and showing me impossible things, breaking the rules of the game that we'd been living with for thirty years. Over and over again, he was crumbling all the beliefs I'd come to know as fact.

"So, tell me, how can you create spells, something that's impossible or the rest of us?"

A hint of a grin turned the corners of Magnus's lips. "I helped design and program the Ouroboros Project; as such, I gave myself a few perks."

I leaned against the table and blew out a short breath. "So that's how you can do so many incredible things. You're cheating the system."

His face darkened as I accused him; a fire raged in his eyes before he composed himself. "It's insulting to call someone a cheater, though I understand how you came to that conclusion. But no, I am not, nor can I cheat the system. I may have given myself a few advantages, but not even I can cheat the A.I."

Bah, I don't know whether to believe him or not, but I guess it doesn't matter. He can do these things, and I can't. It's that simple.

He picked up a couple of paperweights and sat them at the corners of the parchment. "Player-created spells cost a tremendous amount of mana to use, and it's not something I'm capable of anymore, regardless, but that's not what I wanted to talk to you about."

I went over to the side of the desk to look at what he'd unfurled. It was another map, though not half as detailed, and it was mostly unfamiliar to me. I recognized the Isle of Nexus, but there were other landmasses entirely new for me on this map, including a continent that was well over double the size of Nexus. It was labeled "Summervale" in rough scribble.

I pointed at the unfamiliar location. "What's this? I've never heard of it?"

Magnus ran one hand through his shaggy length of hair, his fingers gliding through his golden hair while his other hand drummed in a staccato rhythm on the parchment. He wasn't looking at me; he wasn't even looking to Aliria, who stood silent as a wraith, her cold eyes drinking in the scene unfolding before her. Magnus was looking from his hands to the wall to stare into the soft lambent light of the candles. Anywhere but at me.

His behavior was stoking my curiosity. *If he was going to play coy now, after all he had shown me...must be something big if it's got Magnus so nervous.* My impatience overrode my fear at the answer. "Well, what is it?"

Magnus blew out a breath, long and slow. "What you are looking at was the true size of the world."

I didn't understand. "Was?"

Magnus Inclined his head. "Yes, this is the original map of the world for this server of the Ouroboros Project."

I backed up from the desk. That was too much information at once for me. I was already reeling from his earlier statements, and he went and threw me into even deeper water. I paced around the table, sorting through and dissecting his words. *Okay, you can do this...Gods, I need a drink.*

I stopped my circling and faced Magnus. "Okay, walk me through this. So first off, pretty much everything I know is wrong. Not only was the world much bigger than I realized, but there are other servers than this one?"

"Pretty much."

"What are they like?"

Magnus shrugged his shoulders. "I haven't a clue; I was only involved in creating this server."

"Fine. Whatever. What happened to the world?"

Magnus paused, his face grew slack as if he were nothing but a statue. He stayed quiet.

"Magnus?"

"...I don't know."

What the hell? No, seriously, what the actual hell?

"Okay, okay, okay..." I ran my hands over my temples; the alcohol in my system wasn't enough to stop the pounding headache that was trying to crush my skull. "Okay...not okay, so not okay."

Godsdamn it, I so don't want to know any of this. Magnus took note of my freak out and spoke to Aliria. "Would you have Magnolia or Jasmine bring him a drink? I'm sure he could use it."

Aliria turned and left without a word, leaving me alone with Magnus and with my thoughts.

I faced Magnus, my head pounding. "What *do* you know, then?"

He picked up the paperweights and neatly stored them in a drawer on the desk. He looked at me with eyes that held the weight of a dozen lifetimes and sighed. "All I know is, something happened just over three hundred years ago. A massive system crash nearly destroyed the entire server. Because I had admin access, I received advanced warning from the governing A.I. But things spiraled much quicker than we could repair it."

Magnus bent over the table and conjured his magnifying glass once more. He brought the lens over to the very edge of the map, way out into the Eclysian Depths, the deepest part of the Azure Seas. Where I expected to see endless ocean, I was met with an incredibly strange sight. A creeping darkness at the edge of the sea, water rushed to fill the space but was swallowed whole.

"What is that?" I asked dumbfounded.

"The void, or some variation of it."

I gestured at the table. "I can see that, but what's it doing there?"

"What it does best: devouring everything."

Magnus canceled his spell, and the image before me disappeared with a pop. "When the system failed, we had to make a drastic choice: sacrifice a few for the good of the many, or let the whole thing unravel. You can guess which choice we made.

"Right now, best I can tell, the damage was contained, but it destroyed most of the hard drives. Right now, we're operating on about twenty-five percent of what's left."

"So the system devoured the other continents to save space on the remaining drives?"

Magnus shook his head, holding a very forlorn and pained expression on his face. "Not just the landmasses, but NPCs, players, memories, and even history itself. Anything that was deemed non-vital."

"What?"

He cast his eyes towards with a raised brow. "Have you not wondered at the current state of things? The fact that we don't have an accurate record of history or any concrete time system?"

I coughed, turning away from the weight of his eyes on me. He expected a reasonable answer, which I didn't have. I tugged at my ponytail. "I mean, I guess I've thought about in passing, but there was always something better to occupy my time with than sitting around reading books or theorizing." *There was always something else to worry about. Some new job or quest. Some dungeon to explore while I made the climb to level one hundred. I didn't have any inclination to sit still; it always brought up old memories—my past failures.*

Magnus sighed at my answer before chuckling. "You and most others in this world, though I suppose it's a blessing. If too many people learned the truth, it would be chaos."

"I'm used to dealing with chaos, nothing new for me there. But this. This is beyond anything I could imagine."

Magnus was about to retort but was interrupted by Magnolia, bringing a large silver tray with a large bottle of liquor and two glasses. She set the tray down and bowed to Magnus. My mood picked up at the sight of the bottle, and I walked over and poured a too-generous measure into the glass. I knocked it back and poured another. The booze quieted my rampaging thoughts that were haunted by what I'd just been told. It was too much, way too much for me to handle, and I downed glass after glass in the hopes of finding some sense of normalcy in the world.

It didn't work, and I got nowhere but drunk. *And at this point, I'm okay with that. Damn it all to hell.*

I stood off the ground, how I'd gotten there was beyond me, but I managed to stand after a few tries. The room spun, so I leaned against the magical spy table and tried to focus on Magnus; there were three of him in the room. *Was there always three of him? Odd that I never noticed.*

My vision swam again, and I blacked out.

***

I awoke to pain. My head pounded with the remnants of the overabundance of alcohol in my system. My hangover made even moving a challenge, but the light currently blinding me made it a necessity. I sat up slowly, pushing myself out of the blistering light, and when I got up, resistance clung; soft and warm hands held me.

"Good morning, love," I called to Eris.

I reached down to unstick her from my side, only to find short auburn hair obscuring her face. *Eris doesn't have red hair...wait a second. Oh, no! Tell me I didn't.* I slipped the heavy slate comforter off me. *Okay, still have my pants on. That's a good sign.*

The events of the previous day came crashing into me, and I put the massive existential crisis out of mind for the moment and focused on the naked girl in bed with me.

I poked her gently. "Jasmine?"

A low mumble was her response, and I tried again. She lifted her head. "Yes?"

"What are you doing?"

"Cuddling."

"Why?"

"You asked me to," she said, pressing herself to my side.

"Why did I ask you to cuddle?"

Jasmine shrugged and nuzzled into me. "I don't know. I thought you might have been joking, but I wasn't sure."

I let out a long sigh and tried not to get upset at the maid. *It's not her fault I'm an idiot.* "Okay, well, you do not have to cuddle me again. Best not take anything I say when I'm drunk seriously."

"Okay."

"So you can let go of me now."

She shook her head.

"Why not?"

"Because you're very warm. It's nice."

I tried once more to pull away, but it seemed she was adamant about not letting go of me.

"Jasmine, could you let go of me for just a second?"

"No."

I gave one final attempt to pull myself free, but without putting a considerable effort into it, I wasn't going anywhere. *How the hell do I get her off me?* I was about to resign myself to be this girl's pillow for the next few hours, when a delicious thought struck me.

It was mean and childish, but I couldn't help but smile at what I was about to do. I reached over for the pitcher of water on the nightstand by the bed.

"Jasmine, will you please let go of me?"

Another shake of her head, and she clung even tighter.

I gave her ample opportunity. It's on her now. I moved the pitcher over her sleeping form, snuggled so soundly into me. *What a rude awakening this is about to be,* I thought and dumped the remaining water on top of Jasmine.

The result was better than I could have hoped for. As soon as the cold water touched her skin, she bolted, her eyes open, just in time to be drenched as the rest of the water landed all over her. Jasmine let out a half gargle, half screech of surprise and flung herself as far as she could away from me. The bed was more than accommodating, and she found herself with plenty of room that wasn't now soaked with water.

I stood off the bed and threw on my shirt. While she glared murder at me. I undid my hair and quickly retied it before walking to the door.

"Have a good morning, Jasmine," I said and hastily left the room.

I found Magnolia a short walk later. She asked me about Jasmine, and I admitted where she was, but I hastily assured her again that nothing had happened between us.

"I was worried when she didn't return to her room last night, I'm just glad she's all right."

Without another word, she led me to the dining hall.

Magnus sat in the same spot as last night, in front of him on the oak table were an array of dishes hardly touched. He sipped from a porcelain cup and picked up a piece of parchment, though his eyes rose as I approached.

"Good morning, Duran, I trust you slept well."

I groaned a non-reply and sat down in the same chair as last night, resisting the urge to lay my head down and sleep. Magnus was cheerfully awake, dressed in a vibrant, butterscotch tunic, looking like a man who'd gotten a full night's rest.

I didn't get more than three hours, and he was still wide awake with Aliria when I blacked out. That thought brought a question to mind. "Where's Aliria at?"

He picked up his cup and took another sip, ignoring my question for the moment. As he sat his cup down, he spoke.

"She's taking a bath. I'm sure she'll be along shortly." He lifted his cup and gestured towards me. "Would you like some tea? It's my own special blend. I think you'll find it to your liking."

When Magnolia returned, I almost leapt out of my chair. The door opening was a gunshot to my senses; I flinched at the sound and shook the table. Magnus looked up with a grin and drained the rest of his tea.

By the time Magnolia reached the table, I'd calmed my shot nerves. She sat down a large cup of tea with a wink. "I made it special for you."

The smell rising from it was heavenly—a mixture of black tea, lemon, and a sharp, bitter undertone that I recognized well. I took a large gulp. The tea was delicious, but the liquor was what made me sigh in pleasure. The bite of the alcohol soothed my aching head almost instantly, and I drained the cup in several gulps before setting it back on its saucer. *Guess let's get this over with. I need some answers.*

"Can we talk?"

He looked up from his papers to answer me. "Of course. I'm sure you have many questions."

"That I do."

Magnus picked at one of the biscuits on the plate, tearing it apart with his fingers and flicking the pieces into his mouth. "I'll answer what I can, but as I mentioned last night, there is still much I myself don't know."

"Yeah, I got that, but let's work through what you do know. Before we go off speculating, I'd like to have a good grasp of the situation. It was a lot to take in last night, and I want to fully understand the situation before we add to it."

"Go ahead."

I fumbled with the knife next to me, buttering a half of a biscuit I had no intention of eating. *Let's start with the easiest thing for me to understand.* "So the world used to be much bigger than it is now?"

"Correct."

"And up until three hundred years ago, everything was fine, until something happened. You don't know what, but it caused a massive crash."

"Indeed."

"So the system compensated for this by deleting shit, including people and even history itself?"

Magnus nodded. "A bit more eloquent than I'd have put it, but you have the basics."

"Why haven't we noticed any of this?"

"A few have, but the main reason is that everyone's memories get deleted."

"Wait, what?"

"Memories take up quite a lot of data, and with our limited hard drive space, it was the simplest option."

I paused to consider his words. I got the gist of it, but the technical aspects behind it boggled me. "How does that even work?"

Magnus sighed, rolling up his parchment and sliding into his pocket, giving me his undivided attention. "It's basically on a cycle. We have enough space for about a hundred years of everyone's memories. When the storage starts to exceed our allocated space, the A.I. resets the world."

"It deletes our memories and resets everyone back to square one?"

"Precisely. It hard resets everything back to the first backup, which was made when we reset the world the first time and erases the data."

I pointed a finger at him. "How do you know all this?"

"Perks of being the lead programmer. I've kept all of my memories since the very beginning."

I whistled. "That's a thousand years of memories."

Magnus took a sip of his tea. "It's certainly been a burden to bear. It's hard to make friends when they'll just forget you in the end." He smiled. "Though there are a few exceptions."

Aliria, of course, but there have to be others from the sound of it. I was about to ask when Magnolia returned with more tea.

The clink of china interrupted my chain of thought; Magnolia sat the full cup down on its saucer, and from the smell wafting past my nose, it was at least as strong as the first cup. I picked it up and took a tentative sip. It was more alcohol than tea. I took a big gulp, enjoying the burn of the booze as it went down.

It helped me get my thoughts in order, or at least sort them into manageable chunks for me to digest. *Okay, let's not go off and ask every single question that's running through my head right now. We'll be here for hours if I pester him about pointless things. I need clear, concise, and understandable information.*

"The void at the edge of the world—I'm assuming that's a threat?"

"Not by itself, no, but it's indicative of a much greater problem."

"Which is?" I hedged.

"Chaos, or for lack of a better term, instability. It means something is wrong and the system is compensating again."

"Can't you just use your admin access and find out what's going on?" I asked before drinking another sip of tea.

Magnus shook his head and sipped tea. "I could, if I still had it. I lost my contact with the A.I. and haven't been able to access any higher system functions."

"How'd that happen?"

Magnus paused, his eyes shifted away from me. "I don't know."

Liar. But I didn't press further. It would only anger him, and he was entitled to his secrets. There were much bigger things to worry about.

59

"Are we in danger?"

"Not at the moment, but something needs to be done, or it could turn into a serious problem."

I leaned back in my chair while I digested what he'd just told me. There were things Magnus was keeping from me, it was obvious, but what was also obvious, was that something was wrong. *Okay, so something is going on here. Something big. It's not just Magnus's words, but whatever that's been taking over my voice. I'm being pushed into this, whether I want to or not. I can't afford to sit this one out, even if I had a choice in the matter.*

Wonder what the Aspect thinks? I closed my eyes for a second, reaching down for its presence. *It's been unusually quiet since meeting Aliria.*

Hey, Aspect, talk to me.

It pulsed, keeping me alive, but it refused to answer my call. I pushed, and it sent a spike of frost through my heart. The pain was sharp and took my breath from me before fading and disappearing.

What the hell is going on with it? It was terrified, which in turn terrified me. The Aspect was strong, abomination or not, and it had saved my life more than once, so for it to be afraid meant serious news.

I ran my fingers over the cup of tea, trailing over the smooth porcelain under my fingers. It was a real, physical sensation that helped ground my fear and let me work through it.

As I was about to respond, there was an itch in the back of my head. *Eris is up.*

That thought made me happy for a split second, but it couldn't erase the fear and unease running wild. There was too much unease flowing through me that there was no way I could keep it from her. I was so afraid, and Eris knew it.

She opened our bond, and our emotions mixed. They poured over one another and did nothing to quell each other; if anything, it made things worse. Her misery at my absence only magnified when my terror slipped through. There was no way for me to communicate with her, and her tidal wave of emotions flooded into me, drowning me.

I had to close off our connection, though it pained me to do so. It had to be done. Our emotions would only hurt the other, and it wasn't what I needed to focus on right now. Throughout all of this, I tried to keep my distress off my face, but Magnus saw right through it. He was looking at me with a quizzical expression on his face. He put down his tea. "Something troubling you, Duran?"

Instead of answering him, I picked up the china cup in front of me and drained the contents. As always, the booze helped to calm my racing heart and mind. As I sat the cup on the table, I spoke. "Uh, I'm fine, just a little headache."

My weak lie did not get past him. "Trouble with your wife?"

"That obvious, huh?"

He laughed. "Only to me. Like you, I've spent ample time with an entomancer; you pick up a few things. While I'm not bonded to Aliria, I understand the concept easily enough."

His words surprised me. "I'd assumed the two of you were bonded."

"Oh, by the stars, no. Not that I'm opposed to the idea, but Aliria, for obvious reasons, refuses to be bonded ever again."

Well, with how things ended with her first bond-mate, I can't say I blame her all that much. She doesn't want to end up like me. The door to the dining hall opened once more, and Aliria strolled in, her pale skin flushed by heat, her hair damp, turning the golden strands into tarnished brass. Her hair was tied back out of her face in a ponytail, and she was garbed in a dark crimson dress that

61

flowed down to her ankles, though her feet were bare. *Like mother, like daughter.*

Magnus looked from me at the sound of the door opening, "Ah, speak of the devil. We were just talking about you, dear."

Aliria smiled at his words. "All bad things, I hope."

"All right, Magnus, what do you need from me?"

Magnus stopped mid-sip, his teacup frozen halfway to his lips, and confusion lit up his eyes. "I'm sorry?"

"There's obviously something big going down. Now that I know about it, what can I do to help?"

Magnus looked from me to Aliria and back again. His confusion washed away to amusement as he realized my meaning. He chuckled, but it wasn't his usual laugh; there was absolutely no kindness in it. "I think you've misunderstood things. After our meal, I'll give you a teleportation scroll and send you home."

What? I couldn't stop my anger from boiling out. I slammed my fist down on the table, knocking over my empty cup in the process. The table shook at my outburst. "Excuse me?" I yelled, spitting fury across the wood. "After all this, everything you've told me, just to go home?"

"Precisely."

Magnus picked up his cup and continued to drink his tea as if we were discussing nothing more important than the weather, his face betraying no hint of his reasoning.

"Why?" I tried and failed to keep my voice level.

"Do you want the truth?"

"Obviously!" I said through clenched teeth.

Magnus sighed, setting down his cup and looking me square in the eye. There was judgment and darkness in them.

"You're clearly a capable man, I won't deny that. Tough and strong-willed, but you're also quick to anger, dangerously unpredictable, and your penchant for drink borders on alcoholism. You bring much to the table, but you also leave much to be desired." He paused and took a breath, leaving me in stunned silence. "In short, I have no use for a man like you."

His words stung me, but purely from the audacity of them, they rang hollow in my ears. Magnus clearly didn't understand the kind of person I was. *Alcoholism? Ridiculous. I've never had a problem.*

His words should have enraged me, almost did, but to give in to my anger would have just proved his point. Instead, I countered his accusations with one of my own. *Who is Magnus to levy judgment when he keeps the worst kind of company?* "Yet you employ the likes of Darren, or Liam? Yeah, you clearly have discerning tastes, all right."

Magnus looked up, eyes widened. "You've met Liam?"

"I have."

"Liam's been with me for many years and has proven himself loyal time and time again."

I laughed in his face. "Loyal? Liam was a right bastard. A slaver, like Darren, who preyed on the weak."

Magnus couldn't help but notice my wording, the inflection in my tone betrayed Liam's fate.

"Was?" Magnus asked.

"He got in my way."

"*You* killed him?" Magnus's tone changed from bored to incredulous, as did his face. He didn't believe me.

I inclined my head. *Well, it was a combined effort, but I don't think he needs the details.* Magnus took his eyes off me to stare at his interface. His eyes dropped when he realized I spoke the truth. A flash of sadness, tinged with righteous fury, crossed them before Magnus could compose himself.

"You weren't lying. You must forgive my disbelief; Liam was one of my strongest lieutenants. Few were capable of besting him."

He shook his head, brushing his blond hair from his face as he composed himself. *Even if they were friends, Liam will be back in a few months once he respawns.*

"Well, aren't you full of surprises," Aliria said from beside me before she leaned over to whisper to Magnus.

I strained my ears but couldn't pick up more than half a word or two. Nothing that could help me make sense of anything. As Aliria broke away from him, Magnus spoke.

"You make an excellent point. I hadn't considered that." He turned his head to me. "Very well; you say you wish to help. If you have the skills to defeat Liam, then despite my reticence, I could use your assistance."

I don't like this one bit. I rose from my chair. "Why do I feel like this is a trap?"

Magnus smiled at me, back to his cheerful self. "Not a trap, a test. It'll be dangerous, risky. I won't lie, but if you truly want to help…"

I'm going to regret this, but what the hell. "All right, what do you need from me?"

Magnus set down his cup of tea and pushed the remains of his breakfast away from him. He picked up the pristine white cloth in his lap and dabbed at the corners of his mouth, wiping non-existent stains away. "Why don't we continue this conversation in the war room?"

"The what, now?"

Magnus grinned wide, his eyes sparkling with anticipation. "Oh, you're going to enjoy this."

CHAPTER 4 - JUST ANOTHER JOB

Magnus said I'd enjoy the war room, and what met me as we stepped through the heavy iron door did not disappoint. The room was large, easily the same size as the dining hall or throne room, but there were no windows or stained glass here. No, there was floor-to-ceiling stone. Bright green lights hung along the walls and in gigantic wrought-iron chandeliers from the roof. They all bubbled and frothed effervescent, casting dancing shadows onto the muted gray wall, which came alive with darkness.

The lights were mesmerizing, and it took a concerted effort to pull my gaze from them. I growled under my breath. *What the hell is Magnus thinking?* "Some warning would have been nice, Magnus. Mage lights aren't things to play around with."

He cast a small grin my way. "If you can't handle little mind games, you'd be utterly useless to me."

"Little mind games." I scoffed. "People can go insane from just one, and there's hundreds here."

"You're not people. I stand by what I said, but I now have much higher hopes for you."

As we walked through the room, we came across the first area. The entire room was divided into sections, each one taking up one-fourth of the space. The first one looked like nothing short of a military command center. It held an exact replica table of the one in his study, though this one had a few noticeable changes. From a quick glance, I could tell what this table was for: planning conflicts, assessing threats.

I scanned over it, but I'd already seen its tricks in his study, so it was far less impressive a second time.

When I stood up from the map table, I caught the glint of metal in the far corner of the room, and when my eyes adjusted, I saw what the latter half of the room was hiding.

Rows and rows and rows of armaments. Hundreds, if not thousands of them. What must have been one of nearly every weapon in the world, lined up in neat order next to one another.

A full rack of swords was next to a rack of spears, which continued to a rack of daggers.

None of them were below hero-tier. Which put just one little rack at easily the most expensive thing I'd ever seen.

And there were dozens upon dozens of weapon racks.

I'm staring at tens of millions of gold, just in weapons alone. By the nine kings of hell.

This, more than anything else I'd seen since coming here, terrified me to my bones.

Magnus was a truly powerful man, but his magic was so far out of my purview that I didn't understand it. I was so far out of my depth regarding him, but I understood these weapons. I understood the unthinkable amount of wealth they represented.

If Magnus so desired, he could overthrow the entire Compass Kingdom, could topple the five kings, and proclaim himself emperor of humanity…and he hadn't.

This amount of money was enough to corrupt even the Whisper herself, and I knew deep in my soul that I wouldn't have been so noble; this money would have destroyed me with the power it could grant.

And this was just one-fourth of the room.

The other half was a mixture of over two dozen sets of armor, each one clearly hero-tier, the highest quality that existed. Alongside the armor were quite a few sets of mage robes. All of them humming with untapped power, even to my nearly magicless senses. I couldn't ignore the power they gave off.

And if the weapons and armor weren't enough, the last section of the room was dedicated to miscellaneous items. Potions of every kind. Every one I'd ever seen, as well as many more that I'd only ever heard about. On a large wooden bookcase next to the potions was a small library of scrolls, sectioned off and labeled.

The more I looked, the more I was amazed. Jewelry and charms, magic items that did gods knew what. Everything was neatly organized and displayed like a prized collection, but I knew exactly what I was looking at.

An armory.

This room was an armory, built to wage war, and I believed with my entire being that there wasn't a force alive that could stand against Magnus.

He might as well be a god, and with his unnatural powers, he might actually be one.

I turned to him, my mouth hanging to the floor. "Why do you have all this?"

Magnus laughed. "A product of my nature. I'd rather have it and never need it than find myself wanting."

"If you need this much firepower, I weep for all of us."

Magnus laughed again quietly. "Perhaps. Once Aliria gets here, we can go over the assignment," he said, then busied himself with the table, already lost in his thoughts.

I decided to have a look around at the unbelievable weapons while we waited. Naturally, I was drawn to the swords. I walked over to the rack and admired the gleaming metal.

The first row was dominated by what I would say were the lowest quality weapons, which baffled me to even think about, because I saw a similar sword to the one I carried. And this was just the lowest shelf. The unbelievable quality only increased as I reached the next levels. The top two racks only held a single sword apiece, and these enraptured me.

They were rather plain-looking longswords, without much ornamentation, but they needed none.

The sword that was eye level with me was solid black from hilt to blade, but when I blinked, splashes of red and orange seemed to trickle in and out ethereally. It was beautiful in its simplicity, and I wanted to wield it. It called out to me.

I shook my head and focused on the next sword. It was the inverse of the previous sword, shining silver metal that sparkled even in the dark. The hilt was solid white with a golden pommel, and the blade of the sword shone with soft white light.

However, this weapon made me want to run screaming from it. I recoiled and backed away.

"The hell are these?" I asked, my voice cracking slightly.

"Hmm," Magnus said, looking up. He squinted before his light green eyes lit up. "Ah, should've known you'd take an interest in those two."

"What are they made of?"

Magnus waved his hand, and the black sword was in his grasp. It flared to life as if lit by the flames of perdition itself. "It goes by several names, but I call it hellsteel. It's incredibly hard to forge, but not impossible. Several prominent blacksmiths have managed over the years. And before you ask, no, I won't tell you how it's made."

Damn it, I want one. "Fair enough, but what about the other one? Why do I want to never go near it again?"

His lips turned up in a half smile. "It has that effect on the unworthy."

"What's that supposed to mean?" I snapped.

Magnus held up his hands to placate me, but his eyes lit up with humor, none of it ill. "I meant nothing by it, friend. If it makes you feel better, I can't wield it either."

My eyebrows raised. "How come?"

Magnus snapped his fingers, and the hellsteel sword vanished, only to be replaced by the shining silver one. It floated in the air above our heads, lazily spinning on its axis.

"It's called godsteel, and it's not meant for mortals. Only those with shards of divinity can wield such weapons."

"How do you have it, then?" I asked, not having a clue about what he was talking about.

A small, sad smile met me. "I'm holding it for a friend."

"Who?"

But my question went unanswered as Magnus busied himself with the table. It was clear he would say no more on the subject, despite leaving me with far more questions than answers. *Okay, just leave me alone to unpack literal demonic and divine weaponry.* Seemed like Magnus liked to play it that way, blow my freaking mind and then leave me hanging with questions. *Whatever, just more shit that doesn't make any sense…which is rapidly becoming normal for me.*

"Why don't you get to the reason why you brought me here?"

Magnus brushed my question aside, focusing on his map table, pushing pieces around like it was a chessboard.

"Magnus!" I slammed my palm flat on the table, sending his little pieces scattering across the map. Anger clouded his face, and his eyes darkened.

He glared at me, and suddenly I couldn't move.

I stood stock-still. My airway was clear, but no matter how hard I tried, I couldn't breathe. My lungs refused to operate. I couldn't even fall to the floor; I just stood there and suffocated.

For nearly a minute, I maintained my cool. I'd pissed him off, and I figured he would relent, but after another half a minute, my consciousness waned. Panic quickly set in, and I started freaking out. I railed against my invisible bonds as hard as I could, to no avail. I wasn't moving an inch.

My sight grew dim as my brain starved of oxygen, my head grew heavy, and my thoughts lost all cohesion.

Then he released me.

I tumbled to the floor and lay there choking on the air I shoveled into my starved lungs. It took several long moments before I regained the strength to stand. I stumbled up and clutched at the table to support myself.

Magnus looked me dead in the eye. "You forget your place, Durandahl. I am not someone to make demands of. I may not be your enemy, but that doesn't mean I won't kill you if you cross me."

From the look in his eye, he meant every word, and he more than had the power to carry out his threat. Much as I hated to admit it, he was right. I had forgotten my place. *I'm nothing compared to him. My power is nothing. My skill with the sword is nothing to a man who can kill me without a word. He outclasses me in every possible way.*

I nodded to him, rubbing my throat. "Message received."

He straightened, tugging at the cuff of his golden tunic. "Good. Even with all your faults, I find myself liking you, and I try not to murder people I like, but it happens."

Magnus began fixing the table, placing the toppled and scattered pieces back where they belonged with pinpoint accuracy. He worked with speed; in under twenty seconds he had replaced every one that I had knocked over.

As he situated the final piece, he spoke up. "To answer your question, I am waiting on Aliria…she is bringing something of importance. She should be here—"

The heavy door opened, and Aliria walked in. She'd changed into a radiant crimson dress, accented by a rather simple silver necklace in the shape of a honeycomb that draped across her slender throat.

She smiled at Magnus before turning her gaze upon me. "I hope you two weren't waiting long."

He shook his head, smiling at her. "Not at all. Duran was just looking at my collection," he said, as if I hadn't almost lost my life moments before. "Let's get started. Did you bring her?"

Aliria nodded and placed two fingers in her mouth and whistled.

Soft footsteps from the door caused me to turn at the new arrival.

She was tall for a girl, as tall as Aliria, which put her just under six feet. Her thin black dress left her alabaster skin bare at the shoulders and hinted at the immodest with its plunging neckline revealing the curves of her sizable bust. The girl walked with her head low, hiding her face behind a veil of her jet-black hair.

But at that moment, her appearance didn't matter. Her gait as she walked in is what caught my attention.

The pace she walked and the set of her shoulders screamed nervousness. Her hands twined together in front of her, long, slender fingers playing over each other, again and again. She kept her eyes to the floor and refused to look at anyone.

The girl stopped just shy from Magnus and Aliria, kneeling in supplication.

"You called for me, Master?"

Her voice was heady and sweet, like honey, but it cracked with anxiety. I'd heard it before yet couldn't place where.

"Rise. I have a task I need of you," Magnus commanded.

She bobbed her head in acknowledgment and stood, giving me my first proper look of her. She brushed her curtain of dark hair back and let it drape down her back where it rested just above her thighs.

Her face was soft and kind. Small chin, low rounded cheeks, and downward-turned raspberry lips that were made for smiling—something this room desperately needed right now.

However, the most profound aspect of her visage were her blood-red eyes. I'd have taken her for a vampire, but the red didn't stop at the iris. The color bled to the whites, staining them crimson, leaving only her small pupil and a thin black circle in an ocean of red.

My eyes widened when I realized what she was, and I grimaced.

Our eyes met. Sorrow and regret stared back at me before she hastily looked away. Though her gaze lingered on me when I turned back to Magnus.

A shapeshifter, fucking perfect. Been a long time since I've seen one of their kind, but what's she doing here?

"Why's the shifter here?"

The girl flinched at my words and dropped her head once more. Magnus glanced at me with approval in his eyes. "Raven's here because you will need her help for your task."

Raven? Pretty name for a monster. I frowned, furrowing my brow as I tugged at my ponytail.

"So not only have you not told me what I'm doing, but you expect me to run a godsdamned escort mission with a shifter?" I resisted the urge to pace and placed my hands firmly on the cool wood of the map table. "Enough games and secrecy, what's the job?"

"Nothing terribly difficult for one as talented as you. A simple retrieval," Aliria said, her eyes smoldering with predatory delight.

I barked a quick laugh. "All right, what do you need me to steal for you?"

She smirked at my response. "Such a clever boy."

Magnus tilted his head from the table and chuckled. "Told you," he said to Aliria before turning to me. "You're correct. What I require isn't something I can purchase; the gods know I've tried."

He paused, which set my teeth on edge. Magnus danced around the topic, refusing to outright tell me what I needed to know. And that worried the hell out of me.

All I know is it involves the shifter, which already isn't a good sign. I don't trust them, never have. The price for their power has always been too high.

Someone who's made that bargain has nothing to lose and no line they won't cross. She's dangerous.

Aliria came over to lean against the table next to me. She sighed and placed a finger on the map. On top of Aldrust. "What we need is an emerald, rather large for its size."

An emerald? Why—oh, no. My heart jumped up in my throat, and blood pounded in my ears. *You can't be thinking...oh, by the nine kings of hell.* I stared at her pale finger, at the blood red fingernail pointing at my death.

"You can't be serious. That's a suicide mission for even the most experienced thieves. I'm worse than a bull in a china shop. No," I said, my mouth drier than the sands of the Badlands.

Magnus sighed, disappointed at my answer, but it wasn't a shock to him. He knew exactly what he was asking of me, and he understood. Aliria, on the other hand, wasn't having any of it. Her face clouded with anger at my flat-out refusal, while the shifter stood ramrod straight, not looking at anything but the floor. The tension in the air was so thick, I could've drowned in it.

"You're just backing out?" Aliria asked.

"Damn right, I am. You know what you're asking, right? Lachrymal's Heart, really?"

"Are you afrai—" Aliria began, before Magnus cut her off.

"We know exactly what we are asking, and the risks involved, which is why I won't hold it against you if you decline. You wouldn't be the first."

I'm sure. I'm sure you've sent plenty to their deaths after this fucking McGuffin hunt of yours. Professionals. I'm just a thug for hire, a hammer, not a scalpel. "If you've tried in the past, you obviously would've hired the best the Thieves Guild could offer. No way I succeed where they failed."

"I disagree," he said with conviction.

Something in them had faith in me, despite everything, despite the callous words he had thrown at me an hour ago. He'd told me his truth, that he thought I was unfit to help, yet now he stood there with his knowing eyes that told me I could do this.

I wasn't half as confident.

"Wipe that look off your face. I'm not doing it."

But he still kept his gaze firm and unblinking, staring into my soul. "Even if it could save the world?"

His words hit me like a truck.

"Would you like to help save the world?"

The question that started it all. The one question that brought me to this world in the first place. The question asked of me all those years ago. The question that got me to join up in this crazy experiment. *A thousand years later, and I still don't have any clue as to what the point of any of this was. Why are we here in the first place?* But I had better questions that needed answering right now.

"I thought you said we weren't in danger?"

"We aren't, not right now, but we could be if we don't do something. You said you wanted to help, so help save this world."

"Save the world. You make it so nonchalant, like it's just another job."

Magnus shrugged. "Isn't it, though?"

No. No, it's not. What was being asked of me was beyond dangerous, and if I failed, I wouldn't live long enough to regret it. *Do I want to save the world?* My answer to back then was no. I'd had no desire to save the Earth, only to escape my miserable existence, and now I was being asked again.

Earth was beyond saving—is Nexus any better?

I didn't think so. This world was much the same as Earth, giving humans access to magic and game mechanics didn't change us. As soon as we got our bearings, we set about conquering this world. Killing and enslaving those we thought inferior to us. *We drained this word dry as fast as we fucking could.*

This world was just as corrupt and debased as the one we left. It didn't care about me, so why should I care about it? *Let someone else handle it. I'm going home. You hear that, Ouroboros? I don't want any part of this madness.*

I turned to walk out. To walk away from all of this, half-expecting Ouroboros to stop me, but I met no resistance. "This world doesn't matter to me. Find someone else for your suicide mission."

I left them in silence; the only sound in the room was the echoes of my footfalls. I reached the large iron door that would lead me upstairs and away from this. I had the handle in my grasp when Aliria spoke.

"What about Eris?"

My body froze on its own, nothing stopping me but my heavy heart. *Damn it all to hell.* She knew my weakness and knew exactly how to twist it to her advantage.

The worst part about it was I couldn't even be mad at her. I'd have done the same in her position. I didn't care about Nexus. It was just a place; let it burn for all I cared.

But I absolutely cared about Eris.

I cared for her. For Wilson and Gil. I cared about my friends and my castle. I cared about my warm bed and my balcony view, and I couldn't enjoy any of it if I was dead…but it brought up an important question. *Can I live without them? Can I live with the knowledge that the world might be in trouble, and I could've done something to stop it?*

No. I'd rather die a hundred times than lose my family again.

I huffed, knowing I was beaten. "Fine. I'll hear your plan, but I'm not promising anything."

If I don't have a chance of pulling it off, then I'm out. I'll find another way to save us if it comes to that. I returned to the table with a scowl, only to find Aliria looking quite smug and superior as she plied her power over me. Her demeanor left a sour taste in my mouth, and I needed to find some way to wash it out.

"You know that's your daughter you're leveraging as a bargaining chip, right?"

Her smile fell. *Much better, now let's get back to my need to be committed for even thinking about attempting this.* I took a look at the map and guessed where Magnus had built his castle. I'd only seen a few glimpses of the outside world, so I had nothing but a hunch. I pointed to an open spot on the map, on the far edge of the Badlands.

Right where I guessed Magnus's castle to be.

Magnus didn't smile or acknowledge I was right, but a slight intake of breath told me as much.

"All right, so we're about a four-day ride to Aldrust. Is this a time-sensitive job?"

He shook his head. "Not to you, no. I've been waiting for years. A few days give or take won't be an issue."

That's one thing sorted, but I still don't like this. There are far too many unknowns. "Anything you can tell me about the job, any information I might need?"

"A little. I've got several teams on retainer in Copper Lowtown. Raven is my point of contact for them. So you'll have as much backup as I can provide, but unfortunately my scrying magic doesn't work underground or indoors, so I don't have more actual intel to give you."

Damn, this isn't good. I untied my hairband and ran my hands through my hair before quickly retying it. "Not inspiring a ton of confidence, Magnus. Your team might work for you, but not here. I want my guild in on this. Wilson is one of the best thieves in the business. He could handle this much better than I could."

"Absolutely not. Your Gloom Knights have quite a reputation, and barring a few exceptions, like yourself, I'd sooner do it myself than allow your guild anywhere near this."

Indignation flared through me. My fingernails dug into the soft wood till it hurt. "I trust them with my life, yet I have to work with a team I've never met and a godsdamned shifter to steal one of the most heavily guarded artifacts in the world?"

"In a nutshell."

"Oh, fuck this," I said and pushed off from the table, heading back to the stairwell. "Come get me when you want to stop tying my hands while asking the impossible."

The door was an inch away when a scorching hand grabbed on my arm; it spun me around to face Aliria, whose face was set with a stubborn determination. I jerked my arm from her grasp. "I'm not your plaything. Don't put your hands on me."

Aliria leaned into me, placing her hand on my shoulder this time. My first thought was to pull away again, but something about her demeanor stopped me. She got right up to my ear and whispered, "If you leave now, Eris will die."

"What did you just say?"

Absolute pitch-black rage exploded from my chest in an unrelenting tide. Before I could stop myself, I picked her up by her throat and slammed her against the iron door with a resounding clang. I hadn't called it, but chitin came with my fury.

Subtle scents of the forest flowed around me as it oozed over my forearm and coated my hand and fingers in jagged obsidian.

I squeezed tighter, tearing into her flesh and splashing drops of crimson over my hand. It snaked from her throat to run over my arm to drip to the ground. "Don't you ever fucking threaten her!"

She smiled at me through the pain, which only made me squeeze tighter. I wanted her dead, but first I wanted her to suffer terribly, and I split her pale skin open, drawing even more blood.

Aliria's smile never wavered. She reached out a hand and tapped one finger on my chest, right over my heart. As the first time, my world shattered with pain. The chitin around my arms dissolved to black rain and slunk back under my skin.

I dropped her as my strength waned and blood dripped from my eyes and nose. It spilled metal into my mouth, and I spat it out to join the growing puddle on the floor.

She smirked. Her eyes flashed victorious as she backhanded me. I hit the ground, my cheek landing in nearly scalding blood. I tried to stand, but her foot connected with my ribs and turned me over.

"You don't have the first clue how to use your power do you? What a waste of a knight." She scoffed and walked over to Magnus. "Would you be a dear, love?"

"Of course." He snapped his fingers, and her wound closed as if it'd never been there at all. "Now go apologize to him. You provoked him on purpose."

I stood up, glaring death at her. I hated her, hated her more than I'd ever hated anyone before, in the real world or the virtual. She was nothing but the incarnation of cruelty. And I promised to see her dead before I let her anywhere near Eris.

"You would threaten your own daughter's life, just to force me to cooperate with you. You disgust me."

She barked out a laugh so cold, it chilled my very bones as she wound her finger through Magnus's. "I don't have to lay a finger on her, abomination. You'll kill her long before that."

Her words struck cold fear in my heart, and I wanted to ignore them, storm up the stairs, and flee this place...but I couldn't, and Aliria knew it. *Godsdamn it! If she's lying to me...*

The thick stone floor cracked with every heated step I took. My fury this time, however, burned with cool detachment. My face nearly touched hers when I spoke through clenched teeth. "No more fucking games! Tell me what you mean right now."

"Or what?"

"Or I tear myself to pieces to kill you, bitch. Now tell me!"

Aliria breathed through her nose at me, relaxing her posture to drop her cruel gaze, she stared at me with very human emotions on her face. "I'm not so heartless, you know, to treat my daughter so."

"Could've fooled me."

That garnered me a quiet chuckle. She backed up and looked at me without all the pretense, without her air of superiority. As the cruelty and darkness left her face, she looked so much younger. She actually had a kind face, a face that haunted me.

"I would never harm Eris, not ever. But you will. Whether you want to or not. You're not entirely in control anymore."

Denial was on the tip of my tongue, and I was a millisecond away from denying it with every fiber of my being. But she was right, and I couldn't say otherwise. *I'm not in control of myself anymore, not since I made a deal with the Aspect.*

"But the Aspect is part of the Hive; it can't harm the queen."

"It was part of the Hive, but like you, it's not entirely pure anymore. It's corrupted, and the more power it gains over you, the less it has to obey. One day it will overpower you."

"I won't let it," I said, but my words were hollow. I couldn't stop it; it had already proven as much.

I needed help, but Eris couldn't help me. She'd told me she couldn't.

Aliria could, though, and she knew it.

What made everything worse was that I was playing right into her hands. Whatever game she was playing with me required me to steal Lachrymal's Heart. They needed it, and this was just bait to reel me in.

"What are you offering?"

She smiled, and her kindness disappeared, back to her usual self. "You perform this task for us, and I can rid you of your monster."

There was no room for me to maneuver. She'd beaten me.

I would do anything to keep Eris safe, a fact that was too dangerous for my enemies to know. I was a puppet on strings, dancing for Aliria's amusement, to help achieve her and Magnus's goals. And I couldn't do anything against it. They had me hook, line, and sinker.

I wanted to scream at her, but I calmly made my way back to the table next to Magnus and Raven. I propped myself against the table and stared dead into Magnus's eyes.

"All right, let's steal the heart of a god."

CHAPTER 5 - ROCK AND A HARD PLACE

Eris

It took a few minutes to calm myself down enough to speak without crying or screaming at my own helplessness. I wiped away what few tears managed to escape and composed myself. I took the hands of the children, and it helped.

Gil and Wilson looked at me with a mixture of concern and confusion. The others further down the table whispered about my outburst. Gil scratched his bald head and spoke first, his voice filled with worry.

"Eris, you all right? What's wrong?"

I tried to speak, but my words caught in my mouth, and I choked on them. I shook my head and tried again, but I had to force them out. "Sam's gone."

As soon as the words fled my mouth, my emotions threatened to spill out once more. I fought them down, held back my tears and squeezed Tegen and Chiera's hands tight.

Gil drew his brows together, tilting his head. "Who's Sam?"

Oh no! In my despair, I didn't realize what I'd said. The fact that I let slip his name only sent me further into misery. I couldn't fight the tears that spilled over my cheeks.

"I meant Duran...please don't tell him I told you. He'll be angry with me."

Gil chuckled and grinned, trying not to break out laughing. He looked at me with a smile so warm, it made him glow. "Oh, girl. Have you seen the way that boy looks at you, and you at him? He isn't capable of getting angry at you."

He stood from the table and walked over to me. Gil leaned over and wrapped his humongous arms around me. He pressed his lips gently against the top of my head and whispered in my ear.

"Don't worry your pretty head. I won't tell him." Gil stood up to look at each of the members of the Guild. "None of us heard anything, isn't that right?"

A few yeahs and some nods of agreement rose from the table, all except one. Harper spoke up from further down. His bright orange hair and pale forehead were all I could see of him. "I heard what she said!" His voice held a devious joy in it. As if he was planning something.

Yumiko stood in a flash, her crimson eyes flared with anger. "Shut the fuck up, Harper. You didn't hear shit."

She brushed a lock of her beautiful black hair from her cheek and looked over to me. She gave me a curt nod and a twinge of a smile before sitting back down.

"Thanks, Yu," Evelyn said, humor alight in her golden eyes as she looked over. "Now, what do you mean he's gone?"

"He's not in the castle. I don't know where he is, but I know that it's very far away, and that he's afraid."

"And how do you know this?" Wilson asked from the head of the table, a quizzical expression in his dark gray eyes.

"D and I are connected. He is my bonded, and we can feel each other, no matter how far we are."

Gil whistled at that, which earned him a few chuckles from the others. Though Wilson didn't seem to fully comprehend what I meant, and I couldn't fault that. *Humans don't have a frame of reference for bonding, and I'd be confused if I were in his place.*

"So you can read each other's minds?" he asked, tugging at his full beard.

"No," I said, shaking my head. I'd expected that question and let out a small laugh. "Duran asked the same question when we first bonded, but no, we can't read each other's minds. We can only feel each other's emotions."

Wilson pursed his lips as he frowned, the lines at his eyes and forehead became pronounced as he sighed in frustration. He reached across the table to grab Gil's mug of ale.

"Hey!" Gil protested but didn't stop him.

Wilson chugged the contents and tossed the wooden mug onto the table. It rolled and splashed the last dregs of ale onto the wood, but nobody complained. Everyone was too lost in their own thoughts to worry about a little spill.

"I don't get it, but that's not important at the moment. Duran wouldn't leave without telling anyone, and with how attached the two of you have become, he definitely wouldn't leave without a word to you." Wilson stood up from the table and looked at each one of us in turn. "That means Duran didn't leave here voluntarily."

"There is no way for anyone to get in and out of here without one of us noticing!" Gil shouted.

"That's simply not true. Wilson and I can do it quite easily," Evelyn interrupted.

Gil looked from Evelyn to Wilson. "I call bullshit! We spent nearly two years making sure this place couldn't be infiltrated, and you're telling me the both of you can do it without a sweat."

"Pretty much."

"Of course."

Gil let a groan and buried his face in his hand and reached for his ale, only to realize once again that Wilson had drunk it.

He grumbled under his breath and went to fetch another one, though as he walked passed me, he flashed a kind smile to the children and me.

He came back a minute later, new mug in hand, and immediately started debating with Wilson and Evelyn, with the others swiftly joining in. They got louder and louder, but nothing was getting accomplished.

"All right, all right...settle down, you mongrels," Wilson said, and amazingly, everyone got quiet. "This line of questioning is getting us nowhere, and the answer doesn't matter right now. What is important is that our guild leader has been abducted to gods know where, and we're here bickering like high schoolers."

I didn't know what a high schooler was, but I had to agree on his points. Sitting here going back and forth was stupid.

There was nothing more that I wanted to do than immediately rush off and scour the entire island to search for him, but I couldn't. I didn't have the first clue as to where to start, and I wasn't strong enough to go off on my own regardless.

I hated it, hated my own weakness and inability to do anything to help my bonded, but if I couldn't help Sam...*I'd only be a hinderance, and even if I could, I can't leave the children by themselves. I can't help Sam.* I knew he could take care of himself just fine, and I had to trust that, had to trust that my bonded would come back to me, or I'd never get a moment's peace.

"We can't help the guild leader. Even if we knew who has taken him, we don't have a single lead to follow."

Silence draped over the room as everyone realized how powerless we were to help him. Makenna looked up from her meal to join in. "Who do we like for this?"

"An excellent question," Wilson said.

"I think we all know the most likely suspect," Gil interjected.

I shot my head up, and everyone was nodding in agreement. The answer was so obvious to everyone but me. "Who?" I nearly shouted. *I can't begin to guess who it could be, so how could they?*

Evelyn just stared at me. "Magnus. It has to be."

"Oh," I said. It *was* obvious.

"Duran killed quite a few of his men, so he's getting his revenge," Wilson said.

Gil thumped his large hands on the table, causing me to jump. "What are we going to do about it?" he asked, looking at all of us.

I sighed, trembling as I stood, my heart in pieces. I knew the correct answer, knew what we had to do.

"We do nothing."

Gil's eyes went wide. "What? You should be the first person busting down the gates to get him."

"That's exactly what I want, but what good would it do? We don't have the faintest idea of where to look."

"We could at least ask our informants. They could have a lead for us," Wilson said as he stroked his beard.

"And how well did that go for us the first time around? Might as well be a ghost with how difficult he is to pin down," Evelyn chimed in. "And you can bet no one is going to spill any secrets, not to us. Magnus has too much money to throw at his problems."

Wilson sighed into his hands before his head shot up and he slapped himself on the forehead. "Gods, we're stupid." He motioned with his hand, his eyes staring at something I couldn't see. *His interface, I guess.* He moved his hand for a few moments before growling in anger. "Of course, it wouldn't be that easy."

"What?" I asked.

"I tried to send Duran a message, but his contact card is grayed out," Wilson said, his face distressed, full of anger. He slammed his fist into the stone above the fireplace and cursed as his skin tore and blood oozed out of the wound, which he ignored.

Wilson threw his hands up, which only caused flecks of blood to fly in the air. "Godsdamn it! What the hell else are we supposed to do?"

Evelyn's eyes turned to me with a curious smile. "I think our little queen has an idea."

I had to frown at her. "It's an idea, but I'm not happy about it."

Gil took another drink of his ale. "Well, let's hear it."

"From what I see, there isn't any way to help D. There is too much we don't know, and it would be nothing more than a wild goose chase to try…much as that hurts me to admit, I don't see a way to help him right now. So I don't think we should even try."

"He can take care of himself; I believe that, but I have to do something other than stay here, or I'll be sick with worry. I'm going to take Cheira and Tegen home."

Evelyn perked up at this. "Back to Slaughter Woods?"

"The Silvanus Darkwoods, yes."

She smiled wide at me, her bright white teeth and golden eyes lighting up with anticipation, her whole body awash with the energy of adventure. "I'm so going with you. It's been ages."

I happily accepted her offer. There was no way I could go by myself, and I was about to beg the guild to help me anyway. "Of course. I was going to ask you anyway. I can't go alone; I'll die by myself long before we reach the woods."

Evelyn tilted her in her chair to glance at the other members. "Any other volunteers?"

"You're not leaving me behind," Adam said.

"Of course not, little brother."

Adam scoffed, but he was hiding a smile. "We're twins, idiot."

Wilson chimed in next. "I would love to help, but with Duran gone, it falls to me to lead the guild, so I have to stay."

"Well, if Wilson is too afraid of the big, bad, man-eating woods, then I'll go," Gil said.

I beamed at him. "Thank you, Gil."

He just chuckled. "Can't let my best friend's main squeeze go alone. He would never forgive me. Besides, you've grown on me."

"I'll go too," Makenna said with a raise of her hand.

Everyone looked at the little woman with surprise, to which she flushed with embarrassment. Her face turned as scarlet as her hair, but her emerald eyes held determination and excitement in them. "Just think of all the unusual creatures that live in those woods. I can't miss an opportunity to study them."

Her answer received a round of laughter from the entire guild. "Of course, leave it to the bug freak to want to go," Harper said.

"Shut up," Makenna replied.

"Read the room, you moron," Gil said, pointing to the children and me.

"Oh, right. Sorry, I forgot."

I ignored his words, too thankful for the other members to let anything get me down. "Thank you, all of you."

Wilson stood from his chair. "All right, everyone going, get packed. You know the drill."

Immediately, there was a bustle of activity as everyone filed out of the dining hall, leaving me and the children by ourselves.

Well, best go pack myself.

***

It was painfully apparent that I owned very little. I packed my clothes in a spare bag in Sam's room, but that was all my belongings in the world. *I shouldn't have spurned Sam's attempt to give me money before. I'll probably need it.*

I sighed as I stared at the elegant nightstand by the bed and opened the bottom drawer. *He won't care in the slightest, but why do I still feel like a thief?* I opened the chest of gold and grabbed a handful, tossing it in a small canvas bag with a leather drawstring, and pocketed the money with regret. *I'll pay this back, love. I promise.*

I stood, all my possessions in order, and went with the children to find Gil.

As I reached the inner bailey, I opened the door to Gil's forge. The air was hot, and while the temperature didn't bother me, it stifled the air and hung in my lungs with every breath. Several sets of metal benches sat along the wall, and I told Tegen and Cheira to sit while I went around the corner to speak to Gil.

He was hunched over a grindstone in the corner of the space. The sleeves of his sapphire tunic bunched around his biceps, showing his dark, muscled forearms. Sweat dripped down his head and neck as he worked furiously to sharpen a large, black axe. Sparks arced from the stone, landing harmless on the dirt floor.

I called out to him, but it was drowned out by grating metal against stone. I tried again, louder, nearly shouting.

Gil turned, stopping his work. "Done packing already?" he asked, wiping his brow.

I nodded.

He leaned around me to glance at the meager bundle I had slung around my back, at which he rubbed the back of his bald head and grinned. "Looks like you don't have much. That won't do, won't do at all." He turned back to his work, grinding away at the axe. He spoke between grinds. "Once I'm done with this bastard, I'll see about getting you more gear."

He nearly jumped as if he was stung by a bee. "That reminds me! I have a present for you. I'll give it to you here in a minute!" He turned back to his weapon and started whistling to himself as he worked, a soft but upbeat tune to which he bobbed along, filled with energy.

Gil worked for half an hour while I went and stayed with the children. When he was done, he came around the corner with the massive black axe strapped to a makeshift harness behind his back. He had a box in his hand and set it at my feet with a cheeky grin.

I knelt and pried the lid off the box. It fell to the dirt with a thump, and I gazed at what Gil had been so excited to show me. A bundle of fabrics and leather stared back at me. I picked up the first piece in the box. A thick leather cloak rolled out. It was short and would stop just above my knees. As I picked up the dark brown garment, a slight jangle sounded, nearly inaudible to anyone but someone with my hearing. I turned over the cloak to see the inside was interwoven with chains. *Chainmail.*

"It's nothing fancy. I wanted to make it out of shadowsteel, but I used the last of my supply working on my project. So it's not as good as I would like, but its Aldrustian steel, so it's durable and lighter than average. I also sewed a weight into the hood. It should keep from falling off your head if we have to hide your features."

"It's perfect. Thank you, Gil."

"Think nothing of it." He smiled wide. "As I said, you've grown on me, and you may not realize it, but you being here has had a major effect on all of us."

"What do you mean?"

"I've known Duran for a long time. In fact, I met him at probably the worst period of his life. I've seen him at his worst and what I thought was his best...until he met you. It's obvious to those who've spent so much time with him. He's different when he's with you, and it makes us happy to have some light return to his eyes."

It dawned on me that I didn't know how Sam and Gil met. Sam called Gil his best friend, and I could see why, but I wanted to know their story.

"How'd the two of you meet?"

Gil laughed and tugged on his ear, but his eyes looked away from me. "Um, when he tried to rob me."

I snorted. "Really?"

He nodded but looked at me sideways. "You don't seem surprised by that."

"I'm not. I know Sam used to be a bandit. I don't like it, but it's in the past, and he's not that person anymore."

"True, but anyway, back to how we met," he said and sat beside me. "I was working as an adventurer in the Compass Kingdom. Ran with a guild of gold-ranked players, so we started taking more dangerous quests, trying to earn as much as possible. One day the leader comes back with a quest to guard a caravan of elven merchants delivering goods to and from Yllsaria. The pay was good, so we all agreed and teleported to Siltfall and met the merchants as they came out of the Emerald Ocean. Two days out, and things were quiet."

"Until they weren't," I said.

"Until they weren't. Caravan gets ambushed, and Karen takes an arrow to her throat…she drops, and all hell breaks loose. I rush in with my axe, but it's clear that we're outnumbered. My guildmates are dropping like flies, and then out comes this kid, a wild glint in his eye, sword stained with my friends' blood."

My heart sped up as he told his story, cotton in my mouth. "Duran?"

He nodded. "He fought like a devil, but you've seen what he can do. Second best swordsman I've ever seen."

"What happened next?"

He looked up and to the side, staring off into space. He stood up quickly. "That'll have to wait. We've got to get a move on. Evelyn just sent me a message, and I'd rather not keep her waiting."

Gil gathered up his bag, which hung next to a rack of swords. He took a look at the swords and back at me. "You need a weapon."

I shook my head, standing and going to rouse the children. "I've got magic, so I don't need to carry a sword."

"Magic alone won't help you if an enemy gets close. You need something stabby, just in case."

I chuckled and ruffled Tegen's hair as he tried to go back to sleep. I appreciated Gil's concern, but I'd gotten stronger at controlling my magic, and I didn't need to carry a weapon.

"It'll be easier to show you," I said and held out my hand.

I pulled at the magic that thrummed through my veins. The magic that flowed through time and space, connecting me with my ancestors.

The magic of the Hive.

My hands pooled with smoke and brought the scents of the Nymirian forest spilling through my fingers. The smoke dripped down my hands to cascade around my feet and pulsed with the energy of every living creature under my bailiwick. The descendants of the once-proud Hive.

My children.

I let them rest in their safe havens; I had no need to call them to me. I pulled much deeper into the Hive Mind, drowning myself in verdant smoke and the echoes of the Mnemosyne. I'd never dug this deep into my magic before, and I let the shades of the past whisper to me and guide me to where I thought I needed to be.

A brush of my own Aspect guided me to the spell I wanted. I had never used this spell before, but I tugged, and it came without resistance. The Aspect wished for to me to stay, immerse myself in power at my command, but I couldn't; my magic was fading quickly, and I needed to see this done. I had to prove I could do this.

I brought the spell I wanted with me out of the Hive Mind and departed. As I came out of it, the spell activated, pooling chitin over my skin, burrowing out of every one of my pores. Black chitin wrapped itself around my arm and crawled up my hand to form to my desires—a blade of darkness, sharp enough to sever the very air in two.

Throughout the process, Gil had stood there silent, dumbfounded at my display of power. As the chitin sword finished constructing itself, he whistled appreciatively. He looked at me with a sly smile on his face and wonder in his eyes. "Badass. I've never seen magic used like that. I mean, you didn't even use Script."

Oh, right. Sam voiced the same thought when he first saw my magic, but I didn't see why it was all that special. Liam could use magic without spells, so why was my magic any different? The Hive was ingrained into my soul; why would I need to use an incantation to use a part of myself?

"Hive magic doesn't require such things."

Gil laughed, his eyes still wide at the lingering smoke that drifted down my hands. "Yeah, I can see that."

He once more stared off into space and cursed.

"All right, all right. Jeez, have some patience, woman," he muttered as he turned to me. "I know I promised I'd help you get ready, but I've got some last-minute preparations to handle." He opened the door and pointed at a building across from us. "Head into the storehouse and take whatever you need."

I nodded, but he'd already gone around the corner. I glanced at Tegen and Cheira, who'd woken up from their nap and were now drawing in the dirt, completely disregarding how filthy their clothes were getting. "I've got to go next door, do you want to come with me or stay here?"

"I want to finish the drawing," Cheira said, her voice light, happy.

"Yeah," Tegen replied.

"Okay, but if you need anything, I'm just over there," I said and pointed to the storehouse. "And don't be afraid to ask Gil for help. He's a good human, I promise."

They nodded emphatically, not paying me any mind. I smiled at them. *It's good to see things have changed. The old Hive wasn't like this. Makes me hopeful for the future.*

I got up and left the heated shop. The cool breeze was soothing on my skin; it swept up small leaves and dust that swirled in little clouds as the breeze rolled through. The storehouse was easy to find, as it was the only other building besides the stables and Gil's shop. The wood old and worn, but well-kept, and the thatch roof looked fresh and damp.

I opened the pine door and was bathed in darkness.

To my surprise, I wasn't alone in the building. Adam looked up from one of the many shelves that ran through the large building. It was filled with more items than I'd ever seen in once place; even the store that Sam took me to paled next to this. Nearly a dozen rows of wooden shelves were stacked in a neat and orderly fashion. Potions, tools, clothes, and boxes upon boxes of things labeled in small, neat handwriting that I couldn't make out from this distance. *Oh, this is a lot of stuff. I don't have the first clue what I need.* Thankfully, Adam noticed my utter confusion and graciously decided to show mercy on me.

"What are you looking for?"

I smiled sheepishly at him. "I haven't the faintest idea," I admitted.

He laughed to himself and sat the blue vial in his hands back on the shelf and walked over to me. He looked me over, noticing my clothing, and gave me a nod of approval. "I take it you're needing supplies for the trip?"

I nodded at him.

"What kind of supplies do you need?"

One of the strands of my hair had fallen loose, and I twirled it around my finger. I was a little embarrassed about how utterly clueless I was about so many things. "I'm not sure."

He smiled a tight smile and started looking around the room, using his finger to count the aisles, looking for something in particular. He shook his head and muttered to himself. Almost so quiet that I couldn't hear it. "No, that won't work." He rubbed his hands together and clapped. "I've got it!"

Adam ran over to the wall and grabbed a large backpack. Well, it probably would have been average on anyone else, but it would look ridiculous on my slight frame. He seemed to notice that very thing as he grabbed for it. "Definitely not."

He went through the many bags that lined the wall until he found a small bag that looked like it would fit nicely. It was made of worn leather but seemed quite sturdy. He smiled, and his eyes glazed over and ran through the tightly packed aisles at random, grabbing things by the handful and stuffing them in the bag. I tried to keep up but was almost immediately lost as to what he was putting in the bag. It took him next to no time to fill the bag up completely. In less than five minutes, he returned to me and handed me the bag. I went to take it from him, only for him to snatch it from my hands.

"I forgot something," he said in a rush and went over to the racks of potions on the shelves. He snagged a small red vial and a blue one. On his way back, he picked up what looked like a piece of leather.

"You probably won't need these, as we tend to carry them in excess, but it won't hurt to have them just in case."

He stuffed both vials into the leather cloth, which had pouches sewn into them. He rolled them up and tied them with a thin cord before dropping it into the bag and handed it to me once more, though this time I was much more careful about grabbing for it. "There you go—should have ample supplies for the trip."

I opened the bag and peeked inside. "What's all in here?" I asked.

Adam paced back and forth, scratching at his head as if he couldn't remember what he had placed inside the pack either. "Um, should be your typical adventurers' pack. Tent, pillow, and blankets. Along with two weeks' of dry rations and spices. Flint and steel with tinder. Dungeon delving kit. Fifty feet of tightly wound rope and two torches. Hunting kit with a knife. Along with a first aid kit and one health and mana potion. Should be more than enough."

I tried to cram my meager bundle of clothes in with the bag and just managed to squeeze everything in and close the bag. I hefted it on my shoulders and found it cumbersome, but manageable. I had to untie my cloak to secure the bag to my back, but once I had done so and retied the cloak, I found the thick leather concealed the bag nicely and that it didn't jostle or clank when I moved around. I beamed at Adam. "Thank you so much!"

He looked at me, confused. "For what?"

"For the backpack..."

His eyes lit up with recognition. "Ah, right, right, right. Of course, you're more than welcome."

At that moment, the door to the storeroom opened in haste. It banged against the wall outside with a heavy thump. Evelyn stormed in. She didn't look angry, but the force of the door slam suggested she was. Her posture was one of aggravation, even if she kept it off her face. Her long silver hair whispered behind her back as she strode through the storehouse. The sharp clack of her shoes on the stone echoed, and her bright golden eyes shone with the light of the sun even in darkness.

"There you are. I should have known you'd—" She took note of my presence, almost like an afterthought. "Oh, little queen, you're here as well." She shifted her gaze to my back. "You're all set to go?"

I nodded. "I am."

"Good. Then let's hit the road."

Adam seemed to panic a bit at the abruptness of Evelyn's arrival. "Wait, I'm not ready yet."

Evelyn turned and glared at her brother, her eyes not accepting Adam's excuse. "You've had your bag packed five minutes after we left the dining hall, and you have all of the constructs and creatures that you could possibly need or want, so don't give me that nonsense. Quit dragging your feet and get your ass in gear."

Adam nodded, crestfallen, his head hanging low as he followed his sister out.

What a strange family. I laughed at that; I had no room to talk. I quickly followed the back into the biting daylight.

Chapter 6 - The Salted Mire

The four of us made our way to the stables. Since I was with them, they couldn't take a teleporter, but the others didn't seem upset at the prospect. Adam opened the door to the stables for us, and we walked inside.

The others scrunched their noses at the smell of the stable. The raw stench of manure, sweat, and animal blended together with the body heat of the horses. I didn't mind the smell, though. Evelyn, Adam, and Gil immediately went to separate stalls each one housed a different horse.

The horses recognized their owners and were happy to see them. I didn't have a horse of my own, a fact that became apparent to everyone quickly.

Adam thumbed his finger back at me. "Who's sharing a horse with her?"

I walked over to the furthest pen from the door to see a familiar face. I smiled at the obsidian horse. "Why don't I ride Lacuna?"

Adam laughed. "Don't bother; she hates everyone but Duran."

I leaned over the pen to run my hand over her face and along her thick mane of midnight hair. Lacuna nuzzled against me. "Good girl," I cooed.

Adams's jaw dropped, which caused me to giggle. "Well, I take back what I said."

The others busied themselves with saddling their own horses, while I went to grab Tegen and Cheira.

They hadn't moved an inch, still playing where I had left them. I picked them both up, dusted off their filthy clothes, and carried them to Lacuna.

I sat them on the horse and climbed up; it was difficult but much easier than the last time I tried. *Sam's not here to do it for you. Do it yourself.* It took two tries, but I managed. I let both of the children ride in front of me; they were small enough to fit in the seat together comfortably.

Everyone else was atop their horses. Evelyn rode a deep gray horse with a snow-white mane, while Adam sat astride and beige and chocolate horse with deep brown eyes. Gil's horse was nearly as tall as Lacuna, but where Lacuna was lean and tall, Gil's horse was clearly a warhorse, with a mountain of muscle. It was a deep champagne with black hair that was longer than the others.

They were all beautiful creatures, but none could compare to Lacuna. I reached down to stroke her hair.

"Is everyone ready to go?" I asked.

"We are, but why do I feel like we're missing something?"

Gil's question was answered by a high-pitched scream. "Wait for me!"

The four of us turned our heads simultaneously at the source of the commotion. A shock of bright red hair tied back in pigtails flapping in the wind greeted us as Makenna ran full sprint from the keep. Clouds of dust rose in her wake as she ran with her bag nestled in her arms. She tried to sling it on her back and keep running at the same time, but she tripped and landed in the dirt.

She sat up with a groan and wiped the mass of dust from her traveling clothes.

Makenna wore dark green wool pants that hugged her legs quite nicely, and a black sleeveless tunic only a tad big on her. She was maybe an inch taller than me, and even with the dirt, she was too cute.

She doubled over and tried to catch her breath, gulping down huge lungful's of air. Gil inhaled sharply and muttered to himself beside me, "I forgot about her. Oh, she's so going to poison me in my sleep."

His words both confused me and intrigued me at the same time, so I had to ask. I turned to face Gil. "Why would she poison you?"

I didn't think my question was rude, but Gil shot me a heated look. His eyes pleaded with me, but the damage was done.

"Gilgamesh! You ass! You forgot me, didn't you?"

Gil sighed into his hand. "Shit."

Oh, that's why. I'm sorry, Gil. I think I just got you in trouble.

"I'm sorry, Kenna. I got so absorbed in my work that I tuned everything out."

She huffed, and it was clear she was still angry at him, but she let slip a grin, letting him know he was forgiven.

Makenna still jabbed a finger at him. "Since you have so much time for your side projects, then you have time to get Cinder saddled for me."

"Of course I can," Gil said, hopping off his horse and walking as fast as his legs could carry him back to the stables.

He returned a few minutes later with Cinder in tow.

I found her name to be appropriate. Her coat was such a bright brown that it seemed like fire alight under the eyes of the sun, and she had a mane the color of a burning wick, black, which lightened to a bright auburn as it fell down her flank.

Makenna dropped her pack and ran over to her so she could run her hands over her coat. Cinder reveled in the affection, but the others weren't so accommodating with her. Evelyn hummed under her breath for a few moments, eyeing Makenna before she got tired of it and yelled at her.

"Quit playing with your horse and let's get a move on, we're already behind schedule."

Makenna stood with a jolt. "Right, sorry!"

She leaned to pick up her pack and closed it. She motioned with her hand, and the pack vanished. Makenna expertly climbed onto Cinder, a method that seemed the most natural thing in the world. *I'll have to see if I can get her to teach me that.* As soon as she was in her saddle, Evelyn led the group to the castle gate, which opened from a sharp whistle from Gil. A young-looking man on top of the wall gave a sharp nod and lowered the gate for us.

The heavy wooden gate thumped on the dirt road, sending more than a few clouds of dust spiraling into the wind. The whistling breeze muted the clomp of hooves over the wood; it screamed past our ears like the wail of the dead and brought with it a chill from the lake below us.

I shivered despite the beating gaze of the sun. We rode off the gate, and with a command from the gate guard, the massive gate began to rise back once more. The Gloom Knights all stayed for a moment to make sure that it was secure before we set out.

As soon as the gate shut, Evelyn took off at speed, not bothering to look behind her to see if we were following.

With a swear from Gil, the others raced to catch up with her. I followed along, but at a reduced speed. Just enough to keep them in sight of me while I tried to master horsemanship.

Lacuna was a very smart horse, and she helped me as much as she could. It took around a couple hours or so of riding before I got the hang of it. Lacuna would neigh and speed up whenever I was in danger of falling behind, so she made for a competent instructor.

Once I had learned the basics of horseback riding, I sped up to join the rest of the party. Gil rode side by side with Makenna, while Adam and Evelyn were leading the group from the front. I had no idea the direction we were heading, but at least they did. Gil turned in his saddle to look at me when I had caught up with them.

"Hey, look, who finally joined the group."

Makenna let out a snort of laughter but spared me a smile and a look of solidarity.

"It's okay, took me a few good tries before I got the hang of it, so don't let it bother you."

I nodded my thanks to her. I'd spent most of my attention on learning the ropes of riding by myself and making sure the children weren't going to fall off, and I had neglected to notice that we had been heading in a different direction than the one Sam and I took to the Compass Kingdom.

We'd passed out of the green plains and hills that surrounded the castle and were now in unfamiliar territory for me. There were still plenty of trees and green grass blowing in the wind, but it seemed like with every passing mile, there was a little less life around us.

It took me quite some time to notice, but after three or four hours of mostly silent riding, I had to speak up.

"What's going on with the surroundings?" I asked Gil.

He took a look around as if he didn't understand my meaning.

"Oh, this is your first time being out this way, so I guess it would be a bit of a shock if you've never been here before." He pointed northwest. "'Bout five days ride is the South Kingdom. A brutish place, but home to the largest salt mine on Nexus."

"Why does that matter?"

"Well, the mine is important for a number of reasons. There are a few other salt mines dotted around, but nothing compared to the size of this one." Gil stretched his arms out for emphasis. "I'm talking hundreds upon hundreds of feet deep, with miners working around the clock to haul as much as they can. It's undeniably a profitable business, and it's made King Sykes one of the most influential of the five kings." He gestured to the land around us, a little sadness in his eyes. "But that profit comes at a cost. The salt mined over the decades bled into the ground, into the water, and pretty much everywhere else. Turned the land sour."

Makenna sighed in agreement with Gil. "Welcome to the Salted Mire. Nothing but salt-soaked marshlands for a hundred miles."

I sniffed at the air. It was slight, but hints of salt lingered in the air.

Gil laughed bitterly when I pointed it out. "Get used to it. It only gets worse the further we go."

I frowned at his back. *The smell doesn't bother me now, but if it gets more intense, I may have to cover my nose.* Salt wasn't my favorite; it burned my nose in high doses, and I hoped it would at least be bearable for me. We lapsed into silence once more, though I didn't mind. It let me enjoy the greenery while I still had the chance. I daydreamed as we rode.

My thoughts briefly thought of home, but mostly I thought of Sam. I couldn't banish the worry in my chest, so I wished it would leave me be. It did nothing but ache.

With my heart so low, I tried to focus on other things, but the long stretches of silence left me with little to occupy my time. Gil and Makenna chatted happily to one another, and Adam and Evelyn were engrossed in some form of hushed conversation, but that left me with no one to talk to.

I suppose I could have woken up Tegen and Cheira, who had fallen asleep about half an hour after we'd left, but that would have been selfish of me. Both of them were sleeping comfortably, and I refused to ruin that just for the sake of alleviating my boredom.

The others were oblivious to my agitation, and I couldn't even be mad at them. They weren't excluding me on purpose, so I just kept riding along as the green landscape slowly died to make way to wet and muggy scrubland. The ground squelched underfoot, and water pooled in the tracks we left. The air became stifling and heavy with each passing step we took. The stench of salt grew more pronounced.

My already dwindling happiness was soundly ruined as we got closer to the salt ridden marshes.

I loved nature, every living aspect of it, and after a thousand years of the pitch-black void, I had reveled in nature once more, but this wasn't natural.

The poisoned earth sickened me to my very core. *To destroy the environment for the sake of money is abhorrent. The greed of humans disgusts me.* Life was more important than wealth or power.

This lesson, I learned the hard way.

The entomancer race paid the highest price for our greed. If humans aren't careful, they'll have to pay for their sins someday. The last of the greenery fell away to gray, and so sunk my spirits.

With nothing else to do, I resorted to opening up my Hive Mind. I kept one hand on Lacuna's reins while I let the other rest on her flank, allowing a trickle of magic dribble out of my fingers to drift to the muddy road.

I plunged myself into the small amount of life that lingered here—pockets of resistance to humanity's intrusions. There were very few spiders or ants anywhere near. They clung to the last remaining trees; scorpions and cockroaches seemed to be the majority of the holdouts. However, the scorpions were unhappy at the salt-rich land, and yet, they still survived in the heavy moisture that sunk through the ground. The cockroaches were indifferent to everything and carried on unhindered by the salt. I poured a trickle of my consciousness into them all.

All my little ones, going about their lives. They, too, acknowledged my presence and rejoiced for their queen. I poured as much love as I could into our connection and spent a little time with them while we rode. Having used this particular spell more than the others, it drained my mana the slowest.

I still had to be careful of my mana usage, but I could handle using it better now. The more creatures I touched with the Hive Mind, the more mana it cost me, but as we went deeper into the Mire, fewer and fewer could stay with me. I bid them farewell and was about to sever the connection when I noticed a strange bird on one of the trees.

One of my little spiders watched it from its home in the deadwood. It was afraid of the bird, and though it looked right at my spider, it made no attempt to eat it.

All birds were the enemy of my little ones. *My goddess loves to pit her creatures against each other. So why isn't it eating the spider?* I pooled more of my power into the little spider, trying to get a better look at the bird.

It was clearly a bird, but it wasn't like any I had ever seen before. It was large, black, and menacing. Its beak was a striking blood red. As it looked at the spider, it shifted. Its whole body flickered for a second, like a mirage. The singular bird leaked shadows, bleeding ink out into the world, before it faded for a second.

It was there, then it was gone, replaced by three identical copies.

Each of them looked not at each other, but out in the distance, where we happened to be riding by. The three birds shifted themselves, creating more and more of them as I watched. Dozens of them appeared before one flickered on top of the spider I was controlling and crushed it underfoot.

With the death of the spider, my mind flooded back to my body in a rush and left me with a pounding migraine. I gasped as I came back to myself, jerking in the saddle and managing to wake up both of the children. I looked up from them to find the others looking at me with mixed emotions, from concern and confusion to bored curiosity.

Gil spoke up first. "What's wrong, Eris?"

I didn't know how to explain what had happened. It was confusing to me, and I knew I would just muddle things if I tried to explain what I saw, but I tried my best anyway.

I paused over my words before I spoke. "Um, I'm not entirely sure myself." I shifted in my saddle to point at the tree a few hundred feet away, where even now the birds kept shifting and multiplying. "But there are some strange birds in the trees over there."

Gil and Makenna laughed off my explanation, I guess thinking I was enamored over the wildlife, but Evelyn frowned, drawing a firm line with her pale lips.

"What did they look like?"

I tried to recount their appearance. "Large and black, with really red beaks...and odd. They kept shifting, like an illusion."

Both Gil and Makenna stopped chuckling, and they turned to face me with anxiety on their faces.

"How many were there?" Makenna asked.

I told her. "Just one at first, then they multiplied."

"Oh, shit," Adam cursed.

The others reacted in a similar manner, their relaxed attitudes shattering as they drew arms and climbed down off their horses. I was utterly lost at this point, but I stopped Lacuna and followed suit, dropping to the ground and sinking about a foot into the swamp. The mud and wet earth slid between my toes and covered my feet.

While I had no trouble navigating through the muck, the others were hobbling and taking concerted steps. I went over to Gil, who seemed to be having some difficulty standing upright on the uneven and soft road.

"What is going on?" I asked him.

He looked off in the distance, his face solemn and firm. "We've been marked."

Am I supposed to know what that means? "What?" I asked.

Evelyn inclined her head to the tree line, where over a hundred of the birds perched, staring us down. "Shades."

Adam barked a laugh. "It's about to get exciting."

As if by command, the flock of shades rose in unison from the trees, taking to the skies and unleashing a horrendous caw.

It sent shivers of fear through me and made me want to do nothing but flee and never look back. Their echo reverberated through my skull, and all I wanted to was curl into a ball from the pain. Gil reached me and hauled me to my feet.

"Stand firm. Don't let their mind games affect you. It'll get worse if you don't fight it."

"Here they come!" Makenna shouted.

They sent another debilitating screech at us, and a wave of death descended on us.

Hundreds of the shades swept from the trees to assault us, and with every passing moment, more appeared. Each of them dripped shadows like ink from a giant squid in the water. They blotted out the sky with their shifting darkness, and as they dove down, I jumped out of the way, finding ample footing through the damp muck.

"Tegen, Cheira, hide. I'll find you when this is over!" I yelled at them.

Without a second's hesitation, they bolted from Lacuna and took off into the marsh, sprinting through the reeds out of sight. I regrouped with the guild, who were having a much worse time navigating in the sticky marsh, their feet sunk deep into the soft earth.

Even though they were having difficulty moving, they were far more deadly than I. Each time the birds swooped down to attempt to claw us apart, they died.

Gil swung his glowing axe and slaughtered dozens with ease. Each time his giant black axe struck, sparks flew out and set the birds alight. With a horrendous screech, they burst into flames before withering and turning to shadows.

Even though I was having an easier time moving, I still wasn't faster than the shades. They showed an animalistic cunning, catching me off guard and raking their sharp claws over my exposed arms. I cried out as sharp talons ripped through my skin. Blood ran from the deep gashes to drop down my arm.

By the void, that burns!

Their claws left shadows to stick to my wound, eating away at my exposed blood. *I need to protect myself.* I couldn't enter the Hive Mind in the heat of battle, but I accessed the two spells I had on the top of my tongue: *Chitin Armor* and *Chitin Sword*. More and more of them kept coming, and the five of us had separated in the wetlands.

"Quick, regroup in the trees!" Evelyn shouted and headed into the largest mass of birds.

Something happened to her—a translucent shimmer formed just off her skin. As if controlled by a gust of wind, it blew out in a circle around her. As soon as it touched one of the birds, they simply dissolved, cracking and turning to black mist as they died by the hundreds. Enough to give us an opening to run to the copse of dead trees a couple dozen yards in front of us.

"What are you waiting for? Get moving!"

Gill followed through the hole Evelyn made for us.

I took off after the giant, quickly gaining ground on both of the Gloom Knights as I ran through the mud. I kept pace with Evelyn as we reached the trees. A random dead branch from a tree snagged at my cloak but didn't tear through as we dove behind cover.

It was a short run, but I was panting as if I had run for miles. My nerves screamed at me, and my beating heart drowned out the world around me. The shades circled overhead, screeching in unison. Fear welled in my stomach and my hands shook, and I fought the desire to turn and run. To escape.

Evelyn smiled at me, even though her eyes watched the rest of the guild and the incoming swarm. "You can move, I'll give you that. Now let's see how you fight."

I nodded breathlessly and called upon my magic. Evelyn's eyes rose by a fraction as green smoke flowed from my hands, and black chitin appeared from my skin. I shrugged off my backpack and cloak before the sharp chitin tore through the leather. It crawled up my skin in seconds and covered me from head to toe.

As the chitin slithered over my head, I lost the ability to breathe until it hardened and allowed two small slits under my nose. Chitin didn't have a smell itself, but it carried with it the scent of the forest, and when it formed over my eyes, my vision swirled with green light. In the bright day, it faded, but in the low light of the salt-soaked mire, everything was clear as day.

Coating my entire body with chitin took a massive amount of mana, and when I used it in tandem with *Chitin Sword*, my limited mana pool dropped even lower. With two simple spells, I was down to less than half, which fell by the minute as I kept both spells going. *I doubt I have enough to last five minutes. By the void, I'm weak.*

I'd gained a little bit of control over my magic while traveling with Sam, but I would still be considered a novice when compared to any other member of the Hive. *Even the apocritans and mantearians could use more magic than what I'm able to muster right now. And I'm supposed to be the Hive Queen; the other races would've laughed me right off the throne.*

Makenna lagged behind Gil as they charged over the soggy ground. The squelching mud was overshadowed by the cacophonous sound of hundreds of feathers flapping in unison. The shades gained on the pair quickly; it was apparent that they wouldn't reach the tree line before the birds were on them.

Makenna stopped, drew nearly a dozen long needles from seemingly out of nowhere, each of them tipped with a glossy, dark liquid. With pinpoint accuracy, she flung her hands in the air, and each needle pierced through a shade, killing them instantly.

What was strange was one of the ones she hit was higher than the others, and when it died, nearly a dozen others followed it in death, ones she hadn't touched.

"Go for the puppeteers! They're the controllers!" Evelyn shouted next to me.

"Yeah, we know! But how the hell are we supposed to tell them apart?" Gil asked, swinging his ax.

The shades attacked en masse, but they couldn't do more than superficial wounds as Gil and Makenna were both wearing thick leather armor that held up to the birds' sharp beaks and claws. Gil had donned a full-faced helmet, and Makenna pulled her hood taut over her head, leaving the shades no way to inflict more than scratches.

As before, they showed more intelligence than any bird should have, and when they couldn't swarm their prey, they cawed in unison a grating shriek that sent panic through my body. I wanted to run screaming, but I stood my ground and tried to fight through their tricks.

The others were far less affected by the shades' shout than I was, and Evelyn ran from the trees to join her friends. "Wait for me!" I called and ran after her, not knowing what I was going to contribute to the fight.

When I reached Gil and Makenna, the shades changed. In a fraction of a second, they backed into the sky and shifted again, but this time they folded back into one another, forming five large rolling shadows suspended in the air.

"What are they doing?" I asked.

"Morphing. Shades can take the shape of anything they've seen before. I expect they realized a flock of birds wasn't getting the job done," Gil said.

"What are they going to change into?" I asked as we all waited for the shadows to take shape.

Before anyone could respond, five humanoid shapes dropped from the endless darkness to attack us, and the shadows overhead disappeared to allow some of the muted sunlight to stream in from the overcast. Each of the five shades looked human; in fact, they looked exactly like the five of us, albeit without any concrete facial features, just more twisting shadows. Without a word, we began fighting our doppelgängers.

My shade swung at me with a facsimile of my chitin sword, but it wasn't made of actual chitin, so when I brought my sword up to block, it bit into my rival's shadow blade.

It hissed at me and let out a cry of pain. *Is it using its own body as a weapon?* The answer didn't matter as I pressed forward, stabbing and slashing with all the finesse of a child wielding a toy. I knew I lacked skill with the sword, but I didn't need to be a master to hit a single target.

My sword wouldn't cut through the shade's, but with each landed attack, the shade screamed, and droplets of shadows trickled to the ground. For all the intelligence of the creature, it had no skill with the sword but still landed a couple of good hits.

They glanced off my armor, causing only superficial damage and chipping. *Least it can't get through my armor. I'm safe as long as I can keep it up.* It had been only a handful of minutes since I cast them, but already both spells were wearing me out. Sweat beaded on my forehead, and my arms grew heavy with each attack I made. *If its weapon can't get through my armor, I don't even need my sword; I can just hold it off while the others deal with theirs.*

The rest of the Gloom Knights had a much better time in dealing with their shades. Evelyn was the first to destroy hers. All she had to do was touch the thing, and it disintegrated. Once hers was dead, she just stood back and watched, even though her friends were in danger.

Adam tossed a single crystal onto the ground and easily ducked his shadow's attack. He spoke two words, and before the shade could react, a massive black and silver wolf appeared from the crystal and ate half of the darkness with a single bite. The rest of its lifeless body fell and scattered in the wind.

With a laugh, Adam held out his hand, and the gigantic bane wolf disappeared back into its prison. The crystal snapped back into his hand, and he pocketed it to go and speak to Evelyn.

Gil and Makenna fought theirs just out of my field of view, but I couldn't take my eyes off my own foe to see how they fared. Wind whistled behind me as Gil struck with his ax, and the marsh filled with the acrid scent of fire.

I tuned out Gil and focused on my foe. I let the magic holding *Chitin Sword* fade. My exhaustion waned once the drain on my mana eased up, and I was able to catch the mimic's sword in my hand. I pushed it aside and let it slide off harmlessly off my arm.

I brought my fist up and tried to punch the thing's face, but when I struck, my hand sank in like I was wading through ooze. I eventually pushed through to something very spongy at the center of the shade's head, but my punch didn't do anything besides make it angry.

It warbled a screech and swung at my head. I was to slow to block, and it landed hard against my temple, sending me to my knees.

My hands sunk into the muck as I steadied myself and Gil shouted painfully loud to my ringing ears.

"We have to help her!"

I risked a glance, and both Gil and Makenna had defeated their adversaries. I was the only one still fighting. Gil had his axe and was tense, panicked as if he were about to charge in.

"Leave her be, blacksmith. I want to see what the little queen is made of," Evelyn said.

Gil grumbled and lowered his weapon.

A tear ripped into my heart when Gil stepped back, leaving me to fight alone. I didn't like it, but I understood. *I'm the weak one here; I'm holding everyone back just by being in their presence. I need to defend myself, and I can't rely on everyone else for the rest of my life.*

I attacked the shade recklessly, knowing I was safe from harm while I had my armor up, but I was running out of time. Something solid was in its head, so that's what I aimed for. I tackled the shade to the ground. It was much lighter than I expected, and I hit it with all of my strength.

I took my hands and willed the chitin to form claws. It shifted at my command, but that one change dropped me to less than ten percent of my remaining mana. I reached my clawed hands into its head and dug into the soft substance at the center.

The shade bucked and recoiled in agony as I did, releasing such a terrible scream that I thought my head was about to split in two. I bit down, gritting my teeth, and dug in deeper. I used the pain and my anger at my own helplessness to fuel my strength. I gripped the center in both hands and pulled it apart as quickly as I could.

It came with minimal resistance, tearing in half under my fingers, and I ripped until it was broken. As I pulled it free of the mass of shadows, the shade stopped screaming. It stopped doing anything and dissolved into nothingness, leaving only a squishy, pale yellow ball of sponge in my hands.

I dropped it as a rush of adrenaline surged through my bones, invigorating me and bringing a warm strength to my aching limbs.

"Hey, I leveled up."

CHAPTER 7 - COMPLICATIONS

Sampson

It'd been most of a year since I'd last been to Aldrust, and even in the span of a year, things could've changed drastically. Because the kingdom itself resided far below ground, along with the constant mining going on, the layout changed every so often to reduce the risk of cave-ins and rockfalls. *I can't rely on my previous knowledge of the layout, so we're going in blind.* I had a few friends living in the dwarven kingdom, and the thought of what we were planning left a sour taste in my mouth.

I was about to waltz in and steal their most prized possession, and I was starting with absolutely zero workable intelligence.

My first thought was to call up Wilson or Evelyn; they'd be much better suited to planning a heist than I ever could, but my contacts in my interface were grayed out. I couldn't send or receive any messages. When I asked Magnus about it, he made a corny joke.

"My castle is in a dead zone, no cell service," he chortled.

"Funny," I said and turned back to the map.

The trip to Aldrust would take a little under four days by horse. I wanted just to teleport, but since I had to bring the shifter with me, I couldn't do that, and Magnus flat out denied me when I asked to go alone.

"Why? I can do this alone, and I don't need her help."

Raven tensed at my words, lowering her gaze as she turned away from us. I didn't care that I'd hurt her feelings—I didn't want a tag-along on this job.

Magnus shook his head. "I disagree. Raven will prove herself a valuable tool for you."

"She's only going to slow me down. I can teleport and be there in Aldrust in under an hour. By horse, it will take at least three days."

Magnus held his hand and stared me down, not willing to even entertain the idea. "She's going with you. If for nothing else than to help ensure a smooth delivery."

Ah. It clicked why he wanted her along. *She's there to watch me just as much as she's watching my back. Magnus doesn't trust that I won't abscond with Lachrymal's Heart if I do manage to pull the job off.*

I wasn't getting my way in this, and I relented. There was too much at stake for me to just back out, no matter how distasteful I found the prospect of working with a shapeshifter.

"Fine. You win."

Magnus acknowledged his victory with a subtle nod of his head and the beginnings of a smile. "Your contact in Aldrust will have a better idea of what awaits you when you get there, but feel free to take anything you might need from my armory."

That was very generous of him, but outfitting me was only common sense. Lachrymal's Heart was easily more valuable than any one item here, and since I sorely lacked in equipment, I happily took him up on his offer, though I had to ask one specific question. "Even the hellsword?"

He grimaced but nodded. "If you can use it, though. That specific sword was designed for a magic user, not a knight."

Why would a mage need a sword? Unless you specialized as a battlemage, physical weapons are almost useless to pure casters. I walked over to the rack, anticipation building. I wanted the sword, wanted to wield it. My hand reached out as if it were being pulled by a string to grasp the hilt of the fiery blade. It glowed with delight at the thought of being used, but the moment my hand touched the hilt, it shocked me, sending my hand away from it.

"Ow! Damn, that stings."

Magnus and Aliria both laughed from the far side of the room, chuckling over my pain. Even Raven let out a quick snort of humor, which didn't endear herself to me in the slightest.

"I warned you," Magnus said.

A notification appeared in my interface.

Warning! Stat Requirements Unmet.
Stats Required.
Strength: 90-Met
Constitution: 80-Met
Wisdom: 75-Unmet

Damn it. Oh well. I fanned my hand, trying to dispel some of the pain and numbness. I'd forgotten how much that hurt.

With that sword out of the question, I went through the many racks of swords, searching for one that would be appropriate for me. I discounted the heavier and large claymores and such to focus on the lighter weapons and went down the line, picking them up one at a time and testing them out. A few were nicely balanced and felt right in my hands but were completely ostentatious, adorned with gold, silver, and numerous gems.

I nearly picked the one that was just like my own sword, but I hesitated. It was nice, but it was built for a class similar to Blade Master, something I wasn't any longer. So I tried to find one better suited to my Hive Knight class.

Only a few swords remained when I found the best choice. It was a hand and a half sword, and a little flashier than I was used to, but not overly so. It was slightly shorter than a normal longsword, the blade wide and thick, and it sported a solid heft to it that I liked.

The blade was shadowsteel and a stark black. The handle was polished drake horn, and the smooth gray accented the black of the blade and silver crossguard nicely. Etched into the silver were the branches of a tree, and in the flickering light, they came alive as if blown about in a breeze.

The final and most extravagant aspect of the sword was the pommel, which was also silver and had an emerald the size of my eye set into the hilt.

I found the stone symbolic of the job I was about to undertake and very fitting. I rubbed the gem for good luck and strapped the sword to my belt. The sheath was a pure black with small green lines spreading out like the veins of a leaf.

Sword down, next is armor.

I went to the far side and perused the armor sets. As soon as I took a good look, I immediately found the section I wanted—the medium sets.

These were all made with a mixture of leather and chainmail, but the chest and back plates were crafted from shadowsteel plates. I chose one of the darker ones—black wyvern leather with thick shadowsteel plating. Flipping over the chestpiece revealed something startling. It was backed with thin leather along with chainmail, but as I ran my fingers over the blackened chain, I found it wasn't standard steel, it was shadowsteel. *That's something you don't see every day.*

I equipped it and moved around a bit to get the feel of the new weight. *It's not that noticeable, but I'm slower. The weight is heavier than I'm used to. That could prove fatal if I don't watch it.* But the main ideal feature of my newest equipment was that, despite its heaviness, there was no discernible sound as I moved around. Every single slab of metal separated from the rest. The only sound was from the leather rubbing against itself, but with a little oil in those trouble spots, I'd be virtually silent. *Perfect for a heist.*

Speaking of, if I'm pulling a heist, I'll need some specialized tools. I'd probably need a full burglar's kit, and since I'd be deep underground, it wouldn't hurt to have a dungeon delving kit, just to be on the safe side.

A dull pain throbbed through my skull at the thought of everything I might need for this. My go-to was usually carry more than I could possibly need. *Overkill has never failed me before.* Before I left, I went through the potions. The entire bottom shelves were stacked with health and mana potions, hundreds of them in neat rows. I took ten of each.

Then I went through and grabbed everything I could even think I might need for such a quest.

Potion of the Revenant went into my inventory, along with a lightstep potion, wraithsight, and an invisibility potion. All the ones I might need for this job. I had turned to head out of the room when a thought struck me, and I went back to search the shelves for one more potion.

"Gotcha," I said as I snagged the recovery potion that was hidden behind a few dragonsbane draughts.

Potions secure, I headed for the door.

Magnus and the others had already left the war room, leaving me alone with literal millions of gold. *Is this another test, or am I reading too much into it?* Regardless, my inventory could only store so much, and I couldn't carry away even five percent of the items in this room.

I only took the items I absolutely thought I needed. Though, I would still need supplies and provisions. Magnus would know where I could acquire them. The emptiness of the room amplified the echo of my footsteps on the stone. With the absence of people, the bubbling green mage lights dotted around sent chills up my spine. I ignored the urge to look at them and fled the room. I thrust open the door and almost ran headlong into Jasmine.

"Ah! Sorry, Jasmine, I wasn't expecting you."

She stepped back, her face a little flushed, but she smiled at me. "That's okay. I was sent to bring you upstairs when you were finished with your preparations down here." She brushed a lock of auburn from her face. "I take it you're done?"

I nodded to her, suddenly confused. *She was furious with me this morning—why is she being so nice now?*

"Yeah, I'm done here, though I still need a few things for the trip."

"Of course. Mother is preparing your supplies as we speak."

Good, I'm getting tired of this place. I went up the stairs ahead of Jasmine, but it seemed she was determined to keep up with me. I slowed my pace and let her walk side by side with me. I was fine with the silence, but she kept prodding me for conversation.

"Are you leaving today?"

"Soon as our supplies are ready."

"Are you coming back?"

"Probably."

She pouted at my terse responses and hunched her shoulders but stuck close to me as we climbed the many stone steps, our labored breathing and footsteps breaking the silence. She kept brushing up against me; her fingers lingered on the back of my hand.

I sighed, but didn't stop her for myriad reasons. I wasn't going to reciprocate her feelings, but I also didn't feel like shattering them either. *Though I poured cold water on her this morning. Most girls would have gotten the hint.*

I tried to get my bearings and see if I remembered the way to the throne room when Jasmine locked the door to the stairwell. The lock engaged with a loud clunk. I turned as Jasmine stowed a large brass key into the folds of her uniform, her face slightly flush from the climb.

She noticed me watching her and flashed me a wicked grin, pulling her top down in the process to give me a peek at her chest. Sweat beaded up on her rich skin, glistening in the lambent light before sliding down between the curves of her breasts.

I turned away quickly, my face beet red. *Great! You didn't say anything, and now look where you're at. Stupid, stupid, stupid.* While I berated myself for feeding into her antics, Jasmine led me through the halls, practically bouncing with every step.

I tried to be upset, but it was hard when she seemed genuinely happy, but I was thankful when we reached our destination. Jasmine muttered under her breath, and her mood dropped as she unlatched herself from me and opened the door.

"After you, My Lord," she said with a wink.

"Wouldn't have it any other way."

She smiled and followed after me.

The throne room was busier than I had seen it before. Magnus was, of course, sitting on his throne with a bemused expression playing across his face as he talked in muted tones with Aliria, who laughed at something I couldn't hear. Raven was on the opposite side of the throne, looking as meek and pathetic as she had in the war room.

Magnolia was close at hand to her master, ready to answer any command he might need. She noticed how close Jasmine was to me, and even though we weren't touching at all, she just knew something was up and gave me a knowing smile and a nod.

I tried to ignore everyone and focus on getting everything ready. As I approached the throne, I inclined my head respectfully to Magnus. "Thank you for the weapon and armor. They are spectacular."

He grinned wide at me, his eyes glowing as he took me in. "Of course, friend, and might I say, they suit you. It's good to see them used again. I've kept them locked away for far too long...is there anything else you require?"

"Just some supplies for the trip and the equipment needed to complete the job."

"Right. Magnolia, if you would be so kind."

She bowed low. "Right away, Master."

Magnolia walked past me to leave the room, and Jasmine followed after her, both of them whispering to each other as soon as they reached the door. When they disappeared from view, I returned my attention to Magnus, who looked at me strangely, conflicting emotions in his eyes.

"There is just one final thing you must do before you set out. A necessity, I'm afraid."

"And what's that?" I asked. I admit, he had me curious. Though, the tension on his face suggested I wouldn't like what was about to come.

He shifted his eyes to Raven, and an unspoken conversation went on between the two of them. It seemed Raven was as apprehensive of whatever it was, but she could not win against Magnus's wishes and nodded her head slowly.

She moved from the throne, stepping closer to me, her head low, and even though I was staring directly at her, she refused to meet my eyes.

"Raven will be important in ensuring the successful retrieval of the Heart, but her going with you presents some difficulties."

This again. I don't want her with me in the first place. "Then don't send her. I'll be fine on my own." I all but spat the words out, and Raven sniffed, looking away.

"I disagree."

I tried to keep the frustration off my face, but the sigh of annoyance was audible, and Aliria decided to push my buttons.

"What's the matter, little knight, is she not to your liking? Not pretty enough for you?"

The harsh retort of laugher that fled from my lips cracked like a whip. "I could give a damn about her appearance; nothing good ever comes from working with shifters."

"Well, I'm afraid you've little choice in the matter. She's going with you, much as you find the idea distasteful," Magnus said.

An understatement to be sure, but I was tired of arguing a point that I wasn't going to win, so I resigned myself to the fact that I'd be working with Raven and put the matter out of my mind—or I tried to, but Magnus's next words left me speechless.

"In order to have her accompany you, she will need to be bonded to you."

What! I withdrew from Raven on principle, away from the insanity. "Hell no."

Magnus didn't seem thrilled by the idea either, but I was livid. No way in hell was I going to let yet another person bind themselves to me. Especially a shifter.

I'd accepted being bonded with Eris, accepted being her mate. I'd grown to love her, and for the most part, it'd been wonderful. However, I wasn't okay with binding my soul together with someone I'd just met just for the sake of a job.

"I'm afraid it's necessary."

"Why?" I shouted. "Why do I even need her along in the first place? Give me one benefit to bringing her with me."

Magnus stood from his throne and walked down the steps to stand beside me. "It'll be faster to show you. Let's step back, shall we?"

I didn't follow him mentally, but I did so physically, stepping about six or seven feet back and waiting for something to happen.

"If you would show him?" Magnus asked.

She bowed her head, her blooded eyes in pain as a ruffling of feathers rose from out of nowhere. Two large wings sprouted from her back like the wings of an angel, or a demon, nearly a dozen feet long and as black as Aliria's heart. Hundreds of feathers rained to the stone as she swept her wings in front of her and over her head. The feathers floated down lazily and completely obscured her from my sight. When the last feather touched the floor, Raven was gone, replaced by her namesake.

Standing before me was a monstrous black raven, easily fifteen feet long and terrifying. Raven stared at me with sharp, blood-red eyes that held a startling intellect.

She snapped her beak at me; it was as black as her feathers and caused me to jump back out of reflex.

"Holy…big bird!" I shouted and stumbled over my feet.

Magnus and Aliria snickered at my expense, while Raven stepped forward. Sunlight dripped down her glossy feathers as she walked next to one of the stained-glass windows. As she got closer, I noticed the massive talons capped at the end of her legs.

By the nine kings of hell, that's huge! I didn't think shifters could grow to that size. Seeing Raven shift also clarified her purpose in all this.

"I'm not riding a horse to Aldrust, am I?"

Magnus flashed a devious smile at me. "Nope."

Well, shit. Though, as I gazed at Raven's admittedly majestic form, my heart fluttered at the prospect of flying. For all the fantastical elements of the game world, flying still eluded most of us. *Well, it'll be a new experience at least.*

It overwrote my prejudices about partnering with a shifter just enough that I got lost in my daydream of flight and didn't notice as Magnus walked up next to me, grabbed my wrist, and drew a thin dagger across it.

"Son of a bitch!" I hissed as blood welled to snake down my hand. My health bar dipped by a fraction to register the damage I'd taken. "What the hell, Magnus?"

He didn't answer, just held my bloody arm out to the giant bird, and true fear crawled up from the pit of my subconscious as I stared into Raven's eyes; they sparked as she shifted back to her human form. Raven shook herself and let her feathers fall out once more. When they'd disappeared, Raven the human stood and walked over to us.

She scrunched up her face at the sight of my blood, but and after some prodding from Magnus, placed my bleeding wrist to her mouth and bit down.

I sucked in a breath and fought back a grimace. Raven downed several large mouthfuls of blood before licking her tongue over my flesh. With a look of disgust, she wiped the specks of my blood from her lips and held out her wrist to Magnus.

The Aspect, though silent, made its desire known. It hungered for her blood, and its chill pulsed faster in my veins. My mouth salivated without my consent at the thought of biting into her flesh. I had to squeeze my eyes hard and will the Aspect back into my heart before I lost control and did something I'd regret.

There was no way I could let Magnus spill her blood. The Aspect was too strong already. And it wanted blood. Giving it what it wanted was something that seemed like a demonstrably bad idea.

The blade was halfway to her wrist when I stopped him.

"Stop!" I shouted, trying to keep from having to ingest her blood.

I don't like the idea of bonding with her, but if it has to happen. I refuse for it to be by consuming her blood. I don't want to experience her memories in the Mnemosyne. I didn't want to see the kind of life she'd led.

But more than that, I didn't want to give the bastard in my heart an inch.

Though the only other option available to me left a sickening feeling in my stomach. *It's better than drinking her blood, but ye gods, I don't want to do it.*

Magnus looked at me with a quizzical expression, the knife hanging in mid-air. "Duran, why am I stopping? This has to be done."

"Why? Why can't she just go with me? Why do I have to bind myself to her?"

Magnus stowed the knife back into his tunic and spoke. "Her contract was that she would become mine. She can't leave my side for more than three days without suffering excruciating pain that would render her useless to you."

"That's a pretty ruthless contract," I said.

He shrugged nonchalantly. "The Alice isn't someone you enter into a bargain with lightly."

He had a fair point, and it was the reason I distrusted shifters. *Never make a deal with the queen of the fairies—she'll find a way to screw you over every time. Only the damned or the desperate chose to make that deal.* Still, contract or not, I didn't want to be a part of this. *Here goes one more futile attempt.* "Any chance I can get you to say you'll let me go alone?"

"None."

"Damn it all to hell, but I had to try," I said, marching over to Raven.

"Don't you need the knife?" Magnus asked.

"Hopefully not," I said as I reached her.

She shrank under my harsh glare, and I eased off a bit. She looked ready to bolt from the room at any second, and as much as I didn't care for her kind, I needed her acceptance.

"Look," I whispered. "I really don't want to drink your blood. It would be problematic for a number of reasons. There is another option, but it's not really a better one."

Raven nodded, waiting for me to continue.

"I've found that it doesn't always have to be blood that is required to bond. Saliva works just as well, but that would mean we would have to kiss." I held up a hand. "I don't particularly like either option, but since it seems I can't get out of this, I'll leave the choice up to you."

Her eyes widened as her lips parted just so. "You would give me the choice?" she asked softly.

I nodded.

She paused over the choice for what seemed like ages. When she spoke again, it was nothing more than a whisper.

"Kiss."

All right. It's better than feeding the Aspect, at any rate.

Before my nerve could remind me what an awful idea this was, I grabbed the nape of her neck and kissed her.

It was hardly a kiss. As soon as our lips touched, I brought my tongue into her mouth so our saliva could mix. For half a minute, I swirled around her mouth with no response, and I was about to resign myself to tasting her blood when a force tugged on my heart.

At first, it was only the black magic side of my heart was being drawn out, but it was no longer just one side of magic in my heart, and both came at the call. It flowed through my veins, searching for an egress, the gash in my wrist.

An itch nagged at my arm before tendrils of thin smoked drifted out from my bloody wrist. I pulled away from our kiss as the smoke gathered around my arm and slithered around to enter Raven's mouth.

She jerked as it flowed down her throat and into her lungs. She stopped breathing as it seeped into her bloodstream. She twitched and wheezed when she started breathing again, doubling over and nearly falling to the stone floor. I caught her and lowered her to ground before stepping away while my magic tore through her body. She shuddered and groaned softly in pain but did not cry out. For several long moments, her body was wracked with spasms of pain, before finally settling.

I knew it when it stopped; some twitch in the back of my head told me when we'd bonded. Different than mine and Eris's bond, but similar enough.

All in all, the entire encounter took less than three minutes but left me mentally drained. I was itching to leave, the gray stone walls felt claustrophobic.

I scratched at my beard and left Raven to get up on her own. "All right, Magnus, I did what you asked, now I'm ready to leave. I don't want to spend another minute here."

He nodded. "I understand." Magnus held up his hand and flicked his fingers to the side a few times. "Here you go."

Quest: Steal Lachrymal's Heart
Type: Unique
Difficulty: S
Reward: 48000 Exp!

"I do apologize for demanding it of you, but rest assured, I can undo the bonding if the job gets done," Magnus said after I accepted the quest.

"If?"

"I said when, didn't I?"

"Doesn't matter," I said, turning to leave through the same door Magnolia went through a few minutes prior. "I'll bring you your accursed rock. The Gloom Knights always get the job done."

"Safe travels," Magnus said, smiling.

I was thankful I didn't have to speak to Aliria as I left; I wanted nothing more to do with either of the two lords of this castle. I'd been cooped up inside for too long, and already the outside world beckoned.

I rounded the corner just as Magnolia came into view. She spotted me and walked over, large canvas pack in hand. "I was looking for you, Lord. I was given clear instructions on what needed to go in, so you should find everything to your liking."

I took the pack and dropped it in my inventory. "Thank you, Magnolia. You've been very kind to me."

She smiled. "It's no trouble, My Lord. Though I do apologize for my daughter's behavior. She's been spending too much time with Aliria, and I fear it's had an effect on her personality. Jasmine has also never been around someone her own age before. I think that has caused her to become a little enamored with you."

I laughed and waved her off. "Jasmine's a nice girl, but Aliria could corrupt even the gods with that attitude of hers."

"I like your daughter, but not in that way. I should've been more direct with her. That was a blunder on my part."

Magnolia shook her head. "Don't worry, I'll talk to her about it, make her understand. But I must truly thank you for your kindness towards her. She's never had friends before. I'm grateful."

With those parting words, she bowed and showed me to the exit.

Magnolia led me up to the ramparts of the castle. Once outside, the burning heat immediately brought budding beads of sweat to my skin, only to be swept away by a stiff, salty breeze blowing in from the east. I couldn't see the ocean from the castle, but the wind was unmistakable, and it all but confirmed that I was right about my assessment of the castle's location.

In the distance, the sands of the Badlands loomed. Swirling sand dunes extended as far as I could see; waves of heat rose from the baking surface. On the furthest wall of the castle rose a tower ringed by parapets. Jasmine was at the top already, and we headed over.

We were at the highest point in the castle, and I still couldn't see out past the dunes. The sun scorched mercilessly overhead, and even with the soft breeze, standing around wasn't doing any good. *What's taking Raven so long?*

Jasmine smiled at me, her hair drifting in the breeze as she reached into her uniform and pulled a long emerald green cloth from her uniform. "I have a gift for you."

She held it out to me, and I took it, confused. *Is it a scarf? No. Too long.* Jasmine smiled at my obvious confusion. "It's a sword sash. It can be worn horizontally or across your chest, whichever you prefer."

"Thank you, Jasmine. I'll see you around," I said, removing my sword and wrapping the green cloth around my waist.

After tying it, my new sword slid into the hole by my belt nicely, and the rich green accented the black of my armor well, even if it was a bit too ostentatious for my liking.

"Till we meet again." She bowed and departed with her mother, sparing me a glance just before she went back inside.

She really is a nice girl, but that's not going to end well for me.

Before long, Raven joined me on the tower. It was just the two of us now, and I wanted to set some ground rules. I turned to her.

"I've made my feelings on you accompanying me abundantly clear. I don't trust you, but if we are going to be working together, I want to make sure you understand. You do what I say, when I say. No debates, no discussions. Do you understand?"

She nodded, bobbing her head up and down rapid fire. "Yes, Master."

"Yeah, no. Don't call me that. That's rule two. I'm nobody's master."

"Okay, then what would you like me to call you?"

"My name, if you must. Now let's get going, we're burning daylight."

Without further conversation, Raven backed up and shifted, going into her giant bird form. Her voice came from nowhere, even though her beak remained closed.

"Climb on, Duran. And please be gentle, my feathers break easily."

Grumbling, I did as she asked and hopped on as gently as I could. Her feathers were incredibly soft under my hands and warm to the touch. It was like the world's softest down comforter, and I indivertibly spoke aloud.

"These feathers feel amazing," I said before I could stop myself.

"That's kind of you to say," Raven said.

"Whatever, let's just go."

Raven knelt and launched herself in the air so fast, I had to grab handfuls of her feathers just to keep myself from falling off. She soared high into the sky before opening her wings and leveling out to glide forward.

I looked back to see the castle, already well behind us on the cliff face, the speed Raven at which flew rapidly turned the large castle into a dot on the horizon behind us.

The air was cold despite the heat as we climbed higher. Wind whipped past as we flew through the air. It took more than a few minutes for my heart rate to settle and get used to the sensation of flying, but when I did, I laughed aloud as the sands of the Badlands raced past at frightening speed. I lowered my head and clung to Raven's warm feathers and found a nice balance between the chilled wind and the desert's heat.

The Badlands were nothing but vast stretches of sand, easily hundreds of miles wide, so I settled in for looking at the same hues of brown for a while, and we flew in silence for a few hours.

A shrill tone interpreted my daydreaming. A name flashed across my interface. Miguel.

"Problem with the Gloom Shrooms?"

He laughed, breathing heavily. "Not at all. Delivery went smoothly, dropped off the payment."

"Then what do you need?"

"I have a job for—"

Click.

I closed my interface and stared at the ocean in the distance. By the third hour, I was getting sore and tight from staying in one position for so long, and without a proper harness to sit on, my ass was killing me. I wanted to stop and rest for a few moments but wasn't about to complain in front of the shifter.

I'd just about resigned myself to enduring the aches that wormed into my muscles when we passed low over the wastes. I could make out dozens of small dots below us, walking in disorganized chaos, or shambling as it were.

Roamers, and quite a large horde of them, too. I was itching to do anything other than continue riding at the moment, and a delicious thought came over me.

"Raven, slow up and circle back."

"Of course, but why?"

"Don't worry about it. Just do it."

She slowed down considerably and dipped low over the dunes, kicking up a gust of sand in the process. She lowered one shoulder and circled around, spying the horde of roamers as I had.

"That's a lot of them in a single group. Is that what you wanted to see?"

I grinned. "Yep, it's absolutely perfect," I said, tensing.

Raven tilted her head to look at me, her large, blooded eye staring at me with concern. "What are you about to do?"

"Just a little power leveling," I said and jumped.

"Duran!" she shouted, but I was already in freefall.

Chapter 8 - The Roving Dead

I timed my jump precisely, but my landing was anything but smooth as I dropped on to the top of the largest sand dune. I sank deeper than I was expecting and fell off balance, tumbling down the hill.

"Damn it," I cursed as I spat out a mouthful of sand, the gritty grains fouling my mouth and slipping down my throat. Ignoring the roughness in my mouth for a second, I stood up, dusted the worst of the sand from me and pulled out a waterskin, washing out the remaining sand and spitting for good measure before draining a good fourth of the water. *Next time, make sure I know what I'm jumping on if I'm going to pull a stunt like that again.*

Raven swooped down near me, and I shielded my face against the small dust storm she kicked up in her wake. She quickly transformed back to her human form and marched over, clearly displeased.

"That was reckless of you," she said as she knelt beside me.

"Was fun as hell, though," I said with a chuckle before dropping my smile and focusing on the roving dead.

We'd landed behind the moving horde, and they were brainless creatures who could barely spark enough brain cells to move, let alone think. Pure instinct and need drove them to consume the flesh of the living.

As I peered out at the hundred or so roamers, I found a mixture of soldiers, farmers, and even a few who'd once been mages. All of them in various stages of decay and rot. Black magic kept the somnambulists mobile and slowed the rate of decay, sometimes stopping it altogether if the necromancer was strong enough. *I don't see anyone leading them, so maybe this is an unbound horde. Maybe their creator is already dead.*

Dead or not, I was excited to get to work. Roamers in small groups were chumps, even at high levels, but since each undead lost a quarter of their levels during the resurrection, there would never be an undead higher than level seventy-five, barring a lich or any of the spectral undead. *Easy enough in small doses, but a hundred is more than I can take at once unless I do this smart.*

I eyed Raven, who wasn't much to look at. She still wore her thin black dress and had no weapons. A liability, one that would only slow me down.

"Do you have any armor at all?" I hissed at her.

She flinched and nodded. "It should be in my pack."

I withdrew her pack and tossed it to her. "Get dressed, quickly."

She didn't bother responding; instead, she stripped out of her dress then and there, giving me a brief glimpse of the smooth, pale skin of her abdomen and her ample bust before I could turn my head.

I put her out of mind and focused on watching my prey.

The horde moved at a snail's pace, and there were pockets of open areas in between some of the larger groups. Giving me plenty of room to work with. *Go in from the left, where the horde is the weakest, and work my way through. I'll only deal with a few handfuls at a time.* Best plan I had, at any rate, and considering what I was up against, I wasn't too worried.

I gave Raven a few minutes to change, and she coughed softly when she'd finished. She now wore a nearly skin-tight cotton shirt and pair of pants in mottled hues of dull black and gray under leather armor, dyed a midnight black, with thick padding over her chest and thighs. Any vital spot was covered with leather, but still allowed mobility. As she turned around to grab her bag, two slits stood out from the back of her armor. It was stitched so there was no fraying; her shoulder blades moved under the holes. *Are those for her wings?*

Whatever, don't really care. She handed me back her pack, and I stowed it away. "Don't you have a weapon?"

"Don't need one. So why are we doing this again?" she asked.

"Because I said so. You can either help or stay here. What'll it be?"

"I'll help."

"Then let's go, follow my lead."

I vaulted the sand hill we'd been on and slid down the steep incline. Using the built-up momentum, I hit the ground running and drew my new sword in the process. The black metal gleamed, its maiden bloodletting at hand.

My charge led me right where I wanted to go, and I plowed into a small group of five roamers. Each of them wore Alliance breastplates, and they stopped, turning as my lifeforce washed over them.

They let out haunting groans of hunger. The closest one lurched at me. Half of his face sloughed off as he whipped around and opened his rotting mouth to assault my nose with a miasma of decay. Before he could bring his arms up, I sliced my sword through his neck, and as his head sank into the sand, I stuck my blade through it, splitting the weakened skull.

One down.

The others took their time and stumbled to me in blind hunger. Rotten flesh dripped, and their milky white eyeballs told me they wanted nothing but to taste my flesh. One of them was close enough to grab my armor. His thin, bony fingers gripped as tightly as his failing muscles would allow. I severed his hand at the elbow and whipped my sword back to slice through his head.

That makes two.

One of them tripped over the supine form of his dead-undead friend and met the tip of my sword as I shoved it through his brain.

The remaining two were close now, forcing me to take a step back and goad them toward me. When they moved parallel to each other, I moved. I ducked under their outstretched arms and shoving them into one another, causing them to crash to the ground together. One quick adjustment later to line them up, and my sword slid through the nose of the top roamer and out the back of the head of the second.

Two for the price of one, and that makes five.

Raven gave me an exasperated sigh and shook her head as I pulled my sword free.

I wiped the rotten and blackened brains from the steel. "Got something to say?"

"Not at all. Far be it for me to tell you when you're being impetuous."

I tossed the torn and now soiled piece of cloth from the roamer. "Good, because I don't need another nag in my life. C'mon, we've got some more zombies to slay."

"Zombies?" she muttered as we edged toward the rest of the horde.

I'd created a gap to start whittling away at them from the side, but we would end up biting off more than we could chew if we strayed to close and the others sensed us.

There were a small group of six or seven farmhands that were the closest to us. I slunk along until I was as close as I could be from them without straying into the horde itself. My lifeforce tempted them, and they turned, coming for me, and breaking away from the oblivious horde as I kited them back a good ways.

I was about to engage when a ruffling came from behind me and a shadow passed overhead. Raven floated about fifteen feet in the air in her human form, her black wings stretched out and flapping in lazy rhythm as she stared down the horde.

"Can I take them?" she asked.

I thought about it and shrugged. "Be my guest."

She nodded, and I danced out of range while they shuffled after me. Raven flapped her wings harder and rose a few feet more before bringing her wings down sharply. Dozens of heavy feathers shot out from her wings, spinning end over end like throwing knives as they descended on the unsuspecting horde. She'd put enough force behind them to cause major damage to the seven roamers. A few missed or landed on the soft feather side, but plenty struck properly, sinking the entire shaft into the undeads' soft and weakened bones.

A few took out eyes and hit the brain, killing them instantly, but she'd only managed kill shots on four of the seven. *Huh, not bad for one attack, though.* Raven glided back over to me and withdrew her wings, dropping to the ground. "My apologies. I wasn't able to get them all."

"Don't worry about it," I said, raising my sword. "I'll finish them off."

I ran forward, and with a few quick slashes, I slaughtered the remaining three. *That makes eight.*

One of her feathers stuck out of the sand. I crouched and picked it up. It was heavier than any feather I'd ever held before. I prodded at the tip of the white shaft, drawing a bead of blood. *Holy shit, that's kind of impressive.*

Though sharp, they lacked the heft needed to perform as a true weapon, but Raven had bypassed that by using extreme force. *Damned impressive.*

Before I could do anything else, the feather disappeared, fading away to nothing along with the rest of the ones that lingered over our small battlefield. *Faster than a corpse, but I guess they operate similarly because they're organic.*

I stood up and walked over to Raven. "How many times can you use that trick?"

"Only a few times in short bursts. My feathers grow back quickly, but if I lose too many, I won't be able to fly properly."

"Well, then ballpark it for me. How many times can you use that again right now?"

"Twice more, at best."

"All right," I said, pointing at the largest groups of roamers. "Fly over and see how much damage you can cause."

She nodded, unfurling her wings. "What are you going to do?"

I smirked and summoned my *Chitin Shield*. Thankfully, I had the wherewithal to unbuckle the vambrace and push the leather higher on my arm. I stowed the armor piece away just as the inky darkness slithered out from my pores and coalesced into a round shield on my arm. The shield was muted tones of black, rough, uneven, and the edges sharp as shale. *Wonder if I can take a roamer's head off in one swing.*

"I've had a lot put on me the last few days, and it's only going to get worse from here, so I'm going to go blow off some fucking steam."

Instead of pushing my anger down and letting it fester, I let it come to the surface and boil over. I let out as loud of a war cry as I could, and I charged into the mass of undead.

My shield raised, I barreled into the nearest roamer. I shoved it with enough force that it toppled over into the crowd and took half a dozen out like a row of dominoes. Two walking corpses were right in front of me. I bashed one with the edge of my shield, sinking it just under its nose and crushing its face in until I hit its brain and it stopped moving.

The other tried to take a bite of me but chomped down on my sword instead. With a flick of my wrist, I filleted its skull open. It spilled rancid gray matter and viscous black blood to the sand.

I wiped my blade with my finger and shook the gore from my hand. I turned back to the set of undead dominoes which had forgotten how to stand and crawled toward me, eliciting an unholy chorus of groans. I curb stomped each of their heads to vile pulp, staining my new greaves and boots with filth and rot.

That makes thirteen.

While I took out the group, Raven flew overhead and rained her razor-sharp feathers down on the zombies. I couldn't tell how many she took out, but she attacked, glided out of the horde before rising, and dropped once more.

When she could do no more from above, she circled and dropped next to me as I bashed my emerald pommel into the side of a zombie's face, crumpling the weak bone. It dropped, and I crushed what remained of its skull under heel.

Another rushed us, stumbling over the corpse of its friend.

"Allow me," Raven said and struck with what looked like a finger jab to the roamer's eyes.

The roamer stopped dead, falling lifeless to the sand. When Raven withdrew her hand, she had sharp talons instead of hands. Her fingers were longer than a human's and had glossy black claws where there should be fingernails. I whistled.

"Neat trick. How many more are left?" I asked.

With a flap of her wings, she rose to survey the battlefield. "About eighty, give or take."

"All right, can you fight by yourself or do you need backup?"

She scoffed and flicked her eyes down. "I'll be fine."

"Whatever you say," I said and didn't bother waiting for a reply.

There're zombies to kill.

Between the two of us, we cleared out the shambling horde in under two hours. It took a lot of patience and hit and run tactics to whittle them down, a handful at a time. I had to be careful of my battle fatigue as the fight wore on, so Raven and I took turns when it neared max.

I went through thirty of them just fine, but my sword slipped off a particularly brutish roamer's face and let him get close enough to bite me. It wouldn't have gotten through my armor, but Raven crushed its head before it could even try. She didn't even gloat about saving me as she helped me to my feet.

"Thanks," I muttered and picked up my steel.

She nodded and flew into the air to begin her aerial bombardment.

As the hours ended, I buried my blade through the skull of the last roamer and sighed in relief.

I was utterly exhausted, but I still had the strength to smile at the mound of corpses in our wake. I looked around and spied a large dune to our right. The shadow stretched far and offered a much-needed rest from the sun's beating gaze. I pointed to it, and we both went and sat down, nearly collapsing.

"Godsdamn, but that was fun," I said, pulling out two waterskins and handing one to Raven, who was currently using my shoulder to rest on. I was so tired, I couldn't muster the strength to shove her off.

"Get off me," I snapped.

"Sure, sure," she said and didn't budge but to uncap her water.

Whatever. How close did I come to maxing my fatigue during that last pass?

I opened my interface to look at my battle fatigue meter. *Huh, I still have a little bit left in the tank, but why am I so fucking tired, then?*

I lifted the waterskin to my lips and drank deeply, my muscles quivering. *Ah, my armor is heavier, my sword too.* The shadowsteel plates were much thicker than even my own set back home; it added more than a little weight to myself, and with my stat penalty, I wasn't used to the difference yet.

As my fatigue wore down, my strength returned, little by little, and I leaned back, basking in the soft wind that carried a nice breeze and gusts of sand towards us. *That fight did its job. I feel better. My head feels clear, even with all that Magnus dropped on me.*

I was a fighter; my clarity came at the end of my sword.

While I had the time, I decided to sort through my notifications. I knew after a fight like that I had more than a few waiting for me.

Combat Results!
48 Killed (Roamer): 14,400 Exp!
4 downed: 1200 Exp!
Mercy Penalty: -400 Exp
Total Exp Gain: 15,200 Exp!
Exp: 5100/5100
Level Up! (x3)
Exp: 3700/5400
Level 54
30 Stat Points Available!

Less than I was expecting, actually. With how much Exp Ouroboros has been throwing my way, these numbers look almost normal. Still more than I should get for killing a bunch of roamers, but for what's coming, I need all the boost I can get.

With my stat penalty from being so far away from Eris, putting my points into my main stats would most likely be a waste. *Need more Durability for sure. Maybe more Attack Damage as well.*

I put twenty into Durability and ten into Attack Damage, which brought Durability to thirty-five and Attack Damage to forty. *Not bad. But I'll need to keep working to get stronger.*

"You ready to move?" I asked, tipping the last of my water into my mouth.

"Yeah."

Raven used me as a crutch to help her stand, and I was about to shout at her when she offered me her hand. Still a little pissed, I took it reluctantly.

She walked a few feet out of the darkness, and the sunlight caught her face. She closed her eyes as the wind swept her inky hair back. "The heat feels wonderous, though I bet I'll be cursing those words in about ten minutes."

"Yeah, probably. Hurry and shift before we—!"

I tackled Raven to the ground as my instincts screamed at me and a blast of hellfire scorched the sand to glass where she'd been standing a second before.

The hell? Who's throwing around black magic?

I scanned the area, nothing but sand and dunes in all directions. There was nothing that I could see.

"Ruined!" a sudden voice shouted.

A figure wreathed in darkness appeared from the shadow of one of the larger sand dunes. It was incredibly well-camouflaged, and if I hadn't been searching for the voice, I'd have never spotted it. Inside the shade, a darker shadow told of a hidden doorway in the sand itself. *Is that one of the entrances to the Nymirian Dungeon?*

I held off that train of thought and stood, pulling Raven up along with me.

The figure stalked toward us, tall, his stride purposeful, yet heavy with rage. Though he stood under the blinding light of the sun, shadows clung to the figure, bathing him in midnight. He wore a cloak so dark, it obscured his physique, shrouding him almost completely.

Only his chin and mouth were visible under the shadows that covered his eyes, his lips set in a ferocious snarl.

"Ruined!" he shouted again, his voice young but tinged with maturity and anger that far outshone any mere teenage angst. "Do you two know how long it took me to raise and lead those roamers all the way out here? And you two fucking waltz in and ruin everything!"

From within the folds of darkness, he withdrew a dark wooden stave, unadorned and plain but oozing wicked intent.

My sword was useless at this distance, but I spied a knife in a leather sheath at Raven's lower back. "Mind if I borrow your knife?" I asked.

"Help yourself," she said as the hooded man approached.

"I'm going to make you pay for crossing me. I'm the Shadow King's chosen. I am Ja—"

Whatever he'd been about to say was suddenly cut short by the knife now lodged firmly in his trachea. My throw had been perfect, and I'd aimed at the only unprotected spot he had.

He gasped and bled his life out on the sunbaked sand, the blood mixing with the grains of sand and clumped as it dried.

"Rule number one: never monologue in the middle of a fight."

That earned me a snort from Raven. "You ready to set off?"

"One sec," I said, and went over to the dead man and stole all of his stuff. I didn't bother cataloging the items, I just quick looted him and jogged back to Raven.

I handed Raven back her knife and quickly sorted out the combat results from that encounter.

Combat Results!

1 Killed (Human): 1500 Exp!

Total Exp: 1500 Exp!

Exp: 5200/5400

"All right, let's go."

She shifted, and I climbed atop her. We set off, and I was grateful to be out of the intense desert heat. The wind tore at my face as Raven put a burst of speed into her wings, but I enjoyed the rush as we soared high above the desert. The shift in temperature was enough to make me shiver, but after sweating bullets minutes ago, I wasn't about to complain.

We flew for another hour or so, but the sun was getting low by then, and Raven had slowed considerably, prompting me to lean down and ask to find somewhere to make camp.

"Absolutely, I'm worn out," she said, her voice clear despite the howling wind.

About twenty minutes later, we passed by a high cliff formed of red rock. It was tall enough that nothing I knew of could climb it, and unless wyverns or dragons roosted there, we'd be safe from attack. I nudged her with my foot and pointed toward the cliff. She got the message and swooped down to land.

I took a few tentative steps to make sure the ground was solid everywhere, and when nothing crumbled or moved, I was satisfied and pulled out our packs, trying to get the camp set up.

"Anything I can do to help?"

"Sure," I said, tossing her the pack after pulling the tent out. "Knock yourself out."

We got to work in silence. By the time I set the tent up, I was furious, and Raven had a fire lit and dinner going.

"Give me the bag."

Raven did so at once, and I rooted through it, getting madder by the second. Knowing I wouldn't find anything, I pulled out Raven's and gave it a cursory look, not finding what I was looking for.

"Godsdamn it."

"What?" Raven asked, looking up from her preparations.

"There's only one tent."

"Oh," she said, not at all looking concerned about the fact. "Maybe they did it that way to save space?"

"No, I'm pretty sure it was just to fuck with me," I grumbled and pulled out the one thing that would make the situation bearable.

Whiskey.

I took a long pull from the frankly oversized travel flask Magnolia had procured for me and went to help with dinner.

"What are you making?"

Arrayed on a long strip of cloth were salted vegetables and meat, each separated by individual strips of cloth. Instead of dried meat, we had fresh meat with a fine layer of salt over it to allow it to keep.

Raven asked for the bag back and pulled out a small bottle of red wine and a bevy of spices and bouillon cubes. All of it went into the cauldron over the fire and was allowed to simmer. In just over half an hour, we dug in.

I hated to admit, as the meat fell apart in my mouth, but it was one of the best meals I'd ever had here.

Raven was just as hungry as I was, because she scarfed down three helpings of the meat after I tapped out on one.

"Hungry?" I asked with a smile.

She nodded, wiping broth from the corner of her mouth. "Shapeshifting takes a lot out of me, and I'm not used to using it for extended periods of time. Today was exhausting."

"Well, you fought surprisingly well today," I said, setting down my bowl and spoon.

Raven looked up with surprise, more sauce at the corners of her mouth where the hint of a grin lifted her lips. "What? For a shapeshifter, you mean?"

I pulled out the flask again and took another drink. "Yeah, for a power-hungry leech, you didn't suck," I said, offering her the flask.

She took it and drank a larger gulp than I was expecting and passed it back. "Damn, that's good. Thanks for sharing."

I laughed and gave an exasperated sigh. "All right, spill. What happened to the meek, subservient girl in the throne room, kowtowing to Magnus? Seems like you pulled an alternate personality out of your ass."

Raven laughed and held her hand out for the flask, so I passed it back. She leaned back and glanced up at the incalculable number of stars overhead. There was absolutely zero light pollution, and millions of stars shone bright in the night sky. It took her a minute to speak, but when she did, her voice was filled with fear.

"You haven't been around him long enough, but Magnus is the most terrifying man I've ever met. He's utterly ruthless in the pursuit of his goals, and nothing is off limits when it comes to achieving them...I've found keeping my head down is the best way to avoid trouble."

She took another drink from the flask. "Despite your hatred of me, I'm still grateful, you know. To you."

"Whatever the hell for?" I asked.

"For getting me away from Castle Aliria, even if it's only for a little while."

Castle Aliria? Yeah, she seems the type. I scoffed. "Don't thank me. I'd have left you there in a heartbeat if I could've. I'm just as bad as Magnus, and I don't need your thanks."

My words didn't push her away as I wanted. Instead she looked up at me with a tilted head, her crimson eyes regarding me with intent. "I've been watching you, ever since I was told I'd become your tool. You're not as bad as Magnus. I can say that for certain."

"You're wrong."

Raven shook her head. "I am not. Magnus was cruel when I didn't do exactly as he said or made a mistake. You wouldn't hurt me."

"Don't be so sure of that," I replied.

She scooted even closer to me.

"Then do it," Raven challenged. "Hurt me."

My first response was to laugh at her; she was right, after all. Even if I couldn't stand the fact she was a shifter, I wasn't going to physically hurt her.

But as I gazed down at her pale throat, the slight raised vein on the side of her neck throbbing in time with her heart, my inner demon roused itself from its slumber again at the mere thought of blood.

"Do it, knight. Hurt her. Feast upon her flesh and savor her blood."

I bit my lip in anger at the flood of desire radiating from my chest. *Finally decided to speak after being so quiet? I don't need your influence, Aspect. Back off.*

I forced my eyes away from her neck, but the pull was strong. I wanted nothing more than to feast on her blood.

To lap at her neck and drink my fill.

Get out of my fucking head! You left me to fend for myself with Aliria—I'm not doing a damn thing you demand!

The magic in my heart burrowed free from its shell and filled my veins with ice water as it sought out my brain. The Aspect sought to control me again, its frigid grip on my mind, fogging my thoughts and weakening my resistance.

Pain filled my body and converged on my mouth as if I'd stuck a red-hot coal into my gums and gargled with acid. I backed away and clawed at my face, dragging my nails down my flesh, ripping deep furrows into my cheeks. The pain shifted something in my mouth, and I spat on reflex.

A handful of my teeth and a large gob of blood fled from my mouth.

"What the hell?" Raven asked, stepping back.

The pain receded, and I rode the pain for all it was worth, because it kept the Aspect from taking control of me. Though a sense of smugness came from within.

"Fight all you want, knight. We are one now."

The Aspect faded back into my heart as I pulled out Raven's bag and found the item I'd noticed earlier. A small hand mirror.

Opening my mouth with trepidation, I found I'd been changed once again. My canines had elongated and been joined by another set, side by side in my mouth. *Just like Eris's.*

I had the teeth of an entomancer now.

The mirror showed them in complete detail, and I didn't want to look at myself anymore. I stowed it away and sat back on the ground. Raven had distanced herself from me, and I thought that a wise move.

"I wouldn't put much stock in that theory of yours, Raven. I can hurt you just fine."

CHAPTER 9 - TRAINING

Eris

As the glow of leveling up faded away, I knelt as fatigue set in. I wiped my brow; the hot, muggy air clung to my skin and burned in my nose from the salt in the air. *Oh, that's interesting. My Agility increased by five, and so did my Durability. That seems reasonable, though I wish I had gained a bit more mana.*

"Congratulations, on the level up," Gil said. "What's it at now?"

"Only twenty. I wasn't allowed to take any really dangerous quests growing up, so it took nearly twenty-two years for me to even make it to nineteen."

"Well, the rate we keep going, you'll climb the ranks quickly."

Gil turned back to the others and left me alone.

The yellow squishy thing that'd been inside the shade was by my foot in the mud. I picked it up, wiped the muck off and squeezed it gently, my fingers indenting it. *What is this?* I turned it over and found a slight tear in it—something shiny lay at its center. I tore it open, revealing a single black ball in the center, about the size of a marble. It twinkled even under cover of clouds. I took it from the external casing and stood.

I walked over to the others, who were staring at me with a mixture of emotions. Pride came from Gil and Makenna, while Adam eyed the bauble in my hand with greed, and Evelyn looked quite disappointed.

"Good job, Eris!" Makenna said, beaming at me.

"Good job? That was abysmal. You have literally no technique. I expected that blockhead you call a lover to at least teach you something of fighting, but it was foolish of me even to expect that much," Evelyn scoffed, her tone reproachful.

I couldn't even argue with her; I knew I wasn't a fighter. *That was only my third fight and my first where Sam didn't help me. If I didn't have my magic, I'd be dead right now.* I needed to get stronger, so I had to muster up the courage to ask. "I know I'm not skilled at fighting, and I know that I need to get better and fast. So would you be willing to teach me, Evelyn?"

She sighed at my request but nodded. "I'll have to. I'm not going to babysit your ass." She gave me a half-smile. "Besides, not like you can be a worse student than Duran."

"You taught Sam?" I asked.

"Of course, though he'd developed a few bad habits with the sword, and I had to retrain him from scratch, so you'll be a breeze compared to him."

"Thank you," I told her, but she brushed me off.

"Save your thanks. I just don't want your ineptitude to get us killed. Now, round up those kids of yours and let's get a move on. We still have a lot of ground to cover."

"Right!" I said and headed off in the direction I had last seen them.

Finding the spiderlings was easy thanks to their acute hearing. I barely had to call their names before they came bounding out from the underbrush, covered in mud and twigs.

Tegen smiled wide at me, holding up a six-foot snake he'd caught. "Look what I found, Aunt Eris!"

"I see that," I said, taking the snake and releasing it back into the marsh. It slithered off as Tegen groaned. "Sorry, Tegen. But we can't take it with us."

"Told you," Cheira said, ruffling her brother's fine brown hair.

I couldn't help but laugh as I knelt to brush what filth I could from them, though we were all dirty. *I need a bath, but there isn't any clean water around that I can tell.* With so few insects around, I couldn't use them to pinpoint any freshwater. So I settled in for staying grimy for a while.

I held their hands as we made our way back to the group; everyone was already on their horses by the time we got back. I helped Tegen and Cheira onto Lacuna and was about to hop on myself when Gil called out to me and tossed me something. It was my backpack and cloak that I'd discarded by the trees.

"Thank you," I said, hastily donning my pack and tying my cloak around me. From the look of the clouds overhead, it was going to rain soon. The breeze that blew through the gray marshes began to pick up, so I climbed on Lacuna, and we quickly picked up the pace. The rain would do wonders to wash all the muck off us, but I didn't want to be stuck in the deep mire if it started to flood.

We sped through the damp as quickly as we could, but it still took another hour of riding before we exited the worst part of the marsh. Dying reeds and mud gave way to a breath of greenery as we took a path that, according to Gil, would lead us out of the worst of the Salted Mire.

"The only route to this road is through the deep marsh, but we should be out of the worst of it for now. We're headed to a small town on the outskirts of the Salted Mire about twenty-five miles away, so we have a lot of ground to cover," Gil told me as I kept pace with him.

I was just thankful to have a breather from the salt-laden wetlands. We were finally on somewhat stable ground. The scent of salt was still present, but it was almost as an aftertaste. Another hour of riding, and my stomach was screaming at me for food, but I didn't want to be the first one who complained. So I suffered for a while longer until Makenna spoke up and saved me.

"All right, guys. I'm seriously about to gnaw off my own arm here. Let's break for lunch, shall we?"

I heaved a sigh of relief when Evelyn nodded, and we found a decent spot to build a fire and get some food cooking. While Gil dealt with setting things up, Makenna and I carried heavy pieces of deadwood from the edge of the marsh to the fire pit along with some decent kindling. Once we had the fire going, Gil took out a large cooking pot and metal stands to set it over the fire. He poured in a generous measure of water along with salt and spices and let it rise to a boil.

When the stew was finished, we all gathered around the fire and let the damp dry out of our clothes. The storm clouds had been steadily increasing throughout the day, but the rain held off as we filled our stomachs.

I poured two bowls for the spiderlings first and let them eat while I waited for everyone to get their fill. I slurped down as much of the soupy stew I could stomach before setting back with content. Tegen and Cheira cuddled into me while everyone made polite conversation. With nothing to add myself, I took out the strange rock I'd acquired from the shade and twirled it around my palm, marveling how it shone even without a light source.

"How much?"

At the sound, I looked up to see Adam leaning over on the stump, staring intently at the rock in my hands. I held it up. "How much for this?" I asked.

He nodded, his head bobbing back and forth like it was attached to a string. "Yeah, yeah, yeah. How much do you want for the core?"

"*This* is a core?"

"Sure is!" he said, practically bouncing in his seat. "Do you know how valuable they are?"

I didn't have a clue. I had heard of cores before; they were prized trophies that lucky members of the Hive procured from slain monsters, but I hadn't ever actually seen one before and didn't know the first thing about them. Adam seemed overly excited about it, and even if it was exceedingly valuable,

I had no use for it, so I tossed it over to him. In his surprise, he almost dropped the small core.

His eyes widened as he palmed it. "I can just have it?"

"Sure. I have no use for it, so I don't see why not."

"Wow, thanks!" he said and took out a nearly transparent crystal, and with a long string of guttural words, a glowing blue circle made of light appeared in his hands just under the crystal. He brought the core close to the now-glowing crystal, and before they could touch, the core absorbed into the clear gem, turning it black.

"Where'd it go?" I asked, bewildered.

Adam laughed and scooted over on the log to show me the crystal. "This is a summoning crystal; they're used to store the cores of monsters and the like."

"So you used the shade's core and the summoning crystal to do what?"

"Just watch," Adam said.

He stood up from his seat and walked past the fire while I watched and waited. The others didn't so much as stir from their food. Once Adam had gotten about fifteen feet away, he tossed the crystal in the air.

"Come forth," he called, and the darkness burst from the crystal and rained down to form three individual shades. They took the form of humans and stood still, like they were waiting for something. I jumped to my feet as fear ran through me, but Adam just laughed and told me to calm down.

"They're under my control now, and they won't hurt you. Now, my shades, return from whence you came!"

In unison, they bowed and flowed into a single mass of flickering shadow before returning to the crystal. Adam called the gem to his hand and stowed it away. "Awesome, some new toys to play with."

I had to agree; it was awesome. *Sam said Adam was good with creatures, but I've never seen anything like that before.* "So you have to use a summoning crystal to store cores?" I asked.

Adam shook his head. "Not technically. You can use any gemstone, but they're usually inferior to summoning crystals, which is why they cost so much."

Gil's booming voice shouted over to us. "Hey, Adam, if you're done with the summoning lesson, let's get going. We still have a long way to go, and those storm clouds are getting darker."

After that, we cleaned everything up, dowsed the fire, and set off again, trying to outrun what was quickly turning into a monsoon. Wind swept at our backs for over two hours as we kept up a frightening pace; none of us wanted to get caught in the storm.

But for all our might, we were nothing compared to Mother Nature, and mountainous thunder was the harbinger of the storm. It rolled over us and pelted us with rain the size of rocks. The storm was so fierce, it whipped up debris around us, and we could not press on without fear of injury. We huddled in a close cropping of trees while the wind and rain hounded us for hours. We couldn't even make camp or take shelter under our tents without them getting soaked with water, so we leaned against the trees and suffered under the rain.

At least we were all clean now.

It was approaching twilight when the rain finally let up. The rain drizzled to a stop, and the dense cloud cover faded into the cool evening. I stood from the soggy ground and shook well over a pound of water from my clothes, in definite need of a change of clothes.

Gil spoke up from the next tree over. Both he and Makenna were dripping with just as much water as I was, and they looked miserable. "Why don't we set up camp here tonight? I'll doubt we'll find a better spot, and I'll get a fire going while you girls go and change."

That sounded like a fantastic plan, and I quickly climbed to my feet, as did Makenna and Evelyn. I told the children we'd be right back, and the three of us headed into a nearby thicket to change. After pushing through some thick underbrush, we entered a small clearing just wide enough for the three of us to move without bumping into one another.

I wasted no time in stripping from my soaked clothes, though the leather corset had straps that I couldn't reach on my own, and I struggled for a second before Makenna came over and helped untie me.

"Here, let me," she said as she placed her hands on my back.

"Thank you very much."

"It's no trouble," she replied and got to work.

She'd done this before, and in under a minute had me out of the armor. I placed it on the ground and stepped out of my skirt easily enough, but my shirt stubbornly clung to me and took far too much effort to remove. When I was finally free, I almost shouted in joy. I piled all my soiled clothes together and opened my pack to change.

"Well, don't you look sexy," Evelyn said at my back, I turned to find her naked, staring at me with curiosity.

"I'm sorry?" I asked, unsure of what she meant by sexy.

She didn't say anything, instead choosing to come closer to me. I couldn't help but stare at her while she did so.

Evelyn was beautiful, to a truly remarkable degree. I'd noticed before how lean she was, and how her armor hugged her body, but to see it uncovered was like night and day.

Her skin was flawless, pale like mine, but so much prettier. Hers was almost translucent it was so clear. She had the grace of a dancer and the strength of a warrior, pure functional muscle, but it was smooth and flowed flawlessly from head to toe. Her breasts were larger than mine, not by much, but still enough that it irked me. They were taut, and her nipples were almost invisible next to her skin. She caught me staring but wasn't angry; she looked at me with desire in her golden eyes.

Evelyn stood several inches taller than me, and she trailed a finger slowly from the top of my navel through my cleavage to grab my chin.

My heart beat incredibly fast in my chest, so much that I was sure Evelyn could hear it. She bent low to gaze at me, and her breath drifted across my bare skin to tickle my nose, and I caught the sweet fragrance of peppermint and honey from her mouth, while her skin smelled of rose petals and lavender. She tilted my neck, and I knew she was looking at my scar.

"What have we here?" Evelyn asked under her breath, her fingers playing over the indentation of Sam's teeth. "Seems you like it rough, kinky."

More words I don't understand, but I can't tell her about what happened between Sam and I. Sam hates the scar, and even if it wasn't his fault, I don't want to paint him in a negative light. I stepped back from her, not because I wanted to, but because I wanted to be closer to her. I longed to feel her skin against mine, but I couldn't.

Sam wouldn't like it, and I couldn't do something knowing it would hurt my bonded. He had a thing about only being with one person, and even if I didn't exactly agree with it, I didn't want to betray his trust.

Evelyn kept her hand on my neck but didn't press me, just reciprocated my earlier gawking and looked me up and down.

"You really are a gorgeous specimen, it's a shame you shackled yourself to the one man who would object to having his own harem. He'd never forgive me if I took you for myself," she said, walking back to her clothes.

Makenna watched our exchange with extreme interest, her clothes in her hands forgotten as she stood naked, waiting for something to happen. Her pigtails had come loose; her hair spilled down to cover her modest chest, which was as freckled as her face.

She was adorable, and as she bent over to climb into a pair of underwear, I noticed a shock of vibrant red hair at her crevice. It matched her hair, and I found that amusing for some strange reason. She looked at me when I started laughing to myself but thankfully didn't ask why. I didn't have a good answer for her.

The close proximity to Evelyn had left me heated, but now, alone, the chill left by the storm sank into my skin. My body heat kept the worst away, but the temperature was steadily dropping. I chose my clothes—a white cotton tunic that came down to my knees and a short black skirt—gathered up my belongings, and headed back to the fire to dry them.

Evelyn was dressed more casually than I had ever seen before, a black loose-fitting garment that tied at the waist and a pair of pants in a similar fashion. They looked like pajamas, but they also looked easy to move in, so I doubted they were actually sleeping clothes.

Makenna chose a billowy tunic that was at least three sizes too large, and I would have bet my dinner if it wasn't Gil's. Adam and Gil had also changed; both wore fresh shirts and pants, Gil's a light cream, while Adam wore a navy blue. There were several makeshift racks near the fire that already housed the other's clothes, so I added my own to the pile and went to take care of the spiderlings.

Tegen and Cheira had no other clothes, so I gave them both a shirt of mine and washed out their clothes and set them by the fire.

Once they were taken care of, I went to set up our tent.

I had watched Sam do it enough times while traveling that I thought I knew how to set it up properly, but it still took me about ten minutes of fumbling with the strings and stakes to get them to stay in the saturated ground. When the tent was as good as it was going to get, I stowed my belongings inside and went back by the fire.

While I was gone, Tegen and Cheira had disappeared. Slight panic chilled me when they weren't by the tree, but I quickly calmed down. *Those two are smart and as fast as I am. They're probably just playing. Nearly eight hours in the saddle, I'm sure they just need to burn off some energy.* My hunch was correct as around twenty minutes later, they came bounding out of the underbrush, carrying the carcass of a small doe.

"Look what we caught!" they both shouted in unison. I smiled over at them; they were so proud of themselves that I couldn't help but be happy for them.

"I can see that! Good job, both of you. We'll eat well tonight because of you two."

Gil stood up from beside the fire and walked over to us, kneeling by the deer and giving the children a bright smile. "Good work!" he said, speaking slowly.

Tegen and Cheira couldn't speak the language of humans, but they understood enough to know that Gil was praising them. Though they were still frightened by the giant, they both managed to return Gil's smile.

Tegen had dried blood on his hands, so I led them over to the fire and wiped them clean with some fresh water.

I passed the time until dinner by watching the fire. There was something mesmerizing about watching the flicking flames as they devoured whatever they touched with abandon. I stared into the smoldering coals for long enough that my eyes started to water, and I was brought out of my reverie by a curse from Gil.

"Oh, shit!" Gil yelled.

"What?" both Adam and Makenna asked at the same time.

Gil just held up his hand and stood up from preparing the deer. His hand went to his interface, and he started babbling.

"Hey! D, are you okay?"

My heart leapt into my throat, and I jumped to my feet. "Sam!"

Gil looked up at my shirt and nodded, before holding up his finger, telling me to wait. I didn't want to wait. I wanted to tackle him and demand answers, but I sat back down while my mind ran in circles trying to keep pace with my heart rate.

He kept speaking in low tones, so I couldn't make out what was being said when Gil abruptly shouted again.

"You're doing what?!" The veins on his hands throbbed as he opened and clenched his fists. "You can't be serious! By the gods, are you insane?

"All right, all right. I won't try and talk you out of it, but you watch your ass there. Don't be reckless and get yourself killed, you hear me?"

It seemed their conversation was coming to a close, and I desperately wanted to speak to Sam, just to hear his voice. Gil noticed my distress and took pity on my sanity.

"Hey, before you go, there's someone here who wants to talk to you, and if I hold off any longer, she looks like she's going to mob me," he said and pushed an invisible button in front of him.

Out of nowhere came Sam's voice, his handsome voice that laughed at what Gil had said.

"Hey Eris," he said, and his voice was filled with so much warmth that it made my heart melt.

"Hey, love."

"I'm sorry about cutting our connection. I didn't want to, but it was necessary," Sam said.

"It's okay; I was just worried about you. Where are you right now?"

"Gil will fill you guys in. I've had an exhausting day, but I wanted to touch base with everyone before I passed out. Don't worry, love, we'll see each other again soon."

"I'm holding you to that."

Another deep laugh. "I'd expect nothing less. I love you."

"As I love you. Until eternity, my bonded. Goodnight."

"Goodnight."

When Sam's voice cut out, Gil pressed a button and came to sit by Makenna. Before he could fully sit down, I all but screamed at him.

"Tell me everything."

***

After Gil finished explaining the conversation that went on between him and Sam, we all stared at him, dumbfounded.

"...he's working for Magnus?" Makenna asked.

Gil nodded. "Looks like it, the damn fool."

I didn't know what Sam's reasoning was, but I knew he was no fool. *If he's allied with the man that kidnapped him, there has to be a reason. We just have to figure out what.* I trusted him enough to have faith that he was doing the right thing.

The others were less concerned about why he had sided with Magnus and more about his destination: Aldrust.

"He's attempting to steal Lachrymal's Heart?"

"That's what he said, but I don't see how he can even pull it off."

"Think we should help him?" Adam asked.

Evelyn shook her head. "Impossible. It'd take over a week and a half to reach Aldrust from here unless we teleported, and it's not like we can leave the little queen to fend for herself."

We were all forced to agree with her; we had our own journey to accomplish, even if we could abandon it and chase after Sam.

Everyone discussed more while Gil cleaned the meat, but I didn't join in; I had made up my mind about what I was doing, and I couldn't go back on it.

"Food should be ready in just over half an hour," Gil said.

Good, the stew from lunch hadn't tided me over as long as I hoped. Tegen and Cheira were playing by the fire, drawing in the dirt, and I was about to sit by them when a whistling noise echoed from behind me.

I turned and caught the object that had been heading for my back. It was a sword, but wooden. Just like the real thing but wouldn't end with me getting cut to pieces.

"Nice reflexes," Evelyn called as she stepped towards me. In her hands was an identical copy of the sword she had thrust at me. "Now, come at me!"

Without hesitation, she swung, catching me on the chin with the tip of her sword. My head jerked back, and she used the opportunity to slash at my shoulder, sending me to the ground.

"Dead."

I struggled to my feet and didn't bother holding back as I swung at her. But I was so hopelessly inferior that it wasn't even fair. Evelyn batted my weak attacks aside with ease, not even trying to hide how easy it was for her. "Watch your feet," she said and rapped my shins hard with her sword. I faltered under the pain and stopped for just a second, and Evelyn snapped a kick that sent me sprawling to the wet ground, her sword at my throat.

"Dead," she repeated.

Angry and humiliated, I grabbed a handful of mud in my hands when I stood and tossed it at her when I struck with my weapon. Evelyn grinned and sidestepped both the mud and my attack, whacking my back with her sword.

"Improvisation and underhanded tricks—you're learning. Never be afraid to use whatever options are available to you. Honor means nothing if you get yourself killed," she said, settling back into her fight stance. "Again."

I attacked her, trying to get past her, but no matter what I tried, her sword blocked mine effortlessly. "Don't attack my weapon, attack me. The weapon is just an extension of myself. You're leading with your body. Lead with your weapon, and don't flail. Keep yourself behind your blade and keep your strikes precise."

The two of us went at it for what felt like hours, even when Gil finished preparing dinner and the others tore into fresh venison, Evelyn and I kept up our sparring until I physically couldn't hold my training sword any longer. I fell mid-swing and lay gasping on the ground, aching like my entire body was pulling apart.

Evelyn took mercy on me and called an end to our training. I managed to half-walk, half-drag myself by the fire and let the pouring sweat dry in the heat. I was gross, and so bone-tired that even eating had lost its appeal. I took two bites before exhaustion set in, and I shuffled off to bed. The spiderlings joined me, but I was asleep before they could even cuddle next to me.

CHAPTER 10 - THE GOLDEN-EYED TWINS

If I thought I was sore last night, it was nothing compared to the full body ache that throbbed with every slight movement. My entire body was like a walking bruise, and it made the thought of even more long hours in the saddle so unbearable that I wanted to immediately crawl back into my bedroll and sleep for a week. *Can't do that, though, even if its appealing. The others are probably waiting on me.*

I woke up the children, and we left the tent. Gil stirred a pot over the campfire, while Evelyn and Adam were up and working through a set of exercises. Makenna intermittently napped while leaning against Gil, who looked up when he heard the flap of the tent.

"Morning, you three. Hungry?"

I tried to say yes, but it came out so thick with sleep that even I couldn't register what I'd said.

Gill just laughed. "I'll take that as a yes. Come over here and get a bowl. Stew should just be about done."

"Thank you, Gil," I said, trying to be grateful, but I was tired of stew, and Gil heard it in my voice.

"Don't worry, we should hit the town today and stock up on more supplies," he said before leaning down and kissing Makenna on the head. "Time to get up, Kenna."

She groaned and shoved him in playful anger. "I'm not used to this crap. Fourteen or more hours a day on the road is for the birds."

Her words stung a bit, but I knew that wasn't her intentions. It was because of me that they all had to take the long road, but Makenna would have been mortified if she knew her words had hurt me. So I quickly shook them off and went to sit by the pair.

Evelyn and Adam finished up their training and snagged two bowls of stew before coming to sit by us. Evelyn looked me over and smirked. "How is the little queen feeling this morning?"

"Like I almost wish I was back in the void, so I wouldn't have to feel my body."

Makenna perked up at that. "What was it like?" she asked before blushing scarlet. "Sorry, that was probably incredibly rude."

I smiled at her. "Not at all," I replied, but I paused, trying to work up the courage to speak.

The void was called such for a reason, and I doubted I would ever truly stop feeling its effects. Even now weeks later, it clung to me. Wouldn't fully let go.

I tried to keep my smile, but it fell as soon as I spoke. "The void is nothing. And inside it, I was nothing. I couldn't feel my body, couldn't feel anything, and sometimes, for years at a time, I couldn't even think."

Everyone was staring at me now, food left forgotten in the cast iron pot, boiling over. I wanted to let the story die, as already my mind kept going back there and the ever-familiar weightlessness tingled across my arms once again. I shook my head and rubbed away the goosebumps. As much as I wanted to forget, I couldn't. I needed to get it out and off my chest.

"Centuries passed in what felt like the blink of an eye, but every time someone picked up my prison, I was forced back into the light. Because of the curse placed on me, I had to choose the person who would free me, but that person would also become my master, and I, a slave.

"I was able to get a glimpse at the souls of anyone who picked up my crystal. But it seemed only the worst sorts ever picked me up. People with the blackest souls, who would have used me in the worst ways and brought nothing but pain to my life. Seven men and women. Seven black hearts until the eighth."

"Duran, right?" Gil asked.

I nodded. Thinking of Sam was already banishing the lingering void. I was free and would never go back. "Sam was the first person in a thousand years that was worthy. Though he doesn't think so."

Gil scooted over and patted me on the back. "D is harder on himself than anyone I've ever met, but none of us are exactly the picture of mental stability anymore. You have to understand, the world we came from was a hellish place, and for some people, Duran especially, it's hard to let go of your ghosts."

"I know, it's just…"

I didn't know what I was going to say. That I wanted Sam to stop blaming himself for Micah's death, along with whatever other tragedy that kept haunting him? It's easy for me to say, but here I was letting my own ghosts still have a hold on me. *I'm sorry, my love. You've had to shoulder so much pain, and you refuse to let anyone help. Maybes it's time we both start sharing each other's burdens.*

I lapsed into silence after that, trying to work though my own past, and the others were aware that I wasn't in the best place to keep up a conversation. Everyone turned back to their food and devoured their meal while I only picked at mine. I knew I would regret it in a few hours, but I couldn't stomach another bite when it was in so many knots.

After breakfast, we quickly packed up and set out. The horrible storm from the night before had blown away to reveal bright blue skies and a beautiful day. It was impossible for me to keep sulking when I was surrounded by such beauty, so I soon got over my slight bout of melancholy and perked up to enjoy the day. *Sam, when we see each other again, I promise to lay everything on the table, and I want you to do the same. No more ghosts. I'll help rid you of yours if you help with mine.*

I let the fresh air and sunshine wash away everything and just basked in the open air as we rode. Two hours later, and we came out of the woodlands and found a small town, right where Gil had said it would be.

"Welcome to Odelpha, a town where we best keep an eye on our purse strings," Makenna said.

Odelpha didn't give off any bad vibes as I glanced about the town as we rode in. We crossed back near the Salted Mire, and the scent of salt clung in the back of my throat, but the town itself seemed fine. Most of the buildings were built of rough, dark wood with muted windows and worn wooden roof tiles. A few buildings were made of stone, namely the largest building in the center of town that looked like a house but much larger. *Mansions. I think that's what Sam called them.* It was built on solid ground, while further towards the marshlands, houses and buildings were on wooden stilts raised off the ground, which looked perpetually wet and muddy.

We stayed on the main road and made our way to the largest building next to the stone mansion. From the sign swinging in the wind it looked like an inn. It was a three-story building equally as worn as the others around town, and the windows were too dark to see inside, but even through the thick wood door, music mixed with loud conversation and shouting. We stopped at the front porch, hitched our horses, and went inside.

It was dark. Even though there were a dozen lanterns along the wall and a fire roaring on the far corner, it only helped to cast dancing shadows along the wall. Thirteen tables were scattered around the floor, most of them packed with people. Men and women of all types, but each of them looked worse for wear, like none of them had eaten a decent meal in a few days, and they all eyed us hungrily as we entered.

172

Gill and the others didn't seem to be bothered in the slightest. Each of them wore hard glares as they stared down the inn's patrons. Most of the withering looks faded, and people went back to nursing their drinks and food.

However, it seemed one of the patrons didn't take the hint and gathered the courage to attempt to pickpocket Evelyn. I didn't see the man approach but couldn't miss his screech as Evelyn suddenly moved and grabbed him by the throat. I turned as she lifted him with one hand as if it were the easiest thing in the world.

The man was young, just out of his youth, and clearly the life he'd led had been a hard one. His blond hair was shaggy and greasy, and his blue eyes were hazy, like he was drunk or worse. His teeth were black and rotten as he gasped an apology to Evelyn, kicking and squirming in her grasp.

"I'm…I'm sorry," he managed to squeak out.

Evelyn smiled a frigid smile. "I'm not," she said and produced a small thin knife from out of nowhere, placing it against the man's heart and slowly pushing in.

Blood began to trickle down his chest before increasing to a stream, and it poured down his chest as the blade struck his heart. He struggled in pain but could do nothing against Evelyn and succumbed to death a moment later.

Evelyn withdrew her knife, wiped it on the man's shirt and tossed his corpse aside before going and lounging in the only open table available. The entire inn dead silent, the beating hearts and gulps of fear from men three tables down were audible to my ears as we followed Evelyn and took out seats. Gil gave her a shake of his head and a chuckle, clearly less perturbed about her casual murder than I was.

"Was that absolutely necessary?"

"Of course not," she said with a grin. "But word will quickly spread, and we won't have any more trouble. I'd say that's worth the life of one lowly pickpocket."

Makenna sat down with a chuckle. "I won't complain. Besides, if it keeps the rabble from getting handsy with us, then I say it's well worth the price."

I disagreed wholeheartedly, but I couldn't speak up about it, not when my own hands were stained with blood. *I killed because I had to, because Sam or myself would have died otherwise, but that was murder.* Something I wasn't comfortable with at any level.

Sam himself was a murderer, but he always had a good reason for killing. Evelyn may have had a valid reason, but there were other options available that she could have done easily.

I sat down heavily, the chair groaning as I dropped my weight on it. Evelyn and the other looked up, saw my face and frowned. Evelyn picked up a fork and jabbed it at me. "Don't even think about it, little queen. You'll just waste your breath."

"But…did you have to—"

"Yes. Now I don't want to hear about it again. I've already forgotten it."

With that, she tuned me out and whistled for the barkeep, who had been nervously eyeing us since she'd killed the man. He came over, tray in hand close to his chest like a shield, and tried to put on a fake smile, but it slipped every other second.

"What can I get for you today?" he stammered.

It seemed everyone deferred to Evelyn as she ordered for us. "A round of drinks and steak, and it better be fresh."

He jumped at her tone and nodded before scurrying back behind the bar. Adam looked over at his sister with a sigh and reached over to flick her lightly on the nose. "Your evil is showing, dear sister of mine."

She laughed. "And your point being?"

"Nothing," he said, grinning. "Just being a dutiful brother and pointing out your shortcomings."

Evelyn laughed and began toying with the fork still in her hand, making it balance on the tips of her fingers, looking over at me and my sullen face. She sighed.

"All right, little queen. Because I actually like you and it seems not everyone agrees with my decision, I'll stick to clear, justifiable murder going forward, fair?"

It was probably the best I could ever hope for, so I nodded. "Thank you, Evelyn."

After that, the mood lightened around our table. A few different conversations picked up between the guild. Gil and Makenna talked to themselves, discreetly holding hands under the table, which I thought was the cutest thing I'd ever seen. Tegen and Cheira were sitting together on a chair, each of them fighting for more room on the small chair until I picked up Cheira and put her in my lap.

She smirked at Tegen and leaned back into me. "See, told you Eris loves me more."

"She does not," Tegen retorted. "Right, Aunt Eris?"

I reached over and patted his head. "Of course. I love you both equally."

Cheira's hair was windswept, so while we waited for our drinks, I combed through her hair with my fingers, untangling the knots.

By the time I'd tamed the chaos of her hair, the barkeep returned with an even larger tray filled with glass mugs brimming with a deep brown and red liquid. "Far Trips specialty. Blackberry mead. On the house," he said, setting the drinks down and leaving, going through a door on the back wall that led to the kitchen, from the scents of food that wafted out.

I picked up the glass and savored the bittersweet aroma that drifted to my nose. My mouth watered at the prospect of drinking it, and I was about to take a sip when Cheira grabbed my arm.

"Can I have some?" she asked.

Tegen perked up at that as well and raised his hand. "Me too, me too!"

Should I give them some? It seemed harmless enough, but I wanted to make sure it was okay before I let them have any. I took a sip and marveled at the sweetness of the blackberries before I reached the small bite of the alcohol. It was sweet and smooth, and if they didn't drink too much, I figured it would be fine to let them have a taste.

They each took turns after I warned them of only a sip, and they both delighted in the taste, lighting up and reaching for more, but I took it from them.

As the barkeep passed by our table, I waved him down. "Can I get two small glasses of watered-down mead for the children?"

"Right away, Miss," he said and quickly brought over two glasses.

Soon after our food was ready and we dug in, each of us delighting in the fresh meat and drink. I joined in the conversation with Gil and Makenna when they brought up Sam and Aldrust. They were trying to figure out how Sam could possibly complete his task, but keeping the specifics vague since there was a chance we could be overheard.

I had never been to the kingdom of the dwarves, so I was useless in providing any help, but it was interesting to listen to them talk about it. I knew that most of the city was deep underground, but from the way they were talking about it, it was far larger than I originally thought.

"So you think he has a chance?" Gil asked.

Makenna thought about it for a minute before sighing and shaking her head. She was about to say something, but I interjected. "Of course he does.

He's the most stubborn man I've ever met. human or Hive. He'll be fine," I said, putting as much hope that I was right into my words.

Makenna smiled and patted my shoulder. "You're right. He'll be fine."

We ate, drank, and talked for another few hours, enjoying resting after several days in the saddle. Eventually the number of patrons started dwindling, some heading upstairs with a number of women after exchanging coin. It seemed a strange practice, so I asked Adam about it.

He was taking a sip of mead at the time and coughed and spluttered when I spoke up, causing everyone to burst out laughing.

"Uh, those are…um…prostitutes, women who exchange sex for money."

"What a strange practice," I replied. "Though humans and entomancers view sex differently, so that's probably why."

"What do you mean?" Makenna asked.

"In my culture, because of the way women were treated, sexual intimacy was traded rather than bought. Especially between the nobility. It was used as a way to further secure favors or trade agreements."

"Hold up," Makenna said, setting down her mead. "So your people just passed the women around whenever it was convenient for them."

"Essentially."

"Fucking disgusting," she said, draining the rest of her ale.

"Were you ever treated like that?" Evelyn asked out of the blue, eyeing me intently.

"Oh, um. No. No, I wasn't," I said, blushing. "I was the heir to a powerful family, even before my mother became queen. My purity was too valuable to waste."

"That means our dear guild leader was your first," she said, smiling.

I nodded. "He was."

"I admit, he's pretty good in the sack, right?"

Before I could respond, Gil slammed his mug down. "All right, that exceeds the amount of girl talk I can handle for the evening. I'm heading to bed."

Evelyn and Makenna just laughed, but Adam held up his hands in prayer and mouthed, "Thank you."

The inn only had two rooms available, so we were forced to bunk together, Gil and Adam in one room, with me, Evelyn, Makenna, and the children in the other. Our room was the last door at the top of the stairs and could barely be called a room. It was cramped with two small beds and a nightstand in the middle. From the darkened window, I could just make out the light of the moon reflecting off the bog water in the marshlands in the distance.

Makenna complained about the heat, so I opened the window, letting in the humid night air and chattering of insects. On reflex I opened the Hive Mind and spread my consciousness throughout the little ones while the other two got undressed and Tegen and Cheira crawled over the bed and under it. Despite the rambunctious nature of the children, they were barely making a sound as they chased each other over the covers.

I turned back to the window, leaning out and letting the thick, moist air lick at my sweat-stained skin. It was lovely while I pushed my consciousness further, trying to build my magical tolerance. It was only thanks to this that I got a look at something that made no sense.

There were people out in the marsh, a lot of them. Well over three dozen, and as I pushed my reach, I found they were even more, circling the town. *I don't know what they're doing, but it can't be good. I need to warn the others.*

"There are a lot of men in the marshes surround the town. Dozens of them, maybe more," I said, turning to the others.

As a credit to both women, they were up out of bed and alert in seconds, throwing on clothes and drawing weapons. Makenna pulled a handful of her needles free and started dipping them in some sharp, noxious-smelling liquid from her belt. "I'll go wake the others. Eris, can you use your magic to control the insects in the marsh?"

I caught her meaning at once and nodded, pulling my consciousness to the most potent of my little ones. "You want me to attack them?"

"Yep, slow them down and kill a few if you can."

"What if they're good people?" I asked.

"Kill or be killed, little queen. I believe this counts as justifiable murder to me."

I knew her words were the truth, and I had no reason to expect the people in the marsh harbored anything but ill toward us and the town. *Last time we were ambushed, we nearly died. I won't hesitate like that again.*

With my mind made up, I focused every facet of my being into my creatures. There were simply too many men and women hiding in the swamp lands to get them all, but it seemed they were just waiting for orders, so I went looking for the leader but quickly realized I would never find them just by their attire alone. *Okay, so new plan, I guess. Let's go after the biggest ones, the ones that look the most trouble.*

They all looked like trouble, but there were plenty of large men who oozed danger. There were fewer venomous spiders in the swamp, but I took what few I had and had them crawl up the men. It took a few minutes to get the thirty or so to make their way to my intended targets. When the last crawled up, I gave the order to attack.

Using all the stored-up venom in the spiders, they each bit down on the necks of the brigands. A few pained shrieks slipped from the marshlands, but they quickly quieted. The venom was lethal over time in small doses, but by pouring every last drop into their systems. Their nervous systems would soon seize up and begin shutting down their bodies, paralyzing them and killing them quickly after.

The insect bites were noticed but brushed off as just being outside, near insects. Only potent antivenom would save them, but it was far too late for that.

Gil and the others came into the room, and I released the control of the Hive Mind. One look at me and Gil pulled a mana potion from his inventory and handed it to me. I hadn't noticed, but I was a little shaky, and I greedily drank down the potion, sighing as energy flooded into my muscles.

"Thank you, Gil."

"Don't mention it."

"I managed to bite about half their number, but depending on the individual people, they might still be able to fight even with the venom in their system. Thought the majority should start feeling the effects any moment now."

He walked over to the window, peering out at something, and nodded. "All right. I bet when they see their men go down, they charge ahead and surround the town. That or call off the whole thing, but when has our luck ever gone that way?"

"What do we do?" I asked.

"We get set up, c'mon," he said and left the room.

I followed after him, and we headed back downstairs to the bar. All the tables had been overturned, and Adam had summoned the shades again. They were in the process of dismantling the chairs and turning the chair legs into miniature spears.

Evelyn pulled out a few weapons: a shortsword, two daggers, and a longsword. She was in the process of deciding which one to go with, taking practice swings with each of them. A barbaric yawp sounded in the distance, followed by a war horn. *Guess the venom finally took effect.*

The others tensed at the sound, and Evelyn quickly chose her shortsword.

I looked around, finding one missing. "Where's Makenna?" I asked.

A chuckle from above drew my gaze, though I didn't see anything at first. It took me a second to spot Makenna hidden in the shadows on one of the support beams. What was even more surprising was that Tegen and Cheira were up there as well, grinning down at me.

Both of them had a singular dagger in hand, and I was terrified for them but wasn't going to dissuade them of helping. *They're fast, faster than almost any human. I trust them if they think they can help.* I didn't like it, but if they could help, then let them.

The thudding of boots got louder until a mixture of new sounds joined the pounding feet. High-pitched screams and the clang of clashing steel. A battle raged outside, and too soon it reached the inn.

Pounding loud enough to wake the dead assaulted the door in front of us, and it was strong enough to force the cheap metal hinges to bend inward. Less than half a minute later, the door cracked and was forced out of the doorway. It crashed down to the floor, and half a dozen men and women flooded into the space.

Before they even took a single step further, Makenna attacked, flinging out with her poisoned needles. Four of them hit their targets, but the rest pinged off armor or missed and thudded into the soft wooden floor. While the enemy tried to figure out what had attacked them, Makenna withdrew a small knife with a curved blade and dropped from the support beam, slashing out with her knife as she landed in the center of the mob.

One of the men who hadn't been hit with her poison dropped to the ground with his throat slashed open, spilling a fountain of blood across the floor. The others turned to engage Makenna, but she simply flowed around their weak strikes and consumed their entire attention.

Which is when Cheira and Tegen struck from behind. They were smart and aimed for the ones furthest in back and killed them with brutal efficacy. They dropped, killed their targets, and darted away in three seconds.

I was immensely proud of them.

The men poisoned by Makenna dropped to the ground, lifeless, and she deftly slipped back around our makeshift barricade. In ten seconds, we'd killed the opening wave of invaders, but there were still many more outside to deal with.

"Shades, scout ahead," Adam commanded.

The three wispy doppelgängers marched outside and joined in the fray. A minute went by before a sharp crack of glass shattered through the sounds of battle, and the crystal flew back to Adams outstretched hands.

He sighed and pocketed the crystal. "That's what I get for sending the newbies."

Evelyn sauntered out from behind the bar, drink in hand as if she didn't have a care in the world. She knocked back the liquor and smiled, her golden yellow eyes glinting in the firelight. "Let's go join the fun, shall we?"

We exited the inn to a bloody victory. Even with their decimated numbers, the gang of bandits had made short work of the town. A few villagers who'd fought back were dead, slaughtered like livestock and left where they fell. No building was left unbroken or unlooted, and the few villagers who were left alive were huddled together in the center of a mob.

More than twenty bandits surrounded the inn, the last building standing. All of them had their weapons out and were half a second away from engaging. Gil, Makenna, and I went out first, and the leader of this gang of bandits stepped forward.

He was tall, burly and brutish with hair the color of fresh straw a day after harvest that trailed down to his lower back and a thick beard that obscured half of his face, though his hazel eyes were alight with bloodlust. He wore heavy plated armor and carried a giant sword that was bigger than I was.

He swaggered over to us and laughed. "Couple of fighters, eh? Well then, you'll have the pleasure of facing Bandit King Cassimere in combat," he said with a wide grin. "Who's going to be my first victim?"

"I believe we'll take you up on that offer, Cass," Evelyn said, walking out with Adam by her side.

One look at Evelyn, and Cassimere deflated. His entire personality shifted, and pure and utter terror paled though him. His eyes widened, and his sword fell from his grip.

He dropped to his knees and held up his hands. "I didn't know. I swear, I didn't."

Both Evelyn and Adam's personalities shifted slightly. They gained an air about them that I couldn't identify, but it stopped me from speaking up. I settled back and watched as they approached Cassimere.

"That is a shame, Cass," Adam said. "You were always my favorite, too."

One of the men, a younger man with hair spiked in every direction, marched over, cocksure as could be and loudly proclaimed. "I don't know who the fuck you are, but you need to show King Cass some resp—"

Before he could finish his speech, one of the other men ran him through. The man didn't have time to scream as the blade pierced his heart and he dropped to the ground. The man who'd killed him dropped to his knees and bowed low to Adam and Evelyn.

"Please forgive us, Empress Evelyn."

CHAPTER 11 - ALDRUST

Sampson

"Goodnight," I said and hung up.

I sat back and stared up at the black sky, lonelier than I'd been in a very long time. I used to could spend days without talking or feeling the need to be around other people, but now I was drowning without Eris by my side. *A couple of days, and we'll be back together. I can deal with things for a couple days.*

Though I didn't actually believe that.

I fingered my teeth, running my fingers over them for the hundredth time. *Still can't wrap my head around them. Fucking hell, Aspect!*

It just laughed and sent a wave of cold dripping down my spine. I shivered and took another drink of whiskey, trying to banish its lingering whisper inside.

It was late, and I needed sleep, but Raven had already turned in after the episode with my teeth, and I wasn't ready to share a tent with her just yet.

So I settled for drinking.

We'd reach Aldrust tomorrow, and I'd get a refill, so I polished off the rest of the flask in an hour, and when I was suitably drunk enough to stomach the thought of sleeping next to Raven, I turned in myself.

Raven was out like a light in the left corner of the tent. She curled over on her side and was wearing only a pair of black satin panties and nothing else. The pale of her back was to me, her toned muscles rising and falling with each breath. Her midnight hair covered her torso like a blanket. I put my back to her and climbed into my sleeping bag.

I bunched my pillow under my elbow and forced myself to sleep.

Rustling from beside me woke me what must've been only minutes after I'd fallen asleep, but daylight streamed through the seams in the tent, basking the small room in early twilight.

"Morning," Raven called from beside me.

I rolled over to find her right next to me, sitting cross-legged, still naked from the waist up. Raven had light pink nipples surrounded by a perky, full bust that jostled as she roughly gathered up her hair with a tie stuck in her mouth.

I averted my gaze with a chuckle. "What's with the women in my life and exhibitionism?"

"It's more comfortable sleeping like this," she said, deadpan, as she pulled the tie from her mouth and wrapped it around her mess of black hair.

"You and my wife would get along well," I said, climbing to my feet. "Just get dressed and meet me outside."

I left the tent and began packing our supplies. By the time I was done, Raven had dressed in her leather armor and was ready to go. I broke down the tent, and we set off as soon as it was done.

Raven shifted, and we took to the skies. Even on the second day, it was still exhilarating flying, and I loved it as we soared high above the desert.

We flew for a couple of hours and only slowed when the desert gave way to tufts of greenery and trees. The beating heat of the desert faded to lush grasslands for an hour or two until we reached the edge of Aldrust's territory. A huge wall made of dirt and rock rose up thirty feet in a circle, covering the entirety of the territory of Aldrust. Though ninety percent was underground, there was a standing force on the surface to guard the wall and maintain a few small farms.

"That's a big wall," Raven said as we got close.

"Yeah, but keep away from it, unless you want to get shot down."

"Good point."

Though I couldn't see them from this high up, I knew there were guards stationed around the wall, ready to engage with anything that threatened them.

Raven dipped low, and we landed about a mile away from the entrance to the city. She shifted back into her human form, and we started walking. I was grateful for the exercise. Sitting atop Raven for hours at a time wasn't the most comfortable thing I'd ever done, and from the way she was walking, the same could be said of letting me fly on her.

"Let me do the talking when we get to the gate," I said.

Raven turned and looked at me. Her blood-red eyes bored into mine, and she shook her head. "We're a married couple coming to see an old friend. Magnus has already made all the arrangements."

I sighed and tried very hard not to growl at her. It wasn't her fault she was pissing me off.

"We could just eat her, her flesh looks tantalizing," The Aspect whispered.

Oh, shut up.

"How about you just eat her, then, no biting involved? She has a fantastic body, and I bet she tastes delicious."

You're awfully chatty now that we're away from Aliria.

"I'm thankful to be away from her. She's terrifying."

Well, I wish you'd go back to the silent treatment.

I ignored the snide laughter of the Aspect and kept walking.

"So why are you doing this?" Raven asked after about five minutes of silence.

"Doing what?"

"This, all of it," Raven said, throwing her hands up. "You don't seem like the following orders type."

"Well, I'm not, but something big is going on, and I don't really have a choice in the matter anymore. I've got to figure out what's going on with the world and help stop it, even if that means working with Magnus."

"Even if it means doing bad things to good people?"

I snorted. "I've done a lot worse for much less. At least this time, I'm helping."

Raven didn't respond. Instead, she clammed up and wore a contemplative expression across her face while we reached the entrance to Aldrust.

The massive wall of stone, earth, and grass towered above us, casting us into shadow as we stepped under its gaze. The wall was smooth, completely without blemish as it circled around the territory of Aldrust. Nearly a dozen soldiers stood by the entrance, which was only an entrance if the guards allowed passage—otherwise, it was just another part of the wall.

We got in line behind nearly a hundred others all trying to enter Aldrust. Most of them were dwarves, but a few humans stood above the heads of the others. Time passed as Raven and I inched closer to the gate, and then it was finally our turn.

The gate guard, a taller dwarf male with more muscle than hair, leered at us, calm and collected.

"State your business," he said, his voice rough and graveled.

"We're—" I began, but Raven held up a hand and cut me off.

"We're here on our honeymoon, visiting an old friend. Orryn Drell," she said with a smile.

The gate guard nodded. "Tax is two silver," he said and held out his hand.

Raven pulled out a few gold coins and dropped them into his palm. And even the stony-faced guard's eyes widened at the money. He turned, held out his empty hand, and spoke a short rolling incantation in Script.

His hand glowed a light brown as the Script circle popped into existence and swirled, ethereal, around his palm. When he finished speaking, the circle faded away, and a thick slab of stone opened in the wall.

The gate guard waved us through, and as soon as we were inside, the door slammed shut behind us. Inside the wall was a long passageway made of stone and lined with torches that flickered every couple of feet.

Before we'd taken a single step, I whirled on Raven and shoved her against the wall. My finger pressed against her cheek.

"Don't ever speak for me again, you understand?"

She nodded, a smile pressing at her lips. "I understand."

"Good," I said and backed off her, turning and walking down the hall.

Raven followed, her steps clacking quickly behind me as she caught up. We walked in silence, but there was a pep in Raven's step that hadn't been there before.

"Excited?" I asked.

"What?" she asked, her face flushing scarlet. "I mean, a little."

"Well, we've got some time to kill today. We can look around—it'll be beneficial to get the lay of the land regardless."

"Oh, yes. The city, of course," she said, turning away from me for a moment.

I left the quirky shifter to her own devices and stepped through the heavy wrought-iron door that led to the upper farmland.

The sun was high in the sky overhead, and after being in the cool shadows for an hour, I welcomed the heat. Dozens of large natural stone buildings were all around us, along with an abundance of farmland. The earthy scent of freshly tilled dirt and vegetation permeated every inch. Dwarves toiled away at their farms with smiles on their faces as they worked. And they had good reason for those smiles.

"Why is everyone so thrilled to be doing manual labor?" Raven asked, confused.

"Because each and every one of the dwarves working are Aldrust's best. High nobility, war heroes, Lachrymal's chosen disciples. They've all done something of great importance to have earned their farms."

"That doesn't make sense. Their reward for hard work is more work?"

"Essentially, but the farms are more than just farms. They're status symbols to the dwarves."

She chuckled, shaking her head, but I let her be. It didn't really make sense to me either when I first came here.

We passed by the farmlands and walked to the entrance to Aldrust. It was basically a gigantic elevator that lowered us down to the city, but it was powered by teams of dwarves and their earth magic. We stepped on it, and after some words in Script, we descended.

Elevators didn't bother me, but for someone like Raven who hadn't ever been on one before, she was having a blast. Her head darted around as the stone block we were on grumbled and shook as we went deeper into the earth.

When we stopped at the lower level, Raven's excitement abated, but it surged right back up as we stepped into the city.

Even after seeing it dozens of times, I never really got over its majesty. Everything was carved out of stone. Stone houses and manors rose from the very earth itself. Carved stone formed everything, from the streets and stairways to the lamp posts that held shining blue mana crystals as they lined the winding roads in all directions.

Aldrust was a never-ending maze spreading like the roots of a tree in all directions. All with the level of detail and craftsmanship that would put even the most skilled human hands to shame.

High above us, nestled into the rocky ceiling, stood the largest cluster of mana crystals in the world. The cluster was the size of Castle Gloom-Harbor and pulsed with radiant blue light, creating a facsimile of a sun underground.

"Wow, I've never seen anything like it before!" Raven exclaimed, grabbing my arm.

I nodded. It was always something to behold. I let Raven take in the sights for a long moment while I tried to see through the chaos of the streets.

"All right, enough gawking. Let's get to walking. It's changed since I've been here last, and I want to get a feel for the place."

Raven nodded. "We've got time. Our meeting isn't supposed to be for this evening, so we can sightsee as much as you want."

Well, if that's the case, might as well go visit Thrayl, since I have time. "I want to stop by a friend's shop. It's in Silver Midtown."

She held her hand out. "Lead the way."

While technically, we were already in Midtown, Thrayl's shop would be a couple miles further down. It would take a little navigating to get there. But there was always a pattern with the way the dwarves laid out the city. Even when they remodeled it every couple years, there was always a reason for it.

The streets were filled with hundreds of dwarves going about their day, the men headed to the mines or manual labor jobs while the women minded the shops. We stepped around a dwarf woman with long red hair, carrying a basket of produce. She nimbly wound around us with a wave of apology.

If the women weren't so short, they'd actually be very attractive.

I was careful not to run into anyone and grabbed Raven's hand as we crossed a few streets and wound up at one of the stretches of market.

Thick stone stalls lined the streets with merchants peddling anything we could ever need. There wasn't anything I needed at the moment, so I pulled Raven along and tried to disengage us from the throng of patrons and sellers.

After some careful maneuvering, we'd gotten off Merchant Street and hit the stairs that wound down the city.

"This place is packed," Raven said, sticking close to me.

"Well, despite the size of this place, dwarves like sticking close to one another. I think it has something to do with safety in numbers."

"In case of cave-ins, things like that?"

"Most likely." I shrugged and stepped down the second flight of stairs. Dwarves never made much sense to me, but I didn't bother questioning some of their quirks. They made the best weapons and armor on Nexus, and that was good enough for me.

It took around half an hour to reach Thrayl's shop. I had to do some asking around, and an elderly dwarf pointed us in the right direction.

Thrayl's shop hadn't changed since the last I'd been there. The outside was stone, with wide bay windows on each wall. Even from here, the heat was intense; heavy smoke curled around the gray trim and floated skyward. An attached storehouse contained every tool or instrument involved in crafting, and each hung in neat order along the walls and in specific spots on the shelves.

I crept up to the window, where loud clanging sounded from just inside.

Thrayl sat banging away at a long hunk of metal on an anvil. He was tall for a dwarf, around five feet, and skinnier than most, but wiry cords of muscle clung unevenly to his frame. He had a thin, scarred face from years of metal work and thick blond hair that'd been pulled back into an intricate braid that matched the pattern of his long beard.

"Thrayl!" I shouted between hammer strikes.

He stopped mid-swing and turned, squinting. "Duran?"

"Yep."

Thrayl hopped up from his seat a wide smile across his face. "How's my favorite human?"

"Busy, you got a few minutes?" I asked.

He looked back at his project and to me. "For you, always." He waved me in.

Raven and I went around to the door, a smooth portion of the wall. The door slid under the ground without so much as a scrape and Thrayl stood in the doorway, still smiling.

He took one look at me, and his smile fell.

"You go back to robbin'?" he asked, scratching his head.

"Not that I'm aware of, why?"

He pointed at me with all five of his fingers. "Then how the hell did you come by a set of Arryn Mora armor?"

My jaw dropped. I looked down and back at Thrayl. "No way."

"I'd know his craft anywhere," he said, craning his neck past me to look at Raven. "Good on ya' for settlin' down. Was worried you'd die before you found someone to put up wit' ya'.

"But where're me manners, come in. There's a story here I want told."

We entered his cramped home. My head barely missed hitting the top of the doorframe. Inside his home wasn't much better, and I resorted to a high crouch to avoid bashing my skull against the ceiling. Thrayl led us to his living room and offered us a chair.

While made of stone, the chair was rather comfortable, and the thick woolen cover kept us from freezing.

"So how'd you manage to land such a lovely young woman?" he asked, glancing at Raven.

"Oh, we're—"

"It's a long story," Raven said, interrupting me. "Took too long for me to convince him we were meant to be, but I'm persistent."

"Ha! Good on ye'. He's a stubborn one, but not bad folk, all things considered." Thrayl laughed and slapped his knee. "Let me go grab us a drink, I'll be right back."

As soon as Thrayl left the room, I glared death at Raven. "I thought I told you never to speak for me."

"What else was I supposed to do?" she hissed at me. "We're supposed to be a couple, that's the cover story. Or did you forget what you're trying to do here?"

I gripped my knee, digging my fingernails hard into the leather, trying not to lash out at her. "Fine."

By the time Thrayl got back with three glasses of dwarven whiskey, I'd calmed myself.

He handed me my glass, and I downed the three fingers in one gulp.

"Still like your drink, eh? Never met a human who could drink a dwarf under the table before I met you." Thrayl laughed. "So if you ain't runnin' with the clans again, how'd you get the armor? You can barely afford mine, and Arryn's is a hundred times more expensive."

I was about to explain when Raven turned to me. "Clans? You used to be a bandit?" She frowned, her mouth set in a hard line.

"Long time ago."

She glanced at her untouched drink on the table, grabbed it, slammed it back and stood. Raven walked out of the house without a word.

"What's tha' about?"

"No clue," I said.

I didn't much know or care about what was going on with Raven. It wasn't my concern. Instead, I turned back to Thrayl, and we caught up.

He told me about the day to day comings and goings in Aldrust. I hoped for some usable intel, but it turned out to be nothing but gossip, nothing that would help during the heist. I told him about recent events, leaving out certain key aspects to avoid confusion. I couldn't tell him about Eris because of the cover story, but I told him about Magnus, leaving out his name, and passing him off as just a rich nobleman.

After about an hour of polite conversation, I checked the time and made my excuses.

"Well, why don't you and ye' girl have dinner with me an' the missus before you leave? Della would love to see ya again."

"Could never miss a chance to have more of her cave mushroom soup."

We shook hands, and Thrayl clapped me on the back. "Damn good to see ya again, Duran. Oh! Before I forget, wait right here."

Thrayl disappeared back into his home for a long minute. A few soft curses followed some clamoring of boxes and things being moved around. He came back a short minute later and held out his hand.

"Was a custom order for a customer, but they didn't like the design, so I redid it. Meant to put this one up for sale, but just never got around to it."

He handed me a long black knife forged from shadowsteel in a sleek black leather sheath meant to hang scout-style at my lower back. I was missing my hunting knife, so this was absolutely perfect.

The thought of what I was about to do sickened me, but I fought it down and smiled. "It's absolutely perfect, Thrayl. What do I owe you?"

"Nuthin'," he said with a wave. "Already got fifteen thousand for your last repairs, meant to send this with it as a gift, but I forgot. Just hope you'll stop by more often in the future."

"I will."

I waved goodbye and left. Raven stood outside, leaning against the wall of Thrayl's storehouse. I secured the knife to my belt as I walked over to her. She glanced at me and looked away, quickly.

"Stow whatever your problem is. It doesn't matter and won't help the job," I said, walking past her.

She didn't immediately follow but caught up before I reached the stairs that led to Copper Lowtown.

"Ass," she muttered softly to herself, but it was amplified in the narrow stairwell.

"Sometimes, yeah. What, you don't like that I used to be a bandit?"

She shook her head. "It doesn't matter. Let's just go," she said, pushing past me.

I shoved my hand against the wall, blocking her path. I stared into her crimson visage, into the thin circle of her iris and the black dot of her pupil.

"I've taken lives and coin with little regard for either. There's no justification for the things I've done, but it's in the past. Can't change it, even if I wanted to. Now we have a job to do, and I need to know that I can count on you, that you'll have my back."

"Can we work together, or is this too much of an issue for you?"

Raven stepped back, her heel half on the step above her, and crossed her arms. "I guess I have no choice."

"We always have a choice."

I headed down the stairs without looking back. There was slight hesitation, but Raven followed less than a minute later.

By the time we reached Lowtown, I was dying to stop at the closest tavern and drink away my frustrations, but according to Raven, our meeting place was deeper in.

"What's the place called?" I asked, stopping as we stepped down to the rough streets of Lowtown.

"Low Road Bar," Raven replied.

Well, let's find it, quick. I'm ready for an ale or more whiskey.

We walked the Lowtown streets cautiously, my hand resting on my sword. Lowtown wasn't any more dangerous than walking the streets of Central at night, but if we got pegged as a mark, we were in for a bad time. I just projected confidence and kept an arm around Raven, despite my distaste for her.

Someone takes a fancy to her and that'll just lead to trouble. I don't need to dodge a murder charge today, not when we have a heist to plan. We meandered seemingly at leisure until we found the bar a mile down the street.

It was formed from rock and stone like the rest of the buildings in Aldrust, but the level of craftsmanship in Copper Lowtown was considered shoddy by the inhabitants of Midtown and Hightown. The stone was chipped and hadn't been repaired recently, and the slanted slate roof was missing tiles. There were no windows, but there was a crude pipe wedged into a hole near the roof which belted smoke in a constant stream.

A sign hanging from a broken chain told us it was the bar we were looking for. *The Low Road Bar, this is the place.*

"Let's eat and drink our fill, then let's have the shifter for dessert."

What's with you and blood lately?

"It's delicious and slakes my thirst. Just a couple drops, and I'll be satisfied."

"Oh, hell no," I said and shook off the lingering mental chill the Aspect brought; ignoring the quizzical look from Raven and entered the bar.

Subtle music mixed with the hum of the patrons. The bar was packed with dwarves, humans, and even one of the fae. She was bartending, which was a strange place to find a faery. I turned to Raven and let go of her hand.

"Find your contact and come get me when you're done."

She stopped and paused, raising an eyebrow. "You don't want to go with me?"

"I'd rather drink. Besides, consider this an olive branch. I expect you to fill me in completely when you're done. I'm choosing to trust you. Don't make me regret it."

Trusting her goes against my nature, but right now she doesn't trust me, and that could go bad if we get backed into a corner.

She nodded. "I won't."

I left her to her own devices and made my way over to the stone bar top. Half a dozen other patrons crowded around the bar, all vying for the attention of the faery.

She was unnaturally beautiful, as all members of the fae are. Long, straight mahogany hair framed her refined face and cherry lips. Her hair fell to her waist and swirled as she moved her hips to the beat of the drums and flute. Her ice blue eyes swept over me as I reached the counter, and I shivered under the intensity of them.

"What can I get you?"

"Something strong," I said, pulling out a gold coin and sliding it across the bar.

She smiled and swept the coin into her palm, turning to grab a glass and giving me a good look at her back. Her blue tunic and tight black pants were an unusual style of dress for the fae, but she made it look natural. Two slits above her shoulder blades told me where her wings were, but she'd concealed them with illusion magic.

She returned a minute later with a tall mug with a bright red liquid that bubbled and fizzed as it threatened to spill its contents over her slender chestnut fingers.

"Red Goblin pale ale. A personal favorite," she said as she sat the mug down.

I took a cursory sip. It was tart and hoppy as hell, but delicious. The faery came back with my change and counted it out exactly before handing it to me. I took half.

"Keep the rest."

"Thank you," she said, smiling wide, showing her two rows of pointed teeth.

"Can I ask your name?"

"Tel'ganora, but everyone calls me Tel."

I nodded and smiled before taking another sip of beer. "It's nice to meet you, Tel."

"It's nice to meet someone who isn't gawking at me. I appreciate it," she said before turning to handle the mob of other customers all demanding her attention.

I nursed my drink and listened to the band playing while I kept a sidelong glance at Raven. She sat alone at a stone table in the corner, not talking to anyone, but she kept throwing her eyes my way.

I'm not going anywhere, little shifter; just do your job and we can get out of here. This bar was a decent enough place, but having a creature as beautiful as Tel nearby would only complicate matters. People would do anything for beauty like that, and damn anyone who happened to be in the wrong place at the wrong time.

Though as Tel flitted around her domain, she kept order really well. One of the scruffier dwarves got a little handsy and grabbed her ass, and he swiftly received a fork stuck through his fingers. The screaming, bleeding dwarf was dragged out of the bar and tossed out on the street while the patrons cheered.

Guess she has things under control.

"Let's break her of that control, drink her dry. I bet her memories are sweet."

Oh, godsdamn it! Look, you sadistic little monster, just wait till we get back home. I'm sure Eris won't mind sharing her blood.

A grumbling came from my heart, but the Aspect considered my proposal. *Fine, I'll behave—for now. The false queen's blood is rich and sweet as sin. You can have her flesh as long as I get her blood again.*

Deal. Now keep quiet unless you're going to help.

I finished my drink, and Tel swiftly brought me another one. "How'd you like it?" she asked.

"It was perfect."

She flashed me another sharp grin and went back to work, she sat up straighter as a thick, black-haired dwarf walked in. *So that's Orryn.* He wore a simple brown tunic free of any dirt and a pair of canvas pants. His beard and hair were well-groomed, and his dull green eyes swept the bar in a professional manner. His eyes met mine, and I knew he'd made me.

He looked from me to Raven and back again. He jutted his chin toward the table, motioning me to join them.

Ah, hell. Whatever. I grabbed my drink and ambled over to the table. Raven glanced from me to the contact. "Thought you were going to leave this to me?"

I held my hands up. "He made me, nothing I could do about it," I said and took a drink.

"Can I have a taste?"

I slid her my glass while Orryn sat down. Raven chugged a third of the beer and let out a sigh of content, thumping the glass against the stone table.

"Let's get to business, shall we," I said as our dwarf contact pulled out his chair.

He smiled and leaned back in the chair. "I wasn't told about ya, I was told to meet with a red-eyed woman with pale skin and long black hair. A male wasn't part of the arrangement. I don't like this."

"I'm part of the team. Though I don't know your part in this, I'm sure we'll manage if you want to walk away. Though you would greatly displease our employer, and none of us want that, do we?"

Orryn blanched slightly, paling as he stroked his beard. "All right, ya bastard, no need to get nasty. I just wasn't expecting ya is all."

Fluttering from behind me caused me to turn my head. Tel had climbed out from behind her bar and was dancing elegantly our way with a tray of drinks. She stopped and sat them down before leaning over and giving Orryn a peck on the cheek.

"On the house. This one was a gentleman," Tel said, thumbing back at me.

Orryn nodded and ran his hand over Tel's lower back. "You're a doll, Tel."

She smiled and left, back to man the bar, leaving me angry that we'd been had as soon as we stepped foot inside.

"Tel's your frontwoman, making sure we're clean."

Orryn just gave me a toothy smile. "Love that woman. Vicious, and sweet as syrup. Now we can get down to business?"

Raven coughed, speaking up. "What we need has already been discussed and payment made. We also need a place to set up for a few nights. For an additional fee," she said, palming a small bag that clinked ever so slightly as she slid it to Orryn.

He didn't so much as glance at it before stowing it in a pouch by his waist. "Understood. I have just a place in mind, made with humans in mind so it won't even be cramped. Now that our business has been sorted, I was told to introduce you to the team you're going to be working with," Orryn said.

He placed his fingers in his mouth and whistled sharply, breaking through the clamor of patrons. Footsteps sounded off the stone outside. *Three men, from the sounds of it. The way this job's gonna go, I'll take whatever help I can get.*

The men were all human, scruffy and scarred from years of hard service and questionable decisions.

The two in front were both nondescript, brown hair, one long and wavy while the other was short, nearly buzzed to his scalp. The longer-haired man had bloodshot blue eyes and the other brown. I took them in. Decent leather armor, but worn and scratched, which formed into a rich patina. They had swords belted at their hips, but they weren't the highest quality.

I promptly discounted them. They were nothing but fodder, maybe level forty at best, with mid-tier gear. They wouldn't be worth much.

The third man, however, was a different story entirely.

He was tall and thin. Old Japanese heritage gave him a nearly lanky appearance, but there was too much lean muscle cording down his warm cedar skin. Thick veins writhed to the surface as he clenched his hands tight, flushing the color from his knuckles.

His long, jet-black hair was pulled back in a topknot out of his once-soft face that had been chiseled in recent years as his skin stretched thin over his cheeks and slim, hard-set jawline.

The man locked eyes with me, and cold fury stoked the warm brown in his iris as he strolled across the tavern.

"Mika—"

His fist slammed into my nose before I could even rise from my chair.

CHAPTER 12 - BITTERSWEET BLOOD

My head snapped to the side as the cartilage in my nose burst and spilled red hot agony over my lips. I careened out of the chair and landed hard on my side before sprawling across the floor.

I braced myself for a beating, but nothing more came my way. Mika hadn't moved from where he'd knocked my block off. I stood and picked up the chair before I looked at my old friend.

The tension in the air changed drastically with that singular punch. Raven reacted harshly, sprouting her midnight wings and claws. The others reacted to her and drew arms while I threw my hands up in a panic.

"Hold the fuck up! No one move!"

Though we could've heard the drop of a pin, if anyone had dropped a pin, we'd have torn each other apart just out of pure reaction.

The other patrons of the bar saw the writing on the wall and beat a hasty retreat, leaving only the seven of us.

Raven grimaced, nearly snarling at the others while they stared wide-eyed at her expansive wings and wicked talons. "That man assaulted you. This breaches the contract. Why are we just standing here?"

"Because," I said, brushing the blood off my mouth and spitting what dripped into my mouth on the floor, "I deserved that."

"At least that. But that settles our score," Mika said, cracking a smile as the fire faded from his eyes.

"It's been a long time, old friend."

"Too long. Now you gonna get over here and hug me, or do I have to break your nose again?"

I crossed the room and clapped the man who'd once been a brother to me on the back. Mika wore shadowsteel, like me, which made our hug awkward to say the least, but the meaning behind it was clear.

I let go of him and stood back. "I'd recognize Thrayl's work anywhere, but c'mon, Mika, you look like a damned samurai from the movies back on Earth."

"Even have the katana, though it's certainly an upgrade from the original Takamikazuchi back in the Swords, eh? I call it Taka 3.0."

His armor was black shadowsteel, but his sword was shiversteel. Its silver blade accented by the black tsuka ito wrapped around the handle, it was certainly a beautiful sword, on par with any hero-tier weapon. *Might even give my new blade a run, though shiversteel would chip and crack, even as it bit through my shadowsteel.*

"So we're not fighting, right?" Raven asked, still in a combat stance.

"No, we're not," I replied, waving at her to sit down while I took my own seat. "We're all friends here, barring the hired help over there."

The two rent-a-thugs scowled at me. Their hands twitched to their swords, but Mika held up his hand. "Stand down. He's the leader of the Gloom Knights—you both know what that means."

The two men nodded and sat down without another word. *Godsdamn, have some fucking pride.* Normally I afforded other rent-a-thugs an amount of professional courtesy, but the two men that had been hired were poor excuses for mercenaries.

Their armor and swords were cheap, and they had the battle-hardened looks of seasoned men, which meant they skimped on their gear to save profits. A choice only fools would make.

"I know I joked about your armor, Mika, but at least you know how to play the game."

He snorted and sat next to me. "True, but it's just like you to antagonize your comrades when we're about to go into what sounds like, by all counts, a really fucked up situation. You haven't changed."

I sighed. "I wish that was true."

Mika drummed his fingers on the table. "I know we have business to discuss, but how've you been?"

"That's a complicated question."

"Can't be more complicated than how things ended between you and Lonny," he replied.

I chuckled. "You'd be surprised, but speaking of, I ran into Ascalon not too long ago."

He paused mid-drink. "And how'd that go?"

"Couldn't have gone worse if I'd resurrected Sophia only to kill her in front of him."

"Whisper's lips," Mika cursed. "Though, if you can joke about Soph, you must be doing better."

"I'm getting there," I whispered.

Mika smiled and drained his mug. "Well, we'll have all the time in the world to catch up properly when we've got what we're after and are rich as kings. Your boss is footing the bill for this quest—that means you're calling the shots. What's the plan, D?"

I stood up, and Raven followed suit. "For now, recon. Considering the stakes, I'm not leaving anything to chance. In the morning, we're going to scout the location and assess the situation. What your team could do for me is work Hightown, listen to rumors, monitor foot traffic, you know the drill."

Mika and his team nodded. "Operational budget?"

"Spread some gold around quietly. I'll reimburse whatever you spend."

"Understood."

With that, our business concluded for the evening, and I was looking forward to some much-needed rest. Mika and his team departed with plans to meet up the following day to discuss our plan.

"Well, might as well follow me," Orryn said as they left.

Raven and I stood and swiftly exited the tavern behind him. It wasn't cold enough to fog my breath, but as we stepped onto the street, Raven shivered. I barely noticed the chill. The air outside was fresh compared to the heated confines of the bar, but even with as much wide-open space above us, the air was still a little stagnant.

We caught up with Orryn a short jog later just before he rounded a corner and disappeared from view. He didn't so much as look at us as we fell into step behind him, but he did pick up his speed as we crossed side streets and alleyways until we reached a small residential street. Two rows of houses stood side by side as we walked down the street to the last house.

It was a modest dwarven two story, though I was hoping Orryn's comment meant it would be spacious inside, but it was nondescript, nothing that would distinguish it from any of the other houses on the street. The roof was flat rather than slanted, and I was betting it had a roof hatch so we could escape if needed.

Orryn walked up the steps to the front door, which was nothing but a thick slab of stone, and spoke a few words in Script. The stone slid under the ground and revealed a quaint entryway. He motioned us inside and followed behind us, raising the stone slab with his magic once more.

"I have no clue if either of you can use earth magic, but there are a few scrolls etched with the spell next to the door. Bath is upstairs, but there's limited hot water, just letting you know."

I gave the place a once-over, just making sure we were alone. It was unequivocally dwarven, with a lot of stone furniture and plenty of furs and blankets draped over everything. Wood was a luxury Copper Lowtown couldn't afford, so they made do.

"Thank you. I'm assuming the rest of our supplies will be provided?" Raven asked.

Orryn nodded. "I'll bring them by tomorrow."

With those parting words, he departed, leaving us alone in the quiet stone house. Before we'd really taken a step inside, a loud grumble caught my attention. I glanced over at Raven, whose cheeks flushed with embarrassment.

"Sorry."

"You hungry?"

She shook her head. "It can wait."

I could eat. Been awhile since I had dwarven cooking. I snagged a scroll by the door and waved her over. "Let's grab some food. I know a good place. Do you have any dress clothes?"

Raven nodded. "In my bag."

I pulled it out and mine at the same time. "Good. Let's get dressed and head to Hightown. It's rather expensive, but with Magnus paying, we've got plenty of money."

She didn't put up a fight, and we quickly threw on our clothes. Thanks to Magnus, I had plenty of perfectly tailored outfits and chose one at random. It was black, with light gold around the collar, and hugged my frame nicely. Raven wore a variation on the black dress she'd had on earlier in the day, though this one was more modest, only hinting at her upper chest without dipping down.

When we were both suitably presentable, I led her up, back through the miles of winding staircases, stopping only briefly at each landing so we wouldn't sweat and stain our nice clothes. It took about an hour, and we were both famished by the time we found our way to The Oak Door.

A single-story stone building with gold trimmed tile for the roof, as its name suggested, the entrance housed a massive, incredibly detailed door made from solid oak. It was a testament to how profitable the restaurant was that they could even afford the wood.

We stepped inside and were immediately warmed by the roaring fire in the fireplace by the host stand. An immaculate dwarf in a simple black suit inclined his head to us. "Two?" he asked, holding up two fingers.

I nodded, and he escorted us to our table and brought crystal glasses with ice-cold water and stood at attention as we settled in our chairs.

"We have several dishes on the menu tonight, sir and madam."

He proceeded to list off the meals we could order, but as he listed the third, I knew that's exactly what I wanted.

"I'll have the brown butter-basted steak," I said, trying not to salivate.

"The same," Raven replied.

"Excellent choice. It's one of my favorites," the dwarf said. "Might I recommend a dry red to pair with your meal? The tannins in the wine help bring a near perfect balance with the meat."

I wasn't much of a wine person, but the conviction in which the dwarf spoke left no room for debate.

"That would be lovely."

"I'll bring your drinks out right away," he said and departed.

Raven looked around the room and then back to me. "I have to admit, this is a nice restaurant. Cozy."

"Expensive, but the meal will be well worth it."

I folded my hands together and glanced at Raven, who had a peculiar expression on her face. I opened my mouth to speak but quickly closed it as the silence stretched. *Well, this is awkward. I spent the whole trip distancing myself from her, but now I can't even make polite conversation. Even if she's a shifter, I can suffer through a single meal with her, at least.*

"So how long have you been working for Magnus?" I finally managed to eke out.

"Working?" she scoffed. "Nice way to say 'slavery,' but to answer your question, about five years now."

I shrugged. "Would you call it slavery if you willingly put yourself in that position? No one forced you to sign your life away to the Alice," I began but stopped, my mouth strangling the rest of the sentence before it could spill out. I threw up my hands. "Fuck, I really can't have a civilized conversation with you, can I?"

Raven was about to respond when the waiter returned with our drinks and an open bottle of red wine.

"Enjoy," he said and departed.

I picked up my glass and drained it quickly, barely tasting the hints of cassis and plum as it swirled over my tongue. Raven did the same with hers, and as she finished her drink, she laughed.

"It's okay. I hate myself too, if it matters, but how about, for this dinner, you forget I'm a shifter, and I forget you're an asshole, and we just pretend we enjoy each other's company?"

I laughed louder than I meant and quickly covered my mouth as several of the nearby tables turned in my direction. Raven lit up in surprise at my sudden outburst. Her eyes widened, and her mouth lifted in a genuine smile, the first I'd seen on her.

It made her glow, and for a second, I did forget that she was a shapeshifter. She was just Raven in that instant, and I couldn't fight the smile that crawled over my lips.

But reality set in, and the moment passed.

My smile fell, but Raven's lingered for a moment longer. Our food arrived a short while later, and we both dug in, while discussing meaningless things as we stumbled our way into a facsimile of polite conversation.

We finished our meal, polished off the entire bottle of wine, and half another.

Nothing was waiting for either of us back at the safehouse, so I thought why not stay and enjoy the atmosphere? We both lingered, the wine helping to make us forget what we were here to do.

After the booze had safely settled, I paid and left a generous tip for the helpful dwarf, and we headed back to Lowtown.

The two of us had had enough to drink that by the time we made it back to the house, we were a little tipsy.

Raven plopped down on the couch when we got inside and lay out on the furs. "Hey, this is actually pretty comfortable," she said, sitting back up.

"Yeah, the dwarves know what they're doing when it comes to stonework. They just can't do much about the cold."

"Speaking of, a bath sounds amazing. Care to join me, husband?" she asked, her words ever so slightly slurred.

"Pass, and don't call me that. You're not my wife."

"You miss her, don't you?" Raven asked, sliding from the couch and standing.

"More than I ever thought I would."

She walked over to me and stared at me, her head cocked to the side ever so slightly. "You don't seem the type, honestly. To settle down and get married."

I chuckled and went to the kitchen, where a crude stone refrigerator stood in the corner. Half a dozen frost stones embedded in the stone chilled it to nearly freezing, and Orryn had stocked it with plenty of beer and spirits. I grabbed a glass bottle and unstopped it, taking a sip.

"I wasn't. But Eris didn't care. She bulldozed into my life and gave me something I didn't know I needed."

"And what was that?" she asked, holding out her hand for a beer.

I reached back in and pulled one out for her, reaching across the small dining table to hand it to her. "Acceptance."

Raven took a long pull of her drink, eyeing me with a smirk the entire time. "Isn't that what everyone is looking for?"

I shrugged and drained the rest of my beer. "Not sure about everyone else, but I damn sure didn't think I'd ever find it."

"I accept you, knight," the Aspect said with a smirk.

"Oh, shut up," I growled.

Raven furrowed her brows, blinking rapidly. "What'd I say?"

I grabbed another beer. "Wasn't talking to you."

She threw up her hands and crossed a leg over the other on the couch. "Then who?"

I blew out a breath and set the beer on the stone table. *You want to answer that?*

"With pleasure."

The Aspect slithered into my head, bringing a blizzard to my thoughts. My head jerked to the side as I worked my jaw around. *"He was talking to me,"* the Aspect said, its dark, sibilant voice a harsh echo of my own.

Raven gasped, dropping her half-empty beer. It shattered on the floor as her hand went to her mouth. "What the fuck?" she whispered.

My head snapped round to stare at Raven. *"He certainly has issues with you. Doesn't exactly trust you. Though he has little room to judge, he traded away a part of himself for power too. To save his queen, he made a deal with me."*

"What are you?" Raven asked, standing up.

We moved across the room in a flash to stand over her. *"Thirsty."*

I shook my head, forcing the Aspect out. "That's enough, Aspect. Back off."

It left me, and I sagged down to the couch, running a hand through my hair, pulling the hair tie out and letting my hair cascade around me, blocking me from having to look at Raven. After a moment, I realized I didn't have to stay here. I got up and made for the stairs.

Raven stepped to me and pushed me against the wall. "Oh, no. You don't get to walk away after dumping that on me. I want you to explain, right now."

I glared at her. "Who are you to command me?"

"Your partner," she said jabbing her finger into my chest, her crimson eyes slightly glazed. "Now what did it mean, it's thirsty?"

She kept prodding me with her finger, and my rage broke free. I pushed off the wall and threw her against it, my hand closing around her pale throat. "It wants you. The monster in my head wants to eat you, wants me to gorge on your blood while I take you."

I must've sounded like a lunatic. Raven's eyes went wide for a second before she blinked, long and slow. "Then why don't you?" she asked, her voice no more than a whisper as she wrapped a hand around my wrist.

"Because I'm in control, not it. It's my head, and I will not let it make choices for me."

Her radiant eyes stared into mine for what must have been only a second but seemed like an eternity. Then she blinked and time reasserted itself. "So it wants my blood and my body?"

"Mostly the blood," I said, nodding.

I realized my hand was still around her neck, and I eased my grip, but Raven's hand grew tense around my own and stopped me from withdrawing it. She squeezed my hand hard, curling my fingers tight around her flesh once again.

"What are yo—"

"I was given very specific instructions. Magnus told me to do as you said, to be at your disposal. He meant for the job, and I understood. But Aliria took me aside and told me to seduce you if I could."

Raven sighed. "I didn't want to, but I had no choice but to agree. Though it seemed you had no interest in me, which I was thankful for. You hate me, I understand. As I told you earlier, I hate myself too, but if we're going to work together, we need to trust each other. If your monster wants my blood—" She rose her free hand up, a sharp, black talon elongating from her fingernail. She sliced a groove in her neck in a flash, and a thick drip of blood welled up before spilling down her collar, "—then it can have it."

Her hand stopped me from pulling away as she smiled and twisted her neck, baring the blood to me as it slithered over our fingertips.

Rust and iron filled the air, and I sniffed, drawing the scent in. The scent of blood filled my nostrils and coated the back of my throat. And the Aspect followed it. It flowed from my chest, bringing the frigid tide in its wake. It crept to my head, and I could do nothing to stop it.

"Finally! I was right. Her blood smells delightful." It spoke aloud, curling my lips into a gruesome smile.

My teeth ached and shifted in my mouth. The sharp canines dug at my lips, and the Aspect opened my mouth wide. Raven relaxed as she looked into my eyes and brought her neck closer to me.

I couldn't stop the overwhelming ache of hunger boiling in my stomach, nor the irresistible urge to sink my teeth into her flesh. I bent low, no longer sure who was in control and graced the tips of my teeth across Raven's skin.

She shuddered at my touch, her hands going from her neck to my waist as she pulled me closer. I sank my teeth into her flesh, and she moaned softly, her warm voice tickling my ear as she cried out. Ruby-red life burst like a dam and poured down my throat in a rush. Her blood was indeed sweet. It filled me with a warmth, and I greedily drank it in.

The Aspect made its approval known and greedily slaked its thirst.

For a single moment, I was in the room with her as she grew ever more heated as I drank her blood, then my vision swam, and my mind fell into darkness.

It was less jarring this time around as I entered the Mnemosyne. I was suddenly standing in a small town with a great expanse of forest in the distance. I recognized the variety of trees; they were the towering trees that filled the Emerald Ocean, which housed the elven kingdom of Yllsaria. There were only a few human towns on the edge of elven territory, which made the village either Rodale or Siltfall.

It was a modest town, brightly lit by the light of the sun. No house or building was over a single story. Most of the houses were well-built log cabins, but a few of them were worn and falling apart. A young girl stood before me, carrying a heavy basket filled with carrots and potatoes. Her thin white shirt and brown canvas pants were strewn with dirt, but she held a smile on her face as she walked.

Her skin was darker, her midnight hair a little lighter in the bright sunshine, and her gray eyes had yet to be blooded, but it was still Raven.

She was younger here, not quite a woman yet. She walked carefree, her lips whistling a tune I couldn't hear. She reached a dirt crossroad and turned left, heading to one of the older and worn houses beside the street. A man was on the porch, sitting in a chair with a piece of straw sticking out of his mouth. He was older, deeply tanned skin from years of working outside, but he had a kind face, and there was a hint of Raven in his eyes. He smiled widely when he saw Raven walking up the street. The straw slipped from his mouth as he stood and met her halfway.

When he reached her, he took the basket and knelt, smiling down at his daughter. Joy radiated from her eyes as her father praised her.

An arrow fired from somewhere beyond my sight pierced her father's neck.

Blood splattered across Raven's face, and her look of joy fell to horror and panic. She turned toward the direction of the arrow, and her mouth gaped. A group of bandits rose from the trees and fell upon the town like a plague.

Raven had no time to mourn her father as he crumpled to the ground and soaked the earth with his blood. She ran, ran as fast as her legs would carry her. She ran to a well in the center of town and clung to the rope as she slid down it. Raven stopped just before she touched the water, leaning heavily on a small rocky outcropping. Water licked at the hem of her dress, and her hands bled, soaking into the rope she clung so desperately to.

Time sped up as she hid in the well; minutes flowed to hours, which flowed into days. She stayed down there for two days, making as little noise as possible until the bandits topside had ransacked the entire village and fled.

After the two days, she weakly hauled herself back up the well, ripping open the scabs on her hands in the process. As she climbed out of the well, we both got a good look at the carnage that had been wrought by the bandits.

Bodies lined the streets, left to rot where they died while most of the buildings were broken, doors and windows splintered while a few were set ablaze, and now were nothing but smoldering blackened wrecks.

Tears slid down her cheeks as she stared blankly at the destruction.

The scene faded out as I stared at Raven crying. Her face gave way to darkness as I waited for the next memory to play.

Must've been the Rodale raid that happened eight years ago. Whole village was wiped out by Hal's clan. Though from what I heard, he got what was coming to him.

Light faded in out of nowhere and brought me to the next memory.

Raven appeared in a grove surrounded by lush grass and flowers that bloomed every shade of the rainbow. Raven was a few years older here, leaner. There was a hard set to her chin, and some of the light had dimmed in her eyes. She had the stare that only came with great loss. One I saw every day in the mirror.

She stood in the center of a perfect circle of death cap mushrooms, the white capped fungus forming a faery circle. The mushrooms glowed with a soft blue light, and suddenly Raven wasn't standing in forest anymore.

She was in a rooftop garden, atop a white stone castle. Sunlight bathed the garden in brilliance, and Raven stepped out of center of the faery circle to a smooth stone walkway that led to an archway, which held two soft, rosewood doors. Raven stepped through them and into an expansive throne room.

Raven followed the path, and in under a minute, she stood before a throne made of white marble with brilliant red cushions.

On the throne was a girl, no more than eight years old by appearance. She still wore the softness of childhood in her thin features. Her burgundy hair spilled fine wine down her back and over her translucent dragonfly wings, which cast rainbows over the stone. Her ocean-water eyes threatened to drown Raven as she knelt before the queen of the faeries.

The Alice wore a slender, white strapless dress and leaned heavily on the armrest as boredom played across her face. She gave Raven a once-over and motioned for her to speak. Raven looked up and spoke with pleading eyes.

She continued for a few minutes, before she stopped. The Alice sat up straight and spoke a few words before Raven nodded once more.

With that nod, a deal was struck. And one never bargained lightly with the Alice.

The Alice rose from her throne and stood over Raven. She raised her hands to Raven's face. Her fingers crawled over Raven's cheeks and toward her eyes. The Alice rested her thumbs just above Raven's cheekbones as her fingernails elongated, forming wicked, pale claws. The Alice dipped her fingers into Raven's sockets ever so slightly, puncturing through the cornea and bringing crimson pain to drip down her face.

Raven screamed in pain as her body twisted and contorted, bones snapping and shifting under her skin.

Wings black as sin sprouted from her back as her body stopped convulsing. Raven lay on the floor panting as sweat dripped from every pore. Her fingers wiped the long red streaks from her cheeks, and Raven stood.

With a smug grin, the Alice left Raven and returned to her throne as darkness once more came for me.

The last scene started with Raven walking through the forest alone. She was wearing a version of the leather armor she'd worn around me, and she carried no weapons. She stepped through the forest like a ghost as light from ahead of her cast dancing shadows over her face.

Raven strolled out of the woods and into a campground, a dirt clearing that had over a dozen tents hammered into the ground and fires going. Men and women sat around the largest fire eating and drinking while a massive boar roasted on a spit over the coals. They were too busy enjoying themselves to notice Raven, who'd slunk behind them. She stopped and pursed her lips in what had to have been a whistle, as everyone turned at the sound.

A large barrel-chested man with brown, unkempt hair and tattoos over his arms rose from the log he was sitting on to walk over to Raven.

I knew the man.

Hal had never been the brightest of the bandit kings, but he made up for it in savagery. He didn't care who he killed as long as he got paid. And he stood over Raven, staring at her like a woman to bed, rather than as the threat she was.

Raven thrust out her hips, throwing a lazy smile on her face, and as Hal reached a hand to grope her chest, Raven shot out her clawed hand and ripped his throat out.

Hal tumbled to the ground, his windpipe and bloody spine showing through the torn, ragged flesh as blood gushed over his chest.

When he hit the ground, the others stared in shock, but none immediately went for their weapons. Not that it would have saved them, regardless.

Her midnight wings sprouted from her back as she flew into the mass of bodies, her claws raised as she tore into the bandits with gleeful murder in her eyes. Her jagged black talons shredded through the bandits with ease, and even the few who'd managed to bring their weapons to bear against her were no match.

She flew into the air and peppered them with her razor-sharp flechettes. In minutes, the dozen or more bandits were dead or dying from blood loss.

Raven took her time, going to each body, and dead or not, she pulled a dagger and thrust it into each bandit, again and again.

As the last of them died, she dropped to her knees, crying and screaming at the top of her lungs.

She'd gotten her revenge, but it had cost her everything.

The scene faded out, and as I returned once more to the darkness, I filled in the rest.

The Alice wasn't known for her kindness or mercy. Raven had willingly sold herself, body and soul to the Alice for power, and she in turn had sold Raven's contract to Magnus.

That was the end for her. Raven would never taste freedom again.

I came back to myself, blood stained on my lips with Raven still holding me, my face buried in her chest as she got her breathing under control. I pulled back and she looked up at me with glassy eyes. "That was...it was—it wasn't unpleasant."

"It was good for me," the Aspect said, speaking through me. *"Her memories were so sweet in their bitterness. Did you like the ones I showed you? She had many more, but none were as sweet as those."*

Raven pulled back, her eyes wide. "What? My memories? What are you talking about?"

I sighed, wiping the blood from my lips. "When I drink blood, I get a glimpse into the person's life whose blood I'm drinking."

"You saw my life?" she asked, her voice quivering.

I nodded.

The Aspect was right. Though it didn't leave me much choice, I still made the same choice she did. I judged her without knowing anything about her. I'd have made the same choice. I have made that choice.

Who am I to judge anyone? My sins are greater than hers will ever be.

I stepped away from her, my heart heavy, and started up the stairs. "I'm sorry."

"For what?" she asked at my back.

"I'm just sorry," I whispered.

CHAPTER 13 - SILVANUS DARKWOODS

Eris

It seemed like I was the only one who was shocked by the sudden revelation. I didn't really understand the implications of what was going on, but I knew "empress" was a title that demanded respect.

The others were very nonchalant about the whole thing.

After the threat to our lives had disappeared, the remaining bandits went to loot the houses and the dead while Cassimere stood with a few of his men and talked to Adam and Evelyn.

"What are they talking about?" I asked, sliding over to Makenna and Gil.

"No clue, but it's not my business, so I'm staying away."

"I really don't understand what's going on. Can someone please fill me in?"

Gil sighed and wound his hand over my shoulder, leading me back inside the inn, which had suffered the least amount of damage.

Once inside, Gil picked up one of the knocked-over tables and chairs while Makenna went and got a round of drinks. I just sat back and stared through the broken door frame at the twins while they conversed with the bandits.

Gill thumped down heavily in his seat and propped his chin under her hands. "Where to start," he mused, ruining his fingers in staccato rhythm over his thick chin. "The best place to start would be the beginning, I guess. I already told you how Duran and I met," he said.

"He tried to rob you, right?"

He nodded and smiled, turning his head when Makenna came back with our drinks. "Thanks, Kenna," Gil said and kissed her on the lips.

She blushed and returned the kiss with abandon. It was both heartwarming and incredibly depressing to see. It hurt to see such love and not think about Sam. *I hope he's okay right now.*

I still couldn't feel him since he'd closed off our connection, and I didn't think he needed the distraction right now, not with everything going on. I took a few sips of my mead to try and calm myself, and it helped. By the time Makenna sat down next to Gil a few seconds later, I was much calmer and composed.

"So where did I leave off at? Oh, right, Duran was in the middle of robbing us. We'd fought the bandits tooth and nail, with heavy casualties on both sides. It had gotten bloody and over half of the guards we'd signed on with were lying in bloody chunks next to the pay wagon we'd been sent to guard.

"Most of my guild perished during the initial attack, and for the most part, it was just me and Duran left. One of the best fighters I'd ever crossed, though given his teacher, I never stood a chance. I fought till my fatigue was maxed—the other bandits had already surrounded us and were just watching the spectacle. Duran was just toying with me at this point, goading me to max out."

I winced. Listening to Gil tell his story was hard, only because I knew how Sam fought, and imagining him going against his best friend like that twisted my stomach. I pushed away the mead; its sweetness no longer held any appeal for me. Gil looked over at me, took one look at my face and grinned sheepishly.

"Sorry, Eris. The worst part is already over with. Well, once I'd maxed my fatigue and seized up, the rest of their group were calling for my blood. But something changed in him, and he refused. To this day I don't know why he spared me. Never worked up the courage to ask. Scared of the answer, I guess.

"But Duran did. Even when his king ordered him to end me, he refused."

"What happened after that?"

Gil paused, taking a drink and continued his story. "D fought his clan to the last. Slaughtered them all. Bandit king included. After that, he let me go. 'Course he took the entire pay wagon for himself. But I wasn't in a position to argue. With my guild wiped, I had nothing to go back to, so I stuck with him. Something about him just made me want to follow him.

"We rode together for a few months, but of course word got back to Evelyn about what he'd done, and she and Adam came after us personally."

Makenna let out an involuntary shiver, despite the heat in the air, and Gil laughed. "You have no idea, Kenna. As scary as she is now, it's nothing compared to back then. Evelyn's actually mellowed out quite a bit since those days."

Makenna laughed, snorting as she tried to take a drink and splashing it over the table. She slammed the mug down, flushed with embarrassment, and tried to wipe her dripping face. "I don't buy that for a second."

"Don't buy what?" Evelyn asked, startling all three of us.

She walked through the door as calm as could be, with a look of mild curiosity as she joined our conversation.

"Oh, nothing, we were just talking about how we met," Gil said hastily, shooting me and Makenna a pleading look.

Evelyn smiled a predatory smile. "Oh, you're talking about the time I nearly killed you and the guild leader?"

"I wouldn't put it quite like that."

"How would you put it, then, hmm?"

"That we fought with honor and dignity and gave you hell doing it."

Evelyn threw back her head and laughed, her golden eyes practically alight with flames as she shook with laughter. "Sure, you can think that all you want. Doesn't make it true."

"So what actually happened?" I asked, raising my hand.

"What...what she said. Evelyn eventually caught up to us and beat us black and blue. But the stars aligned, and she felt merciful that day. She didn't kill us when she could have and instead decided to ride with us for a while."

"We'd gotten bored at the top of the pyramid," Evelyn said, stealing my mug of mead and tipping it back. A line of purple trailed from her chin down her pale throat as she gulped down the drink.

She tossed the empty glass on the table and leaned over. "Fast forward a decade, and here we are. Now that's enough of story time. I've convinced the bandits to escort us the rest of the way to Slaughter Woods. So I suggest we all get some sleep. We ride at first light."

After her words, her and Adam headed upstairs, leaving us downstairs with a gang of ruthless killers just outside.

"Who's up for bunking together?" Gil asked, craning his neck to peek outside the inn.

***

I rubbed my eyes and yawned, trying to breathe some life into my tired bones. I hadn't slept much; the hollering and looting of the bandits had gone on till the early hours of the morning. Tegen and Cheira had huddled close to me, scared to sleep with all the new humans around.

"It'll be okay," I whispered into their hair as they nodded off to sleep in the saddle in front of me.

Lacuna huffed and snorted as we left Odelpha, wary of the new additions to our little group. The bandits had stolen all the surrounding horses and joined around us, herding us as we left town and skirted along the marsh.

I don't think any of us, other than Evelyn and Adam, liked having the scruffy men and women close by. They talked too loudly and about the crudest of things. I developed an instant distaste for them, but there was nothing I could do or say to get rid of them.

It was Evelyn's show now.

So I kept close to Makenna and Gil. They were nearly as unhappy as I was about the situation and kept talking in hushed whispers, so I trotted Lacuna close to them.

"I don't like this. We were fine by ourselves," Makenna hissed.

"Yeah, I know, but fuck else we can do about it."

Gil eyed me as I approached but relaxed when he noticed it was just me. "Morning, Eris. How are you and the kids?"

"Tired, and more than a little concerned, if I'm being honest," I replied.

He nodded and swept his eyes over the dozen or so bandits. "Bad luck on our part, but they won't dare defy Evelyn, and hell, they'll take a few arrows for us, so I'm not going to complain too heavily if it means we get to keep ourselves safe."

I pondered his words while we rode past endless gray trees and long stretches of muddy road. *Gil's right about that, as callous as it sounds. But am I okay with people I dislike dying in the place of my friends and family? Does it make me a bad person if I am?*

His words had brought up a question I wasn't sure I wanted the answer to. And I shied away from it, focusing on Lacuna and the road and making sure the bandits weren't about to lead us into an ambush.

A few drops of magic pooled out of my fingers as I took control of the scant few insects in the trees and burrows by the road. I tried to expand my reach as far as it could go, pushing my consciousness a few miles in every direction, but there was nothing but more miserable swamp and a few shades too far away to notice us.

"There's nothing into the woods but a few monsters, and those are too far away to be threats," I told Gil, leaning over in the saddle to whisper to him.

"Thanks for keepin' an eye out, but the bandits won't dare try and go against Evelyn. She'd tear them apart if they tried."

"Yeah, I'm beginning to see how dangerous she actually is."

We rode in mostly uncomfortable silence for a few hours, passing out of the last of the marshlands and back to stable ground. The stench of salt fled from the air as a cool breeze blew through the grassy plains we rode onto.

I breathed in deep and couldn't help the smile that broke upon my face as the wind swept my hair back. Our time spent in the brackish swamp had reminded me that even after centuries in the void, I had taken fresh air and sunshine for granted.

We continued for a few more hours until we were well and truly away from the Salted Mire. By the time the sun was highest overhead, I think we were all ready for a break. Luckily, I wasn't the one who complained first.

"All right, I've had enough of this godsdamned saddle," Gil bemoaned, twisting side to side and stretching. "Hey, oh mighty empress, let's break for lunch!"

Before any of us could react, a sheathed dagger flew like an arrow and struck Gil in the center of his forehead.

Gil's head rocked back from the blow, and he nearly careened off his horse. "Ow, fuck!" he shouted, rubbing his forehead where a welt was already forming.

Evelyn didn't react further, and we pressed on for another hour before she deigned to allow us to stop and rest.

We stopped in a glade of tall trees, and with a single whistle from Evelyn, the bandits got to work setting up a fire and getting lunch going. There were a few dead trees that had been knocked over in a storm, their roots pulled up from the ground like veins. I walked over and sat down with the children.

Makenna came over and sat beside me. Tegen and Cheira had gotten used to our group, and Cheira crawled into Makenna's lap while she laughed.

"Seems they don't mind us so much anymore. Shame it's only when we're about to arrive at their home."

My heart fell at hearing that. I hadn't realized we were so close. "How much further?" I asked.

"Maybe a day, maybe less if we keep pushing like we have. We'll be there tomorrow at any rate," she said, letting Tegen hang off her arm like a monkey.

"I see..."

Makenna looked over to me and smiled, rubbing my shoulder. "Cheer up. It's not like you'll never get to see them again. I bet once we take them home, you'll be allowed to visit them whenever you want."

Despite her obvious attempts, her words did make me feel better, and as I watched them play together, I smiled. *This isn't the end. It's the beginning of something great. The Arachne still live, and that means that the other Hive could still be out there. Maybe they're even with the Arachne.*

Grayson Sinclair

The apocritans and mantearians were the weakest of the Hive and would have likely taken refuge with either the Arachne or the scorpius clans. *Maybe more of the Hive will be waiting for me. I hope so, at least.*

I was so consumed with my thoughts that I nearly failed to pay attention to the object sailing through the air towards my head. I caught it on reflex and sighed when I looked down at my hands.

"Do we have to?" I asked, standing up.

"Of course. I can't whip you into shape if you don't practice, and babysitting isn't my strong suit," Evelyn said, sauntering towards me, practice sword raised.

Before she could take another step, I launched myself at her and swung with all my strength. My wooden sword connected with hers just before I'd have slammed it into her neck. She stepped back, absorbing the impact and counterattacked. The tip of her blade jammed into my stomach, taking the breath from me.

I doubled over, fighting to stay on my feet, but a swift kick from Evelyn, and I was on my back, wondering where I'd gone wrong. Evelyn frowned when I got back on my feet. Her furrowed brow and downturned lips cast doubt towards me.

"What?" I asked, my voice cracking.

She shook her head, still holding her soured look. "Again."

I brought my sword up like she'd taught me and tried to play it cautious instead of aggressive this time. I stepped toward her slowly, watching for any sign to predict her movements. Her body poised perfectly, she gave me no hint as I crept closer. Each inch brought my heart rate skyrocketing, because I knew I could never beat her, but I had to try.

228

Evelyn shifted, her hips tilted to the left, and her foot slid forward half an inch. It was just enough to let me know which way she was attacking, and I stepped to her right, thrusting my sword toward her exposed ribs.

My practice sword fell from my numb hands as Evelyn rapped me hard across the wrist with the flat of her blade. It tumbled to the dirt and kicked up a small cloud of dust.

I flexed my fingers, trying to work out why they weren't responding. I picked up my sword and stood, settling back into my stance, but Evelyn shook her head.

"Hand me the sword," she commanded.

I did as she asked but had to ask. "Why?"

"Because the sword isn't your weapon," she said, her tone terse. "I can make you a half decent swordswoman, but you'll never excel at it. You're strong, and have decent reflexes and coordination, but the sword isn't for you."

Heat crept up my cheeks, and my heart beat fast as I fought to keep her cold gaze. She laid out the facts in a mechanical fashion, and I appreciated her blunt demeanor, but I couldn't lie that it didn't sting to hear.

I kicked at a pebble near my foot, tearing it from its home in the ground and sending it on a short journey to rest by a patch of grass.

"So what weapon is for me, then, if not the sword?"

Evelyn finally lost her frown. A slow smile spread from the corners of her mouth, and she bared her blindingly white teeth to me. "That's what we're going to find out."

A half dozen weapons later, and after a half dozen new cuts and bruises marred my pale skin, we'd finally found a weapon that suited me, according to Evelyn.

"Nice shot," she said, after I fired my third arrow at the target stuck to the tree.

"Thank you," I replied, blushing crimson.

Evelyn's praise was just as off as her cold contempt, and like it, I didn't know exactly what to make of it, but I was happy that she was pleased. After three hours of disappointing her, it was nice to succeed in her eyes.

She walked over, took the arrows out of the tree, and brought them back to me, holding them aloft. "That bow is the only one I had on hand. I'm surprised you can draw it back. It's got a sixty-pound string on it—that's not light for someone of your size."

"Thank you," I mumbled.

"Just be careful with it. It's made from the horn of a storm dragon, so it's damn near priceless."

Her brilliant eyes swept over my body and rested at my arms and shoulders. She walked behind me and placed her hands on the nape of my neck.

"Your form is off a tad, but that can be easily fixed."

Her hands traveled down my skin, pushing or pulling my arms and shoulder blades. She lingered over my hips, and her warm fingers dug into my thighs as she twisted them into the proper position. I trembled under her touch, wishing in the back of my heart for her to keep lingering, to explore my flesh further.

A stiff breeze blew through the trees, chilling the beading sweat on my skin and causing me to shiver. It snapped me out of my reverie and back into the present.

Focus! I'm just wasting her time if I don't pay attention to her lessons. Thankfully, she didn't notice my lapse in concentration, as she was focused entirely on correcting my poor posture.

When she finally stood, she stepped back and looked me over. She smiled. Just a tad at the corner of her mouth, but it was unmistakable.

"Do you feel how your hips and feet are positioned, how precise your spine and shoulders are aligned?"

I focused on my body, tried to feel each individual muscle as I stood stock still and absorbed the difference in how I felt now versus my posture before. I was more grounded now. I had much better balance, and it felt good.

I nodded just slightly, not moving too much in case I slipped and put myself off balance. "I feel much more stable. It's night and day compared to before."

"Good. Now, draw back your bow."

I did, focusing on all of my muscles. From my neck all the way down to my toes, dozens of muscles worked in tandem as I drew back the string and aimed an invisible arrow at the tree. It was easier than before. As easy as breathing.

"Okay, carefully release tension on the string, but do not let go. Never dry fire your bow," Evelyn commanded.

I released the string and let out a breath. Tension flooded out of my muscles as I lowered the bow.

"Good, now staying in position, nock an arrow and draw it back."

I did exactly as she ordered, never faltering as I plucked an arrow from my quiver at my back and drew it back.

"Don't release it just yet. Hold it, and just breathe, listen to the world around you."

My hearing was better than most, and I picked up the sounds from a hundred different sources. The horses, grazing in the plains, and the dozen of men and women milling about, cooking, talking, and drinking. Gil and

Makenna, off by themselves, whispering sweet nothings to each other away from most everyone's prying ears.

Adam was in the field, playing with his shades, trying to better control them.

And Evelyn was next to my ear. Her sweet breath tickled my nose, her heartbeat loud in her chest.

"There's too much noise. I can't concentrate."

She nodded. "Of course there is, but you have to focus, eliminate the unnecessary noise and focus of the one sound that truly matters."

"Which is?" I asked, straining from holding the arrow back for so long.

"Your heartbeat. It's the most important sound to an archer. Listen to its rhythm. Feel it pulse in your breast, down your veins and in your fingertips. Feel it pulse through the bow, and in the space between heartbeats, release your arrow."

I focused, ignoring my screaming muscles to listen to the beat of my heart. It was just as she'd said. It pumped loud in my ears, flowing through my chest toward my hands, and it thumped against my bow again and again.

I waited until I knew exactly when the beat would end, and I loosed the arrow.

It sailed through the air, uttering a soft whistle as its war cry and slammed home in the center of the paper target fifty feet away.

A cheer rose from a group of bandits who'd stopped to watch Evelyn train me. And despite them being bandits, scum of the earth, I couldn't help the little bit of pride that welled up inside from their cheers.

Evelyn clicked her tongue. "Not bad, not bad."

I wanted to keep practicing, keep the momentum going, but my aching muscles and screaming stomach said otherwise. We'd been training for so long, and we'd neglected to eat anything, so I was ravenous beyond compare.

Gill and Makenna made room for me on the log next to them and offered me a bowl of charred meat and vegetables. It was bland, the chef not having half the cooking skill of Sam or the others, but food was food, and I was starving. I scarfed it down while watching Tegen and Cheira as they scampered around the woods.

We'd spent hours training and wasted most of the light we'd had left. So we set up camp here for the night. I helped where I could, carrying huge armloads of firewood and helping to set up our tents, but we had more than enough manpower, so there wasn't much for us to do. Evelyn ran the bandits ragged, and they were too scared of her to argue.

I was weary from the training and called it a night early and headed to my tent to get some rest. As I lay down, though, my mind began to wander. My body was bruised and aching, but my thoughts raced like birds through my mind. *Calm down and get some sleep,* I told myself, rolling over and shutting my eyes tight.

But it was to no avail. I was awake despite my protests.

All right, well if I can't sleep, then I guess I'll keep practicing with my magic.

I sat up, crossed my legs, and closed my eyes, feeling for the magic in my soul. It came at my call, spilling from within my chest to crawl its way toward my mind. It submerged me in a pool of verdant mist, and I was no longer in a tent in the woods. I was home.

A tidal wave of thoughts, emotions, and spirits flooded around me, drowning me in their need to be answered, but they weren't what I needed, not tonight, at least.

There was a specific spell that my mother used often, her chitin sword, but I knew there was more than that lurking below the surface, I just had to find it.

"How may I assist you, my queen?" the warm voice asked next to my ear.

I need spells, Aspect. Weapons.

With a subtle tone of acceptance, the presence of the Aspect faded away. I floated in a sea of warmth for a time until a tug pulled my soul deeper in the mist. I was pulled further and further in, when I suddenly slowed, and a dozen thoughts floated past my face. Each one was a spell, but I needed to find the correct one and pull it out with me.

It took some time, but I found the one I needed and reached out my hand. It dissolved into nothingness when I closed my hand and filled me with insight. I had what I'd come for, and I'd stayed too long. I couldn't linger in the Hive Mind, or I risked not being able to find my way out again.

When I came back to myself, I was weak. My body shook with fatigue, and sweat poured in rivers down my face and neck.

But resting in my hands was a glossy black bow comprised of chitin, gleaming even in the darkness.

"Beautiful," I said, smiling down at it.

I let the spell fade back under my skin and downed a mana potion from my pack. With my shaking limbs calmed, I turned in and got some sleep.

In the morning, we packed up camp after a light breakfast and set out at a steady pace to try and make up for lost time. The bandits rode in front, and the five of us brought up the rear on Evelyn's orders as we approached the Silvanus Darkwoods.

They came upon us quickly, and tall, wide trees rose up in an ocean as we approached.

Gil whistled appreciatively. "Damn, never been this close before, but those are some big-ass trees."

Makenna snorted, and the others burst into laughter.

"You're not wrong. For a place named Slaughter Woods, it's really rather quaint, isn't it?" Evelyn asked to herself.

Cassimere and a few of his men circled around and went to speak to Evelyn as we reached the edge of the woods.

"What do you want us to do?" he asked, his speech faltering as he kept casting glances over his shoulder at the tree line.

"Send a few men in, see what happens," she replied instantly.

He sighed, looked over at his men, and shouted. "Ricky, Jones, go check it out!"

Two burley men with tanned skin and unwashed hair shouted in response but broke from the main group and edged their horses closer. As they reached the edge of the trees, they stopped turned back around and just glared hatred at Cassimere before heading into the woods and out of sight.

Nothing happened for a long moment, and everyone held their breath, just waiting for something to happen.

An ear-splitting shriek pierced the air, followed immediately by another one. And then there was silence once again.

"Well," Gil said, turning around to stare at us. "At least we know we're in the right place."

Chapter 14 - The Widow

When the two bandits never came back out from the forest, it was clear we would have to go in next. I volunteered, because with the children, I had the best chance of getting through without harm. The others, Gil especially, were vehemently against the idea.

"It doesn't make sense for us all to go in when that risks everyone," I said, raising my voice.

"What also doesn't make sense is letting you and the kids run off by yourself and you winding up dead. Duran would kill me if I let anything happen to you. Not going to happen, missy."

I wanted to argue more, but when Makenna and even Adam rallied against me, I knew I was fighting a losing battle.

"All right, fine. You win."

"If you're all done arguing, we're going in," Evelyn called from the center of the bandits.

With nothing else to do, we headed in.

The four of us brought our horses towards Evelyn so we'd all be together. I didn't like the idea of us being separated when something inevitably went wrong.

We pushed into the forest, and I was surprised. For a place that was touted as evil, with a nickname like Slaughter Woods, it was actually remarkably lovely. The trees were tall and luscious. Dense foliage and thick, winding branches gave the appearance of a web crisscrossing multiple trees in a random, yet beautiful pattern.

The forest was beautiful, yet still, as if nature had sensed a predator and hidden itself away. There were no birds chirping or animals scurrying. It was a quiet place, and that set my teeth on edge.

I didn't like the quiet. It meant something was wrong, and I quickly told the others what I was feeling.

"Well, why don't you use your magic and see what's up with the place?" Adam suggested, leaning toward me to whisper.

"Whispering is pointless, Adam. The Arachne have nearly as good hearing as I do, and I'm sure they're already well aware of us."

He replied, but I didn't hear what he said. I was busy concentrating on my flow of magic, letting it pour from me as I scanned the surroundings. I quickly took hold of the nearby insects and found exactly what our problem was.

I broke out of the spell and raised my hands sharply. "Everyone stop!" I hissed, waving at them frantically to quit moving.

Makenna and the others listened instantly, stopping their horses in seconds, but a number of the bandits either didn't hear me or didn't care enough to stop. They continued to ride forward across the pristine jungle floor, unaware of what loomed just overhead.

As they crossed some imaginary line, death descended from the treetops.

Dozens of Arachne warriors dropped right onto the foolish bandits, slaughtering them with practiced ease. Most of the bandits died in seconds, torn to pieces right in front of us. A few escaped the initial massacre and ran for their lives, screaming at the top of their lungs. They didn't get very far.

The Arachne hadn't changed much in a thousand years. They still looked the same as I remembered. Each of the warriors were lean and agile. Rippling muscles and no hint of fat on their frames. Each one was tan, though the shades varied, and they all wore fibrous clothing, woven from nature. It clung to their skin as if part of their bodies as they stared us down with calm dispassion.

Their faces were the most striking part of them. Long, angular, and regal features that only accented their eyes. They pierced through us, small and slanted as every color of the rainbow stared back at us.

One of them, a tall, broad-shouldered male with red and yellow spotted eyes, spoke in a harsh voice. "Get the stragglers," he commanded in Rachnaran.

He bore a rough, puckered scar on his shoulder in the shape of a triangular hourglass. It denoted him as the commander of the Widow's guard. Which made him the best fighter of the Arachne. He would be strong and fast beyond measure, and even with my considerable strength, I didn't have the skills to beat him, let alone match him.

"Be careful, he's dangerous," I said.

The others nodded, but Evelyn stared him down and smiled. *Oh, she's not thinking…oh, yes, that's exactly what she's thinking.* Evelyn was sizing him up as a challenge, and that wouldn't end well for anyone.

"Peace!" I shouted in Rachnaran. "Peace!"

The warriors stopped when I spoke, confusion abounding on their faces until Tegen and Cheira bounded from Lacuna to them. Both of them spoke in hushed whispers that even my hearing couldn't pick up from that distance. Before a minute passed, the Arachne stood down and motioned me forward.

I climbed off Lacuna and threw my hood down, letting them get a good look at me. A few raised their eyebrows, and a few gasped. They stared at me as I walked toward the commander who was taller than I'd originally thought. He nearly matched Gil in height alone.

"An entomancer?" he asked, flicking his eyes up and down.

I nodded, trying to keep the fear off my face. It was difficult when I was staring up at a warrior bred for combat and who could probably kill me without blinking.

"You rescued our brood from slavery?"

"Yes, though not without the help of my bonded."

"I understand, but this is not my decision to make. You will come with me, and the Widow will decide your fate."

He spoke with such conviction and finality that if we questioned him, or tried to argue, I knew we'd be dead before we could get the words out.

"Of course," I said and turned back to my friends, walking to get back on Lacuna. "We do as they say and follow them. If we don't, we die."

"I can take them," Evelyn said, scoffing.

"No, you can't. They're strong, well-coordinated, and will swarm us before we could even draw our weapons. Trust me on this," I pleaded.

She looked like she wanted to argue, but Adam rode beside and smacked the back of her head. "None of that now, sister of mine. Let's listen to Eris and not start a war with the spider people, shall we?"

"Fine," she grumbled, easing into a more passive stance.

Our exchange did not go unnoticed by the warriors who stood a dozen yards in front of us in a large pool of blood from the bandits. With a jerk of his head, the commander ordered us to follow him.

We rode through the bloody remains as the stench of blood filled the air. "Ugh, it'll take forever for the smell to leave my clothes. This is why I like killing with poison. It's less messy," Makenna said, pinching her nose as our horse's hooves squelched underneath the dead flesh.

"I just wonder what they're going to do with the bodies?" Gil asked.

"You don't want to know," I replied.

"Now I'm more curious."

I didn't really want to answer; it was a barbaric custom, but he wanted to know, and it wasn't my decision to keep the information from them.

"They eat them," I said, sighing.

"Lovely."

"You asked."

Gil and the others thankfully quieted down as we rode through endlessly thick forests. The only thing that made traversing through it possible was the small and worn trails we crossed as the Arachne led us deeper into the woods.

After a few hours, the trees began to thin slightly, and there was more space to move around as the trail widened and we entered what could only be a city. We broke through the trees, and dozens of buildings rose up from the forest floor.

They were all wooden, but it wasn't the mechanical, perfectly designed homes of the humans. These buildings had been carved and shaped like sculptures. They were all smooth and circular, with wide, open windows and door frames with no doors. They reminded me of the buildings we'd lived in so long ago. They weren't nearly as well-crafted and were smaller in comparison, but it was incredibly reminiscent of home.

The rest of the warriors scattered, vanishing into the city like ghosts, and we were left with just the commander. He turned, speaking slowly to me. "We are alerting the guards to your presence, but if you wander off, you will be treated as hostile and will be killed without mercy." He spoke the language of humans, but it was slow and with a strange inflection.

The others jerked in surprise at his words, but I just nodded for them. "We understand and will obey."

"Good. The Widow has been made aware of you and will see you."

He led us through the city as we passed a number of Arachne, each of them staring at us like we'd grown three heads. *I guess it is strange to see humans in a forest that forbids entrance to the other races. I just wish they wouldn't look at me like that, though. I guess I must be the first entomancer they've ever seen, and that has to come as a shock to them.*

241

As we rode deeper into the city, we reached our destination. It was a large dwelling that dwarfed the much smaller surroundings by at least double. Though it was larger, it wasn't designed with any more elegance than the other buildings, but it bore numerous windows as it rose towards the treetops.

"The queen's palace, eh?"

"Most likely, but please, let me do the talking when we meet the Widow."

"The Widow?" Evelyn asked.

"Yes, it's what the monarch of the Arachne is called. You'll see why when we get inside."

With further discussion, the commander hissed at us and opened the double doors. It was the only building that actually had doors, and as we went inside, I found out why.

Half a dozen guards stood on the other side of the door, weapons of all types raised menacingly close to our faces. I tried my best to ignore the guards and focus on the room.

It was tall and winding; staircases rose on either side of the room to spiral off higher and higher to the many other floors. The walls were smooth and glossy as if they'd been waxed. As we walked toward the throne, we passed a library. Books written on mashed leaves and bound in tree bark lined the walls on either side of me, rising to the other floors.

I wonder what they say? There's so much history that's been lost. I wonder if those books hold the answers.

The throne room was small and thin. It was basically a walkway wide enough to let supplicants come and speak to their queen. Wooden stairs at the end rose up to a dais, and on an elegantly carved wooden throne sat the queen of the Arachne.

She was stunning. So stunning that my breath caught in my chest for a split second before I remembered how to breathe. She wore a similar style of dress as her warriors, a slim fitting black shirt that left most of her upper chest and neck exposed, and pants that hugged her slender body.

Her pure white hair draped like silk over her tawny neck and collarbone. Her skin was rich enough that it looked like it should melt in the sunlight cascading through the windows, and her face was gorgeous, yet softer than I was expecting.

Her ears, like the rest of the Arachne race, were long, but not as long as mine and slightly curved as the tips pulled back toward the base of her head. She had a thin, kind face that should have been laughing with joy but instead stared us down with cool, detached eyes that sent shivers up my spine.

Eyes that marked her as the Widow of the Arachne, their queen.

They were pitch black, almost like mine, but where mine were compounded, hers were smooth. In the center of each eye was a small red hourglass that formed her iris.

She leaned back in her chair, a slender hand under her chin in thought as her unblinking gaze welcomed us to her castle. Her sight flicked over each of us until she finally landed on me.

"An entomancer," she said, forgoing her native tongue for our benefit.

Her voice was husky and rich as she spoke, holding both bitterness and a subtle sweetness as it slithered into my ears. She had an intoxicating voice.

She clicked her tongue sharply against her teeth. "Just my luck to have to deal with another one in my lifetime."

Her words shocked me, and whatever else had been running through my mind at the time was blown away as a single thought shattered my world.

Another one? Another one!

Without thinking, I broke free from the group and ran the distance between me and the queen. I hit the steps at a jog and only managed to slow myself as I reached the throne. "There's another entomancer? Where are they? When did you see them? Please tell me!" I shouted, getting right in her face.

In my excitement and lapse in sanity, I didn't realize the overwhelming error I'd made, and a dozen Arachne warriors appeared from the shadows and were next us in an instant. The commander held a thin-bladed dagger to my throat, and if I so much as turned my head, I'd likely lose it.

The queen held up her hand. "It's fine. Thank you, Elra. But I'm perfectly capable of taking care of myself."

Elra removed the dagger from my neck and bowed low; immediately, all the warriors vanished as swiftly as they'd arrived.

She smiled at my eagerness and shifted in her chair, crossing her legs and leaning on the armrest. "My name is Reinaera, but I prefer Reina. Now tell me who you are, entomancer."

I gulped, suddenly nervous as I stared back at Reina. "My name is Eris. I'm the Hive Queen, and up until a few seconds ago, I thought I was the last entomancer left alive on Telae—or Nexus, rather."

At that, Reina titled her head back and laughed, a throaty laugh that filled the room with music. She came back up still chuckling and smiled at me. "You almost had me there. Eris, was it? But you are not the Hive Queen. I've met the queen."

"What?" I asked aghast, taking a step back. "The other entomancer is a girl?" I shook my head. *Doesn't matter right now, stop fixating on that.* "That's impossible. My mother was the last queen of the Hive, and when she died, the mantle transferred to me. I am the queen."

Reina stropped smirking and tapped her finger on her chin. "Your words ring of conviction, but I've met Aliria, the true queen, and so you must be deluding yourself."

"Aliria?" I asked.

"Yes. You don't look all that different to me, but she is the queen, not you."

I shrugged my shoulders. "I've never heard of her, but I'm not lying."

"That's no concern of mine," Reina said, rising from her throne.

Her attached spider limbs uncoiled themselves from around her waist where they'd been blending in with the dark fabric. Four thin, black limbs protruded from Reina's spine, each of them five and half feet long, ending in a tapered point which concealed two sharp pincers. Reina used them to push off from the chair as she stood, her spider legs suspended in the air by her waist.

The others recoiled and gasped when they noticed, and I didn't blame them. They hadn't seen them before because most of the Arachne kept them concealed or covered. Reina was disregarding tradition by leaving hers out in the open.

She came to stand before me. Reina was taller than me by half a head, and that, coupled with her standing on the wooden steps, put her collarbone at just above eye level. Her revealing shirt gave me a peek at her moderate chest.

I shouldn't be focusing on that right now! There're too many other, more important things to worry about right now than how nice her breasts are. Eris, control yourself!

I flicked my eyes away from the view and back to Reina, whose own widowed eyes seemed to be taking in me as well. She smiled sweetly at me and leaned in closer. "What to do with you, hmm? I think there's a lot for us to talk about, and I want you to tell me everything," she said, her smile not leaving me any room to negotiate as her face crept closer to mine.

I nodded, sweat beading on my forehead. "Let's start at the beginning."

And so, I told her everything.

I retold my story from the very start. My life a thousand years ago till that day, and through it all, Reina didn't say a word until I'd finished my story and sat back up in her throne.

She smirked and turned toward me. "How far the once-mighty entomancers have fallen. Your entire species has been eradicated, just like the rest of the Hive—"

"Really? There's none left?"

Reina shook her head. "The apocritans and mantearians have been gone for centuries, since long before we settled these woods."

"What about the scorpius?" I asked, my hands shaking.

"Gone, too. Like us, some survived, but peace couldn't be had, and they left."

"When? Surely some must have survived all this time."

"I don't know. There isn't anyone left alive from those times, and our records were destroyed in a fire. We have nothing left of our history, but stories passed from parents to child."

It wasn't what I wanted to hear. In fact, it was the exact opposite; the worst thing I could have been told was that the history of the Hive was scattered to the wind.

"Why don't you consult the Hive Mind, queen? I admittedly don't know much about your kind, but the old stories told of your abilities. Surely the history is stored somewhere in that head of yours."

I sighed, resting my palms on my thighs while resisting the urge to drum my fingers. "It's not that simple. The Hive Mind is complex, mesmerizing in its vastness. If I linger or drift too deep, it becomes harder to pull myself of out. That and my limited magic makes trying incredibly dangerous."

Throughout our conversation, the others had been very patient, letting me do the talking while they stood and listened, but Gil kept fidgeting, shifting balance from foot to foot, and Makenna had pulled out a book to read and sat cross-legged on the ground. Evelyn and Adam were barely listening; instead, they were absorbed in their own conversation. I was trying to not leave them out of the conversation, but Reina had no interest in them, and I had so many questions to ask that I forgot that they were with us in the room.

"Hey, Reina. Why do you insist on picking on her? You've been taking stabs at her this entire time," Gil said, his deep voice only amplified by the echo in the room.

Reina scowled, her eyes shooting over to glare at Gil. "Human, while I'm thankful for your part in returning Cheira and Tegan to us, it is not enough to allow such insolence. Speak to me like that again, and I will devour you alive."

The atmosphere in the room changed in an instant. The Gloom Knights shifted from abject boredom to defensive in a heartbeat, and Reina unfolded her limbs and revealed her sharp claws. The tension in the room was palpable, and I had to do something.

"Whoa, we didn't come here to fight," I blurted out, standing in a panic. "I came here to return the children and to meet you and the other Arachne. We're friends."

"Friends?" Reina asked skeptically. "Hardly. You're a nuisance who dropped herself on my doorstep and complicated my life more than it already was. We've governed ourselves just fine for centuries, and all of a sudden, you entomancers come to fuck everything up."

"What's she like?" I asked when we'd all settled down.

"Aliria? She's strong, capable. She waltzed in and overpowered my best fighters like it was nothing. She and her human lover both were unbelievably powerful."

"Human lover?"

Reina nodded, grimacing at the thought. "You're not the only one who's taken a liking to the humans. But Magnus was something else. I honestly don't know which was stronger."

Her words hit me like a lightning bolt. And a collective gasp echoed from our side of the table. *Magnus? Again? Who is he? And how does he tie into Aliria? What's going on?*

Reina furrowed her brow and pursed her lips slightly. "I take it you've heard of him."

"He's made our lives fucking hell for the last few weeks. What do you know about him?" Gil asked abruptly.

"Interesting," she replied, her eyes lighting up with something I couldn't place. She smirked and rose from her chair. "Let's take this conversation outside, shall we?"

Without a word, Reina rose once more and walked past us as she headed toward the door. I gave the others a look. Gil shrugged and nodded, so we all followed after Reina.

She pushed open the doors and turned back to us as warm sunlight lit up her skin and eyes. "They came here around eight years ago now. Offering an alliance of sorts. The way Magnus spoke led me to believe he thinks something is coming—a war, or gods know what—but I refused. I didn't trust him."

"Why? What's coming?" I asked as we shuffled outside.

She didn't answer at first. Instead, she sauntered over the well-trodden dirt and went around the side of the palace to where a large stable was located. It was just as detailed and elegant as the palace itself. Our horses were hitched inside, and several Arachne men and women tended to them with care.

Reina went over to the first stall and led her horse out, a beautiful brown colt with a chocolate mane. As she mounted her horse, she spoke with a shake of her head. "I don't know. Magnus wouldn't say. But he felt off to me. Something about him nagged at me, though he was talkative and charming, for a human. But he never answered my question, and I wasn't about to drag the last of my race into a war when I didn't even know who we'd be fighting."

She motioned for us to do the same and follow her. We all climbed onto our horses, and Reina led us out of the stable and down a long stretch of dirt road that led through the center of the city.

Before we'd gotten a dozen feet, the commander of the guard sidled up to us.

"My Widow, please allow me to accompany you."

She shook her head and craned her neck. "I'm in no danger from these humans, and is that Foard I see? I'm glad he's back from the farms. Go and spend time with your bonded, Elra. And please give him my best."

Elra bowed. "Thank you, Widow. I shall."

I processed what Reina had told us over the last few minutes. *Who are Magnus and Aliria? How did she survive the eradication of our species? It was a thousand years ago, so she couldn't have been alive back then, so where are her parents? There could be more than just us left. I have to find her.*

The commander left, and we continued on, past a number of shops and wooden buildings. Dozens of Arachne went about their day. Most wore green cotton tunics, though more and more had their arachnid limbs bare or visible, wrapped around their waists like belts.

"Why do you leave your limbs uncovered? That was always considered taboo."

Reina laughed. "That may have been so during the time of the Hive, but the times have changed. It's far more convenient to leave them uncovered."

"How strange," I said, scratching my cheek.

Reina let us take in the sights as we rode. We slipped through the city as so many of the Arachne went about their day. Most manned shops in the city, but the city was small, only a few square miles, and as we got to the outskirts, more and more farms cropped up.

There were so many different kinds that it was a little impressive. Chicken, cattle, and even a few pig ranches. Mixed in between grain and vegetable farms. Dozens of them. The Arachne didn't want for anything that I'd seen.

"I don't imagine you using human currency, so how do you pay for things?"

Reina shook her head and slowed her horse so we could ride side by side. "That's true, we don't. We barter for things we need, trade favors or services in exchange for the things we need. Everyone has something that someone else wants or needs, so it works well for us. Though we only number in the low thousands. I have no idea how it would work if there were more of us."

I nodded. "It's the same as the Hive of old. Though do you also barter people?"

Reina's eyes went wide. "Morrigan's feathers, no. We would never treat our people in such a way."

I smiled as relief washed over me. "Good. The old ways were abhorrent. I'm glad to see the Hive can progress unburdened by the past."

"I don't mean to interrupt your conversation, Eris. But back on topic, where can we find Magnus and this Aliria? There's a lot we need to ask them," Gil said.

"Magnus is owed some retribution from us, and I aim to see it done," Evelyn said, a grin on her lips.

"I'm afraid it isn't that simple," Reina replied. "You and yours did us a favor by returning our spiderlings, but that doesn't mean we owe you anything. And as I said before, I'm not getting in the middle of whatever Magnus and Aliria are planning."

"So you're just going to hide away in your woods like cowards?" Evelyn asked suddenly.

Reina looked over to her and paused for a second or two. "You know, for a human, you're quite striking."

Evelyn chuckled. "You threatened to devour my friend earlier, now you want a bite of me? Any other time and I might've let you eat me, but business before pleasure."

"Oh, well," Reina said with a sigh, speeding up as we took a turn down a wide stretch of dirt. The trees growing thicker as we left the city behind. "You call it cowardice; I call it protecting my species. You want to get involved, fine, but that information isn't going to come without a price."

"That's fine. We've got plenty of gold," Gil said, taking a large bag out of his inventory, and shook it, the coins inside clinking as they shifted.

Reina didn't even glance at it. "Weren't you listening? Keep your worthless human money. I have no need of it. No, what I need are assurances."

Gil stowed his gold away, his face scrunched in confusion, unsure of where Reina was going.

"All right, what *do* you want, then?" Makenna asked, glancing over at us.

Reina smiled a wicked grin, her four spider limbs curling around her waist. "If I tell you what I know about those two, that would be the same as betraying them in their eyes if they found out, and I won't go against them without knowing I'm on the right side of things. You want my help, then you'll first prove yourselves to me."

We just won't let them find out, not until we have Sam back, at least. I turned to the others, who were already nodding their heads. *Guess we're doing this.*

"All right."

"Then let's not waste any more time. We still have a few miles to go, so let's pick up the pace."

We followed Reina as she led us through the winding roads of the forest and to a large clearing surrounded by worn and moss-grown stones that resembled an arena.

Reina dismounted her horse in a flash and disappeared into the treetops.

"Welcome to the trial of visitation!" Reina shouted from somewhere among the trees. "Step into the circle, and the trial will begin."

The five of us dismounted and walked over to the stones, squeezing through the thin gap available between the sporadic rocks, and entered the field. It was a once grassy plain that had been worn through to reveal rough brown dirt underneath. Some grass still grew at the edges, clinging to the tall rocks that surrounded us in fear of being trampled away as well.

We walked to the center, waiting for whatever it was that we agreed to participate in to begin.

Slowly, a number of Arachne began to appear at the edges of my vision, creeping in from the tree line like spectators to an execution. They surrounded us, never speaking or uttering a sound, just staring down at us silently.

The whole thing set my teeth on edge, and I dug my fingers into my palm to keep my nerves from getting the better of me. I didn't like this. I was afraid because I didn't know what was going to happen, and the silence only magnified my fear.

Then Reina appeared, walking along a branch that hung high above the arena. "You have accepted the trial, now let me lay down the rules. You are not confined to the arena if you so choose, but Rachnara and the surrounding farms are off limits. Going to the city will forfeit the trial. Also, you may use whatever tools you have at your disposal, but there will be absolutely no use of potions during the trial, no health or mana. Is that understood?"

We all nodded, though we had yet to be told what we were actually going to be doing. The five of us stood and stared up at Reina, waiting.

She smiled down at us. "And you will now face the guardian spirit of the Arachne, the protector of the Hive."

Oh, no.

"Everyone, draw your weapons, quickly!" I shouted, already calling upon my magic to pool my chitin into weapons and armor.

It crawled black up my skin and encased me in a second. Next came my bow, which formed slowly in my hand, slithering to its shape and solidifying. Next came my arrows, which coalesced on my back in a quiver.

I need to be careful. The arrows are made from chitin, and each one takes away from my armor. I can't be reckless with my shots.

In four seconds, the five of us were ready to face one of the strongest beings the Hive Kingdom possessed. An entity once worshipped as a god by the Arachne.

It rose from the shadows cast by the leaves as the sunlight scattered through the trees. Earth rumbled and shifted as it clawed its way from the ground. The others took one look and backed away, tensing and getting ready for combat as the monstrosity clawed its way from the earth and stood, moving its hulking, bulbous body to face us.

A giant spider, twenty feet long, stood before us, its pearl-white skin nearly transparent as it opened its chelicerae and bared its dagger-like fangs at us.

They dripped deadly venom as its yellow eyes stared unblinking at us. Its bloated abdomen hung behind it as its palps dragged along the ground by its head.

"Fuck, what is that thing?" Gil asked, panicked.

"That is Misumena, the voracious guardian."

Chapter 15 - Planning to Plan

Sampson

After a quick bath, I changed into a plain black tunic with cotton pants and found my bedroom. It was small with only a stone desk, a bed, and a nightstand with an oil lamp. The bed was a stone frame with thick straw wrapped in cloth that was sewn shut.

I let my sword rest on the nightstand and slid the knife Thrayl had given me under the mattress. It was too dark in the room without any windows, so I lit the oil lamp. As the room filled with soft light, I curled up and tried to fall asleep.

My interface crashed into my vision, and I cursed at the name. *By the nine kings of hell, Miguel, what now.*

"What is it?"

"Just calling about the job."

"I'm already on a job," I growled. "Look, if I'm not dead or in prison by this time next week, we can talk."

"Okay, sounds—"

I hung up and tried to get some sleep.

Which, after an hour, seemed like an impossibility. No matter how much I willed it and shut my eyes tight, all I was doing was tossing and turning.

My thoughts were consumed by what the Mnemosyne had shown me. I couldn't unsee it; my stomach twisted in knots, and my chest grew tight with guilt. *I've been a right bastard to her, and she didn't deserve it.* I shook my head and forced myself to stop thinking about it. It was in the past.

Godsdamn it! What I would give for one night of peaceful sleep?

One more failed attempt to sleep later, and I groaned and flopped out of bed. *Maybe a nightcap will settle my nerves.* I walked downstairs, and it was hard to see. As my eyes adjusted, one of the windows let in some soft light from the mana crystal outside, bathing the living room and kitchen in a radiant blue light that shone like the moon.

"Can't sleep, huh?" Raven asked from the couch. She was curled up, wearing a soft white chemise made of silk that clung to her skin like it was painted on.

"Something like that. Want a drink?" I asked.

"Sure."

After what had happened between us earlier, I expected heavy tension between us, but there wasn't any. She was rather calm and composed. I went to the fridge and brought back two bottles of beer. Raven shifted over on the couch, making room for me. I leaned back and handed her one of the beers.

"Huh, this couch is kinda comfy. For stone, at least."

"Yeah, but it's a bitch to sleep on," she replied, taking a sip of beer.

I leaned back and stared at my beer, willing myself to take a drink. After a few seconds, I sighed and set it down, trying to find the right words.

"Look, I'm sor—"

Raven held a finger to my lips, silencing me. "It's okay. I do understand, you know, even if you were an ass at times."

I nodded and held out my hand to her. "Fresh start?"

Raven let out a small laugh and finished her drink, before pointing at mine. "Only if you share."

"Have at it," I said with a chuckle.

She leaned over me, her arm brushing against mine as she grabbed the bottle. She leaned back with a smile and took a drink. When she put the bottle down, Raven took my offered hand, her slender fingers cold and wet from the condensation on the glass.

"Clean slate." She smiled widely at me and took another drink.

256

"I will say the dwarves know how to make good drinks."

After taking a drink, she set the bottle on the table in front of us and tugged her tie out of her ponytail, letting her black hair fall over her prominent collarbone and down her back. She ran her fingers through it, strands of hair drifting away from her to fall lazily to the ground.

"Much better," she said and looked at the window. "What time is it, though?"

"Almost three."

"Damn, we're going to be exhausted in the morning."

"Why don't you take the bed? I doubt I'm going to get much sleep tonight."

"Why's that?"

I shrugged. "Haven't had a decent night's sleep since this whole fiasco started. At least some things are consistent."

She laughed and finished her drink, setting her empty glass next to the first on the table.

"Well, since you don't hate me anymore, what's say you and I act like adults and share the bed? Its plenty big enough for both of us. We slept in the same tent last night, what's the difference?"

I didn't answer right away, instead getting up to grab another drink, trying to find a good reason to say no but only coming up with the fact that she was a shifter. My prejudices were not fading so quickly. I popped the top and took a long pull before sitting back down.

Raven smiled at me, fanning her eyelashes and drawing my eyes to hers while she deftly stole my drink from my hand. She took a sip and laughed. "Oh, c'mon, coward. I don't bite."

A hysterical fit of giggles threatened to burst from my lips. I held my laughter and chuckled.

"I do."

She snickered. "Yeah, tell me about it," she said, her pale fingers rubbing her neck as she stood and handed me back my drink. "Offer's still open, though."

Raven head up the stairs, the silk of her chemise clung to her hips as she took the steps slowly. I turned away from her and picked up my beer, staring at the brown bottle.

"Damn it," I sighed, rubbing my stinging eyes.

I'm exhausted, have been for days now. And tomorrow is planning for the heist. I need to be on top of my game.

"Fuck it, I need sleep," I said, downing the rest of the beer and following Raven upstairs.

Raven was curled up next to the wall as I walked in. She scooted over and sat up on the lip of the bed. "Which side you want?"

"Don't care," I said and climbed out of my shirt and flopped on the bed.

I took the side by the wall, turned over on my side, and slid my hands under the pillow. Raven lay on her side next to me and shifted closer to me. Her back brushed my chest, and she shivered.

"Gods, you're warm. It's like sleeping next to a furnace."

I snorted with laughter; I couldn't help it. "Eris runs just shy of boiling, so I understand how you feel."

"I won't complain, though, it's nice when it's this cold," she said, snuggling closer to me.

"Just don't get any funny ideas."

"I would never."

After that, I settled in and tried to get some sleep for the second time. It was admittedly easier with Raven leaning against me. I had no special feelings for her, but the mere presence of her skin so close to mine helped, and before I knew it, I was fast asleep.

Raven woke me in the morning, and my eyes jolted open. Her hand was on my chest, and I grabbed it on reflex.

"Oh, sorry," I said, yawning.

"Don't be. Seems like you needed the rest," she said, fixing the shoulder strap on her chemise, which had slipped down her bicep.

I sat up and swung my legs over the edge of the bed and stood. I stretched when I was on my feet and sighed. The exhaustion that had crept up on me was mitigated, if not gone all together. *I feel pretty good this morning.*

I knew for a fact that Eris wouldn't care in the least that I had simply slept in the bed with another woman, but it still wasn't appropriate. *First Jasmine, and now Raven. I'm sleeping next to a lot of women who aren't my wife...I miss Eris.*

It was the first thought in my head every day, and the last thought before I went to sleep. I missed my wife, and the fact that I couldn't see her really pissed me off.

"All right, let's get dressed. We've got a big day ahead of us."

I headed down the stairs to find a slew of items waiting for us on the table by the kitchen. A few packs lay bulging on their backs, just waiting to be opened. Raven padded down the stairs softy behind me. She wore a gray shirt and pants, and she'd tied her long onyx locks out of her face into a ponytail. Raven followed my eyes to the table.

"Guess Orryn dropped by early this morning."

"Yeah," I replied, rubbing the back of my head. *Damn it, if he'd been an assassin, we'd be dead. I shouldn't have slept so hard.*

I was slipping. The slightest noise should have woken me, and it hadn't. *I've gotten too comfortable around other people. The years of solitude trained my senses, but they've dulled since Eris came into my life.*

I need to retrain them. Just another thing to add to my to-do list.

"Duran, come and check over everything. Magnus is thorough, but even he has blind spots sometimes."

I'd grabbed everything I thought I might have needed back in the war room, but more supplies could only help, and maybe there was something I was missing.

I picked up one of the packs at random and dumped its contents out; they spilled and clanked out across the table. Several vials of potions: wraithsight, invisibility, fleetfoot, lightstep and a few *Agility* and *Stealth* enhancers. It covered every angle of what I might need, but there was no way I could take them all. Potion sickness would begin to kick in after the third potion, and system overload would follow a potion after.

Nice to have, but too much. Least I'll have them if I need them. I turned my attention to the other items on the table, which were much more mundane in comparison. A tightly coiled length of rope, torches and matches, a lockpick and burglar's kit so exquisite they put the one I carried to shame, and a few teleportation scrolls.

"Seems like everything we need for something like this," Raven said as she looked over the items.

"Yeah, but too many people have already failed attempting this. Magnus sent thieves with far more experience than me, which tells me there is something that we haven't accounted for. This isn't going to be easy."

"We might die."

"Maybe, but at least I can come back," I said with a slight grin.

Raven smirked and smacked me lightly on the arm. "Ass."

I quickly packed up the bag before stowing it in my inventory. "All right, let's get a move on. It'll take us a while to get to Gold Hightown, and then we have to scout the area," I said and headed for the door.

Raven sighed deeply behind me. "Least my life isn't boring," she said softy before following me.

***

Gold Hightown hadn't changed much since I'd last been there. While Lowtown festered in destitution, Hightown thrived in opulence.

The air was even sweeter, less polluted with heat and the stale scent of poverty. There were still plenty of stone buildings, just more refined and well-designed, but it was in Hightown where we started seeing wooden houses and manors as well.

It was the only place in Aldrust where the dwarves built their buildings with wood. It wasn't that expensive to buy, but to have it transported, constructed, and maintained in the cool underground cost some serious coin. Only the wealthiest dwarves had the coin or were vain enough to attempt building a house out of wood.

Most of the buildings were still stone, but it wasn't just stone, most had marble or wooden accents to their houses, especially around the roof and windows. It was a less expensive method of showing off wealth, but status was status, no matter where.

The streets were smooth and had been freshly replaced—not a single crack or chip in the flagstones.

"It's gorgeous here, and the air is sweeter. Warmer, too," Raven said, glancing around.

"We're closer to the surface, so more fresh air gets let in from the vents that run through the rock to the surface. As we found out last night, Lowtown doesn't get the luxury of fresh air, so it stagnates and rots on the lower levels."

The walk to the Iron Cathedral was a long one, and I was already nervous. *Why did I agree to this again? Oh, right, I didn't really have much of a choice.* Raven shifted her eyes to mine, and I knew she could tell I was feeling the pressure, and she tried to keep me distracted.

"It's like night and day," Raven said as we passed a rather large three-story manor constructed of dark rosewood.

"Nobility is the same no matter what race you are. If someone can have something, then there must always be someone who doesn't. It's the way the world works."

She picked up her step and walked along side of me, nudging me with her elbow. "Waxing philosophical, are we? Still, the wealth of this place is staggering compared to Lowtown."

"Says the girl working for the richest man in existence."

She snickered. "Touché."

As we stepped along the smooth cobblestone streets, I kept my eyes open. Humans were welcome to go mostly wherever we pleased in Aldrust, but there still wasn't a huge number of us in the city. Raven and I would stand out to any casual observer, and that was the last thing we needed before we cased the Iron Cathedral.

We passed numerous dwarven nobles going about their day. The style of dress had changed slightly, and tailored button-ups with colorful mantling around their shoulders seemed to be in fashion for the dwarven males, while the ladies wore flowing dresses that stopped mid-calf. *The dwarven nobles have always had their eyes on the latest trends, but I can't see how mantling has caught on.*

I ignored most of the looks we got as we passed by, none of them hostile, merely curious. But eyes were eyes, and the less on us the better. So, with a groan that slipped from my throat and gritted teeth, I slid my arm through Raven's and wound my fingers through hers.

She jumped with mild surprise at my touch and stopped walking. She stared up at me in confusion.

"We need to give everyone a reason why we're here. A couple on a stroll is much less suspicious than two humans walking with a purpose."

Raven smiled showing me her pearlescent teeth. "Told you so, husband," she replied cheekily before getting closer to me.

I tried to ignore her smile as we walked, tried to ignore how smooth and soft her fingers were around mine. The way her shoulders rose and fell with each languid breath. She was damned annoying when I paid attention to her.

She wasn't who I'd made her out to be in my head, and I couldn't even fall back on the fact that she was a shifter anymore. Not when I knew why she'd made the deal.

"Just don't forget why we're here. This isn't a date."

"I'm well aware, but that doesn't mean we can't enjoy ourselves at least a little, right?"

"Guess not." I shrugged.

"Good," she said, pulling me along with a smile. "Then let's get going!"

The path up to the Iron Cathedral was sequestered away from the main road that led to the shopping and residential districts. We went through a gate that opened to a singular path that led to the cathedral. It was a bit of a hike as we climbed about a thousand steps, but at the top stood the Iron Cathedral.

It was the single most elegantly designed building I'd ever seen; it put both mine and Magnus's castles to shame in the quality of the stonework and design. Pristine white stone rose to two towering spires on either side of the basilica. Heavy buttresses ran from the spires to the main body of the church like fingers of a god digging into the stone blocks. High above us, stained glass sparkled from the radiant light of the mana crystal. Emerald green motes of light danced across the façade.

"It's breathtaking," Raven said.

I could only nod. "Without a doubt, it's a gorgeous place, disconnected from mortality. Almost a shame what we have to do."

She placed a hand on my shoulder, squeezing gently. "I agree, but neither of us have a choice here."

"We always have a choice."

With those words, we stopped staring at the beauty of the architecture and went inside. The door was comprised of solid stone only a hair's shade off color from the rest of the stone. Nearly a hundred polished emeralds were embedded around the door. It opened at our approach and our footsteps on the stone lip of the frame echoed for a second before our feet hit the plush carpeted green rug that ran the length of the entryway.

Ribbed vaulting ran the entirety of the hall's ceiling until it widened at the center of the cathedral. Where Lachrymal's Heart resided.

Even from the entrance, the lingering foreboding that slithered over my shoulders was amplified by the mere presence of the Heart. Its insidious whispering and high-pitched tone were barely audible from where we stood, but they were still present, sending shivers up my spine.

"Gods, what's that feeling? I don't like it," Raven said, crossing her arms and rubbing them.

"That's what divinity feels like. Just ignore it for now. The more you think about it, the worse it gets."

"Why?"

"We're in the presence of something not meant for mortals, and especially not meant for human mortals. The dwarves have an innate tolerance; we're not so lucky," I said, lowering my voice.

We weren't alone here. There were several priests tending the church and the parishioners, and that wasn't counting Lachrymal's Chosen.

The stoic-faced guards were all clad in shadowsteel armor with a single large emerald in the center of their chests, right over their hearts. Each carried their own preference of weapons, swords, axe, and even a few maces. Each would be a master of their weapon, having fought for dozens of years, maybe even a full century before they were allowed the honor of serving Lachrymal.

I started walking through the nave that led to the Vault of Tears, the resting place of Lachrymal's Heart. Raven stopped glancing around and caught up to me a few steps later.

"I don't like this place. We shouldn't be here," she said, her hand going to mine for comfort.

I gave her fingers a squeeze. "You're right, but we have to. I told you, don't think about it too much. You're letting it get to you."

She jerked head, breathing in and out deeply, but her heartbeat pressed through her fingertips and beat fast against my own rising drum. *Take your own advice—get out of your head about this.*

"As thanks."

Before I could ask the Aspect what it meant, a chill seeped from my heart to my head. it wasn't like before when it took control of my body, but it was a soft breeze that settled my turbulent emotions and brought rationality to my thoughts.

My heart settled, and I wasn't concerned by the tonal screeching that had been steadily rising as we got closer to the vault. The cold, logical side of the

Aspect bled through my mind, and I picked up the pace, nearly dragging Raven along behind me.

Though we had to stop as we reached the vault. The door was similar to the entrance of the cathedral, but the emeralds formed a teardrop in the center. Flanked on either side of the door were two of Lachrymal's Chosen. Standing at four foot nothing, they still radiated the calm grace of a lifetime warrior.

Their eyes flicked over us mechanically. They filed us both in either threat or non-threat category, and I knew exactly what category I was shuffled to: the same one I'd put them in.

But the Iron Cathedral was a public place, even for humans, and they couldn't outright deny us entrance, but the one on the right shot me a warning look that said in no uncertain terms that they would be more than happy to bring heavy violence upon my person if I stepped out of line.

With a nod and a swift chant in Script, the door thudded and slid below the floor to reveal the Vault of Tears.

As we stepped from the plush carpet and back onto stone, the thuds of our boots resounded through the mostly empty chamber and melded with the subtle whine that permeated the room. White stone faded to gray as the slabs led to the center of the room, where the object of our heist lay situated on top of a small, rocky obelisk that rose from the earth itself to cradle the gemstone at the zenith.

Lachrymal's Heart was huge for a gem. It was roughly circular, shaped like an egg about the size of my head and weighed at least twenty-five pounds. It was smooth around the center with precise lines cut along the edge which refracted light in the geometric patterns as we approached.

Raven tugged on my hand which stopped me in place. I turned back, confused. "What?"

"I don't want to be here, it hurts."

I realized then that I hadn't heard the insidious infrasound that the gem emitted since the Aspect had lent me its chill. Raven didn't have such luxury and was feeling the full impact of the oppressive weight of the Weeping God.

I pulled her close and held her hand tighter. "Feel that. Just focus on the tactile feeling of my hand and tune out everything else."

She nodded, unsteady and wound her fingers through mine before gripping my hand with both of hers. I let her have the hand while I focused on my surroundings, to do what we'd come here for.

The room was large, full of mostly unused space, especially around the obelisk itself. A couple dozen pews were arranged around the room in a circle for when church was in service, but beside that, the ground floor was mostly barren.

Getting in from the ground floor wouldn't be an option. There was too much open space and nowhere to hide or run to if I fucked up. Above was my best bet.

The ceiling was high overhead, at least twenty feet, which would hurt like hell if I fell, but there wasn't anything I could do about it. Arched support beams just below the ceiling stretched across the entirety of the room. A few more jutted out and crisscrossed here and there but were for decoration rather than holding the weight of the building.

All right, that'll be their downfall. It'll be cramped, but like I assumed, those beams are going to be my best bet.

The stone beams were high enough and the light low enough that unless anyone looked directly at us, we could potentially hide for a while and scout out the area. There were also a few stained-glass windows that were close enough to the beams that I could leap and grab onto.

Cut through the glass and jump to one of the beams. It'll be a broken leg if I miss, but at that point I'm pretty much dead anyway. All right, we'll scout more when we come back, but there aren't any guards in the vault itself. So I've got my entrance—that's what we came here for.

Mika's team will have info on who comes and goes and at what hours to give us our window. Let's get out of here.

I let go of Raven's hand and approached the obelisk before sinking to my knee and bowing my head. *Let the guards at the door see I'm just a worshipper of Lachrymal and get them off my case.*

I rose and the two of us left. Raven practically clung to me as we left the vault but regained some of her composure the further we got from the heart. When we exited the cathedral, she let go of me and stood on her own.

"Thanks," she muttered, her cheeks red.

"Yeah, don't get used to it, though."

"What, the kind and endearing side of you? Being a decent person for more than a few minutes at a time? How awful would that be?"

She started snickering to herself, letting her blushed cheeks fade away as we meandered down the path back to Hightown.

"I can be kind for more than a few minutes," I protested.

"Just not to me?" Raven asked, tilting her head toward me.

"I don't like you that much," I said, teasing her with a smile.

She laughed, picking up her pace as she stepped over a loose rock and nearly lost her balance. Her legs wobbled a bit, but she recovered and turned around while walking backwards down the steps, a devious smile lifting on her lips. "You say you don't like me now, but that wasn't the case last night."

"The hell are you talking about?"

"You move in your sleep. You held me against your chest for most of the night. Guess you unconsciously wanted to be closer to me," she said, her voice dripping saccharine.

"Bullshit!" I shouted, my face growing hot.

She just kept up her smile and turned back around as we reached the last step. "Guess you'll never know."

I sighed as a dull pain radiated from behind my eyes and my mouth went dry. Her flippant attitude irked me to no end, but I didn't think she was the kind of person to outright lie.

"I could make you tell me, you know."

"How's that? By force? You gonna take your knife to my skin to spill my blood and secrets?" she asked, her voice lifting ever so subtly.

Her tone was light, but there was a dark undertone to it when she spoke. I ignored the tone and focused on the question as we passed out of the gate and back onto the main street of Hightown. I was quiet for a few seconds as we passed a crowd of wealthy dwarven nobles on a shopping spree. The dwarven butler was breaking his back to carry about a hundred pounds of parcels behind the group.

When they were well out of earshot and the street was mostly clear again, I spoke. "Through our bond, I could order you to tell the truth."

Raven paused as her teasing eyes dropped. *Didn't think of that did you?* She shook her head slightly and smiled again, drawing closer to me. "There's no need for that, master. I'm yours to do with as you please."

"Watch the m-word!"

Raven chuckled, her crimson eyes sparking a fire as she covered her mouth to keep from laughing. "Then don't threaten me with commands unless you actually intend to follow through with them."

I snorted. We both knew I wouldn't ever make good on my threat. "Fair point."

By the time we reached the Low Road, I was dying for an ale, and I still had to plot the heist before we went later that night.

It was far too early for the bar to be open, but Orryn told us we had access anytime. I unfurled one of the earth scrolls he'd given us, and with a flash of sandy brown light, the Script circle flared to life and disintegrated in my palms as it activated, and my slight mana bar took a hit.

The door opened as if on hydraulics and slid seamlessly into the wall, and we walked in. The bar was desolate. The stone tables were clean, and the chairs were empty. No one there.

Tel wasn't behind the bar, and she couldn't stop me from slinking behind it and grabbing two bottles of beer.

Raven sat down at a table in the center of the room. I handed her one of the bottles and pulled out the chair opposite her. I popped the top and drained half of it before leaning back with a satisfied sigh.

"All right," I said, pulling out our bag of supplies for the heist. "There's a map of the cathedral in the bag. Let's compare it to what we just witnessed."

"If we had a map the whole time, why did we need to go and see the place for ourselves?"

I opened the bag and pulled out the thick, rolled canvas. With a flick of my wrist, it unfurled, and I used our beer bottles to weigh down the sides.

"Never rely on what someone or something says. Always verify for yourself. This map could be outdated, and if we based everything solely on what we thought we knew, we'd be screwed when we got there and found things different. It's the same principle I'm taking with the plan. There's no sense concocting a complex plan, because it will all go to shit the moment a complication arises."

Raven stood and bent over the table looked the blueprints over. It was simple, drawn by hand, but by an expert's hand, and it matched what I remembered from the Iron Cathedral to a T.

"It looks the same to me," she said, tracing her finger along the rough fabric as she stared at the entrance until she got to the Vault of Tears. "And why do you think there's going to be a complication?"

"Because Magnus has already sent men after the Heart before, professional thieves that were probably incredibly skilled in their fields. They all failed, which tells me there is something none of them considered—the same thing I'm not considering—that got them killed."

"Any idea what it could be?"

"Could be any number of things, but I'm betting a trap, something the thieves couldn't see, and they tripped it on accident."

She nodded, sitting back down. "Makes sense, but what do we do about it?"

"Nothing we can do but have each other's backs. A lot is riding on this. Can I trust you?"

"With your life."

"That's exactly what I'm doing. You've got skill, and you've maintained your composure well so far, but when our backs are to the wall and all hope is lost, I need to know you're in my corner."

She nodded, holding my gaze as she dipped her head. "I am yours."

An uncomfortable weight settled in my chest but faded as she broke eye contact and started pulling out the items in the bag and cataloging them once more.

"There isn't anything we need that we don't already have," she said, as the table filled with our gear. "I'm assuming we're going in from above?"

"Of course. It offers the best avenue for infiltration."

"So we have the gear, the map, and a semblance of a plan. What are we waiting for?"

"The others. We need to go over the plan with them. I don't know about the others, but I've trusted Mika with my life before. I know I can count on him."

Raven rubbed at her chin, huffing as she leaned her elbows on the table. "Well, he needs to hurry the hell up."

"Antsy?"

"A little. I don't like sitting still. My bones start to ache if I don't move around every now and again."

Footsteps sound on the stone outside, and I turned in my chair as Orryn walked through the door, followed by Tel.

"Ah, good you're here already," he said, tersely.

"Good to see you again, Duran," Tel said, smiling as her wings appeared in a shimmer of rainbow light and she flew over the bar top. "And I see you've helped yourself to some of my stock, have you?"

"I'll pay for it," I replied taking a swig and trying not to laugh.

She shrugged, a short laugh building in her throat before she looked at Orryn and clammed up. "I'll be in the other room if you need me."

Mika and the hired muscle swept in behind Orryn, geared up with hungry glints in their eyes.

As soon as everyone settled around the table, I looked at each one in turn and smiled.

"All right, let's go over the plan."

CHAPTER 16 - OLD GODS, NEW MONSTERS

Eris

As the thud of Misumena's many limbs drew closer, I snapped out of the slithering dread that had sunk into my skin and nocked an arrow as fast as I could. I loosed it as Misumena reared her translucent head back and opened her chelicerae to reveal menacingly long fangs.

My aim was true, and the arrow slid into her open mouth, and a thick spurt of pale blue blood squirted out and dripped down. Misumena screeched in pain, a grotesque whine that split the air like a whistle.

The shriek, however, was enough to break Gil, Makenna, and Adam out of their spell. They'd been standing still, staring at the gigantic spider approaching without even touching their weapons. Evelyn had drawn hers but was looking at me for directions. *This is new territory for me! I don't know what to do!*

Even in a world filled with monsters, I guess even the humans chosen by the gods to come here could be baffled by something.

"We need to spread out, grouping up will only make us easier to catch!" I shouted, backing away from Misumena as she shook in pain before closing her mouth tight. A faint snap resounded, and when she bared her fangs once more, the shaft of my chitin arrow had been split in two.

I couldn't just fire at will; my chitin wasn't endless, and every arrow I fired weakened my defense. The arena was large, but Misumena took up nearly a third of the space by herself, and had good reach with her legs. We had to spilt up, but we would need to work together to survive.

"Evelyn, what do we do?"

"That's what I'm trying to figure out!" she shouted back as she nimbly ran forward towards the spider. Misumena had her eyes on Gil, who lumbered sideways and drew his massive black battleaxe, keeping just out of range of Misumena's claws.

She scuttled suddenly towards Gil, flashing out with her front limb. Her jagged pale claws deflected off the head of Gil's axe just as he brought it up. The impact pushed him back, leaving two lines in the dirt, but Gil remained standing.

"Woo! Damn spider has some skill!"

Gil backed away, even more cautious of the bulbous beast.

"Don't get your head torn off, darling. I don't think I can love just your body," Makenna said as she danced near Misumena as she scurried around.

"Not what you said last night," Gil replied with a laugh as he twirled his axe to catch Misumena's gaze.

She flicked her wrist, and four needles flashed in the midday sun as they streaked towards the center of Misumena's body. They jabbed into the hard carapace with ease, but the tiny poisoned needles weren't long or sharp enough to go any further.

"Damn it," Makenna cursed as she took another handful of needles out of her cloak. "I can't pierce her body, and even if I can, my toxins were designed for humans and normal creatures, not fucking twenty-foot-long giant spiders!"

"Having some trouble?" Reina shouted from the thick tree branch that hung over the battleground. She'd sat down and was dangling her legs over us, a broad smile plastered over her smooth sandstone skin.

"Fuck you, spider lady!" Makenna shouted, her face taut in distress. "Guys, I'm useless here."

"Calm down, Kenna. Did you forget who we are?" Evelyn asked.

"We've got this," Adam said cheekily and tossed three small black crystals into the center of the field.

The summoning crystals landed and cracked sharply, releasing a small cloud of glass that sparkled like hundreds of small rainbows before falling back to the ground. When they landed, three bane wolves joined us.

Each at least six feet long and rippling with lean muscle, black and silver fur rose as their hackles raised, and they bent low to the ground, growling at the massive crab spider.

"Bane wolves? Really? Why didn't you summon the void golem?" Evelyn asked, her voice rising as she ran forward and sliced a thin groove across one of Misumena's legs.

Her sword was unmistakably high quality, and the silver of the blade shone like a mirror, but even it wasn't enough to do more than scratch the spider.

"Abby's still on cooldown. I told you this weeks ago!"

"Like I can keep up with every single bit of your nonsense on a daily basis."

While those two shouted at each other, I had to think of something. Evelyn was the best fighter and strategist here, but even her weapons weren't strong enough to pierce the hard carapace, which meant her strength alone wouldn't cut it. *C'mon, think, Eris! None of them knows more about Misumena than I do. There has to be something I can do to help!*

In the enclosed space, we were basically trapped in a cage. And sooner or later, we'd lose.

One of the bane wolves lunged forward and clawed at Misumena's bright yellow eyes. Before it could even lay a paw on the crab spider, Misumena surged forward, wrapping her powerful front legs around the entirety of the bane wolf, sinking her fangs deep into the wolf.

Bones snapped as the wolf let out a pained howl before the venom took hold and worked its way to the wolf's heart.

The bane wolf died a quick and very painful death.

When the life fled from the beast, it dissolved into ash and flowed back to its crystal.

"Shit, that thing's strong," Adam said as the crystal returned to his hand.

"She's a clever hunter, but she relies on deception and camouflage. Misumena's slow to move, but incredibly strong when she does. We have her out of its element, but that only helps us so much," I said.

"Dammit!" Gil cursed.

He tried to sneak around behind it, but a leg darted out and left a vicious gash across his arm.

"This thing's a walking tank," he said as he retreated.

"I don't know what that means, but we've got to come up with a plan."

"Fuck this," he replied and gripped his axe tight.

Gil ran at Misumena, and as he kicked up tufts of dirt and grass, his axe head glowed a bright silver. "How about a taste of *Steel-Breaker!*"

He swung his axe down at Misumena's abdomen, and with a sickening crunch, her carapace buckled and cracked under Gil's attack. Misumena let out an unholy scream as blood oozed from her damaged side.

Having dealt a heavy blow, Gill tried to pull his axe out, but it had gotten stuck inside Misumena, and he couldn't free it. Misumena lashed out with her leg, catching Gil in the side and sending him flying to the dirt a few feet away.

He groaned as his hand went to his side; the leather and chainmail had been punctured, and a sliver of Gil's life stained the armor red.

"Are you okay?" I asked, running over to him.

He brushed me off. "Never better," he said through a pained smile. "I'm a berserker. More damage I take, the more I can dish out. Don't you worry about me."

"And you just blew your ace up your sleeve. Save *Stun Shout*—we might need it soon," Evelyn snapped.

"I know, but I figure now's a good time for *Bloodletter*, don't you?"

Evelyn nodded and stepped back. Her swords disappeared, and her dragon-horn bow materialized in her hands in their place. "The little queen has the right idea by keeping out of range. If she's slow, then we can just stay back and pepper her with arrows. The two of us will hold Misumena's attention while you get ready."

Adam ordered his remaining wolves to back up. We couldn't get through her tough carapace, but she did have weak spots.

"Go for her mouth and eyes. Besides the underside, they're her weakest spots."

I took my own advice and grabbed another of my chitin arrows. I nocked an arrow as Evelyn did the same. We circled around, and as Misumena eyes flashed to us, I released my arrow. It sunk in just below her eye. Evelyn's arrow hit dead center in Misumena's eye and blinded her as a thick trail of blood arced toward us.

Evelyn readied her next shot as I nocked my own, and we fired at the same time. We'd both aimed for its eyes again, but as our arrows sailed towards their target, Misumena shifted.

She ducked her head and snapped her front legs, knocking our arrows out of the air.

"Well, shit. So much for that plan," Evelyn whispered.

"Like I said, she's smart."

"I've got an idea," Makenna said as she ran towards us.

Her hands disappeared inside her cloak. When they reappeared, her fingers were wrapped around two large vials of what could've only been poison. The muted brown and gray liquid sloshed inside the glass as she tossed me one of them and Evelyn the other.

I stretched out a hand, but before I could catch it, the vial shattered in midair. Evelyn's also burst, and she stepped back out of the noxious rain before it could land on her silver hair or armor. We both looked up when Reina laughed.

She kicked her feet languidly and wagged her finger at us. "No potions. I told you the rules."

"Those were poisons, not potions!" Makenna shouted, her face going as red as her hair.

Reina shrugged, yawning. "Doesn't matter, same thing. No more cheating, or you'll fail."

I stopped myself from yelling in anger, but only just. *Can't get angry, I need to keep a calm head. They're counting on me!*

Our attack had done what we intended and successfully distracted our quarry as Misumena covered her head to avoid more arrows.

I took a quick glance over at Gil and gasped.

Gill had a small dagger in his hand, and he brought it to his exposed skin again and again, slicing large gashes down his arms and his face and neck. A slight red aura pulsed just off his skin, and as the blood flowed across his dark skin, it didn't drip to the ground. It slithered over his hands and up the axe, defying gravity.

As it covered his axe entirely, Gil let out the most horrifying scream I'd ever heard, and I jolted in pure terror as a wave of fear slammed into me. I wanted to run, to hide myself away and never come out again.

Then the shout faded, and rationality bled through my fear, and I fought to keep my eyes on Gil as he launched into his attack.

He was ferocious as his blood covered him, and he charged forward as Adam's bane wolves circled around to flank Misumena. Gil leapt into the air and brought his axe down. A wave of pressure swept over us, kicking up a cloud of dust and tearing grass from the dirt as a thundering crash rang painfully inside my ears.

Misumena's legs shuddered under the weight of Gil's attacks, and blood poured freely from her wounds as she howled in agony, but it wasn't enough for her to go down.

A fact that Gil realized too late.

She reared back with savage speed, and Gil didn't have the balance to hold on. He sailed through the air and hit one of the stones encircling us with a heavy thud and dropped to the ground, lifeless.

"Gil!" Makenna shouted and ran over to him.

I held my breath as my heart drummed fast in my chest and drowned out any other sounds. Time stretched as I waited for Makenna to tell me he was okay.

She sighed and smiled as Gil spluttered, his eyes shooting open. *Thank the gods!*

"Guys, we can't stay here, it'll just wear us down, and we don't have the space to stop and think. If we can leave, I say we retreat and come up with a plan!" Makenna shouted as she half-carried Gil.

It was the exact same thing I had been thinking, but she said it faster than I'd thought it and put it into a plan of attack in under two seconds. I was so impressed that I couldn't even bother to be annoyed that she'd beaten me to what I was going to say.

Whatever. No time for that. We need to get moving—now.

"On me!" Evelyn shouted and sprinted toward the far wall.

Everyone followed Evelyn's lead and took off towards the rocks that separated us from the greater jungle.

Evelyn gracefully climbed over the rock and balanced atop it before mentioning us to hurry. "Let's get some distance between us before the giant spider catches up!"

I sped forward as the five of us took off into the woods. Reina and the other Arachne shouted at our backs, but I was too far away to clearly make out what was said, but I was betting it wasn't something nice. Rough overgrown grass and vines rose from the worn dirt path, and we were in the thick of the forest.

It didn't seem like Evelyn had a destination in mind as we all ran full sprint through the brush and heavy flora. Monstrous, primeval trees stood like stalwart bastions, watching over the forest which no human had ever trespassed.

We ran for a few miles, and even though it looked like Evelyn wanted to push deeper in, we couldn't keep running. Misumena was strong and devious, but it wasn't fast on its feet. We had time to stop and think up an idea or two.

"Guys, we can stop!" I shouted, nearly clothes-lining myself on a low hanging branch as I ran.

The others slowed up, and Evelyn turned back to face me. "Not yet. I haven't found the perfect spot yet."

"For what?" I asked, huffing as my heart rate settled.

"For an ambush. Back in the arena, we were playing by its rules, but once we draw it into our desired location, we can trap and kill it."

I glanced around at the endless sea of trees that stretched skyward with hundreds of thick, gnarled branches and shrugged my shoulders. "What's wrong with right here?"

Evelyn sighed, pinching her fingers just under the bridge of her nose. "Does someone other than me want to explain to her the basics of tactics and strategy?"

"Easy there, sis. I've got this. Don't have an aneurysm." Adam ran his hand over her shoulder and smiled widely at me. "She's really a nice person once you spend a few decades with her.

"But basically, this location is poor because it offers too much cover and open spaces," he said, motioning around him at the wide-open spaces and lush foliage which obscured anything beyond. "We couldn't control which area—Misumena, was it?—comes from, and if we can't control that, our entire ambush fails."

"So where would be a good place to set up be?" I asked.

"Somewhere with limited access and preferably some high ground," Adam said.

"Which is what I was searching for before you stopped us," Evelyn snapped.

I held my hands up in apology. "Let me help," I replied with a smile, already taking control of all the nearby insects in the forest.

"Do what you gotta do, Eris. But we need to hurry. We're losing our head start," Gil said as he struggled to heft his mammoth axe on his shoulder.

"Gil, you need to rest," Makenna said.

"Don't think it's going to let me stop and catch my breath. Don't worry about me. Once the bleeding debuff fades, I'll be right as rain."

I tried to pay attention to the conversation some more, but the magic already flowed through me, and I saw through my little ones' eyes and tried to find a spot that met Evelyn's demands.

It took a while, and I had to push the bounds of my consciousness as I pushed further out, but after a few minutes of searching, I found a place that would have to do.

"All right, follow me!"

Without waiting, I took off to my left through the dense foliage.

"Shit, wait for us."

"Eris, hold up! I'm short, godsdamn it!" Makenna shouted a second later.

I slowed my pace and let them all catch up. From surveying the area, I knew the best route to the location, and we made excellent time as my feet found the exact purchase they needed to keep my pace as I rushed over the roots and vines crawling from the earth.

It took us around fifteen minutes to reach the area, but it was even better than I'd seen through the eyes of my insects.

As we broke through the dense vegetation, the forest opened up around us. The roots and vines fell away to soft grass and then to gray rocks that lined the riverbank. Rushing water roared as the crystal blue waters swept over the large boulders that dotted the low points through the wide river.

The wide river snaked and disappeared behind an outcropping of trees a dozen yards away while the mouth of the river gaped and plunged down a steep drop, falling to crash in a shallow pool far below us.

It was serene, an oasis in an alien place, but I was in love with the beauty of it all.

"Not bad, little queen. It'll do as an ambush site."

Right, the fallen god that's chasing us. With one last forlorn look, I sighed and walked back to the others, who were in the midst of discussing a plan; the details of which were soon lost to me as I struggled to keep up with them.

I wouldn't add anything to the conversation anyway. I'm a sheltered girl, not a warrior or tactician. Even as the strongest entomancer, why didn't you ever teach me how to defend myself, Mother? Oh, right, you had such absolute confidence in yourself that you thought I'd never need it. Though even you couldn't save me in the end. Couldn't even save yourself.

I shuddered as ice dripped down my back and chilled the sweat from the muggy heat that beat down on us from the blazing sun. "Get out of your head and get to work," I said, slapping my cheeks and brushing of the phantom chill etched down my spine.

"What can I do to help?" I asked as I approached the huddled group.

They broke apart and looked me over. Four pairs of eyes studied me and assigned me a task instantly. "Wood, lots of it," Gil said. "Long, thick branches. As many as you can grab."

Makenna snickered, and everyone tilted their heads in confusion. She blushed and grinned. "It's nothing, ignore me."

"Hm," I muttered and walked back into the forest on a log hunt.

It didn't take long, as the forest was rife with plenty of wood for me to choose from. It took maybe twenty minutes of ambling about to find about as many logs and branches that I could carry, which turned out to be quite a lot.

Periodically I'd check my surroundings with magic to make sure Misumena hadn't crept up on us, but it was all clear. She would find us eventually; it was a certainty. She was probably already aware of us through our vibrations and smell, but she couldn't move her lumbering body quickly through the thick forest. We would likely hear her coming, but I wanted to make sure she couldn't surprise us.

I wobbled a bit as the strain of holding well over a hundred pounds of wood in my arms caught up with me. My muscles burned with fatigue, and my hands started shaking just as I reached the waterfall. I dropped them, and they clattered against each other as they tumbled from my weak grip.

"I need to exercise more," I said, leaning over, my hands on my knees as I panted, gasping for air.

"You did good, though. And let's be honest, running for your life is a full-body workout," Gil said as he came and knelt by me.

"How are you feeling?" I asked.

Gil smiled at me. "Better. Washed the worst of the blood off in the river, and the bleeding's all but stopped. So as long as I'm careful, I'll be fine."

He dug through the logs with a craftsman's eye and selected several of the longest and thickest branches I'd brought back.

"What are you going to do with them?" I asked.

"Well, with the location being what it is, our best bet is to lay a series of traps in an attempt to corral the big bug where we want her to go."

"Which is?"

"Right over the waterfall and onto some very sharp sticks."

"Though Misumena's carapace is thick. Do you think the sticks are sharp enough?"

Gil laughed, placing his very large hand atop my head, which should have been condescending, but it was actually very soothing, and I knew the giant bear only had the best of intentions with the gesture. "Hopefully, it'll work in our favor. The tensile strength of her carapace has already been weakened by my attacks, and theoretically, the distance of the waterfall should be far enough. That and Misumena's mass coupled with the speed as she falls should be enough to penetrate its hard shell."

I didn't really get what he was saying, and it must've shown on my face because he gave me a dopey grin and sighed.

"I don't have time for a physics lesson, but trust that Evelyn wouldn't concoct a bad plan."

I trusted them both implicitly, at least when it came to battle. Trusting Evelyn in other areas, maybe not so much.

Gil laid out his bundle of broken branches and pulled out a small kit wrapped in canvas. He unrolled it to reveal a slew of knives and other strange tools I'd never seen before. He picked the largest knife and began to shave slivers off the bark.

"Need to thank Duran again for his gift, though it's actually the first time I'm ever using it," he said before he froze and snapped his head around, eyes wide. "Which you didn't hear, right?"

"Not a word," I replied, doing my best to keep from laughing.

"You're too good for him," he said and turned back to focus on his work.

I smiled at him, and then it dropped as I was left standing around while everyone else was busy with something. *Guess I'll go and see if there's anything else I can do to help.*

***

It took well over an hour for Misumena to get close, which was more than plenty of time with Evelyn leading things. She ran us ragged as we worked furiously to get everything set up. By the time we were finished, I was dripping sweat and shaking with fatigue, but I was the lookout, and I had to keep my eyes and ears open for when she showed up.

The low thuds and rustling of trees were a dead giveaway, but I had already alerted the others. I'd spotted her through the eyes of a fly clinging to a vine nearly fifteen minutes ago and immediately told everyone.

Misumena ambled through the jungle as fast as she could, which was rather slow. But sooner than I'd have liked, she trampled over a few trees as she broke free from the woods. She had changed color slightly. Her translucent white body was now a very light shade of green that matched the forest that surrounded us. But it was wasted on us—we were in open ground, and her camouflage was useless against us.

Her body still bled from the wounds we'd inflicted, but her eyes were open and utterly enraged. As before, she didn't move fast. She inched forward towards us, rightfully cautious and calm. The small wounds we'd dealt her already had trickled, leaving light streaks of blue on her leg and chelicerae.

She didn't change her tactics, which I was thankful for.

Because it played right into Evelyn's hands.

An arrow launched from the massive tree just overhead from Misumena and struck the top of her head, taking one of her eyes. She writhed in absolute pain, letting out an inhuman squeal as one of her many eyes ruptured, spraying azure blood into the air.

Misumena lashed out in unhinged rage, slamming her leg against the tree Evelyn was in hard enough to crack the wood. Splinters of wood and bark coated her leg when she retracted it and scurried faster than she'd ever moved before. She tried to return to the forest, but Adam had prepared for that.

A shrill roar echoed through the valley as a great winged beast swooped down from the clouds. It was long, serpentine, draconic.

Thick scales the color of fresh moss glowed in the summertime air. It whipped its reptilian head around to glare at Misumena with too-bright yellow eyes. The beast had a thin, spiked tail and powerful legs with long ivory claws at the end, but it was missing arms. Where they should've been were two leathery wings that it tucked in as it dropped from the sky.

The wyvern was terrifying to behold, but having met an actual dragon once upon a time, it couldn't hold a candle to them.

Still, Adam assured us that it was the right creature for the job.

The wyvern dipped low, and like a bird of prey, extended its legs and sunk its talons deep into Misumena. The wyvern attempted to pick up Misumena, but the weight of the creature was many times more than the wyvern, and it couldn't lift it high. It groaned and let out another roar as it kept attempting to follow Adam's orders.

With a sudden twist, Misumena snapped its front legs and wrapped around the wyvern.

It struggled in vain against the powerful legs of Misumena, and it couldn't escape. It couldn't fight back as Misumena sank her fangs into the wyvern and began using her chelicerae to tear into the flesh of the dragonkin.

"Damn it!" Adam cursed as he held out his hand.

The wyvern dissolved and returned to its housing before Misumena could kill it.

"I thought you said it would work!" Evelyn screamed.

"How the hell was I supposed to know the thing was strong enough to take out Wynonna? She was my best flyer!"

"What about one of your golems?"

"I only brought Abby and Lawrence!"

Evelyn screamed while holding her breath, and her face turned a very unflattering shade of purple. "Just use the damn lava golem!"

"And burn down the entire forest?"

Evelyn mimed choking Adam and then threw her hands up. "Anyone got any brilliant ideas? I'm all ears."

Misumena was wary now, and she'd stopped her advance, afraid of any more surprises, but we had none. Our game plan was to get her over the waterfall using the wyvern, but now we were back to square one.

Well, nearly square one.

"I really hope this works," I said and took off toward Misumena.

Gil and the others shouted at me, but I ignored them and raced across the grass until I was right in front of Misumena. My chitin wormed from under my skin and crept over me in half a second. Fire burned in my limbs as the power of the Hive strengthened them. I leapt high, putting the entirety of my strength into the jump. I sailed over Misumena's head and landed on her abdomen. She reared back as my weight settled on her, and she tried to shake me off, but as soon as I had my balance, I formed spikes on the bottom of my feet to keep me anchored. They sank in only a fraction of an inch, but it was enough.

I knelt down on all fours and crawled my way toward her front. Misumena's legs couldn't reach me, and I didn't have any trouble as I reached her head. Evelyn's arrow had done its job and punctured through at least two of her eyes, but I needed her blind for what I was about to attempt.

I said a quick prayer to my goddess, because despite everything, Misumena was still of the Hive, and she deserved respect.

With a grimace, I summoned dagger-like shards of chitin in my hands and sank them into her remaining eyes. Her bloodcurdling scream tore at my ears, and I curled in on myself until the pain stopped swirling through my eyes. I wasn't in any danger of falling off, thanks to my chitin, so I just had to endure the screeching pain until it ended.

As blood gushed from her torn and gored eye sockets, I withdrew the chitin around my fingers and dug them into her. I reached for my control magic, let it spill through my fingers and enter Misumena. She was not a descendant of the Hive, was not a creature that technically fell under my bailiwick. She was a goddess of the Arachne, a being worshipped by tens of thousands at one point. But Misumena was Hive, and that put her under my control.

My consciousness slipped from my mind and traversed into Misumena. Her consciousness was expansive, a twisting, convoluted maze buried underwater. Misumena was aware of me, and she was furious that I dared to attempt to subjugate her. I hated it as much as she did; this was an intelligent being, not one of my little ones who had degraded to nothing but instinct. What I was doing was wrong, was the worst thing I'd ever tried to do, yet I had no choice. For us to succeed, Misumena had to die.

Her consciousness fought hard against me, but this was in my blood. It was what I was born for. No matter how wrong it was, I was good at it. I smothered her will against my own and suffocated her until she gasped for air. As the holes formed in her psyche, I slithered my way inside and broke her spirit.

As I finished working my way through her mind, she slumped over onto the ground. Her mind retreated in on itself as I bludgeoned my way through her. I'd done irreparable harm to her, and the brute force method had broken part of her psyche. I would have to control her manually if I wanted to get her to go over the edge.

Reina said dead, not disabled. If we want to beat her trial, this has to happen. I steeled myself and let all of the chitin in my body flow out of me and through my feet into Misumena. My body was light as a feather after the heavy chitin entered Misumena and molded itself over most of her body. I focused on the limbs and pushing my magic as far as it could go through her.

She rose on my command, but working two separate forms of magic at the same time was the most exhausting thing I'd ever done, and not even a couple seconds after I'd completed the spell, I started shaking as my mana fled from me.

Need to hurry. I lumbered the shell of Misumena toward the edge of the waterfall. Her legs scuttled into the river, and with each step, they splashed more water into the air to rain over me. When we reached the edge, I spared one last look at the Gloom Knights, who were rushing toward me, and I pushed Misumena over the ledge.

The fall was much shorter than it looked as I rode atop the nearly brain-dead carcass of a fallen god towards what I assumed would lead to my death.

My world was a blur of blue as the rushing water kept pace with us as we both aimed for the shallow and rocky depression at the bottom of the cliff.

With a bone-jarring, teeth-gnashing crunch, we hit the bottom, and I went sideways as my legs forgot how to work properly. My bones ached, and a dull, throbbing pain radiated up my entire body and squeezed until I nearly suffocated, but I was alive.

I was alive, and Misumena was not.

For a while, I lost track of time as I fought to keep consciousness as my head ached with the backlash of being inside Misumena while she died.

Before the fight, Gil had rappelled down the waterfall using a length of rope tied to a stake and had sunk his numerous giant spikes into the ground in a wide circle. His trap had been very effective.

Misumena landed on nearly half a dozen of the sharpened wooden sticks, four of which hadn't broken in half when she landed on them. They stuck through her body, the tips protruding through her carapace dripping with blood. One of them had come half an inch from sinking into my calf, and I heaved a sigh of relief, which turned into a hacking cough as even more pain coursed through my lungs.

But I was alive.

When my body stopped shaking with the brush from near death, I shivered as blistering cold water droplets from the spray of the waterfall hit the nape of my neck and slid down my back.

"Cold!" I shouted, nearly jumping out of my skin.

I shouldn't have moved, because the act revealed I was far weaker than I'd noticed at the time, and I sagged to my knees as a sharp pain thrummed through my head and my vision swam as a wave of dizziness rolled over me. *Mana depletion. I'm still holding onto the spells. Need to cancel them before I pass out.*

"Shit! Eris, are you okay!" Gil shouted.

Gil, along with the others, was standing at the edge of the waterfall, leaning over it to stare down at me.

"I'm...I'm fine," I said, my voice dripping fatigue.

A tide of emotions flooded through me as the wall between my mind and Sam's tore down. He was in tremendous agony.

Sam!

"Gil, call Sam!"

I let the magic controlling Misumena ooze out and fade away. The spell that allowed me to manipulate my chitin took longer to unravel, but the control spell was what took the most out of me. The chitin liquified and slowly started seeping back though Misumena and back to my body.

Misumena jerked in the throes of death, her arms spasming and coiling in on themselves.

Something hard poked me in the stomach, but I barely noticed. "Ow, that stung," I said, rubbing at my stomach.

Something warm and wet clung to my fingers. I glanced down at whatever had hit me.

One of Misumena's translucent legs was sticking into my abdomen. *I don't think that should be there.* A low ache spread from my stomach to my spine, and I couldn't hold my body upright anymore.

Something caught in my throat, and I coughed, trying to dislodge it. A river of blood poured from my lips. *What? What's happening?*

My mind caught up with my body, and I screamed through a mouthful of iron. A frigid winter settled over me, and then nothing else mattered. I was tired and wanted to sleep.

So incredibly tired.

Endless sleep called me, and I answered.

CHAPTER 17 - HEIST OF THE CENTURY

Sampson

For the second time that day, I found myself in front of the Iron Cathedral. Though not hitting as powerfully as the first time, its majestic beauty still wowed me. Mika and the hired help followed behind us, keeping a good distance so as not to arouse suspicion. By the time we arrived at the gate that led to the walkway to the church, the streets were barren.

The nearby shopping districts were closed, and the nobility were at home or one of the numerous parties we passed walking up the cobbled street. The loud music coming from inside the houses was muffled only by the heavy stone walls.

Once we were in front of the gate, I double checked that the street was empty, and trusting my gut that no one was watching us, Raven and I hopped the chest-high stone wall. The others would follow in ten minutes and keep an eye on thigs while the two of us stole the Heart.

Raven landed beside me with practiced quietness and slid me a sly grin. "You ready for this, Duran?"

"As well as I can be. Just have my back, and I'll have yours."

"Let's do this," she said and crouched about fifteen feet in front of me.

With a low ruffling of many feathers, Raven transformed into her bird form. Her raven form was smaller this time, just over ten feet in length. She bent low to the ground to hide her large shadow and tilted her head towards me.

"Hurry and get on before someone sees us."

I climbed atop her and nestled in the crook just before her wings expanded. Raven didn't wait for me to settle before she followed her wings and launched off the ground.

We flew into the air, but instead of flying higher, she kept low and glided, rather than flew. Raven only flapped her wings when it was absolutely necessary, and in only a few minutes, the Iron Cathedral loomed over us.

"Circle around. The window we want is on the other side," I told Raven.

The plans of the church were clear, and I knew exactly where I needed to enter to give us the best shot at success. Raven flapped her wings once more and rose to the roof of the cathedral. She landed on one of the few non-gabled spots, and as soon as her feet hit the stone, I slid off her.

The location where she landed was part of the main cathedral itself, and it meant we would have to do a bit of climbing to reach our entrance point, but there were precious few places for a bird of her size to land on the heavily sloped roof.

I took a look around while Raven shifted back to her human form. We had a long and thin, flat roof that spanned the majority of the church but slanted on all sides, which would lead to a long fall and a short stop if we went over the edge. Risking a glance, I scuttled on my knees as a gust of wind slapped at my face.

High above us was one of the many vents that led to surface and brought fresh air to the underground kingdom. I peered over the edge at the rocky ground a hundred feet below us. Large slate-gray tiles lined the slanted roof and were thick enough to offer handholds to grip if I somehow slipped off, but even as the renowned craftsmen the dwarves were, I didn't want to trust my life to a roof tile.

"We need to be careful crossing. One wrong slip, and that's it for us."

"For you, maybe. I can fly," Raven replied, a snarky smile on her lips.

"Then you're responsible for catching my clumsy ass if I fall."

We both laughed for a second before the realities of our job wiped the smiles from our faces. *No sense waiting around, let's get this job done and get the hell out of here.* My pep talk did nothing for my hammering heart and nerves. Sweat rose on the nape of my neck as a chill that had nothing to do with the cool air sent goosebumps down my arms.

I looked over at Raven and despite the fire in her irises, the fine hair on her arms stood on end. I reached over and took her hand in mine, giving it a squeeze. "We've got this."

She gulped and nodded.

"Stay back until I give the all clear," I said as I let go of her hand and pulled a potion from my inventory. Lightstep was lime and grain alcohol with a bittersweet undertone, but I drank it with a grimace and crept over the stone roof.

Lightstep wouldn't stop me going over the edge, but it would help muffle my steps, and it gave me more stability over uneven ground.

I moved slowly, cautious of anything out of place. It wasn't likely, but I wouldn't put it past the dwarves to have trapped the roof. But as I slunk along, keeping as low to the ground as I walked on all fours, I found no traps or any detection magic.

Foolish of them—and a grievous mistake on their part. Though maybe the sides of the building are trapped. Not many thieves have access to a raven shifter, I imagine. As I reached the end of the stone, I waved Raven over and planned my next move.

The end of the roof sloped down about ten feet and ended in about two inches of stone that formed the lip of the building.

"Not much room for error," I whispered as Raven caught up and peered over the edge.

"Better not fuck up, then."

Too true. Not waiting for my brain to catch up with my actions, I vaulted the stone and slid down the tile. The rough edges dug into my side, leaving bruises as I dropped down. My right foot hit the side of the lip just fine, but I misjudged the left, and it glanced off the edge and sailed down to open air.

"Shit!" I cursed as my weight shifted and I found myself falling.

I scrambled, flailing to find any purchase I could as my body tempted gravity. My hands grabbed hold of one of the tiles in desperation, and I stopped falling, but my body was halfway on the roof and halfway off. I was supporting myself on one foot as I gripped the stone tile.

And I thought this was going to be boring. I lifted up as gently as I could, but as I put most of my weight into my arms, the stone cracked and broke off.

I hung onto the broken half, still attached to the building despite the sharp edges slicing into my fingertips. The cracked part of the tile tumbled off my arm and into open air right down towards the rock below me.

If it hit the ground, that would be it for us. The crack would be loud enough to alert anyone inside, and our job would be over before it even began. I had one chance, and as the chunk of thick tile fell by me.

I kicked with all of my might.

My foot connected with the slate. The vibrations shook though my bones, and I accidentally bit my tongue. But I sent the tile flying dozens of feet away from the cathedral. It landed far enough away that only the hushed echo of the stone shattering reached my ears, and I sighed in relief.

"Are you okay?" Raven asked in a hushed tone.

"Peachy-fucking-keen."

"Then stop hanging off the building like an asshole already."

I hastily climbed back up and slid over to make room for Raven. She slid down on her back, and as soon as her feet touched the lip, I thrust my arm out to stop her from going over the edge.

"Holy crow! Maybe your method was better, though I'm not complaining."

"Why?"

"Look where your hand is."

My hand was holding quite firmly to Raven's right breast. It was a complete accident, and I pulled away quickly, not thinking about how incredibly soft it was or how it filled up my hand far more than Eris's petite chest.

"Ah, I'm sorry."

"Don't be."

Raven smiled at me. The light from the dim mana crystal shimmered off her midnight hair as it fluttered in the stiff breeze. I ignored how radiant she looked and focused on getting into the cathedral.

I couldn't think about her words at that moment, not when I was about to infiltrate and attempt to steal Lachrymal's Heart. *Don't think about how pretty she is or the fact that we actually get along really well. This is really not the time.*

I was really tired of having only two inches separating me from death. "Get your head in the game."

"It is in the game," she replied. "I think you're the one who's flustered."

I didn't have a retort; she was right. I shook my head and focused on the job. Anything less, and we would die.

We lapsed into silence and skirted the edge of the cathedral until we came to the stained-glass windows that looked down into the Vault of Tears.

The ledge widened to allow for room to change any chipped or cracked panels in the stained glass. I paused and pulled out both my burglar's kit and wraithsight potion. There wasn't enough room for both of us on the windowsill, so Raven still had to cling to the side like a frightened animal while I unrolled the kit and drank the potion.

Wraithsight went down sweet. Caramel, honey, and vanilla formed the base with the bitter aftertaste of gin. My sight slowly dimmed, darkness creeping in from the edges, but an ethereal green leapt from the shadows as the potion took hold. Figures in the main room of the cathedral stood out from the backdrop.

Six guards in the next room, two right by the door. If we make any noise, they're liable to come running. I focused on the window, and nothing stood out to my enchanted sight. *No enchanted traps—or physical ones, for that matter. All right. I've got five minutes. I want to make sure we're in safely before it runs out.*

I selected a blade specifically designed to cut glass from the oilskin tool roll and began the painstaking task of removing each pane of glass from the grooved lead pattern with the knife to make a hole wide enough for us to climb through. Once the glass was out of the way and safely stored in my inventory, I began knocking the cames out by wrapping a cloth around the lead and breaking it apart.

It took over two minutes to do, but we had our way in.

I slipped in while Raven perched on the sill waiting for me to move. I had no room to maneuver. If I stepped an inch forward, I'd hit open air. My target was the beam directly to my right. It jutted out seven feet away and just over my head. *If I miss, it's game over. Well...let's roll the dice.* I crouched and jumped.

For a second, I hung over open air. Twenty feet below me lay my death if I crashed to one of the pews, but I'd timed it right, and I hit the stone beam.

My fingers gripped the coarse stone, and I hung there by just my fingertips. Once the jarring stop settled, I pulled myself up and over the edge. My feet found holds, and I was about to haul myself onto the beam when a soft prickle ran over my left hand.

I leaned up, and with wraithsight active, the six magic traps were visible to my heightened eyes. My hand was mere centimeters from touching one and spelling our doom. *I didn't think they'd have trapped the beams, but it's what I'd have done. I'm just lucky the vibrations from my jump didn't set them off.* I had to deal with them before I could climb up; there wasn't any room where I could ascend that wouldn't set off the traps.

"What are you doing? You need help?"

"Stay there!" I said, panic nearly causing me to shout. "The beam is trapped; likely all of the others are as well. Need to deal with them before I can climb up."

Raven glanced around trying to see what I could and failed. She huffed and crouched down, her raven wings coming out to rest around her like a cloak. "I'll catch you if you fall."

"Be careful! The gusts from your wings could set off the traps, and from the Scriptwork, these are nasty little bastards. Paralysis fields. Petty black magic, but effective this high up."

"Can you nullify them? Do you even have magic?"

I've got something better. I smiled to myself and activated *Aura of the Antimage*. The invisible bubble expanded in a flash, and as it touched the magical traps, they popped with a subtle hiss as the antimagic wave swept through the room.

I don't think I got all the traps; the radius wasn't enough to go through the entire room, but it was enough for us to reach Lachrymal's Heart.

I swung up and onto the ledge and crawled forward to let Raven get on. She extended her wings and jumped, rising to smirk at me before lowering gently onto the beam.

"Do you want to do the heavy lifting?"

"You're doing a fine job all on your own, darling."

I tuned her out and focused on my prize. The Heart was in the center of the room, only a couple dozen feet in front and below me. I slid around the support beams and crept along the spider's web of stone until we were right above it.

"We need to hurry. If the person who set those traps is awake, then they felt their mana return to them. I'd rather believe they're awake and are on their way. So that speeds us up."

Raven nodded. "What do you need from me?"

"Stay up here while I grab the Heart. I'll need you to pull me back up when I have it."

With a final glance around the room and beyond to get a read on the guards, wraithsight faded, and the darkened room lit up once more as my normal sight returned. A slight pressure settled in my head before fading away. *Any more potions, and I'll get sick. Won't risk it unless I have no choice.* I pulled out my burglar's kit and about fifty feet of rope.

I measured the distance and cut the length I needed. Lying down on my stomach, I tied the rope around the beam and knotted it tight. I gave the rope a few tugs to test the weight, and then I added a loop for my foot to rest when I descended the rope.

When the preparations were complete, I tossed the rope over the edge and gripped it tight. My nerves stood on end.

"Ready?" Raven asked.

"As I'll ever be," I said and lowered down.

The coarse rope dug into my palms as soon as my weight pressed into it, but I grunted away the agitation and began my descent. Heights had never been an issue for me, but as I lowered down at the slate floor far below me, I could understand the fear that plagued people. I ignored the urge to close my eyes, fought down my nerves, and before I knew it, I was at the end of the rope and Lachrymal's Heart was right in front of me.

It was even more beautiful up close and twice as terrifying as from afar.

As if knew my intentions, the insidious infrasound broke through whatever resistance the Aspect had given me. It increased in pitch until it vanished for a second. Pain vibrated through my brain, and warm blood poured from my ears, my eyes and nose. It began to descend, and it went after my own heart. Something tore inside me, and blood filled my lungs.

What the hell is happening?

The torment pulling apart my organs only continued, and my strength abandoned me. I was being torn apart from the inside, and I had to hurry, or I was going to die.

I reached out and put my hand on the Heart.

Something popped into existence in my interface as whatever force that was rupturing my body stalled for a time.

Do you wish to take Lachrymal's Heart?
Yes/No

Yes!

Do you accept The Weeping God's Curse?
Yes/No

What? A curse? Then it clicked. *This is why the others failed. This is the surprise I wasn't expecting.* The prompt hung in the air in front of me, just waiting for my answer. I had no clue what it would do, but I knew it would only hurt me. But I had no choice, I had to accept it.

Yes.

Warning! Curse of The Weeping God Active.

-25 to all Main Stats for the duration of bearing Lachrymal's Heart.

-50% Battle Fatigue

Acquired the Wrath of the Chosen: Lachrymal's Chosen deal 100%
damage to the bearer.

Well, shit. The emerald shank to the size of my palm and vanished into my inventory. As soon as it vanished, the infernal whispering disappeared, and the Weeping God's Curse activated.

I tried to get ready for it, but I was woefully unprepared for the further drain on my stats. Weakened from the damage to my organs and the loss of my strength, the rope slipped from my fingers, and I fell.

The ground came for me faster than I could blink. I tilted when I fell off the rope and sideswiped the rising obelisk that formerly housed the pilfered gemstone in my pocket.

My ribs broke upon the stone, and then I tumbled off and smashed into the thick pews, bashing my head in the process.

The world didn't matter anymore, the job didn't matter anymore, all that mattered was the agony that ripped me apart. I forgot how to breathe, or my lungs forgot for me. I might've blacked out for a second, but the pain was so intense that it woke me back up.

My health bar flashed a bloody crimson in my eyes, the sliver of my life draining to the abyss.

Let it. I just wanted the pain to stop.

A floodgate opened in my mind. It was Eris, and she'd broken through the block I'd placed on our connection. The mere thought of Eris was enough to snap me out of my pain. I could barely move, but I'd have crawled through the nine hells themselves for her.

I brought a health potion to my lips and downed it, not caring that I would mostly likely trigger potion sickness. I had a job to do, a wife to return to; death would only get in the way.

My health stopped just before death came to collect and returned to the green after a second or two. My bones and organs stitched back together, and the pain vanished as a timer appeared in the corner of my vision, counting down from three hours.

Knew I'd hit it. Oh, well.

"Are you okay?"

"Yeah I'm fi—"

My heart stopped.

I sank to my knees, not understanding how the potion failed. My world went sideways, and as my body shut down, I realized it wasn't my body that was dying.

It was Eris.

I was just along for the ride.

Terror struck like lightning through me, but I wasn't concerned for myself. I didn't care about my life, not when Eris's was also on the line. I could come back if I died—she couldn't.

No, no, no, no, no. Not again, please not again. I'll do anything. I can't take anymore, please, just take me!

I begged. I didn't care who I begged to, the gods, Ouroboros, or even the god that abandoned Earth and left us to die. I pleaded to them all to spare her and take me instead.

I fell back to the ground and stared up at the ceiling, at the intricate stonework and stained glass. I stared at Raven and her panicked face as her eyes filled with worry, for my sake.

I was wrong to mistreat you the way I did. And for that, I'm truly sorry.

Raven jumped and used her wings to glide down to me. she dropped to her knees and pulled my head into her lap.

"What's wrong? What can I do?" she asked, pleading.

There was nothing to do, I couldn't rescue Eris, could only hope and pray for a miracle to save my beloved.

'I've done what I can to slow the progress, but I can't stop it. If she dies, we both follow," the Aspect said.

For too many long moments, I hung in a state between life and death, one foot in both.

And then my heart started beating again.

My body started working properly, and I took in a heaping gulp of oxygen. I sat up quickly and coughed until my throat ached.

It was subtle, but her presence was still in the back of my mind. Eris was still alive.

She was healing and would be okay.

I nearly fainted as relief washed over me. I was lightheaded and took a knee as my mind tingled with the rush of chemicals flooding it. *Thank the gods. Whoever or whatever saved her. Thank you.*

I sat up off the ground as my breathing returned to normal. Raven's concern turned to relief as I stood on my own.

"What just happened?"

"A lot, all at once. Eris nearly died, and I was cursed by this fucking bauble. But talk later, let's get the hell out of here." I looked up at the rope dangling a dozen feet above us and had to reconsider our escape plan. "Can you lift me up?"

"Not in this form, and there isn't enough room for me to transform right now."

I cursed and tried to figure out how I was going to climb up to the rope, when a thud echoed through the Vault of Tears.

I whirled around to find that we hadn't been as quiet as I'd have liked when my broken body landed. *Shit. They'll unlock the door in seconds.* I ignored the pain wracking through my body and sprinted to the door and shoved the nearest pew in front of it.

Won't hold them for long. We need to leave.

But I quickly realized one thing.

There wasn't a way for us both to escape. But there was a way for one of us to.

"Take this," I said, passing Raven my invisibility potion and lowering my voice. "The Heart curses the bearer. Can you handle it?"

"If you can bear it, then so can I."

I passed it to her, and she took the palm-sized emerald without hesitation.

Alert! The Weeping God's Curse has been removed.
Alert! The Wrath of the Chosen has been removed.

Raven grimaced and slumped her shoulders as she accepted the curse. But she kept standing. "Don't worry, my level is in the upper eighties. I'm probably stronger than you."

"Good, now go. Fly out of here and use the potion to escape Aldrust. Take the emerald back to Magnus."

Her grin slipped from her lips. "What about you?"

I turned away from her to the door that would open any second. "If you get the chance, find Eris and tell her I love her, and I'll see her as soon as I can."

"I'm not going to leave you to die here!" she shouted, running over to me.

"Go! Now. That's an order from your master!"

As if I'd shocked her still, she froze. Distress twisted her face as tears welled in her eyes. She bowed to me and shot up into the air. With one lingering glance, she flew through the broken window and out into the night.

"All right. Aspect, let's give them hell."

'I'm not one to take orders, knight. But I happen to like that one. Let's feast on their blood!"

The door burst open, knocking aside the heavy pew I'd shoved in front of it.

All six of Lachrymal's Chosen stood before us as they swept into the room, weapons drawn.

Oh, hell.

They took one look at me and then at the obelisk.

"Defiler!"

"Thief!"

"Forsaken!"

They all shouted at me, wide-eyed that the relic of their god was in the hands of a human. My hand went to my sword. *This isn't going to be easy.*

I'd fought similar odds before, but my past foes were chumps compared to Lachrymal's Chosen. They were the elite of the elite, warriors through and through. They deserved my respect, but I was about to give them my blade instead.

Warning! Forceful activation of Ability.
Chitin Armor.

A burning itch spread over my body as the chitin poured from beneath my skin. As black and glossy as an oil slick, it covered my body and wormed over my head. As it slithered over my hair and ears, a bright green slid over my eyes. The dim room lit up like I'd lit a torch, and I could make out every individual face of the warriors in front of me.

Most of them were men, but two of them were women. All of them held the rugged confidence only years of combat could grant.

They took a step back, surprise blossoming on their faces as I changed.

The Aspect took control and laughed, a grating, malicious laugh that only hinted at my actual voice. *"Come to me, mortals. Let me taste the marrow of your lives!"*

I drew my sword. Its muted black blade slid wordlessly from its sheath. The leaves of my hilt danced ethereally as the light hit it, and together, me and the monster in my heart went to war.

Chapter 18 - Another Time, Another Place

Eris

I wanted to sleep, but screaming and violent shaking wouldn't let me rest.

Every time I closed my eyes, I was roughly shoved awake. I opened my bleary eyes to Gil kneeling over me, the others in the background.

"Eris, godsdamn it, stay awake!"

"Don't wanna," I said, waving him off, or I tried, but I couldn't move.

Something lifted me off the ground, and then the cold blanket that draped around me was yanked off and replaced by a burning pain radiating from my stomach.

"It hurts."

"I know it does, but just hold on."

"It hurts, it hurts, it hurts." I wanted to scream; the pain was too much.

Five points of fire flared across my stomach, and I gurgled a half groan. "Looks like her chitin is plugging the hole and keeping her spine from separating. it's the only reason she's still alive, but blood is pooling inside her. She needs a health potion, and quickly!" Evelyn said.

"Looks like it," a new voice said from somewhere outside of my line of sight. I couldn't see them, could only stare at the too bright sky. "But she sustained the injury during the trial, and potions are forbidden."

"Reina! Damn you! She'll die if we don't do anything!" Gil shouted, his heavy footsteps thudding away from me.

"Then she dies and proves she was unworthy of the mantle of Hive Queen."

"No. Fuck you, I'm not going to watch one of my friends die in front of me. You can go to hell!"

Metal cleared leather, and everything got quiet fast. *I'm so sleepy, but I need to stay awake. Gil told me I had to stay awake, and he wouldn't lie to me.* I fought the exhaustion and mana depletion and tried to summon my magic. I could heal my injury easily with a spell, but I only had drops left—not enough to control a single spider, let alone heal a grievous injury.

I was dying, and there was nothing I could do about it.

And the others were a second away from going to war with the Arachne to stop it.

"Stop!" I yelled, spitting out a mouthful of blood. I wasn't going to let them kill themselves to help me. If I was dying, so be it. I was already dragging Sam with me; I couldn't bear anyone else. *I'm sorry, my love. But you can come back, and that's enough for me. I'm sorry I won't get to see you again. I love you.*

I used the last of my dwindling magic to form a single blade of chitin down my finger, and I raised my hand to take my life so no one else would have to suffer for me.

I plunged the blade toward my throat, only for resistance to stop my hand just before I pierced my skin.

Evelyn let out a throaty chuckle, her iron grip wrapped around my arm. "None of that now, little queen. Don't be so dramatic."

"I won't let anyone else get hurt for me," I said as I struggled like a mewling kitten against her grasp.

"And you won't," she said, turning her head away from me. "No potions is the only rule, correct?"

"Correct," Reina replied, her voice smug, superior.

"That's all I need to know." Evelyn knelt over me and pulled my head into her lap. I stared at her ethereal form though half-closed eyelids while the chill returned. Pins and needles crept up my fingers and toes, and once more, sleep called for me.

Evelyn brought her hand back into view, and she clutched a thin knife in her hand. She brought it to her wrist and split her skin with a fluid slice. Blood welled from her pale skin, but the color was off. It was tinged with fire like a ripe blood orange. It dripped warmth over my cheek, and she lowered her wrist to my mouth.

"What are you doing?" Reina asked.

"Not using a potion." Evelyn's skin pressed against my teeth, and a drip of succulent blood slid down my mouth. It was warm, rich, and utterly delicious. It put even Sam's tangy blood to shame, and I knew beyond anything else that I wanted more.

I opened my mouth wide and dug my teeth into her flesh, breaking the skin to spill even more of her delicious blood over my lips. It invigorated me like nothing I'd experienced before, and I jolted awake, wrapping my hands over her forearm.

Something shifted inside of me, and a warmth spread through my veins as my organs righted themselves and my spine fused back together. It was so wonderous to feel my body again that I didn't question what was happening to me.

And then my mind slipped into the past.

The darkness that accompanied the Mnemosyne was too similar to the bleak, unending void, and like I had when I tasted of Sam, I froze, my heart stopping as unhinged terror threatened my sanity. I curled in on myself as the familiar loneliness crept from the furthest reaches of my mind. I opened my mouth to cry out, but before I could, I was falling.

The memory slunk in with bright tones. I was back in the world Sam came from; that much I knew. It was too different from what I'd come to know as my reality.

The buildings were tall, lifeless gray masses that rose higher than the birds could fly. It unsettled me to have them looming overhead as soft moonlight reflected off shattered glass in the broken windows above me.

The smooth, black street I stood on came to a crossroads where three people stood, their heads darting around as they scanned the darkness for something I couldn't see. Two of them were male, one taller than the other by just a few inches. The tall one was cute, bordering on handsome, but still had too much youthfulness in his face. His dark hair hung past his gray eyes, and he brushed a tanned, muscular hand across his bangs.

I didn't know him, but I felt like I did, something about him was incredibly familiar.

The shorter one was someone I knew I'd never met before.

He was thin, wiry, with shaggy blond hair only a shade or so lighter than mine that framed his sharp face. His green eyes were hidden behind a pair of square glasses, and the beginnings of stubble sprouted from his jawline.

They pointed to a building and shuffled across the road, their movements slowed by their armor. It was obviously armor, but not like I'd seen before. It was sleek, muted black that covered their chests and left most of their upper arms bare. Strapped to each forearm was more of the material, but I had no clue what it was.

In their hands were weapons, that much I knew, but they were blocky, a glossy gray, and they hefted them with respect.

As they crossed the street, the final member of the party checked behind them and followed after.

She was tall, almost the same height as the tall boy, but off by an inch. She had the same dark hair, but hers fell past her chest. Familial resemblance reflected in her features that she shared with the boy, but her eyes were shot through with jade rather than the muted gray of the boy's.

I knew who she was, who they both were then. Because I was seeing Evelyn's memories, the girl had to be Evelyn, and the boy Adam. Gone was the pale skin, the silver hair and golden eyes that I'd come to associate the twins with, but as I stared, it was undoubtably them.

The blond boy shouted in alarm. "Over there!"

The group raised their weapons as a pale, monstrous creature leapt onto a broken, red machine with metallic wheels. It crumpled the metal and let out a piercing howl from its too-wide jaws. Its needle teeth sparkled from the light of the moon down its throat.

It was a ghoul, one of the creatures that destroyed Sam's world and took the person he loved most from him.

A shrill blast of pain rang through my ears as fire bloomed from the weapon Adam carried. A heavy gout of flames shot faster than I could follow and stuck the ghoul. It hissed a wretched scream as the fire blistered and blackened its skin as it spread up its shoulder to the side of its face. In a second, half of its body was a mess of oozing black skin that burst open with vile white blood as it spilled down its legs.

"We're too far away," Evelyn said, her voice taking away any doubt that it was her.

"Retreat?" the blond boy asked.

"Nick, that's a goddamn great plan, but we've got company," Adam replied, motioning with his weapon to the shadows near a decrepit building that sold something called "pizza."

Four or five new creatures appeared, covered in darkness.

They resembled the ghouls only in their hideousness. They looked human, but like walking skeletons. Their pallid, emaciated gray skin stretched tightly over their pronounced bones. Lanky arms ended in five wickedly sharp ivory claws while they stared at the three with soulless, pitch-black eyes.

A low hiss rolled from their mouths as they shambled out into the light.

"Shit. We've already got a ghoul to deal with—I really didn't want to add the fucking grim on top of it."

"Run?" Nick asked.

"Run," the twins agreed.

They turned as one and sprinted to the nearest building, a towering giant with the words Windigo Industries written in giant white letters. They hopped through a broken window and ran down a white-tiled hallway with a lamp overhead that shone with bright light.

Adam stopped, turned, and tossed a small, cylindrical canister down the hallway as the monsters burst into the room.

The canister exploded with a raging inferno. A torrential fire filled the hallway and started eating through the walls and ceiling. The charging ghouls stopped in their tracks, petrified by the flames, but the skeletal grim kept their pace as they dashed through the flames after their prey.

Evelyn and the others rounded a corner as the monsters chased after them.

The room they entered was long and thin with an equally long and thin wooden table surrounded by plush chairs attached to little balls that rolled out of the way as the three of them shoved the table towards the door.

The grim ran headlong into the table and toppled over it. Adam, Nick, and Evelyn raised their weapons, and my hearing failed me.

Rapid explosions punished my ears as I fought to keep my eyes open. Bursts of blood splattered from the grim as chunks of gray flesh disappeared in seconds as whatever weapons they wielded ended the monsters' lives.

Five shredded corpses lay strewn in pieces with muddy blood coating the doorframe and wall.

"Damn, James. These new guns of yours are something else," Nick said, turning to Adam.

"Thanks, though I couldn't have made them without your help."

"Enough standing around, guys. We need to get out of this death trap. That ghoul is still outside, and if there's one, there's a dozen more nearby. We need to grab what we came for and get back to the lab. Sunrise is too far off for us to be out right now."

"You're right," Adam said, looking down at his wrist. A circular silver object wrapped around and lit up in a bright orange color as he held it close to his face. "Edna, scan the building and show us how to get to the vault."

"Of course, Master Bell. The door behind you leads to the elevators. The room you seek is fifteen floors down. I've already hacked into the system and opened the doors," a soft-spoken woman's voice replied.

The light from the device at his wrist faded away, and he shouldered his gun. "You heard the lady. Let's get our asses in gear."

My vision distorted as they left the room and the darkness crept back in.

I didn't know what to make of what I'd seen. I didn't understand most of it; Earth was a strange and chaotic place filled with danger and horrors beyond my understanding, but its technology was truly beyond my comprehension. I was lost in the implications of talking guide spirits and weapons that could obliterate anything in their path. It made my head spin.

And that was just the first memory. There would be two more, and I didn't know if my mind could take it.

The second memory came slowly. I found myself in a gray room with nearly a dozen tables strewn with bits of things I had no names for, huge hunks of metal and thin copper wires wrapped in bright colors and hundreds of other similar things that piled up on the tables as they stretched around the room. Adam was seated at a chair in the middle, hunched over the only table that was remotely clean. His hands and clothes were stained with grease as he held a tube with a spout that sparked with blinding white fire.

There was a knock on the door, and Evelyn walked in. She wore a long white coat over dark pants and a thin purple shirt. She strutted across the workshop and leaned heavily on Adam as she peeked at whatever he was working on.

"No luck?" she asked.

"Not even a scratch," he said, setting down the fire-making device and picking up a pair of metal tongs. "I even poured thermite over it, and it didn't even get hot, so I don't know what to make of them, but watch this."

The tongs clacked together as he picked something up and held it away from him. Clutched at the center of the tongs was a small orange crystal. It was a deep, rich amber, rough cut, and it glowed even in the dim light of the room.

He took the amber shard over to a separate table where a nearly identical crystal sat on the bare table, waiting.

He placed the new crystal next to the one lying on the table, and before he could even move the tongs, the amber shards pulled closer to each other and melded together like liquid glass, leaving only a single larger crystal in their place.

"The hell?" Evelyn asked, taking a step back.

"Yeah, beats the hell out of me. That shouldn't be possible, and I don't understand how, but that's not all that I discovered."

"More surprises?"

Adam leaned over in his chair and grabbed a large mallet off the table next to him and whacked the large crystal. It shattered with a resounding crack, and slivers of the gem went over the table as it broke in half.

The two halves and the countless minuscule pieces shuddered, and the slivers pulled toward the larger shards. And like nothing had happened, the two crystals sat whole and unbroken.

"This is impossible," Evelyn said, staring wide-eyed at the gems on the table.

"Yesterday I'd have said as much, but I can't deny what's staring me in the face."

"What do we do with them?"

"Nothing," Adam said, picking them up with the tongs and placing them into individual cloth bags he pulled from his pocket. "I don't trust the Narghuul, and I'm damn sure not just going to follow along with their plans for us.

"No, we take them to the bunker. We lock them up and keep them safe until we decide to use them—if we decide to use them."

"All right, brother. I'll trust your gut on this."

The bags disappeared into Adam's pocket as the memory faded away.

I couldn't put my finger on it, but even though I'd never seen them before, I knew whatever those gems were, they were important.

The final memory came in quickly.

The whitewashed walls of the room shook. Dust rained from the cracks in the ceiling as it buckled. Desks and chairs toppled to the ground as a low pounding thrummed with each pulse of my heart.

Evelyn and Adam were in the center of the room, their guns in their hands as they stood back to back.

"Why the hell did I let you talk me into following you?" Evelyn asked as something flashed by the cracked, grimy window that looked out to midnight sky.

"Because it was this or death. Edna said this building had the best bet of keeping us safe."

"Actually, I said that this location offered a thirty-two percent chance of survival, which was marginally higher than any of the surrounding buildings," Edna chimed in from the device at Adam's wrist.

"Fucking perfect," Evelyn said, her gun booming as another flash crawled over the window. There was a spurt of blood, a long howl of pain, and then a bone-crunching thud a second later. "They're going to swarm us in the next five minutes if we don't get out of here!"

"And go where? The street's crawling with dozens of them!"

Adam pressed a button on the side of his gun, and it changed with whine. A ghoul I hadn't seen crawled into the room, and Adam jammed the front of his gun into its mouth and pulled the trigger.

It exploded into a cloud of ash and fire.

"Damn it, you know what we have to do."

Evelyn nodded, ejecting a slim block from the bottom of her gun and replacing it with an identical one. "I don't like it, don't know what it'll mean for our future, but it's this or not having a future at all."

Adam let out a heavy sigh, sounding ancient as he pulled the bags holding the gems from his pocket. He tossed one to Evelyn and held the other in his palm. "You ready for this?"

"Nope," she said and tipped the bag over, letting the bright amber gemstone rest in her hand.

As soon as it touched her bare skin, it began to glow. A bright orange light radiated from the center of the crystal, and the same light pulsed from Adam's hand as well.

"Shit!" Evelyn hissed as the shard began smoldering and seared her flesh as it burrowed into her palm. With one last grunt of pain, the gems was gone, leaving behind a single thick scar in each of their palms.

"By the nine kings of hell, that hurt like a bitch," Adam said, clutching his hand.

"Agreed, but is that it?"

"I don't kn—" Adam began but let out a low groan of pain.

"James!" Evelyn shouted and took a step toward Adam, but she sunk to her knees in pain.

They both stared at each other, and for a split second, their eyes light up a bright gold, the golden tint I'd come to know them by.

Before they could speak again, bright orange light spilt from their chests and illuminated through their veins. They both doubled over, whimpering as the light grew until even I had to avert my eyes.

The light built and built until it became a blazing white and obliterated my entire view.

It threw me out of the Mnemosyne, and I bolted upright, gasping, holding back a scream.

I was in a room that I'd never been in before. The natural wood walls and iron chandelier that hung above my head reminded me of Reina's palace; the hand-carved furniture matched as well.

"You're finally awake," Reina said from beside me. She was sitting in a chair with a hand-sewn green cushion, reading a book bound in smooth bark. She looked up and put down the book as I sat up properly. "You've been out for a while."

Before I could even form a reply, an itch crept from the back of my head. It was panic, an overwhelming amount of panic. I smiled despite the worry my bonded was feeling. *Sam. I'm all right. I promise, my love.* I poured as much love and reassurance I could to him, and when his sweeping relief swept over me, I knew he knew I was okay.

Reina noted my smile and drew her lips up to mirror me. "Your human lover was quite worried about you. He kept 'calling' the big, ebony human, trying to make sure you were okay. Though from what I heard, he has much bigger problems to worry about right now than you."

"What?" I asked, nearly shouting at her. "What's going on with Sam?"

"I don't care."

Reina rose from her chair and place a firm hand on my shoulder as I attempted to get out of bed.

"Not so fast, Eris. We still have much to discuss."

I calmed down and checked over myself, making sure I was okay. It was then that I realized I was clean—and completely nude.

"Where are my clothes?"

"Ruined, given the giant hole in them. I'll have some fresh ones brought in for you once we finish talking."

"Okay…what do you need to talk to me about?"

She sat next to me on the bed, her body turned toward me. "You accomplished something I thought impossible for you. I was sure you were going to die at Misumena's hands, but you surprised me and killed her instead. First and foremost, you have passed the trial and are worthy of the title Hive Queen. Even Aliria couldn't defeat Misumena, though she was alone."

"So you'll help us?" I asked.

"We'll see. It's not in my nature to take sides before I know the stakes, but honestly, I'd rather support you than her. She was strong, but so cold. We value strength above all else, but strength must be equal to temperament, or we will follow the same path as the Hive of old.

"You seem a far kinder queen, but also a far weaker queen."

My jubilation fell as she reached the end. I was happy to have even a modicum of her support, but I couldn't deny the reality of the situation. I was weak. I'd known this, but now it was staring me in the face as an immutable fact.

I nearly died. I was so close to death, and I could do nothing. If not for Evelyn, I would have perished. The life I'd built in such a short time was more precious to me than anything, and I'd almost let it slip through my fingers.

That couldn't happen again.

"Reina, I have a favor I must ask of you."

Her smile deepened as she leaned ever so slightly closer to me. Her black widowed eyes glistened with interest. "You need my blessing."

I nodded. "How did you know?"

"It's obvious, and it was the first thing Aliria asked for as well, so I assumed."

I sat up on the bed, disregarding trying to cover myself with the sheet. It didn't matter. "I need the Arachne's blessing if I'm to get stronger. Will you give it to me?"

Reina didn't answer right away, instead she plucked a strand of her snow-white hair and twined it around her finger as she looked away and back again. Her eyes trailed hungrily over my skin, and when our eyes met, there was desire in hers.

"Have you forgotten our ways? Favors are not given, they are bought."

"But I have noth—"

Reina leaned swiftly, and before I realized how close she was, her lips pressed firmly against my own in a kiss.

The suddenness along with the passion surprised me, and for a second, I lost myself in the need of another's touch and returned her kiss. Reina's lips were soft, her mouth willing as she ran her tongue across my mouth.

Her hand went to my neck while the other cupped my breast. I moaned as her firm hand squeezed, taking my nipple between her fingers. As she pinched down, I let out a shuddering gasp at the slight pain.

Reina pulled back a moment later, uncoupling our mouths with regret.

"You have one thing," she said a little breathless.

I shook my head. "I can't."

"Why?" She cocked her head to the side as she tapped a finger on her lip. "Because of your human?"

"Yes." I nodded.

She scowled in annoyance, brushing her fingers over my hand that pulsed with the rapid beat of her heart. "I don't understand why you would hold yourself to human standards when you are so far beyond them."

I frowned, folding my arms over my chest. "That's not what I'm doing at all."

"Isn't it?" she asked, blinking rapidly. "Tell me, do you find an issue with sharing a bed together?"

"Well, no, but—"

Her fingers silenced my lips as she smiled widely. "Then you are absolutely holding yourself to an ideal you don't believe in to appease your human. You are the Hive Queen, yet you act like you have no power."

"Because I have very little…"

Reina surged forward and grabbed me around the throat, her fingers gripped tight as fire filled her eyes. "If you have no power, then take what power you can. I'm offering you power. Take it. Or do you want to continue to be what I thought when you first appeared? A false queen?"

I grabbed her wrist and forced her hand away. Reina was strong, like all of the Arachne, but she couldn't match the strength of an entomancer.

"I am the Hive Queen!"

She gave me a fierce smile. "Then act like it."

Her face was so close to mine, and I wanted nothing more than her lips. Logic and desire took the fight from me. Reina came closer a second time and pressed her forehead to mine. Her lips barely touched my own before I pulled her into my embrace.

***

"Do be sure to say goodbye to Tegen and Cheira. They've grown fond of you," Reina said as she stood in the doorway. "You are free to enter and exit the Darkwoods at your leisure. You can even bring your human next time. I'm anxious to see the kind of man you decided to bind yourself to."

Then she left and I was alone with my conflicted thoughts.

I sat on the edge of the bed with my head in my hands. *Did I just ruin everything?* I didn't know. I loved Sam more than anything, but I didn't always agree with him. I understood his ideals and respected them, but Reina was right. I wasn't human, and I shouldn't hold myself to them.

But I also knew that what I'd done was a betrayal to Sam. I'd betrayed him, and that thought sickened me.

I hope you'll forgive me, my bonded, and that you'll understand.

Despite how I felt about it, I was undeniably stronger now. Reina's blessing flowed through my veins and brought a new life to my limbs. It was powerful, but it might have cost me everything.

Not a minute after she departed, there was a knock at the door, and russet-skinned man with long braided hair entered with a bundle of clothing. The man was familiar to me. I'd seen him with the commander.

"Where is your bonded?" I asked.

"He's scouting the boundary of the forest, making sure everything is in order for your departure," he said, laying the clothes at the foot of the bed. "Have a fair day, Hive Queen."

He left, and I dressed quickly. Reina had provided me with an outfit similar to the one she wore. It was a pair of tight, dark pants and a flowy tunic that left most of my upper chest bare without revealing anything. I dressed and left the room, trying to find my friends.

The long wooden hallway was sparse. The only decorations were the covered oil lamps that provided light through the corridor. I rounded an corner and found Evelyn waiting for me.

She looked over at me when I came barreling around the corner but didn't move.

"We need to talk, little queen. About what you saw in your Mnemosyne."

With what happened with Reina, I'd nearly forgotten what I'd seen, the sights I couldn't fathom. I didn't know exactly what I'd seen, but I knew one thing for certain. I just needed her to admit it.

I settled on the wall next to her. "Tell me, Evelyn. I need to know. Are you human?"

Her eyes fell from mine, and she sighed. Her usual calm aloofness faded away as her luminescent eyes stared at the ground.

"Once. But that was a very long time ago."

CHAPTER 19 - IRON BOUND

Sampson

I activated *Chitin Shield*, and the chitin on my left hand shifted, melting and reforming in the shape of a smooth concave circle on my forearm. I raised it as the frontrunner charged me, a long-haired blond with a trimmed beard. He raised his one-handed axe and brought it down. Its curved blade clanged against my shield and chipped a sliver from the chitin. I batted it aside as it struck and thrust with my sword.

My blade slid though the side of his neck, nicking his carotid.

He clutched his bleeding neck, but it wasn't deep enough to kill him quickly. One hand gripped his neck as blood slipped through his fingers, and the other hefted his axe once more.

I kicked his leg out from under him, and he stumbled back, landing on his ass. I raised my sword to finish him when the equivalent of a freight train took me off my feet.

I flew into the air and got a glimpse at what had hit me. One of the dwarves was a mage and had used earth magic to turn the floor itself into a weapon. A jagged stalagmite rose a few feet from the ground.

I rolled when I hit the ground, nearly clipping a pew as I stood. I shook off being flung and settled back into my stance as another dwarf charged me.

The aubergine-faced man growled in anger as he thrust with his spear. I sidestepped, but he nicked my sword hand, and I dropped my weapon. I didn't bother attempting to retrieve it. I shuffled into his space before he could whip his spear around and brought my shield down on the metal. Chitin met steel, and the inferior metal sheared under my strike.

The dwarf dropped his spear and tried to regroup with his comrades. He'd made a mistake in engaging me and had put a row of pews between him and them.

I had him.

I lashed out with a clawed hand and sank my fingers deep into his face.

The sharp chitin tore through flesh with ease until resistance met me as I hit bone, and then I forced my hand deeper. The frontal bone resisted as my fingers carved divots in the ivory. It held for as second before cracking under my strength. I broke through and sank my fingers into as much brain matter as I could get in my hands before I yanked it free.

Half of his frontal lobe came, clutched in my claws as red blood and scraps of gray brain stuck to my chitin. His jaw hung slack as I pulled my hand from his pulped and ruined face.

The dwarf tipped over as soon as my hand no longer supported him. Vile chunks of brain oozed out, and I shook the gore from my hands.

I knelt and retrieved my sword before the blood reached it and leapt over the pews.

They were too spread out for me to use *Dance of the Immortal*, and I'd added enough points to my battle fatigue that though I still had a lot of fight left in me, I didn't know if I could take all five of them. Even counting the one whose neck I'd cut. They'd swarm me quickly.

"'Let them. Slow time and devour them."

And how do I get out after I drop from maxing my fatigue?

The Aspect shut up after that and left me to deal with the rest of them.

I focused on the injured one. He would go down the quickest, and one less to deal with would only help me.

He'd retreated, leaving a thick trail of blood on the floor along with his axe. He was currently trying to staunch the bleeding while the other four guarded him.

"Who's next?"

Two of them flanked around me. One, a taller dwarf with dark hair and darker eyes, unstrapped a shield and hefted his sword at me. The other, one of the women, a blonde, wielded a bow staff comprised of shadowsteel.

While devastating against unarmored and lightly armored opponents, her staff wouldn't be able to generate enough force to crack my chitin, and it was flexible enough to distribute the impact so my brain wouldn't turn to mush if she managed a lucky hit. My chitin, along with the leather and shadowsteel underneath meant I was relatively safe against her attacks. Which meant I discarded her as the immediate threat and dealt with the shield bearer.

I quickened my pace and stepped to the side, keeping the dwarf with the shield between me and Bowstaff. He lunged with his sword while holding his shield tight. His blade aimed for the right side of my chest. I brought my shield to intercept it when he struck me in the hip with a surprise kick. I stumbled back, and his shield smashed straight into my chin.

My head snapped back from the blow, and my ears rang. Bowstaff ran forward and used the back of Shielder as a springboard and leapt into the air. Her staff angled toward my head.

She'd made a mistake, and I capitalized on it. In the air, you're at the mercy of physics, and she couldn't change her direction. I grounded myself and covered my head with my shield, raising my sword. Bowstaff tried to correct herself with her weapon, but it slipped off my shield, and my blade speared through her side. Shadowsteel met shadowsteel, but gravity was on my side, and her momentum pushed my sword through her armor and into her flesh.

Her weight hit my shield and drove my blade deeper into her. She cried out in agony as my blade slid past a couple of her ribs and slid into her heart.

Her eyes widened as I punctured her heart, and she coughed as blood splattered across my face. I dumped her corpse off my shield and stood, just as a sword hit me in the chest.

Shielder had closed the gap me while I'd dealt with Bowstaff. His blade slid through my chitin, but thanks to my increased *Durability*, he didn't have the strength to puncture my armor.

As he gaped at the fact I wasn't bleeding out, I pivoted to my left, breaking his grip on his sword. He'd left himself open to a counterattack, a sloppy move.

I brought my own blade up to slice across his throat. He backed up, going for his neck, but I grabbed for his discarded weapon and jammed his sword through his nose and out the back of his head.

He toppled to the ground, dead.

I'd taken three of them, but I was tired. My battle fatigue rose quickly with the shield active, and it was over halfway full.

The battle was only going to get harder as it wore on.

The remaining three Chosen grouped by the open door.

My target was the one whose throat I'd cut. He had a health potion in his hands, and I didn't want him healing.

I reached for the knife Thrayl gave me and realized I'd forgotten it back at the safehouse. *Shit.*

Can I throw my shield?

"What? No. What a stupid question. Who would want to throw a shield?"

I snorted. *Saw it in a movie once.*

"A what? Never mind, just go and devour them already!"

With a curse, I canceled my shield. I couldn't justify the added weight.

The last female, an older dwarf with red hair shot through with gray, raised a hand and spoke a rolling incantation in Script.

Can't let her finish that spell!

I changed my direction and went after her instead. Her eyes widened at my approach, but she kept up her chant as my sword arced toward her.

A dwarf stepped in front of her and caught my attack with his two handaxes. He was the oldest of the six; age had weathered deep lines in his face and left too many streaks of white in his once-black beard.

"You will suffer in agony for defiling our most sacred treasure!" he spat through gritted teeth.

With a twirl of his wrist, the dwarf hooked the head of his axe on my quillon and tugged, taking my sword from my grasp. It hit the stone a few feet away and skidded to a halt underneath one of the pews.

Fuck!

I backed up as his twin axes cried out for my blood as they sailed toward me. I stepped back as the blades bit gently into the soft stone, scoring shallow grooves where my foot had been. The dwarf came back up with a snarl. I pivoted into a crescent kick, striking the head of his axe.

It forced the axe aside, and his wrist buckled, sending the blade of the axe to his unprotected forearm, slicing a heavy gash across his arm. He cursed and dropped his axe.

As it fell through the air, I dipped low and snagged it before it hit the ground. Now we both had a weapon, and the playing field was back in my advantage.

The axe wasn't my preferred choice, but I knew it better than most other weapons. I swung it light, as the dwarf sidestepped. He brought his axe overhead as he tried to go for my unprotected side, but I shifted on the balls of my feet and leaned back as steel passed two inches from my face.

I clamped my left hand over his wrist to stop him from bringing his blade back up and sank my stolen axe deep into the nape of his neck.

It didn't behead him, but I'd at least severed his spinal cord, as he dropped lifelessly to the ground. I left the axe buried in its owner and quickly retrieved my sword from where it had landed. When it was back in my hand, I turned to face the mage. Our fight had taken less than a minute, but it had given the woman all the time she needed to complete her spell.

A dark brown light flared from her hands as she grinned triumphantly.

Low rumbling shook the earth as the spell took hold. A mass of rock and stone rose from the floor and formed a rough shape.

It started as a massive blob, but within a second, it became humanoid with two legs, arms, and a head. The next second it had fully formed, and the stone golem stood silently, staring at me with empty sockets where its eyes should've been.

The stone golem stood nearly ten feet tall, relatively thin compared to its size, reminiscent of an artist's sketching mannequin. Craggy rock formed its skin and bald, faceless head as it lumbered towards me. Unlike Adam's creatures, this golem was crafted from the earth, but it was animated solely by mana.

I had to destroy it or the caster to get rid of the golem.

It raised a heavy fist and brought it toward my head. I threw myself into a roll as it sailed past me, landing heavily on the stone floor and cracking the slate into dozens of pieces. I came out of my roll and sliced its leg with my blade.

I hewed a thin groove from it as my shadowsteel ripped through the rock, but as soon as I brought my sword back, the rock shifted. My slice faded as liquid rock dripped from its chest and repaired the minuscule damage I'd done.

"Well, fuck."

It kicked me in the chest, and I went flying. I landed a few feet away when my back crashed into a pew.

Damn, it's faster than I gave it credit for. New plan, then. I wasn't going to destroy the golem, not without *Aura of the Antimage.* And if I used *Dance,* I'd have solved my immediate problem, but I'd be helpless after, and I wasn't that desperate yet.

I'm stronger now. I can handle this. Probably.

Chitin Armor held up to its kick, though I didn't think my organs would relish a repeat performance. I stood from the pew and clenched my sword tight.

What if I run in between its legs as it attacks? It took a second or two to recover from that last smash, so I'd have at least a few seconds to kill the mage before the golem turns and crushes me to a pulp. It was the best plan I could come up with that didn't involve me maxing my fatigue.

I raced headlong to the golem, my sword raised.

Glass crashed from above and drew my attention. A figure jumped through the window and swung down on a rope. As the stained glass broke against the ground, the figure hit the floor and rolled, his katana blade glowing an exquisite, ghostly blue.

Mika stood and slashed through the golem, his blade phasing through it like it wasn't even there. When his sword passed through the entirety of the golem, it dissolved, turning back into nothing but a pile of lifeless rock and stone tile.

As the mage and the dwarf whose neck I'd cut stared at Mika, I just laughed.

"*Null Blade,* really? You're still rocking the primordial swordsman class?"

"Saved your ugly, bug-lookin' ass, and besides, if it ain't broke..."

"I had it under control, but let's deal with the rest of them and get out of here."

We charged the remaining dwarves.

"Dibs on the mage!" I shouted as Mika engaged the one with the slit throat.

"Fine by me, I got Bleedy!"

I tuned his fight out as I focused on the woman. She backed up, her hands going in front of her face, but I knew she was close to mana depletion. She had to be after summoning a golem of that size and strength.

A muddy brown Script circle flared to life, but it was small; she didn't have the time to build a proper spell. She recited a short incantation, but my sword cut her voice off before she could finish it.

As the light from her circle fizzled out, so too did her life.

I ripped my sword from her neck and turned back to the first dwarf, the one who'd gotten away.

He was in half, both sides glowing cherry red and smoking as Mika withdrew his glowing white sword. The sharp tang of burning metal and roasting dwarf stung my nose, and I coughed.

"Sorry, Mika. I forgot to bring anything to the barbeque."

He laughed, waving his hand in front of his face. "Shit, I forgot how nasty it is to use *Volcanic Thrust* indoors."

"Well, let's get the hell out of here. We need to be far away before the alarm is raised. We'll never get out if that happens."

Mika sighed, sheathing his sword. "Too late for that. Guards already on the way. I came in here to warn you while I left David and Johns to guard the gate," he said, heading for the door out of the vault.

I followed his lead, sheathing my sword and heading out. As soon as I housed my blade, the Aspect decided that I was no longer in danger, and

Chitin Armor faded back under my skin. Mika glanced over and whistled. "Seems like we've got a lot to catch up on."

"You're telling me. You think the rent-a-thugs are okay?" I asked as our footsteps echoed in the empty cathedral.

"I'm guessing they're already dead or will be soon enough."

"Harsh. Accurate, but harsh."

He snorted, a laugh bubbling from his chest. "They were insufferable—and not very good at their jobs. I was going to ditch them after this quest anyway."

We reached the entrance to the cathedral and pushed the heavy wooden doors open. We were alone, but that wouldn't be that way for long. The gates in the distance opened, and dozens of guards poured in from Gold Hightown.

"I'm guessing they didn't make it," I said, deadpan.

"Five silver says you're right."

We looked over at each other, and I grinned despite the situation. "Just like old times."

He nodded. "Let's get the fuck out of here."

We turned and booked it off the stone path and toward the wall. If we could reach the wall and climb over it before the guards saw us, we could escape and head back to the surface without incident.

We rushed into the night. Once we got off the road, the ground became rocky and dangerous, as there were protrusions and dips at random. In the dark, with only the faint glow from the mana far above us, we could barely see.

I banged my knee on something at least five times and nearly fell into a hole, but the inky drop was just darker than the rock next to it, so I hopped over it at the last second.

A handful of minutes later, and we had reached the wall. It rose from chest high at the gate to at least eight feet of stone that we had to clamber over.

"How're we getting over this?" Mika asked.

"I've got an idea." I grabbed the rope from my inventory and cut about a foot and a half off it. "Boost me up and then wrap the rope around your hand. I'll fall, and you use the momentum to climb the wall."

Mika laughed and crouched. "You always were quick on your feet."

"Yeah, too bad I'm an idiot, or I'd be really dangerous," I said and stepped into his hand.

He lifted me up, and I hauled myself over the wall and wrapped part of the rope tightly over my fist while Mika did the same. I dropped over the ledge, and Mika climbed over it. When we were both safely over the wall, we jogged a short distance and took shelter in the alleyway.

"Man, it's always fun working with you. What are you going to do, now?" he asked when we'd caught our breath.

"Thinking about risking the surface, but I don't know how smart that plan is."

"Raven has the Heart, right? Where's she at?"

"Heading back to the surface to deliver it. If I can just get topside, I can teleport away, but I'm sure humans are going to be stopped and questioned leaving Aldrust.

"I touched the Heart; it had a curse on it. Even though I don't have it anymore, I think it left its mark on me. No way I get clear if they stop and check me. I might just head back to the Low Road, lie low for a few days till security lightens up."

"I think I'm going to risk it. I never even saw the Heart. They've got nothing on me, so they can't hold me." He nodded and offered me his hand.

"I guess I'll be going, then, before it gets crazy. It was good seeing you again, Duran, truly."

I took his hand firmly and shook it. "Same. I'll see you around."

He took off, but before he rounded the corner a thought struck me, and I yelled at him. "Hey, you looking for a guild?"

Mika paused and leaned against the wall of a nobleman's manse. "Not, not looking. You got a spot you need filled in the Gloom Knights?"

"A few."

"Every adventurer worth their rank knows to stay away from Gloom-Harbor territory if they know what's good for them. Your guild's got quite the nasty reputation, but I think we've come a long ways since our time in the Swords."

"That mean you're in?"

"We'll see. I'll stop by and see what's what," he said, walking away.

"You remember the passphrase?" I asked.

Mika waved me off. "If you haven't changed it in fifteen years, yeah," he replied as he disappeared from view.

I smiled at his back. *He certainly hasn't changed.*

"I bet his blood tastes bitter. Why don't you follow and find out?"

Pass. You already had Raven's blood. Isn't that enough for you?

"Worth a shot. And I did help you today. I do like to be rewarded, you know."

Maybe if you were less psychotic, I'd reward you.

Giving Mika a few minutes to get a head start, I leaned against the stone wall and pulled up my interface to check my notifications.

Combat Results!
5 Killed (Dwarf): 9000 Exp!
1 downed: 1800 Exp!

Mercy Penalty: -600
Total Exp Gain: 10200 Exp!
Exp: 5400/5400
Level Up! (X2)
4500/5600
Level: 56
20 Stat Points Available!

Best bet is to keep pushing my sub-stats since I'm still under penalty. I added ten points to *Durability* and ten to *Attack Damage.* I changed out of my armor and donned my nicest set of clothes. A set Magnus had made for me. It was the solid white silken set I'd first worn when I met him. And it would at least help me blend in, or at least not stick out.

I sauntered around Hightown for a while. Even at this time of night, there were still a few places open. I stopped and had an expensive dinner at the restaurant Raven and I had gone to. I had a lovely meal, and after, I took my time getting back to Lowtown.

By the time I returned to the Low Road, it was late by Aldrustian standards, and the bar had been long closed. I didn't have any elemental scrolls to enter, so I had no choice but to head back to the safe house and wait until morning.

There wasn't a single soul on the streets as I made my way to the house and used the specific scroll I had for the house to lower the door. I went over to the fridge and took out an ale. I sighed in bliss as I drained half of it and sat back on the stone couch.

Shit. Can't believe we managed to pull that off. Hope Raven got out okay.

I hadn't been home for more than two minutes when a knock at the door interrupted my thoughts.

Orryn stood perched in the doorway, hand raised as he tapped lightly on the stone. "Can I come in?"

I shrugged and finished the ale. The glass bottle clinked as I set it down and eyed Orryn. "What're you doing here?"

"Just came to congratulate you on a job well done. It's not reached the public yet, but Balthazar and his council are abuzz with finding out who took the Heart."

I feigned surprise. "Lachrymal's Heart was stolen? That's awful."

He laughed and ambled over to the fridge, grabbing a beer and offering it to me. I nodded and as he was walking back, I glanced over at the door that he'd left open.

"Could at least shut the—" I began but stopped as the clink of metal against metal drifted in from the street. Soft, but unmistakable.

Orryn noticed my look and squinted, tilting his head slightly, still holding the drinks.

"You didn't?" I asked rising from my seat.

He sighed, dropping his hands. "Didn't have a choice. They were at the bar less than half an hour after. They took Tel. Had to give 'em something," he replied listlessly.

He released the bottles, and as they clattered to the ground with a torrent of shattered glass, he whistled.

"You just damned yourself, Orryn. I'll kill you for this."

"Don't matter. Long as Tel is okay, that's all I care about."

Nearly a dozen armed Aldrustian soldiers stormed into the cramped house with their weapons brandished. I couldn't have killed them all even with *Dance*. *Could make it to the roof, but once* Dance *ends, I'm just as screwed, and I'd rather save it for when I know I can use it.*

With a heavy sigh, I raised my hands and let them take me.

***

They'd left me in a dark, nearly airless hole in the wall for hours while they convened the council. The wall slid aside, and several dwarven jailors bound my hands and feet in chains and all but dragged me to the forum. It was a polished building with white marble tile and columns that rose to the open ceiling that looked out to the center of Aldrust. The giant mana crystal hung silently overhead, pulsing with light.

I was tossed into the center of the floor and chained again to the spike buried in the marble. As I looked up, in front of me was the polished silver panel where the council and king sat. King Baltazar who had fury written plainly across his face as he gazed down at me.

Balthazar was rough around the edges like his features had been carved from the very stone around us, but there was undoubtably a regal set to his eyes and jaw. His swept-back hair had salt and peppered since the last time I'd seen him, but it gave his statuesque features depth. His sharp blue eyes looked down his small, hawkish nose as he bit his lip in anger.

A bead of blood rolled down his lip and dripped, invisible on his tailored burgundy shirt.

"Durandahl, once I called you friend to the dwarves, a man who did what we could not and saved us in a most dire time. If anyone had told me that you planned to betray us like this, I'd have had that man imprisoned."

"I didn't hear an accusation."

A metal-plated fist smacked across my face hard enough to rip my skin. My head went sideways, but my chains kept me from falling over. "Insolent wretch," the guard shouted next to my already-ringing ear.

"You bear the mark of Lachrymal's Wrath. But the Heart is clearly not in your possession. Tell us where it is and return it. If you do, in light of your previous achievements, I'll be lenient with you."

It was a generous offer, especially from Balthazar, as he wasn't known for his kindness. But this wasn't about me, not anymore. Whatever was going on threatened the entirety of Nexus. It was bigger than me, and besides, Raven was halfway back to Castle Aliria by now.

I spat a gob of blood onto the pristine white marble and rubbed my aching cheek. "I won't talk."

"He had a girl with him. Pale skinned, red eyes. Not a nocturnal, but definitely not human," a voice said from the crowd.

I jolted up at the voice, and my eyes scanned the crowd until they locked with Thrayl. His normally well-groomed locks were in disarray. *Must've raced up here.* He stared me down, betrayal clear in his eyes. I opened my mouth, but nothing would come. I didn't have an excuse to justify what I'd done.

"How could you?" he asked.

I hung my head as my stomach dropped and shame flushed in my cheeks.

The council members all started yelling at once at Thrayl's revelation, but Balthazar sighed deeply, looking like a disappointed father. "Find her. Meanwhile, question Orryn again. Make him tell us what we need to know. Remind him the consequences of lying."

Balthazar spoke quickly, issuing commands left and right as his men bustled around the room, rushing to fulfil them. It took a few long moments before the forum quieted enough for him to speak again. "Don't make me do this, Duran. You, more than most, know that we have ways of making you talk."

"And having performed several of your methods myself, you know that by the time I break, it'll be too late. If it isn't already."

"Just be honest with us. This isn't you."

"Yeah." I fingered a loose canine in my skull and just decided to pull it. It clattered to the ground as I hawked another thick stream of blood onto the floor. "You're right about that, but I didn't have a choice.

"And right now, you think you have a choice. A choice about what to do with me. You think you can get me to talk, but we both know it won't be quick, and it won't be easy."

He snapped his fingers, and several guards strolled in. "Fine, then. I can make you talk. But I also know just how strong your will is and how long that might take. If what you say is true and the gem is lost to us for now, then I'll just have to settle for making your life as miserable as I can. And we both know I'm well-versed in making misery.

"Take him to Tombsgard Mine!"

Chapter 20 - Tombsgard

Once again, I was manhandled and dragged from the room and loaded into a wagon. Whatever small discomforts they inflicted at that moment were nothing compared to what waited for me in the depths of Tombsgard.

It took a few more hours after my impromptu trial to reach the entrance to the mine. It was always in a sequestered portion of the city, miles away from civilization in an unmapped location away from prying eyes. Only a select few had permission to enter. I was kept in the dark, but I could tell when we descended by the drop in temperature. It was just above freezing at all times in the mine, and that was just the first of the torments that awaited me.

When we finally stopped moving, I was unloaded. Torches lined the walls and continued as the road curved and disappeared into the black abyss.

The guards here wore heavy, fur-lined cloaks and gleefully smirked at me when I was told to strip.

"Fuck you."

One of them stepped up and whipped a thin knife across my chest. It was shallow, an expertly placed cut that stung like hell but did no actual damage to my muscle.

"Strip!" he commanded.

My impertinence would only lead to blood loss, and down in the mine, I needed every bit of strength available. I did as the dwarf demanded and stripped completely. After a rough, incredibly thorough and unneeded cavity search, I was handed a thin and itchy pair of beige trousers and a matching tunic one size too small.

I winced as the guard shoved me and led me down the tunnel to a gate manned by a team of guards, and then once we were through, we stopped at a second gate with even more guards. By the time we were through, I was exhausted and chilled to the bone. I shivered, and the guards laughed.

"Get used to it. You're in for much worse."

We went through the last gate and entered Tombsgard Mine. Aldrust's maximum security prison.

The gate slammed shut behind us and locked with an ominous click.

Tombsgard was a wide cavern that branched into dozens of other smaller tunnels. Hard at work were nearly a hundred prisoners, dwarves mostly, but there were humans and even a few elves in the mix. Each was dressed as I was and carrying pickaxes as they hammered away at the iron ore buried in the rock.

We were high above them, and the only thing separating the guards from the prisoners was about twenty-five feet and a stone railing. The guard motioned for me to step onto a solid stone platform that would lower me down.

I peered over the edge at the prisoners who'd stopped working to watch the new guy.

"Don't get comfortable. None of them are your friends. They all know what you've done and have been promised time off their sentences if they catch you doing anything. So you better not use your magic storage while you're down there."

I turned around, smiling cheekily. "And if I do?"

"Then your water rations get revoked. You do it twice, we chain you inside a cell with about two feet of freezing water and see how long you last. Of course, you can stop this right now, and just tell us where the Heart is."

"Nah, a little manual labor won't kill me."

The guard laughed sickly. "Let's see you keep up that attitude in the next couple days when you're starving and exhausted."

With that, he spoke a chant in Script, and the platform shuddered and lowered me into hell.

Crudely made wooden furniture littered the space. Tan ceramic plates and cups lay forgotten as every eye was on me as I stepped off the platform.

As I was about to take a step, raw emotion flooded through my connection with Eris. It was slow to build, but unmistakable. Pleasure and lust flowed from her to me, and my heart nearly stopped for a second time in as many days.

I stiffened as it rolled through me. My throat burned as my vision blurred as heat settled into my chest as I fought back my tears. I dug my nails into my palms hard enough to bleed, and it still wasn't enough to match the pain in my heart.

My breathing increased as my heart broke. Unbridled rage filled me as I shut off our connection. I gnashed my teeth and strolled into the prison yard.

Waiting.

It didn't take long; I knew it wouldn't. Whether on Earth or Nexus, prison was prison, and the top dog always had to make it known.

A low whistle sounded to my left, and a dwarven male with more scar tissue than face and a heavily broken nose drained his cup and tossed it aside. It shattered on the wall as he stood and sauntered over to me. The man came up to my chest and had the audacity to stare me down.

"Oi, new blood. Let's get somethi—"

I didn't let him finish before I sank my knee into his face, breaking his already-ruined nose. As blood rushed down his chin, a warmth spread over my right hand, and when I looked down, it was encased in chitin.

Before he could react to his shattered nose, I reached low, grabbed a handful of the dwarf's most precious asset, and clenched my fist tight. The color drained from Nose's cheeks, and he gasped, spluttering as a rapidly growing red stain appeared between his legs.

With a vicious yank, my hand came free, clutching what no man wishes to ever part with. I tossed the bloody, useless organ away as Nose stumbled back from the shock.

It wasn't enough.

I grabbed him by the collar of his thin tunic and slammed my fist to his face. Nose crumpled, his blue eyes rolled back inside his skull, and he sank to his knees. Blood streamed over the burst cartilage to soak into his shirt.

It wasn't fucking enough.

I knelt and slammed my fist into his face again. And again, and again, and again. I hit him over and over. I hit him until my chitin ripped flesh from his face and caved in his skull. I hit him until bone crumbled under my fist and I reached his brain. I obliterated his entire skull, and it still wasn't enough.

I sank to all fours, my breath came in ragged gulps as sweat dripped down to sting my eyes and drip salt onto my lips.

Why? Why? Why?

I didn't have an answer.

After a long time, I stood from Nose's corpse, my arm covered in blood and worse to nearly my bicep. I ripped a stretch of relatively clean strip of cloth from Nose's shirt and wiped the gore from myself.

As I turned back to the others, I tossed the rag aside and stared everyone down. Not a soul moved, even dared to breathe. It was quiet as a mausoleum. Everyone gaped at me.

I was about to scream when a notification slammed into me.

Alert! Arachne's Blessing Unlocked!
+15 to Strength and Agility
Unlocked (Hive Mind) Special: Arachnid Limbs

The rush of power to my body melded with Eris's high as she rode her orgasm and left me weary and energized at the same time.

I didn't know how to feel about it; my rage still burned too brightly for me to make any form of rational thought. I had to let it out, or I'd go mad.

A tortured scream filled the silent room as I tried to tear my vocal cords. A dozen shrieks of surprised flowed with my scream and sank into the stone, never to escape.

By the time it faded away, I rubbed at my aching throat and sighed, letting the rage flood away to cool detachment.

Put it aside. It won't help you here.

I stood and walked center stage.

"Let's get one thing straight!" I shouted to the stunned crowd. "There's been a regime change. I'm the godsdamned king now!"

A twisted laugh rose from my heart.

"I'm starting to like you now, knight."

***

The first day was pretty easy. I'd asserted my dominance, and most of the prisoners left me alone to work. I slammed the pick down, chipping away at the rock looking for iron.

It wasn't the first time I'd worked the mines; it was a skill nearly every adventurer had to pick up at one point or another. Whether mining for mana crystals or precious metals, swinging a pickaxe was a necessary skill on Nexus.

I just wish I'd kept up the practice. I wiped my brow with the back of my hand and stepped away from the craggy rock. The constant physical exertion kept my mind from wandering most of the time, but as I settled into a rhythm, I had nothing to do but think.

Eris loves me. That's an immutable fact. She wouldn't betray me without cause. And I could guess at what that cause was. *The Arachne queen. That new blessing.*

I pulled up my interface and looked at the Hive Knight class, quickly finding what I was looking for.

Arachne's Blessing: +15 to Strength and Agility
Arachnid Limbs Unlocked
Scorpius's Blessing (Locked)
Mantearia's Blessing (Locked)
Apocrita's Blessing (Locked)

So that's what they are. I meant to ask Eris but didn't get the chance. So she slept with the Arachne queen to gain her blessing.

It happened so soon after she nearly died. *She had to have a good reason for it. I believe that. I have to, or I won't survive.*

I couldn't take losing her. It would kill me.

With a too-heavy swing, I stopped mining. *Time for a break.* My pick clanged against the ground, drawing a few curious eyes, but they swiftly turned back to their tasks as I went to the table.

The rough wooden chair scraped on the ground as I sat down and poured a cup of water. It was stagnant, barely drinkable, but I drank three cups before sitting back in the chair to rest for a moment.

I really didn't mind the punishment as it was so far. I could handle manual labor all day long, and after my brutal display, no one wanted to get within six feet of me for fear I'd do the same to them. But those were the easy parts—the hard part would be after a few days when I'd be starving.

I wasn't allowed food, and even though I had plenty in my inventory, I couldn't touch it.

Though I was relatively obscured in the tunnels because the guards never dared come down here, I couldn't risk eating for fear that the others would turn me in for a chance to gain favor.

Some of them would be more afraid of me than the guards, but not all of them. and I couldn't risk it, not right now at least.

Raven will get to Magnus eventually. All I have to do is be patient. I didn't like relying on Magnus to facilitate my release, but he probably had the best chance of doing it without bloodshed. Should the worst come to pass, I'd call the Gloom Knights, and we'd slaughter everyone. *Not an ideal plan, but I'll do it if it comes to that.*

I was lost in thought when someone joined me at the table I was at.

He was young, but that told me nothing. Tall and thin. His shoulder-length greasy and lank dark hair covered his lean, starved face and bloodshot brown eyes.

"The fuck are you?" I asked, fire in my voice.

"A friend, hopefully," he said with a smile.

"I don't need friends, so get out of my sight before I get angry."

The man held up his hands, his eyes softening. "I promise, I mean no harm. Name's Maus."

I stood up, knocking over my chair in the process. "Don't care. Leave. Now."

He nodded. "Fair enough, but come see me if you change your mind. I have an interesting proposition for you."

Maus left, and I went back to work, carving through rock a sliver at a time.

By the time it was time to call it quits for the day, I'd worn my muscles out and was ready for some rest and water. I was getting hungry, but going without food for a couple of days was something I could deal with later. It was barely more than an annoyance at that moment.

I settled back against the wall and drank my fill of water while watching the other prisoners come and go. They ate sitting around the same cheap wooden tables, nothing more than thin soup and a heel of bread, but it was more than I was getting.

By the time dinner was through, I was ready for sleep, and I leaned back against the rock, closing my eyes for just a moment.

I slept rough, only to be woken up by the bell in the morning, signaling another day's work. It went much the same as the first. I worked my body to the bone mining, and my hunger only got worse as the day progressed.

The Aspect did what it could, helped take the edge off the worst of the pain, but it could only do so much. At the end of the second day, I stumbled over a loose rock and nearly toppled over. It was a simple mistake, but that was all it took in a place like that.

I'd just shown that I was weak and vulnerable to a pack of predators.

It didn't take long after that for the first hopeful king slayer to approach.

A dark-skinned human with long black hair shoulder barged me as we passed. I turned, grabbed a handful of his greasy mane, and wound it around my wrist. I jerked hard on his locks, and he stumbled back. I kicked the back of his knee and sent him to the ground.

I let go of his hair and curb stomped his throat, collapsing his windpipe.

The man's eyes bulged as his hands went to his neck as he gasped and wheezed, trying to breath.

I left him to choke to death and walked past him.

The others took one look at him, and they backed up. I went to my corner and sat in my chair, keeping an eye on everyone while I clicked on the blinking notification.

Combat Results!
One Killed (Dwarf): 1800 Exp!
One Killed (Human): 1500 Exp!
Total Exp Gain: 3300 Exp!
5600/5600
Level Up!
Level: 57
2200/5700
10 Stat Points Available!

Might as well keep bumping up my Durability, *but I need to start putting some points in* Battle Fatigue. *I'm hitting my limit on nearly every prolonged fight. If I have a bit more* Battle Fatigue, *I could use* Dance *without fear of maxing my fatigue.*

I dropped five to *Durability* and five to *Battle Fatigue.*

As the dead man jerked in his final death throes, I leaned against the wall and sighed. If it happened once, it would happen again. It was only a matter of time, and I would only grow weaker as the days wore on.

I'm going to have to keep my guard up, or I'll find a shiv in my neck while I sleep.

The next few days went by in a blur. I'd work, drink as much water as I could and then go to bed hungry. By the third day, I was starving, and I couldn't keep my strength up no matter how hard I tried.

In the morning, the first of the attacks started.

A glint of light off the pickaxe was the only warning I had before it came down, aimed at my spine. I stepped back on reflex as the pick glanced off stone and lashed out with a kick. I took my attacker in the side, snapping a few ribs. He stumbled back from the blow, dropping his pickaxe and giving me a good look at him.

A stubby dwarf with a thick beard and bald head. He winced as his shook off the pain. I shuffled forward and swung my pick. It connected with the side of the dwarf's head, piercing through his temple and coming out his eye.

Blood and gore slid down his nose to stain his beard, and I ripped my pickaxe free, tearing through bone and cartilage.

He dropped to the ground dead, or wishing he was. I raised the pick once more and brought it down on his skull, splitting his head wide open to reveal bloody bone and brain.

I left the pick where it lay stuck in his worthless body and knelt, snagging the dead dwarf's pick and continued my work as if there wasn't a dead body leaking blood and bile two feet from me.

After the first two failed attempts, I'd have thought the other prisoners would have gotten the message, but attacks still came my way. One or more a day, and I was running on fumes.

This went on for three days, and I'd killed half a dozen prisoners. I was tired, but I had no choice but to fight. It was that or roll over and die.

As the day's work wound down to a close, I dropped my pick and left the tunnel back to the main room. I was going to sit at my table when I found it occupied by four men. Each of them held the look of lifers, scarred, ruthless men who'd committed heinous acts and were now made to pay for it.

"Get up," I demanded.

"Or what?" a man with a squished, ugly face said, sneering.

"Or I rip open your throats and gorge myself on your disgusting blood, you inbred fucks. Now. Move."

I'm going to need your strength to fight.

350

"Delicious. But let's try out our new ability. I'm anxious to see it used."

Fine by me.

A pleasant heat spread from my chest to my back and along my spine. It tingled, and then something rose from my back.

Four black limbs forged of chitin entered my vison, and I glanced side to side at them. They were long and thin, broken only the dorsal hinges as they flexed. Sharp points of chitin tipped the ends like four razor shard dagger points.

Okay, these are kind of badass…and terrifying.

"Let's bring terror to them!"

One question, how do I control them?

"Like any other appendage, you fleshy meatbag."

It was correct. I found I just had to put a little bit of focus into them, and they moved just like my own flesh and blood arms.

The four men stood transfixed at the sudden appearance of four new limbs from my back, but they could do nothing now. They'd made their choice.

The first man stood just as my foot connected with his tanned chest. He went headfirst over the back of his chair and cracked his thick skull on the rock floor, tearing a long gash on the side of his head.

By the time the first man hit the ground, the others rose from their chairs and attacked. I stepped to the side of the second man's swing. The dwarf's attack went wide, the extra force throwing Second off balance. I struck his unprotected side as he tried to right himself. I speared into him with two of my new limbs. They slid between his ribs with ease, slicing across his ribs, tearing through his lungs and puncturing his heart.

I jerked my limbs free, and they came with a spurt of blood. Second fell to the floor, barely missing hitting his head on the wood as he dropped. His eyes went wide with pain before they dimmed.

Third tried to go around Second's body, but I shoved him into First as he picked himself up. Both of them tumbled to the floor. Fourth snarled, his blackened teeth set in a fierce grimace as he leapt over the table.

I grabbed the chair I'd been sitting on like it weighed as much as a feather and bashed Fourth across the face as he landed from his jump.

His jaw dislocated with a crunch, and he sprawled on the ground, joining his friends. The chair still in hand, I brought it down on his kneecap, shattering it.

While Fourth screamed in pain, I slid my arachnid limbs into his neck and ripped his head from his shoulders. It thunked on the table and gushed blood across the worn wood.

With two of the men dead, I dealt with the remainder. The cavern plunged into silence as everyone stared at the mess of blood and bodies I'd left in my wake. The guards overhead watched with dispassionate gazes and went about their day, not fazed by the deaths of the inmates.

First shoved Third off him and stood. His wild hair was flecked with blood from one of the men I'd killed. He didn't care that I'd dispatched two of his friends with ease; he charged me.

I caught his unhinged swing and dislocated his arm at the shoulder. I let go of him as I brought two of the chitinous limbs down and into his back. I forced him to the ground as I sought his heart. With a flick, I tore it to pieces and retracted my spider legs.

As First bled out, I dealt with Third. He stared at me in terror as his eye flicked from me to his dead friends.

He turned to run but stopped.

352

Third stood very still for a long moment before he stumbled and fell to the side.

Standing in front of him, wielding a bloody shiv, was Maus.

He knelt and wiped his bloody hand. "Sorry about stealing your kill. I know that's not cool, but I figured I'd save you the trouble of chasing after him."

"I didn't need your help," I spat.

I used one of the dead mens' tunics to clean the blood off myself and walked over to the nearest table where three men sat staring with unblinking eyes.

"Move."

They shot up like a bolt of lightning and were gone in a flash. I sat down and helped myself to their untouched waters.

"That was fun."

It wasn't boring. Now let's catalogue my notifications, I'm betting I leveled up from these past few fights.

Combat Results!
5 Killed (Dwarf): 9000 Exp!
3 Killed (Human): 4500 Exp!
1 Downed (Dwarf): 1800 Exp!
Mercy Penalty: -600 Exp!
Total Exp Gained: 14700 Exp!
Exp: 5700/5700
Level Up! (x2)
Level: 59
5400/5900
20 Stat Points Available!

After I sorted my stats, ten to *Durability* and ten to *Battle Fatigue.* I let the adrenaline wear out of me and let the chitin flow back under my skin. I laid my head on the rough wood, in desperate need of a nap.

"That was some fight. I know its impolite, but I have to know. What's your class?"

I looked up and blinked my weary eyes at Maus, who'd taken a seat next to me on the table.

"I'm too tired to deal with your bullshit. Just tell me what you want and get the fuck out of my sight."

"I'm here to offer you a friendly hand," he said, putting a smile on his face.

"I'm fine. I don't need your help," I said, waving him off. "Why the hell do you keep showing up, anyway?"

Maus shrugged, glancing up at the guards, who weren't paying any attention. He held out a cup of water for me. "Because you're the most capable person in this damn place, and I've been stuck in here for too long. I want to escape, but I can't do it alone."

"Why me?" I asked, draining the cup.

"Us players need to stick together."

I snorted and sat up, leaning back on the rickety chair. I was too worn out to have the strength to force him away. Maus sat up and shifted chairs coming to sit by me and leaned his head in close. With another quick look around, he held out his hand. In his palm were a few scraps of dried meat. it was just a handful, but to my eyes it was a feast, and I greedily snapped them up.

It wasn't much, but it eased the worst of the hunger and breathed a meager amount of life into my limbs.

"Thanks," I muttered. "I still don't see how I can help you. No one escapes Tombsgard. It's impossible."

"Normally you'd be correct, but I have firsthand knowledge that it might be possible. I just need a partner, someone I can trust."

I wiped at the corners of my mouth to make sure I didn't have any residual crumbs or bits of food around my lips or in my beard. "And what makes you think you can trust me, or that I can trust you?"

He pointed at me, a smile framed his lips. "Because you haven't taken the easy way out. You could let any one of these men kill you and respawn, but like me, you've stuck it out. That means that whatever's waiting beyond these walls is more important than you nearly starving to death."

He had a point, but he knew that. I paused over his words, not trusting him exactly, but he was the only one in the entire prison that wasn't trying to kill me.

"And if he tries, we eat him."

Exactly.

I was a little worried with how in tune me and the Aspect had been the last week or so, but in a place like Tombsgard, its brutality was exactly what I needed.

"All right, Maus. We have a temporary alliance, but cross me, and you know exactly what I'll do to you."

"That I do, and I'll thank you to leave my giblets where they're at. We're a team from now until we get clear of this hellhole."

"What happens after we get clear?" I asked.

He chuckled. "Poor choice of words. We have a cease-fire. Don't attack me, I won't attack you, and we can part ways as uneasy allies."

"I think I can work with that. So what's this plan of yours?"

Chapter 21 - Home Again

Eris

As the first day of our return trip came to a close, I tried once more and failed to understand what Evelyn had told me. I sighed. *She barely explained anything, just told me it had to do with those strange crystals.* I'd tried to bring it up with her again, earlier, but she reacted badly.

I rubbed my neck, hoping her fingers wouldn't leave bruise marks from how hard she'd grabbed me. *I never thought she'd actually threaten me, let alone look at me so callously.*

"I like you, little queen. But you weren't meant to have that knowledge, and I will kill you if you even think about telling anyone. Do you understand?"

I nodded, and her grip on my neck eased. "What about Sam?"

She shook her head. "Especially him. He'll learn about them in time, but it's not the right time."

Then she let me go with a piercing glare that commanded me to heed her words.

I shivered at the thought, at her words when she told me she'd kill me.

She'd do it without hesitation.

I glanced over to her as she rode next to Adam; they were engrossed in a conversation, and as Adam's eyes flicked to mine every so often, I could guess the topic of conversation.

A nudge interrupted my thoughts. Kenna leaned over Cinder and poked me with her finger. It pushed into my thigh in lazy rhythm. "Lost in thought?"

"Just have a lot on my mind," I replied.

"Ah, well, get out of your head and talk to me for a while. Gil's still a little sleepy from the health potion. I'm bored."

I laughed, and it felt good. She was right. I needed to get out of my head. I couldn't do anything about what Evelyn told me, and it wasn't like it changed anything. She was still Evelyn—she just wasn't what I originally thought she was.

"I miss the spiderlings," I said, my voice low.

"Surprisingly, so do I. But you saw how happy they were to see their mother. They're back where they belong."

"Yeah. Izella and her bondmate were very nice. They promised I could see Tegen and Cheira whenever I came back."

"See, told you it would all work out." She poked me again.

I swatted her fingers away playfully, and we both chuckled. "Did you at least have fun?"

"Uh, sort of." She smiled as she leaned down to run her hands over Cinder's flank. "While you were recovering, I talked with a few of the Arachne, managed to snag a new poison, but I didn't like all the eyes on me."

"What do you mean?" I cocked my head to the side.

"We had at least three Arachne guards on us at all times. They were skilled, used the trees and shadows well, but they couldn't hide from me. Hive Queen or not, they'd have tried to kill us all if Reina had given the order."

"And they'd have died very painful deaths," Evelyn said, turning back to look at us as we rode.

Our eyes met, and I hastily looked away.

Adam sighed and reached over and flicked his sister on the head. "She won't say it, so I'll say it for her. She's sorry for making you feel uncomfortable."

"No, I'm not. I meant every word, but do chin up, little queen. It's in the past."

358

"What are you guys talking about?" Makenna asked, glancing between us.

"None of your concern, Red. Let's get moving, I want camp set up before nightfall."

We rode in silence while the sunlight faded below the horizon. After another few minutes we stopped and set up camp.

I went and set up my tent with Kenna while Gil worked on dinner. It was nothing but trail rations and dried meat, but after many hours of riding, I didn't care. It was delicious.

When dinner was over, Gill and Makenna volunteered for first watch while I turned in to get some sleep. I crawled into my tent, but as I lay back on my pillow, the emptiness kept me awake. It was the first time I'd slept alone since being freed from my prison, and I couldn't stand it.

Though the trees rustled, and the nocturnal animals chittered away happily, I couldn't help but feel completely alone. I tossed and turned for a few minutes before I sighed and got up out of my tent.

I peered out of the tent where Gil and Makenna were chatting happily close to each other next to the fire. "Hey, Gil," I called out.

He turned at my voice and smiled. "Whatcha need, Eris?"

"I'm sorry to ask, but would it be okay if Kenna slept with me tonight?"

He laughed, his baritone voice rumbling to echo through the forest. "Can't sleep without someone next to you, I get it. But who're you missing more, Duran or the kids?"

"Both," I answered honestly.

Gil thumbed over to Makenna. "She'd poison me in my sleep if I spoke for her, ask her—"

She smacked Gil playfully on the arm. "Only when you deserve it, you big lughead," she replied, leaning over to kiss him deeply. "Love you."

"Love you more."

She hopped up from the log and skipped over to me. I went back inside, and she followed. I lay back down as Makenna stripped to her nightclothes and removed the hair ties from her pigtails. She shook her crimson hair out and lay down next to me. "Holy hell, you're like a furnace, Eris!"

"Is that a good or bad thing?"

"Well, it means I won't get cold during the night, and I thought Gil ran hot. You must have fire in your blood." She threw off the blanket and snuggled up next to me. "Though it's kinda nice. Gil snores in his sleep, makes it hard to sleep next to him sometimes."

"You're good together, though."

Kenna blushed furiously and couldn't hide the grin that bloomed on her face. "He's something special, but you know what that's like, don't you?"

I smiled at the thought of Sam, but it fell when what I'd been trying to forget came to mind. "He's not doing well. He's weak, cold and hungry. And so very angry. I'm terrified for him, but I'm also terrified of what's going to happen when we see each other again."

Kenna froze, her eyes widened. "Something happened didn't it? Between you and Evelyn?"

I shook my head.

"So with Reina."

The words were on the tip of my tongue, but I held my mouth closed and looked away from her waiting gaze.

She pouted. "Don't stop at the good part. what'd you do? Never mind, I can guess. Did you?"

"Yes."

There was no way for me to hold them back, the word came spilling out along with too many tears. "Sam's so angry." I sobbed. "What if he hates me?"

Kenna came over and wrapped her arms around me, her warm cheek pressed against mine as her hands came up and brushed my hair. "It'll be okay. I don't think he can hate you." She pulled back and wiped away the tears that fell to my chin. "Just be honest with him. Make him understand, and if he rejects you after that, then you know you did everything you could."

She held her hands up quickly. "But he won't reject you. I can almost guarantee it. He cares too much about you to hate you."

"I'm worried about him."

"It'll be okay, Eris. He'll be fine. Duran is reckless, rough around the edges, and a truly terrible guild leader, but he's the second toughest bastard I've ever met, and if I'm guessing things went wrong, and you said he's cold and hungry, then he's in Tombsgard. A nasty prison, but if anyone can thrive in such conditions, it'll be him. Don't give up hope, and have faith in him. He'll return to you."

"Thanks, Kenna."

She leaned over and placed a kiss on my hair. "It'll all work out, trust me."

With that my eyelids grew heavy, and I drifted off to sleep listening to Makenna's deep breathing.

In the morning, Gil woke us up by barging into the tent.

"Sorry for the rude awakening, but Duran just called."

I was awake in an instant. "What'd he say?"

"He was only able to talk for a second. He said he'd be fine and not to call in the calvary. Said he has a way to escape."

"Escape Tombsgard?" Makenna said, rubbing the sleep from her eyes. "It's possible, but I don't know how Duran could pull it off. He's not exactly the slip in and out unnoticed kind of guy."

"He'll do it. I know he will," I said.

Gil nodded and gave me a reassuring smile. "I'm gonna go let the twins know while you two get dressed. We hit the road in twenty."

After we got dressed and had a very light breakfast, we set off towards Castle Gloom-Harbor.

We spent most of the week on the road back to the castle. It was mostly a quiet trip back, broken by only a few random monster attacks. When we crossed back into the Salted Mire, we accidentally stirred up a nest of over a dozen rougarou in the swamps.

They rose up from the muck as twisted, mangled hybrids of wolves and dogs. Their matted fur was filled with mange and clung with mud and bits of swamp. The sudden appearance of them surprised us, but all of us leapt off our horses and into battle.

I personally killed one of them with a lucky headshot when I drew my bow and loosed an arrow at one of the rampaging beasts as it came toward me. The others dispatched their foes quickly. I fired a few more times, but I missed more than I hit.

It was quick, brutal, and over in a handful of minutes, leaving me with a sense of accomplishment that I'd helped—and a mess of muck and mud in my hair and over my clothes.

"I need a bath," I said to myself, but my words carried over the silence.

"Truer words, sister," Makenna said.

After we cleaned ourselves off as best we could, we climbed back on our horses and continued out of the swamps. The scent of salt clung to my skin and the back of my tongue with every inhale, but there was nothing we could do about it but grin and bear it.

By the time we made it back to the castle a few days later, all of us were exhausted from the trip, and when the heavy wooden gate shut behind us, we all heaved a sigh of relief.

I led Lacuna to the stables and spent an hour or so brushing her down and praising her like Sam did. She was a wonderful horse, and I was thankful for her. I made sure she knew it too.

When I was finished, I shot straight to the third floor and into our room.

It was empty, vacant without Sam here next to me, but I ignored my rising dread and focused on getting myself clean.

After a week of not having a proper bath, I was in desperate need of one.

I slid out of my last pair of semi-clean clothes and tossed them in the wicker basket by the door. The steam invited me to join it, so I lowered myself and proceeded to take a very long time bathing. When I was done, I just lay on my back and drifted, unsure of what I should do next.

This is my home now, but why do I feel so much like an outsider without Sam by my side? Everyone here are my friends, part of my family now, and yet most of them are strangers to me.

There was a knock on the door that interrupted my thoughts. "Eris?" a feminine voice called out, muffled by the closed door.

"Come in."

The door opened, and Yumiko walked in, wearing a tight-fitting jade shirt and black pants. Her black hair fell freely past her pale skin and crimson eyes.

I didn't know why she was here, and it must've showed.

"There's a guild meeting in a few minutes about everything that's happened. Figured you would want to be there," she said, her voice quiet.

"Thank you for letting me know. I'll be there."

She nodded and was about to depart when I shouted, "Wait!"

"What?"

"Um, I wanted to apologize. When I first met you, I didn't like you. Vampires and my kind have never gotten along since we have fundamentally different concepts on blood. Because of that, our kinds were always at odds with each other. And I carried that mistrust over to you. For that, I'm sorry."

Yumiko shrugged. "Hey, forgive and forget. I didn't exactly choose to become a nocturnal, either. So I can't exactly blame you for your prejudices."

"How did you—"

She coughed. "The meeting is going to start soon. Wilson will have a stroke if we're late," she said quickly and left, shutting the door behind her.

Guess we all have things we'd rather not talk about. I hurriedly climbed out of the water and got dressed. I chose a long-sleeved royal purple tunic and a pair of Sam's black cotton trousers. They were several sizes too big, but I tied them tight with the drawstring. They were clean, but the dresser where they'd been kept had a soft lingering scent of Sam that clung to the wood and settled into his clothes.

When I was dressed, I made my way down the stairs to the first-floor guild hall. Very few of the others were inside when I entered; only Wilson, Levi, and Yumiko were present. They were making small talk when I entered, but it got quiet as the doors closed.

"Is it okay if I sit in Sam's chair?" I asked.

Wilson inclined his hand and motioned at the chair beside him. I sat down and smiled at him, trying once again to get him to like me.

"How have things been since we've been gone?"

"Busy. To say the least. We've got a lot to discuss."

After that he flicked his hand up and stared blankly ahead, using his interface. He promptly ignored me and left me to wait in silence till everyone else arrived. They trickled in at the pace of a melting glacier, and I drummed my fingers on the table while everyone filed in.

The other members of the Gloom Knights took their seats, and Amber came in carrying a tray with ale and water. She sat a glass of water in front of me, and I took a polite sip while she served everyone before departing.

"All right, first on the agenda is our newcomer," Wilson said, whistling.

At the shrill tone, the doors opened, and a man I hadn't seen before came in. He was handsome, but his dark eyes told a different story. He looked worn down, jaded by life, and his dusk brown skin bore the scars to prove it.

He wore a plain black shirt and pants that matched his tied back hair. The man came and stood along the wall by the table.

"Most of you know him, but for those who've been gone, let me introduce Mika. An old friend of Duran's."

The name tugged at me, and I remembered the conversation Sam and I had shared about his previous life. "Takamikazuchi, right?" I asked.

Mika looked up, eyes lighting up in surprise. "Yes, that's right. How'd you know?"

"Sam—Duran told me. You were a member of the Swords of Legend with him."

He smiled. "You must be Eris. He spoke of you fondly."

Wilson cleared his throat. "Be as that may, let's get to what you told me when you arrived."

"Right. I was hired to provide support for a retrieval job in Aldrust. I didn't know what we'd be stealing or who I'd be working with until I got there. You can I imagine my surprise when I got there and saw Duran but was also told that our target was fucking Lachrymal's Heart.

"Duran and I had an account to settle, but after, we got to work planning the heist. We work the town, make sure there are no hiccups and the time comes to pull the job and D and the shifter infiltrate the Iron Cathedral—"

"Shifter?" I asked. "A shapeshifter? Who?"

"Girl's name was Raven. Gorgeous, black hair, pale skin and blood-red eyes."

Her description told me nothing. I hadn't had much experience with shapeshifters or the fae. *Mother always warned me never to make a deal with a faery. That they couldn't be trusted.*

"Anyway," Mika continued. "They were in there for a while, and I thought everything was going well before dwarven soldiers started flooding the streets. I left the guys I was working with and went to warn Duran. He fought off nearly six of Lachrymal's Chosen by himself." He paused, and a smile form at his lips before he started talking again. "He was a beast, but one of them summoned a stone golem, and I stepped in. We took care of the rest, and I helped him get out of there. We spilt up, but that was over a week ago now, and I thought he'd have been back by now."

"What happened with the Heart?" Gil asked.

Mika shrugged. "Duran said Raven had it, was taking it back to their employer."

"Magnus," I hissed.

"No idea. Never learned their name, all I know is that they paid incredibly well."

I sat back in my chair and drank the rest of the water. Sam had once again shut off our connection, and even though I could have broken through it at any time, I didn't want to know what lay beyond. I was didn't want to know what he was feeling right now.

"Duran isn't answering, but his contact card is still available so it's going through. Gil filled me in on where he's at, but I still don't like leaving him in there. It's not a forgiving place."

"Well, the guild leader, while he may be a complete imbecile, is capable enough, and I'm sure whatever situation he's managed to get himself stuck in, he can get himself out again," Evelyn said, standing up. "Is that all, Shadow?"

Wilson raised his glass to his lips and nodded. "Until Duran gets back, there isn't anything else to go over."

"Very well. Little queen, samurai, come with me. Right now."

Evelyn's tone left no room for disobedience, and I got up immediately.

"Don't break them," Wilson called as Evelyn strolled from the room.

I followed her, while Mika lagged behind. Evelyn led us to the second floor, and after passing a number of doors, she stopped and motioned us inside.

The room was sparse, but not barren. Padded mats littered the floor with humanoid training dummies placed at random throughout the room. On one side of the room was rack after rack of nearly every kind of weapon I'd ever seen before.

"All right, newbies. I'm going to find out what you're made of. I already know the little queen's strengths and weaknesses, but I need to find out how capable you are, samurai."

Mika scoffed and walked up to Evelyn, who was shorter than him by half a head. "I'm game, though don't say I didn't warn—"

Evelyn lunged forward and slapped the blade of her palm against Mika's neck. As Mika gasped and spluttered, Evelyn shifted on the balls of her feet and turned, bringing him with her. Evelyn lifted Mika over her back and slammed him against the mats.

With one hand still pinned, Evelyn calmly placed the arch of her foot against his throat. "I believe I am victorious."

Mika struggled viciously against Evelyn, but the more he fought, the more pressure Evelyn applied. After a minute of fighting, Mika ran out of air and started choking. He surrendered quickly after that.

Evelyn stepped back and returned to the center of the room. "As I was saying. Let's get started. Samurai."

Mika picked himself off the floor. "That wasn't us getting started?"

"That was just to put you in your place."

He chuckled and bowed low, keeping his eyes on her. "Forgive my conduct. That was incredibly rude of me."

Evelyn laughed. "You're forgiven."

"Just go easy on me next round. Please."

She smiled, her frosty eyes chilling the room. "I refuse."

CHAPTER 22 - MICE IN A MAZE

Sampson

After the fourth day in Tombsgard, my body simply couldn't handle it anymore.

"By the nine kings of hell, I'm so tired," I muttered to myself.

My trembling hands slipped, and I dropped my pickaxe. It clanged loud against the stone and drew the nearby worker's gaze.

"The fuck you looking at?!"

They jumped and quickly got back to mining. I left my pick where it lay and dragged myself over to a nearby table. I sagged into the chair and nearly passed out from exhaustion. *The king of the mine, and I'm withering away to nothing.*

"You look like hell," Maus said.

Maus sat beside me, and checking the coast was clear, pulled a bit of bread from his inventory.

"I feel like it," I replied as he stuffed the crust in his mouth.

"You should get some sleep; I'll keep watch for an hour or so." Crumbs of bread stuck to his lips and scattered to the stale air as he spoke.

"Thanks."

I leaned my head over onto the gray stone and was asleep before Maus could dry swallow his next piece of stale bread.

"Hey, get up. It's time to go," Maus said, roughly shaking me awake.

It seemed like I'd gotten less than a second's sleep before I had to open my bleary, sleep-encrusted eyes, and they stung as the dim light of the mine shaft came into focus.

"I'm up, godsdamn it."

"Good, 'cause it's dinner time."

I got up from the creaky wooden chair and shuffled in behind the growing line of prisoners filing out of the tunnel. The faint ring of the dinner bell sent a hypnotic miasma over everyone, and like rats to cheese, they followed without question.

As we reached the common area, the guards were all lined up on the railing overlooking us, bows at the ready while two soldiers stepped onto the stone elevator with today's meal. Even from here, with the packed reeking bodies, the strong aroma wafted from the steaming cauldron. Lentil soup—vegetarian, if my nose was leading me straight. I'd have killed every last prisoner in here for a nice, juicy steak, or ye gods, a godsdamned ale.

The inmates lined up as the platform descended, and the guards cupped soup into tiny metal bowls for them. As the line thinned, Maus stepped up to receive his bowl, but as soon as his fingers curled around it, one of the soldiers, a wiry, pinched-faced man, knocked it from his hands.

"Oh, my bad, Maus. Don't worry, I'll go fetch you a fresh cup right away," Bayln said.

Maus hung his head and walked over to where I was sitting, which didn't go unnoticed.

"How about you, king? You look hungry, your majesty, please, let me go fetch our finest suckling pig for your refined palette."

"Keep laughing, Bayln," I said, holding up my hand. Without even needing to voice it, black chitin formed a wicked-long set of claws over my hand.

I drummed my talons over the table rhythmically, carving shallow divots in the wood each time my fingers struck down. "You won't find it so funny when my hand is writhing in your guts, rearranging your intestines."

Bayln paled a tad and took a step back, visibly stopping his hand from going to his sword. He realized what he was doing and stood ramrod straight, putting a false mask of confidence over his features. "Whatever, king. You're stuck in the hellhole. You can't touch me!"

He glanced up and nodded to one of the men. Within a second, the platform rose once more, and Bayln spared once last sneer at me before leaving.

"What a fucking prick," Maus said, leaning back in his chair.

"Yep, but most of them are that way. Bayln isn't special, he's just an ass. Speaking of, thank you for the assistance, Aspect."

"You're welcome, knight. Though I expect to be repaid in blood."

I promise, I'll get you as much as you want—within reason—when we get out of here.

Maus looked at me sideways. "You have a weird fucking class, Duran."

"You're telling me, but it beats out infiltrator," I snapped back with a wry grin.

He couldn't help his smile. "Screw you."

Our rumbling and aching stomachs stole the smiles from our faces. It had grown from hunger pangs to gut-ripping agony as the days wore on. The little bits of food we snuck staved off death, but only just. We were going to die if we didn't do anything. Either from hunger or one of the prisoners.

"We need to leave tonight if we're going," Maus said.

"Yeah, but don't get your hopes up. I'm betting it just leads to a dead end."

"Let me be the judge of that. Besides, what else do I have to look forward to in this pit of decay? A slow, painful death by starvation or a shiv in my back. I've been here six months already. I'm not going to survive another six months."

"Fair point. We'll check it out on night duty tonight. We'll have a couple hours before anyone comes and checks on us."

While the other prisoners got to sleep in bunks in an antechamber connected to the mine, we had to stay awake and keep working, and every so often a different prisoner was voted to come and check on us. Some would keep their mouths shut, but I knew at least a few would spill their guts at the first opportunity, so it was constantly a gamble to try and get some sleep.

"Oi! Get back to work, your highness. Enough lollygagging!"

I glared up at the guard but sighed and stood. "Looks like our break's over with," I said before shouting, "Food was delicious as always, Bayln. But next time use more spit, really adds to the flavor!"

"Fuck off, king. Get back to work before I have you beaten."

Maus and I left the common area and headed back into the shaft. I snagged my pick where it had fallen and started swinging away at the rock. After an hour of chipping away at the wall, soft footsteps echoed from further up the tunnel. *Right on schedule.*

A dwarven girl with short brown hair and a missing ear peeked her head 'round the corner and glared at us before popping back under cover and scampering back to the others. As soon as she was out of sight and her footsteps faded away, I traded grins with Maus.

"Give me five minutes, and we'll switch," I whispered.

He nodded and took my pickaxe, hammering in a stilted chaotic cadence while I ducked into a small shaft near us and sank against the wall until I hit the ground. I pulled out a large portion of meat and my waterskin and downed them as fast as I could while I gathered what remained of my strength.

The five minutes passed like seconds, and with a soft whistle, I groaned and picked my weary body back up and shambled over to Maus. He handed me the pickaxes and went to rest. I broke the rock apart and collected what ore I could in a large wheelbarrow that rested beside me. Normally there were rewards for bringing in a good haul, but per Balthazar, I got none of them no matter what I brought up.

When Maus's time was up, I whistled and handed him back his pick. We contoured the slog until the next prisoner came and checked up on us. As they departed, and the coast was clear, I dropped my pick.

"Let's go. We don't have long."

Maus smiled and tossed his tool next to mine, and we headed deeper into the shaft.

The tunnel we were heading for was at the deepest part of the mine and had been abandoned when there was no ore to be found. It was closed off by a slab of smooth stone that set it apart from the rest of the craggy and uneven rock surrounding it.

Maus and I had taken turns going at the stone until we'd broken through the day before. A rush of moldy, stagnant air rankled my nose, and I knew we'd found something that hadn't been touched in years. Maybe it led to nothing but a dead end, or maybe there would be something hidden inside.

It took us over ten minutes of walking till we reached the tunnel. It was decided that this section of the shaft was barren, and as such, there were no tools or digging equipment around. It was just endless gray rock. We took a right when we reached the cavern, and in another few minutes, we were at the sealed-off tunnel.

Maus peered into the crack I'd made and recoiled. "Told you this would lead somewhere!"

"Yeah, but we still don't know if it's an escape. This could just be a waste of time."

"Oh, ye of little faith."

"Then let's take a look," I said and reached into the crack. As before, chitin crawled from my pores, and I gripped the hunk of rock and yanked hard.

It crumbled under my fingers, bringing loud chunks crashing to the floor with a cloud of rock dust that clung to our throats as we inhaled. I spluttered and coughed to clear my airway, and when everything finally settled, we got a good look at what was behind the sealed door.

It was pitch black; we couldn't see a thing.

Maus laughed as we stared into the abyss. "Got a light?"

"Well, if we're breaking the rules anyway, might as well break them completely."

I pulled a torch from my inventory and got it lit. The biting flame illuminated the wide corridor and chamber behind us, but only banished a couple dozen feet of darkness before it curved.

"Well, let's get a move on. Once it's discovered we aren't working, they'll come looking for us."

"Good point, let's scout it out and get back."

We both stepped into the cavern and began our descent. It was wide enough for several people to move side by side, so it held with our theory of being an abandoned mineshaft, but I hadn't seen one purposefully boarded up like it was, so I was wondering what the warden was trying to keep hidden. Signs of heavy mining littered the walls as we went deeper in, but after about three minutes of walking, the excavation slowed and then stopped all together, by the time we reached the end.

"Look at that," Maus said, pointing upward.

Just above my head was a pretty large vein of iron, completely untouched.

"Well, we know they didn't close it because the shaft ran dry, so there has to be something here they didn't want discovered."

"But what?" Maus threw up his arms and spun in a semi-circle. "We're at the end, and there isn't anything here."

A thought struck me. "Maus, what abilities do you have for infiltrator?"

"A few," he replied warily. "You know I'm not going to tell you them, though."

"No, man." I shook my head. "Screw game etiquette, do you have *Layout?*"

"Oh! You think something is hidden away here."

"Has to be something along those lines."

He nodded and knelt, holding his hand out, palm facing upward. A subtle brush of wind licked at my skin for a second before being whisked away by the stale, still air in the bottom of the mine shaft. Maus chuckled as he stared at the invisible map in his hand, which quickly turned to full-blown raucous laughter. "You were right. There is something beyond the rock."

"Don't keep me in suspense."

He closed his fist and stood up. "I don't know what lies beyond it, but *Layout* showed empty space, and that means there's something other than rock. That's all I care about. Whether it leads to freedom is another story, but it gets us the hell out of here."

He walked over to the back wall and rapped his knuckles on the stone. "That's hard rock, though. Getting through it is going to be a bitch."

I smiled. "Well, we best get started."

***

With one last heavy swing of my pick, we carved a hole just wide enough to squeeze through.

"That was fucking miserable," Maus said, as he doubled over, panting.

"Yeah, no kidding."

It had taken us most of the day to excavate the wall. We took turns wailing at the unyielding stone until it relented and bent to our desires. We'd worked in shifts, mining until exhaustion to get the hole cleared. We'd been gone for hours, and the prisoners were sent into the mine looking for us, but thanks to Maus's *Chameleon* ability, we were able to disguise the hole we'd made in the start of the shaft and stayed quiet until they left.

But after twelve hours, we'd knocked a hole four feet wide and five feet deep and finally broke through to the other side.

The downside was that we were both utterly spent. I could barely move, let alone fight, and whatever lay beyond the hole was uncharted territory.

"If we go through right now, we go at our worst, and I don't like our chances," Maus said.

"If we stay, we risk capture by the prisoners and being turned over to the guard."

"Both just terrific options," he replied with a weak chuckle.

There weren't any better options. Either we stayed and recovered, risking being found and captured, or we took a chance on the mysterious hole to nowhere.

"I vote the hole, but I'm not going to fault you on your decision."

Maus wasn't my friend, wasn't part of my guild. I owed him as much as he owed me: nothing. We were tied in mutual bondage, but what he chose was his will, as was my own. I wasn't going to stay one second longer.

I stepped through the hole and looked back. "Your choice, Maus, but I'm getting out of here. I've been away too long. I refuse to stay when freedom is right here."

He glanced back up the tunnel and back at me. "Fuck, you're right. Let's get the hell out of here, exhaustion be damned."

He followed behind me, and we slid through the crack. The tight wall brushed on my chest and back, making breathing difficult. For a few seconds claustrophobia tempted my heartbeat, but then I was through and standing on the other side.

It was just as dark, and I'd had to stow my torch to make the climb. I pulled it out and relit it. The darkness recoiled in surprise, and the biting orange flame illuminated our surroundings and danced along the walls.

More of the same rock on this side, but it spread in a rough circle around us, and our little bubble had been carved by hand, rather than nature. The sharp scrapes and tool marks that riddled the space told me as much. *What the hell is this place?* My question had to wait as Maus slid out behind me. He coughed and hacked up a gob of phlegm onto the floor.

"Damn, what is this place?" Maus stared and scratched his head. "Not a part of the mine, the markings aren't from mining. They're from excavation."

I peered closer at the marking and realized he was correct. And that they were old, years and years old. But that alone didn't tell us anything. "Let's keep going, see if we can find a way out of here."

We pushed forward and eventually came to the end of the room, and on the far wall, was smooth stone bricks, worn and crumbling from age.

"Shit, do you know what this has to be?" I asked.

"A building buried deep under the earth, housing some ancient Lovecraftian monstrosity?"

I laughed, despite the pain. "Hopefully not, but this has to be a forgotten part of old Aldrust, something that was left over when the dwarves rebuilt it."

"Okay, but how does that help us?" he asked, exasperated and exhausted.

We were both at the end of our rope and struggling just to stay on our feet. The days of little food and sleep had taken their toll.

Rushing wind split the still air, and I turned at the sound, going for my sword, only to find it not on my waist.

I was slow turning, too slow to react fast enough.

A small hunk of rock grazed my forehead as it sailed past, ripping a rough tear across my scalp. It clanked against the stone behind me as I hastily equipped my steel.

"The hell was that?" Maus asked, stating it into the darkness.

"I've got an idea," I replied as the adrenaline of battle flooded through my veins.

My hunger and exhaustion didn't matter anymore; the only thing that mattered was the sword in my hands and the blood I was about to spill.

Another rock flew toward me from the abyss, and I angled the flat of my sword just in time to deflect it.

"Quit hidin', you bloody coward!"

"Maus, shut it and draw your weapon. If there's one, there'll be more."

He shot me a questioning look but did as I told him and donned his mottled gray and black armor, drawing an elegant dagger. I couldn't wear my armor; it was too heavy and would sap my strength like nothing else. I needed mobility for what was coming for us.

They clung to the darkness like ghosts, but only one thing would be this deep below the earth, and they travelled in clusters.

One of them scuttled into view of the torch, lighting their malformed features.

It was tiny, moving quickly on six legs. Its spindly lower half ended at its waist, and a childish torso slunk into view. A wide head with no mouth or nose stared back with eight sets of lidless eyes. Dull white irises reflected the light of the torch.

"The fuck is that?"

"A knocker," I replied. "Be fast on your feet. They'll chuck rocks fast enough to crush your skull if they hit. They're territorial little bastards, and we've just intruded on their domain."

More stone cut through the air, and we scattered as they pinged around us. There wasn't any cover in the room, and there was no way we could shimmy back through the gap in time before we got brained by one of them.

Our best bet was to retreat rather than engage. They wouldn't stray far from their home, which meant if we could get far enough away, they wouldn't follow us.

Maus dodged a volley of rocks, but he tripped, and one of them smashed into his forearm. A sharp crack echoed sharply, followed by a tortured scream as Maus clutched his limp wrist. Bloody bone split his skin, and crimson rose around it to spill down his fingers.

It's broken, but at least it was his off hand. We didn't have any more room for mistakes, but we couldn't stay in the room. It was a deathtrap, and sooner or later we'd exhaust ourselves and our luck.

"Maus, get to cover!"

"Where?"

My eyes scanned the darkened cavern, and besides the enclosed space we resided in, there was nothing but the wall in front of us. *If we can get inside, they'll be forced to come down from the ceiling to attack us.*

"Follow me!" I shouted, running for the other end of the room.

Lend me your power, I need it.

"Of course."

I skidded to a stop when I reached the smooth gray brick of the long-forgotten dwelling. With my hands encased in chitin, I tore at the mortar that held them together and ripped them apart with ease. The wall came down like clay in my hands, and in a handful of seconds, we had our egress.

Maus filed in after me, and we paused in what had once resembled a workshop. Stone tables were strewn with a heavy layer of dust, and the rusted remains of iron lay in scattered chaos.

I kept an eye of the entrance while Maus pulled a health potion from his inventory and downed it in seconds. His labored breathing evened out as his bones reset in his arm, and he wiggled his fingers, twisting and bending his wrist.

"Much better."

"Good, 'cause we've got company."

Four thumps landed on the roof, and many legs scuttled towards the gap I'd made. They crept over the lip, clinging to the ceiling. When they spotted us, they fell to the floor and raised their slender appendages.

They scraped them along the edges of the floor and walls, and the rock bent to their will, forming heavy clumps of stone at the tip of each limb. As they reared back to throw them, Maus threw himself to the side, and I activated *Dance of the Immortal*.

What little color that existed in this gray landscape bled away to mix with the stone around us. Maus froze mid-roll, his chin tucked to his collarbone. The knockers froze before they could loose their homemade projectiles at us.

I had ten seconds to kill them, it was more than enough.

They had grouped up, making my job easy for me. I crossed the room and arced the edge of my steel through the neck of the first knocker. It hung in the air as my blade passed through it and the momentum carried my swing to the second monster.

The tip scored a deep gash in the second's cheek and split its jaw in two, continuing until the metal lodged in its throat.

I pulled my sword free and vaulted over the split-mouth knocker to engage the final two. For my encore, I rammed my blade through the chest of the one on the right and grabbed the final knocker in my blackened hand.

I crushed its windpipe, tearing through its soft skin to shred and pulp its flesh and arteries. Too-dark blood sprayed from the wounds I'd inflicted, and the color stuttered, telling me my time was up.

I left the carcasses of the creatures to fall and ran back to my original position, just managing to wipe the blood from my blade before the world restored its dominance, and I sagged to my knees.

"The fuck?!" Maus shouted when he came out of his roll and saw the blood-strewn bodies.

I couldn't muster the strength to even speak, and my sword slipped from my fingers as my battle fatigue jumped to nearly max and I fell to the ground. Maus raced over to me and pulled me out of the path of the pooling gore.

"What just happened?" he asked, his voice frantic.

I tried to form words, but using *Dance* had taken the last of my strength, and I lost consciousness.

When I finally opened my eyes, I hurt everywhere. The nap I'd taken had only exacerbated my exhaustion, and sitting up brought aching misery to my bones and muscles. Maus sat cross-legged by a fire.

"Where are we?" I asked, looking around.

We were in a building, equally as decrepit and worn as the workshop, but it wasn't the same building. The roof was convex, rather than flat.

"Still in the cave, just a lot further in. Had to carry your ass when more of those knockers showed up after the others died. Which, speaking of, how the hell did you do that?"

"Do what?" I asked, feigning ignorance.

"Don't give me that," he said, waving a thin wooden skewer at me, its tip blackened by flame. "All four of those things die at the same time and then you collapse like your battle fatigue maxed out. I know you did something, just can't figure out what."

I shrugged and grabbed one of the skewers that still had a bit of food on them and dug in. The meat was bland, absolutely no seasoning, but I was ravenous and inhaled it as fast as I could chew.

"Don't know what you want me to say," I replied with my mouth full.

He gave me a sideways look and smirked. "Fine, then, keep your secrets."

Maus didn't pry more after that, and I was thankful. He'd revealed a bit about his own class, but that was only because it was necessary to us getting out of Tombsgard. He'd dragged me out of a bad situation, and I owed him, but I wasn't about to spill one of my trump cards to someone I didn't trust.

Haven't killed a knocker in a while. Let's see what they gave me.

Combat Results!
4 Killed (Knocker): 3400 Exp!
Total Exp Gained: 3400 Exp!
Exp: 5900/5900
Level Up!
Level: 60
2900/6000
10 Stat Points Available!
1 Ability Point Available!

Finally made it back to sixty. Good. Though I need to think about what ability I want next. I grabbed my sword and looked down at the slight trickle of poison.

Poison Blade *has been helpful, but not all that useful since I've increased my* Attack Damage. *Might think about removing it and choosing something else.*

But that can wait till I'm not so exhausted.

We stayed there for a few hours, just gathering our strength and napping in shifts. The threat of being discovered was mitigated by the knockers. Even if anyone from Tombsgard found the hole we'd made, the knockers would keep them from following us.

When our strength returned, we set off again through the forgotten and abandoned ruins. They were falling to pieces; some of the very stone itself crumbled under our feet when we stepped on it. It took nearly a full day of exploring the maze of streets and buildings, but we finally found a passage that connected to a section of the new Lowtown.

It took some digging and Maus using *Layout* nearly fifteen times over the course of eighteen hours, but we finally broke through the stone and reached civilization again.

As the dust cleared, we climbed through the wall and stood in the warehouse district for Lowtown, only a few miles from the pleasure district, where I had a score to settle.

The two of us dusted ourselves off and made sure no one was around before moving.

Before we'd gone three steps, Maus turned, holding out his hand. "Thank you for all your help, Duran. I'm glad to have made an ally in that misery, but this is where we part ways."

"You sure?" I took his hand and gave it a firm shake. "I can't convince you to come back with me? Could always use someone like you in our guild."

He laughed and clapped me on the back. "Coming from the leader of the Gloom Knights, that's a fine compliment, but you've got a score to settle, and so do I."

I knew the look in his eye, knew I had no chance to convince him otherwise. So I didn't even try.

"All right, but it's an open offer. And I won't forget you pulling me from that place. You ever need help, just call," I said, handing him my contact card.

With a final wave, he vanished into the stone. *Good luck, Maus.*

Okay, time to go settle accounts.

CHAPTER 23 - RETURN

I kept to the shadows as I made my way to the Low Road. But there were hardly any citizens out at this time of night. Through the stone window, I found Orryn and Tel sitting by the bar, drinking.

The stone door was closed, but it was thin, easily broken if I put my all into it.

Ready?

"Drink her dry, drain them both."

I was angry enough that the Aspect's words were tempting, enticing even.

The heat of a furnace brushed my skin, and soon I was covered in the obsidian armor. I dug into the stone with my claws and pulled it from its frame with a grunt and resounding crack. It crumbled to nothing in my hand, and I stepped through the cloud to stare down the man who'd wronged me.

"Hey, Orryn. We need to talk."

Both turned when I ripped the door free, but Orryn didn't panic till he heard my voice. He knew it was me, even if I looked like a demon. He knew what awaited him.

His fear was palpable in the air, sweat and adrenaline drifted out with every hitched breath.

"Duran?"

"You remembered me, though it has only been a few days. Glad to see your memory is intact."

"I had no choice, I swear!"

"Doesn't matter. You betrayed me. For that, you die."

He sold me out, and I refused to let that stand.

I walked toward them, calm in my steps. There was only one entrance or exit, and they would have to get past me to escape. The end of the line.

"Fuck you!" Orryn shouted, hands outstretched as he began muttering in Script.

Tel followed his lead and dropped her illusion over her wings. With a shimmer, her dragonfly wings beat faster than my eyes could follow, and she rose to float over the bar. Her bright blue eyes shone in the candlelight as she scowled at me. She mirrored Orryn and began her spellcraft, both speaking in rolling tongues.

As their Script circles appeared in front of their hands, I chuckled and activated *Aura of the Antimage*. It blew across the room and shattered their nascent spells before they could finish. They stared in shock as their colorful magic dissolved back into the ether before their eyes, and they gaped at me.

"What?"

"How?"

I just laughed. "Easily."

With their magic broken and their mana drained, Tel could no longer hold herself up, and as the rainbow glimmer dimmed along her wings, she lowered back to the ground. Orryn snarled a curse and charged me. His wiry black hair clung to his sweaty face as he attacked.

Orryn swung aiming for my chin. I leaned back as his punch went wide and raised my jagged talons. As his arm sailed past, I hooked my fingertips into his bicep, just above the crook in his arm. Resistance tugged at my hand before giving way and sliding deep into his flesh.

Blood rushed from the wound, fleeing from his severed artery.

Before he could fall or retaliate, I kicked the back of his knee and brought him to his knees. "I cut your brachial artery. You'll be unconscious in less than half a minute, dead in under two. It'll be quick."

Blood pooled at his legs from the river soaking into his once white tunic. Orryn shot a final look at Tel and then back to me, his eyes unfocused and distant. "Sorry...don't hurt her—"

Orryn collapsed over to the floor from the blood loss, his eyes closing one last time.

I left him to his fate and crossed the room to stand in front of Tel, who stared at Orryn's body with tears streaming down her face. Only when my shadow darkened her features did she meet my gaze.

Panicked, she squinted her eyes, and a burst of rainbow light flared to life through her wings and they flitted, trying to fly. With the last drops of magic in her system, she tried to escape. Her feet lifted an inch from the ground before I reached behind her.

I took hold of the base of her wings and ripped them from her spine.

Tel wailed in tortured suffering as sinew and muscle tore free from her and stuck to the ends of her wings, dripping blood. I tossed them aside and clamped my hand over her mouth to silence her screeching.

"I only came for Orryn, but you had to interfere. I'd have left you alone, but you got in my way."

"Let me have her, let me taste of her, let me savor her sweetness!"

I sighed, but I owed it for lending me its power. *Just make it quick, we need to leave.*

"With pleasure."

***

I wiped the macabre stains from my mouth and spat, trying to remove the salty sweetness from my tongue. "I hope you enjoyed that, because I'll never get used to it."

"She was delicious. Her memories even more so."

Glad you liked them, but I really didn't need those memories, Aspect.

It chuckled darkly. *"They were some of the best she had. The others were...tame."*

I shook off the twisted laughter and left the Low Road. I needed to leave Aldrust, but it wasn't going to be easy. The entrance would be heavily monitored, and I was sure mine and Maus's escape was already spreading through the city. *It might turn into a fight if I try to leave that way, but I don't have much choice.*

There were still a few things I had to grab back at the hideout, namely the knife Thrayl had given me. I'd left it under the bed, and I didn't want to leave without it. Thrayl hated me now, so it would probably be the last thing I would ever own by him.

As calmly as I could, I slunk through the streets of Lowtown till I reached the house. I had a few scrolls left, and after the door slid away, I bolted through, eager to get in and get out.

My foot hit the stairs when a shuffle came from my right, and a heavy weight bore down on me.

Something incredibly sharp dug into my neck hard enough to draw blood, and I froze. They had me dead to rights. I risked tilting my neck to get a look at my assailant and sighed in relief when I saw her pale skin and bloody eyes.

"By the nine kings of hell, Raven. Scared me to death."

She flinched as if I'd shocked her and jumped back. Her wicked talons reached for the lantern by the couch. When light filled the room and she got a better look at me, she let out a breath and retracted her claws.

"Duran, thank the gods," she said, crossing the room to pull me to my feet.

Before I could respond when I stood, she wrapped me in a crushing hug.

"I'm okay, Raven. No need to try and squeeze the life out of me," I said, my voice strangled.

Raven pulled back, but her hands lingered on me. Her right cradled my neck, and as she stared up at me, a decision crossed her eyes and solidified.

Her fingers tensed and drew me closer to her as she pressed her lips to mine. They were incredibly soft and only a little chapped. Raven's mouth lingered on mine, but it was chaste, loving. It was a kiss that made clear her feelings for me.

Ones that I didn't know if I could reciprocate.

She pulled away a lifetime later with a subtle pop as our mouths uncoupled. Her breathing was uneven, her pulse raced, but she wore a wide smile as she backed away and dropped her hands.

My hand went to my lips as a whirlwind of emotion writhed in my chest. I was conflicted, so very conflicted.

"I'm sorry for springing that on you, but I wished I'd done it back at the cathedral, and I swore if I saw you again, I would find the courage to do it."

"I—I don't—we can't…never mind. What are you still doing here? I told you to leave."

"I did, and I came here. I was going to take the Heart back to Magnus, but I couldn't. I couldn't abandon you, not when you risked your own life to save mine."

"So you still have it?"

She nodded.

I sighed and went to the fridge to grab the last ale. I took a long pull and went and sat on the couch. *We don't have time to be sitting around, but I was planning to bust through the gate solo. I can't do that if she's beside me, let alone carrying the godsdamned Heart.*

"This complicates matters. I don't have a plan for getting us both out of Aldrust."

Raven plopped down next to me and snagged the ale as I was about to take a sip. She took a drink and passed it back. A small smile curled the edge of her lips. "I've got one."

"Oh, do tell."

"We use the vents."

"The vents? The air vents?"

"Uh-huh."

"You're insane, there's no way that could—" I tugged at my unruly beard, lost in thought. "Well. Okay, that might work."

I paused, working the logistics out in my head. *There isn't anything but a series of nets to keep debris clear from the vents themselves. In theory, it's a straight shot to the surface, though we'll have to break the metal encasing the shaft at the bottom and top to escape.* I didn't know how it would play out, but it was a better plan than rushing the guards and slaughtering them.

"All right, we'll get moving as soon as I get a bath. I don't even want to think about how nasty I am right now." I got up from the couch and turned to head up the stairs when Raven's hand closed around my wrist. "What?"

She frowned. "We're not going to talk about the kiss?"

I huffed and scratched my chin. "What do you want me to say, Raven? I'm already in love with someone, and even if I like you, it doesn't change that."

"But you do like me."

I sighed. "Yes, I like you, happy?"

She beamed at me. "For now."

I climbed the stairs and quickly drew a bath. As I hopped in, I sat back and let what just happened sink in.

That's not going to end well for me, I just know it. I'd hated what she was when we met, didn't want anything to do with her, but she was a lot like Eris. Not so much in their personalities, but she didn't give me any choice but to like her.

Especially now. After what Eris did, it's only fair I'm allowed to do the same. I shook my head. *Don't be ridiculous, I couldn't. I can't.* Eris had a good reason for what she did, I just knew it. I couldn't let that and whatever feelings I had for Raven influence my thoughts.

I knew Eris wouldn't care one bit about sharing, but that was something I didn't know if I could do.

It was every man's fantasy, but I was loyal to my partner, and even kissing Raven was a betrayal to Eris.

But she betrayed me first. I blew out a very long breath. *Worry about your love life after we get out of the city that would see us dead.*

I cleaned myself thoroughly and finally got rid of the beard. It had grown out and was filthy. *Never liked it to begin with. I only kept it because Eris liked it.*

When I was clean, I changed into a fresh set of clothes and raced to the bedroom to grab my knife from under the bed. I glanced at the black metal for a brief second as a wave of regret came over me before I stowed it away and went back downstairs.

Raven was waiting by the door, and as soon as I came down, she walked out. *Let's get going.* Raven glanced around the dead street before transforming. With a cloud of feathers, she became the giant black raven and lowered to let me on.

"We need to hurry; it's going to be hard to fly straight up with you weighing me down."

"Right."

I hopped on she took off in a single smooth motion. In a handful of seconds, we were soaring high above the sleeping city. I wasn't worried about anyone seeing us. There weren't many people out at this hour, and we were high enough up that we blended well into the shadows cast by the earth and rocks.

We flew past the giant cluster of mana crystals embedded in the ceiling; our reflections multiplied with the pulsating light. It was gorgeous, and my skin prickled with the condensed and stored up mana that leaked out ever so gently.

"It's even prettier up close," I said, staring as we passed by.

My remark didn't earn me a comment from Raven. Either she didn't hear me, or she was busy concentrating on flying. The closest vent came upon us quickly, and I let the chitin flow over me as we approached. The vent stuck out like a thick metal tube many dozens of feet wide. A thick cap clung to the tip of it, and a wire net prevented us from entering.

"I'll make a pass, and you climb onto the vent and create an opening," Raven said.

"Got it."

I readied myself, and when I was right underneath it, I leapt and clung to the vent like my life depended on it. Which it did.

I did an incredibly stupid thing and looked down. Far, far below me was Aldrust, and my stomach lurched, roiling with nerves. My skin went clammy just as cottonmouth dried my tongue and I fought to keep from hurling.

"Holy shit!" I swore and focused on anything other than the many hundreds of feet that separated me from becoming jelly on the pavestones.

With my claws, I set to work slicing through the dense wire, careful where I cut so I wouldn't cut away my lifeline. The string dipped and buckled as I severed it, and I clung ever tighter as I made a hole more than wide enough for Raven to fly through.

When I was finished, I slowly crawled up through the hole and perched on the lip of the metal while I caught my breath and my nerves quit screaming at me.

It only took a few moments before Raven flew up through the hole and landed beside me.

"That was kinda fun," she said.

"Yeah, but look up."

The tubular shaft stretched up and up; more nets like the one I'd just gut through hung on brackets every hundred feet or so. We had plenty to cut through to get out of this place.

"Well, we best get started."

This is going to take a while.

***

"Woo!" I screamed as we shot through the vent and out into the blistering daylight. "Freedom!"

It had taken several long hours of hopping from net to net before we reached the top, and by the time we were done, we were both slick with sweat and beyond exhausted. But soaring through the open air once again was more than enough of a reward for our hard work.

"I'll fly as far away from Aldrust as I can, but we'll have to find a place to stop and rest soon."

"Understood."

I sat back and relaxed as the cool wind whipped the sweat from my face and arms. The sun was bright and high in the sky, telling me it was mid-afternoon. I basked under the sun's rays as they brushed along my skin. We flew for an hour at least before Raven's tempo faltered and she slowed. She'd worn herself out and landed in a grassy field in the middle of nowhere.

As soon as I climbed off of her, she transformed back into her human form and sagged to the ground.

"Fuck, I'm beyond exhausted," she said, leaning back on her hands.

"I'm just glad we got away. Seems like whenever I leave a place these days, it's because people are chasing after me. You know, a month ago, my life was actually pretty simple. Now it's world-shattering conspiracies and power the likes of which I don't understand."

"You can't say it's not exciting, though."

"Ha, you know, back on my world, there was an old two-part curse that went something like that: 'may you live in interesting times.' These are certainly that."

Raven laughed as the breeze lifted blades of grass into the air around her and clawed at her gorgeous dark hair. "What was the second part?"

"May you find what you're looking for."

"Doesn't sound like much of a curse to me, but then again, my threshold is set at a terrifying little girl gouging out my eyes."

I chuckled and pulled out my bag, trying to find some food and drink. "Touché."

There was still a bit of dried food and water left, so I split it among us, and we scarfed it down while letting our fatigue fade.

"We better hurry," Raven began, fifteen minutes later. "I'd rather not reach Castle Aliria in the middle of the night."

"Hey, hand me the Heart."

She did as I asked, taking it out and passing it to me. I took it and grunted as the curse set in, but the reduction of my stats was nothing new, and I grinned and bore it. I stowed the gemstone away and stood up.

"I was fine carrying it. Why'd you take it back?"

"Because we're not going back to Magnus," I told her.

"What? Why?" she asked, climbing to her feet.

I had to admit, I liked Raven. Her personality and mine got along well, and I would be the first to admit I was wrong about her, but at that moment, none of that mattered if she was loyal to Magnus.

"I just spent the last five days working myself to the bone in Tombsgard. I'm tired, angry as hell, and I want to go home. Magnus has waited for his bauble long enough. Another day or two won't matter.

"Now the question you need to answer is where do your loyalties lie? If they're to Magnus, then you can run back to him like a good little slave." I held out my hand to her. "Or you can come with me."

It wasn't even a decision for her. She took my hand without hesitation, and my heart swelled.

"Then let's go home."

We set off and spent half a day flying. When I spotted the Rolling Hills in the distance, I knew I was home.

The sun faded under the horizon when we glided over Lake Gloom. The cool air was tinged with moisture, and it beaded along my skin and clothes. Castle Gloom-Harbor was the same as always, but I'd never seen it from on high like this, and as we dipped and flew over the gate, shouts rose from our men at arms.

Raven landed in the outer bailey as a group of guards approached in charcoal and purple armor, each of them brandishing their weapons.

"To the king who walks in shadow," I shouted before they made a foolish mistake.

At once the assault halted in its tracks. The man lowered his weapons. "Sorry, lord. We didn't know it was you."

I smiled at the rabbitman. "It's okay, Lyahgos, you were just doing your job, but speaking of…"

"Right, lord," he said in a rush, and they went back to their posts.

Raven transformed once again, and when her human form presented itself, she smiled. "You probably gave them a heart attack."

"You're the one who shifts into a big-ass bird."

She doubled over with laughter, and I was about to join her when a notification blared in front of my face.

Warning! Proximity to Hive Queen less than a hundred meters. Stat penalty removed.

Eris!

In that instant, I didn't care about anything else. I didn't care that she had slept with someone else, or that I was angry with her. It didn't matter in that moment.

I ran for the doors and arrived just as they opened. It seemed nearly every one of the Gloom Knights came to greet me as Gil and Wilson pushed open the doors, weapons drawn, with Evelyn, Adam, and the others close behind.

They just stopped and stared at me, eyes wide.

"Duran?"

"Hey, guys."

Wilson went to respond, but a voice silenced everything else in my world.

"Sam!"

Eris rushed through the crowd like oil through water and was suddenly standing before me. Her large obsidian eyes filled with tears as wind swept at her unruly golden mane.

Then she was in my arms, and everything was right with the world again.

I cradled her against me as she sobbed in relief and brushed my fingers down her hair as she shook. I didn't even care that she'd said my name in front of everyone. I no longer cared. All I cared about in that moment was Eris.

We stayed that way for only a short time, and after what must have only been a few seconds, she let go of me and stood. Though her eyes never left mine.

"I've missed you."

"As I you, my bonded."

I pulled her close and kissed her, telling her with my lips how much I loved her. And I knew that no kiss could ever hope to measure up to it again. Even though my entire world consisted of Eris, I became acutely aware of the eyes of the audience behind us, and I realized our touching reunion had a few more guests that I'd anticipated.

I broke the kiss with a final brush over her mouth and stood up. My fingers found hers and intertwined as I walked over and greeted my family.

"So what's new?"

Gil just laughed; his baritone echoed throughout the bailey as Wilson rolled up his sleeves of his black tunic, revealing his multitude of tattoos as he crossed his arms.

"Seems we have a lot to discuss. If we could all adjourn to the guildhall…"

"Oh, goody. A meeting."

***

Saying there was a lot to cover was an understatement to say the least. Since I'd met with the puppet master himself, I went first. I told them nearly everything. About meeting Magnus, the power he wielded, and the staggering amount of wealth he possessed. And stealing Lachrymal's Heart. I left out anything about Aliria, and I especially left out the fact that we'd been here for nigh on a millennia, at least for the time being.

Magnus had promised answers, and when I had all the facts, then I would share them.

And then they told me of their journey to Slaughter Woods and meeting the Arachne queen. Eris told me of their fight with the gigantic spider Misumena.

I winced when she told me of getting impaled.

"That explains what happened in the vault," I said.

"What?" she asked.

"I had the Heart in my hands when my own stopped. I fell, and things got...complicated." I knew the forlorn look on her face and stopped her. "Wasn't your fault for getting stabbed, love. Don't even think of blaming yourself."

She chuckled and squeezed my hand. "You know me too well, my bonded."

Neither of us broached the topic we knew we needed to discuss. It would come later, and I just wanted to enjoy being next to her for a while longer.

"Can we see the Heart?" Wilson asked.

"Sure," I replied and pulled it out of my inventory. It retained its size, sitting comfortably in my hands. "Just be careful of it. It's no mere gem."

I slid it to the center of the table, and everyone stared in wonder at it.

"Kinda small, don'tcha think?" Harper asked, his hands absentmindedly running through his short hair.

"It's always about size with men," Yumiko joked, snorting with barely suppressed laughter.

"Har, har."

"Adam, look," Evelyn said, nudging her brother.

"No, I see it. But how would he know?"

Evelyn shrugged. Her golden eyes dimmed as she squinted at the emerald on the table before they widened. "Couldn't be. Guild leader, this Magnus— what does he look like?"

"Uh, average, I guess. Not tall or short, medium build. Shaggy blond hair, green eyes."

Her eyes lit up in surprise, which was the most emotion I'd ever seen in them, and that terrified me.

"Excuse us," Adam said, standing from his chair.

They both left the guildhall before I could ask them what the hell was going on.

The rest of us stared after them until Wilson spoke up. "Well, I guess that concludes this meeting. I'm going to grab a bottle of brandy and try not to think too hard."

I stowed the Heart back in my inventory, and grimaced as the curse set in. *Guess I'll go grab a shower and some sleep. Though I still need to introduce everyone to Raven.*

I'd only briefly explained her presence, and that she was a shifter. The others took that fact much better than I had, though there was still plenty of distrust towards them.

"You can come in now," I called out.

Raven came in through the open door, followed by Mika. We exchanged nods.

"Glad to see you decided to take me up on my offer."

He laughed. "Well, I wasn't busy. Figured why not?"

Wilson cleared his throat. "So is everyone in agreement about allowing Takamikazuchi entrance into the guild?"

My hand shot up first, followed swiftly by everyone else's.

"Then it's settled. Welcome to the Gloom Knights, Mika."

"Glad to be here."

Eris came up and placed her hand on my lower back. "Who's your friend?"

"Oh, right," I said, motioning towards Raven. "Eris, this is Raven. Raven, Eris."

Raven smiled and held out her hand. "It's a pleasure to meet you. Duran wouldn't stop talking about you. All good things, of course."

Eris took her hand and jumped like a bolt of lightning struck her. Her eyes flicked down at their hands and then over to me. "So that's what that feeling was. You've bonded to my Sam."

Raven nodded and looked over to me. "It wasn't exactly by either of our choices, but it can be undone when we return the Heart."

She shrugged. "Oh, I don't mind. I completely understand. The Alice isn't known for her kindness, and I'm sure her contract was probably as ruthless as she is."

"That's putting it mildly," Raven replied.

"Anyway, Sam trusts you, and that's good enough for me."

"How do you know that?" Raven asked.

Eris smiled at her and let her hand go, turning to me. "Because we are bonded, I can feel what he feels, but even without that, it's plain in his eyes, his bearing. He relaxes around you, which tells me he trusts you, and that's all I need to know."

Raven beamed at her. "Thank you, but I still think Duran isn't exactly comfortable with the arrangement. If it's his choice, I will unbind with him."

"I think we can table that discussion for another time," I said, gesturing around the empty room. "I'm in desperate need of a bath and to catch up on my sleep. We can talk more in the morning."

"Of course."

We filed out of the guildhall and to the third floor, I showed Raven to her room, the one Eris had been staying in when this all started. I told her to come get me if she needed anything and bid her a good night.

After heading back to our room, Eris and I took the longest bath ever, and by the time my pruned and shriveled skin had soaked up a gallon of water, we got out and dried off, falling into bed together.

"Sleep," I moaned.

"Not quite, my love," Eris said, despair filling her eyes.

"Right." I sat up and pulled the tie from my hair. *Guess we'd better get this over with.*

I couldn't stop the anger and betrayal from creeping back from where I'd locked them away. They came willingly, and my heart burned in anguish.

"You slept with someone else. The spider queen, if the notification is any indication."

"I did," she said with hardly any emotion.

I shot up from the bed and whirled on her. "Why?"

"Because I needed her power, and that was the price she asked of me. That doesn't excuse what I did, though. I knew it would hurt you, but I still chose to agree to it." Eris paused. "I'm sorry I hurt you, my bonded. I am. But I needed Reina's blessing."

"So that makes it okay?"

I threw my hands up and paced the room, trying not to scream at her. The pacing helped while I waited for her response.

Eris didn't say anything for a long time, her head down and her arms folded over her chest as she sat on the bed.

"I nearly died, Sam. It was so close, and I know you felt what I felt. I nearly died because I'm weak, weaker than anyone here, and that can't continue. I refuse to let it continue." She stood and padded over to me, her hand found mine and she gave it a squeeze. "I love you. I love you as much as I've ever loved anyone, but Reina reminded me that I'm not human. And I shouldn't hold myself to human ideals.

"There is absolutely no love between Reina and I. It was simply an exchange of favors. My kind thrived on the practice, as I told you. It was business."

Her response was clear, logical, and I hated it. I hated that I understood her motivations. *But I knew she wouldn't have just done it because she wanted to. She isn't that kind of person. I knew she had to have a very good reason to sleep with someone else. My anger is just because she did it.*

My rage boiled to the surface, and I turned away from her, slamming my fist into the wall. Bone cracked, and the skin over my knuckles split open. "Godsdamn it, Eris. I get it!"

I turned and sagged to the ground, completely ignoring the pain in my hand. She was right, and I hated it.

My rage slipped out as cold apathy gripped me. I was too worn down. Too much had happened in the last few days, and I couldn't handle it. I brought my knees to my chest and laid my head on my arms.

"You're right. You're not human, and I can't stop you. Do whatever you want, I don't care."

CHAPTER 24 - ACCEPTANCE

Eris

Sam's words cut deeper than any blade, and I sucked in a breath as a cold weight pressed down my chest. As he hung his head, his voice defeated, I couldn't stop the tears that rushed over my cheeks. I'd hurt him so bad, and I didn't know how to fix it.

I dropped to my knees and crawled across the stone to him. My hands tugged at his warm skin. He tensed as I touched him, and my heart broke again. I grabbed for his hand, the one he'd damaged.

I tore my shirt off and ripped a long strip from it. He gave me the hand I gingerly wrapped and tied a knot to keep the bandage from falling off. When the blood stopped dripping, I just held his hand in mine, unsure of what to do.

Sam refused to look at me, his head hidden by his knees.

I couldn't take it. I pushed in between his legs and cupped his head in my hands.

"Sam, look at me."

He didn't move, and my desperation grew.

"Sam, please." My voice broke and I choked as I sobbed. I clutched at him, my hands digging into his shirt. "Please."

His head lifted as I devolved into hysterics and bawled into his chest. "I'm sorry, I'm sorry, I'm sorry." I didn't know what else to say, and my voice failed me as I cried.

Sam's powerful arms wrapped around me and brought me closer. I only cried harder at his touch and clung to him with everything I had.

His warm cheek brushed against mine, and he held me for a very long time before he spoke.

"I forgive you."

I only cried harder at his words, I cried until I had no more tears to cry and my throat hurt from the strain. Sam eventually picked me up and held me tight as he took me to our bed.

He didn't say another word as he leaned back against his headboard and ran his fingers through my hair. We stayed that way for hours, until eventually the emotional drain and exhaustion settled in and I fell asleep, still holding onto him.

***

I didn't know what time it was when I finally awoke, but from the way my eyes stuck together, I guessed we'd been asleep for a very long time. The events of the night rushed back to me, and a well of emotions rose in my chest.

Sam had forgiven me; his words and his touch told me that, but I wasn't sure if I'd forgiven myself, not of the act itself. I knew that I'd made the right choice there, but the pain that I'd caused him was something I didn't know if I could ever forgive myself for.

Sam breathed gently as he slept on his side beside me, his bare back presented to me. I never tired of staring at him, at his muscles as they rose and fell with every breath.

I placed my hand in between his shoulder blades and caressed down his back ever so slightly, just to make sure I wasn't dreaming. *Words can't express how much I missed you, Sam.* I leaned over and kissed his cheek, trying not to let his stubble tickle my cheek.

"Sleep, love. You've earned it," I whispered.

It was early, just after sunrise, and I should've been tired considering how much I'd slept the night before, but I guess we both needed the sleep. I'd never felt as refreshed as I did now. Though a slightly soured stench wrinkled my nose. *I need a bath.*

When I was clean, I dressed in a copper-colored tunic that perfectly matched Sam's hair and a pair of black pants that Yumiko had let me borrow.

Sam hadn't had an easy time the past few weeks, so I let him sleep.

Guess I'll train. I tied back my hair and crept out of the room to pad down to the second-floor training room. I was alone when I entered and quickly began warming up like Evelyn had taught me. When I was limber, I started on several exercises, called calisthenics, in order to increase my endurance and flexibility.

They were tough, and afterward, I was heaving and dripping sweat. *All right, stretching time.*

It was another of Evelyn's routines, and after I spent nearly thirty minutes trying to dislocate my limbs by contorting them to every possible angle, I was ready for my archery training.

I grabbed a washrag and doused it in a metal bucket with a sliver of fire stone inside to heat the water. I cleaned the sweat off as best I could and drank deeply from a waterskin hanging on a nail by the door.

The archery range was outside the castle in a courtyard beside the inner bailey. By the time I reached the walled-off stone area, the sun was bright over a cloudless sky. I ignored the rising heat and grabbed a wooden recurve bow from the covered rack next to the range.

I nocked an arrow and lined up at the circular straw target twenty-five yards away. The world dimmed as I focused on what Evelyn had taught me, slowing my breathing and waiting for the space between heart beats. I released the arrow, and it struck home several inches off center.

"You're tensing at the release," a voice said, breaking the silence.

I jumped and whirled around, trying not to shout as I stared at Yumiko, bow and quiver in hand, leaning against the side wall next to me.

She laughed and smiled at me. "Sorry, didn't mean to sneak up on you, but I figured with your hearing, you'd have heard me coming. I wasn't quiet."

"I was focused on my breathing and listening to my heartbeat."

Yumiko came up beside me and slung her quiver over her shoulder. She drew and nocked an arrow in a flash and released it just as quick. It struck dead center in her target.

"The way Evelyn trains isn't wrong. Hell, she taught me most of what I know, but her method isn't exactly right for you, not with how adamant you are about sticking close to Duran—and given his penchants for trouble, you'll be getting into more fights and don't need the beginner's version of her training.

"Here, let me help you."

She set down her bow and came up right behind me. Her hands were light on my skin, but her thick calluses rubbed roughly as she adjusted my form ever so slightly. "Now, nock and draw."

I did as she told me and readied my arrow. I sighted up my destination and waited for her instruction. "You're holding in your breath while aiming and letting it out too fast when firing. It's causing you to twitch just so. It takes practice, but you must keep breathing. In slow and out slow, fire at the end of the breath. It takes a lot of practice, but it'll help you when you can time your shots to coincide with your breathing."

She backed off and told me to give it a shot. I focused on what she told me and didn't hitch my breathing while going through the motions. I had my shot, and I released at the exhale. It landed just above the center, but it was closer this time, and it was smooth, rather than jerky.

Yumiko brushed a loose strand of hair over her ear and nodded. "Better. You won't master it overnight, but you've got the basics down enough. Just keep practicing, every day if you can. You'll get there," she said and began her own training. "Oh, and one more thing. Never let Harper try and train you. That idiot is a damn good shot, but his skill can't exactly be taught, and he has too many bad habits."

I told her I would only let her or Evelyn teach me, and we spent the next hour or so going through dozens of arrows. Little by little, shot by shot, I was getting better, more comfortable with the weapon in my hands. Even Yumiko praised me a few times, and that made suffering under the beating sun all worthwhile.

When I'd done as much as I could, and my arms started shaking with fatigue, I called it quits and went to take a bath and wake Sam. He was still sleeping when I came in, so I padded over and kissed his hair before taking the second bath of the day. It was much shorter than the first, and by the time I'd changed, my stomach was rebelling at the lack of food.

"Sam, time to get up," I called as I exited the bath.

"Ugh, don' wanna."

I chucked as I changed clothes and slid next to him in bed. I kissed his neck all the way up to his lips and lingered just above his lips. "Don't make me get the spiders," I said, teasing.

His eyes bolted open to see my smiling face peering down at him.

"You're evil."

"Yep." I kissed him softly. "Now let's get up. I'm starving."

"Uh-uh."

So fast I didn't have time to react, Sam grabbed me and locked his legs around the back of my knees. He rolled with his whole body and pinned me to the bed.

I yelped in surprise as he smiled down at me, all traces of the anger and pain last gone from his eyes. Only love remained, and it mirrored the look in my eyes.

"We have unfinished business, love," he said with a smirk.

"And what would that be?"

He leaned down and pressed his lips to mine. I returned his kiss and pried his mouth opened with my tongue, meeting his and pulling him close to me. I ran my tongue around his mouth, and my eyes widened when I passed over his teeth.

I pulled back, catching my breath before I spoke. "Sam, your teeth?"

He shook his head softly, letting his copper strands fall over us like a curtain. "We can talk more later, but I think we both deserve a proper homecoming, don't you?"

I couldn't agree more, and I told him with my touch as I grabbed him by the collar and pulled him down to me.

An hour or so later and after another bath, we got dressed.

Sam went to fix his nest of copper hair. By the time he came out a few minutes later, he looked much more refreshed. He wore a royal blue shirt and gray washed pants. As I was walking toward the door, his hand grabbed mine and stopped me.

"What is it?" I asked, my stomach gurgling loudly.

His expression darkened. "There's something I need to tell you, should've told you yesterday, but we had so much going on I didn't want to add to it. But you need to know, and I don't have the right to keep it from you."

Sam's expression was forlorn, pained. Whatever he had to tell me was hurting him, and that worried me. "What is it?"

"When I was brought to Magnus, I met someone. Her name is Aliria, and she's y—"

"She's an entomancer. I know, Reina told me about her."

He paused, his eyes haunted. "No, Eris. Aliria is your mother."

That familiar age-old pain shoved a dagger through my chest and caught my breath. Chills crawled over my skin, and my mouth went dry. "What? That's—that's impossible."

"I know, I can't explain it either."

"No!" I shouted, my hands going to my temples as blood pounded too loud through my head. "I watched her die; you watched her die in the Mnemosyne. It's not her, it can't be."

He stepped to me and pulled me close, holding me tight while my strength failed me.

I had no more tears to cry, and after a while of fighting my emotions and trying to understand what he'd told me, I finally took a deep breath. *Calm down. I need to calm down.* I dabbed at my puffy eyes and blew my nose as Sam stroked my hair and cheek.

"Are you sure?" I asked, terrified of the answer either way.

His chin pressed to the top on my scalp as he nodded. "She looks just like you, and she knew things that make it unquestionable. It's her."

"How?"

"I don't know. My first guess is Magnus. His power is unlike anything any of us have seen before. He said he wasn't, but I think he's manipulating the system somehow."

I wrapped my hand around his. "What does that mean?"

Sam sighed, his breath blew soft through my hair. "I can't really explain it; it wouldn't make sense to you. But basically, I think Magnus has powers that exceed the bounds of this world. He can do things that shouldn't be possible, but are."

I stood from the bed, too many conflicting emotions running through my head. I needed some time to think, to process.

"Thank you for being honest with me, but I think I need to be alone right now," I said, my heart in tatters.

Sam came over and kissed the top of my head. "I'll be here when you need me."

I left the room, unsure of where I wanted to go, but knowing I couldn't just sit in Sam's room. I'd fall to pieces if I did. I wandered around at random, barely acknowledging the presence of the maids and guards who walked by. I soon found myself outside, along the walls of the castle.

The gray stone shrank in the sunlight overhead and tempted my skin with sweat. I walked around until I faced Lake Gloom. A subtle breeze rolled through, bringing the pungent scent of the water rising to my nose. *It's peaceful here. The sun is hot against my skin, and I'm surrounded by nature.*

Mother is alive.

She's alive.

I couldn't put into words how that made me feel, but it was something that I had to face, had to deal with. I just didn't know how.

The sun sat high in the sky when I arrived, but by the time I roused myself from staring at the water, it had begun to fall back over the horizon. I'd spent hours trying to sort through my emotions, and I was no closer than when I started.

Maybe this isn't something I can understand. Maybe I just need to go see her. I'll understand everything then.

It wasn't much, but it was a goal. Something I could wrap my head around and push toward. It would have to be good enough, and if it wasn't, I knew

Sam would always be there. Despite my actions, despite the storm I stirred up with what I'd done, we'd both come out the other side relatively unscathed. I was grateful for that, that we could still be ourselves after what happened. *That's really all I need. We can work through anything as long as we're together.*

My spirits were up, which was the best I could've hoped for, and I turned to head back inside when I found someone walking towards me.

It was Raven, the shapeshifter Sam had befriended. We hadn't spoken but briefly when he arrived back. She was gorgeous, but that hardly mattered when it came to my bonded. He said she was kind, and that was much more important. *Though, her beauty isn't a bad thing.*

Her silken pitch hair was so dark, it could rival the void; her face held a softness that didn't match her blood-red eyes. They were the eyes of those who'd seen the worst of the world. They mirrored Sam's eyes perfectly.

I snorted. *Mine too, probably. We've all seen things no living creature should witness and survive, yet we have, and somehow found our way into each other's lives. Maybe it's fate.*

"What's so funny?" she asked quizzically, her eyebrows pinched together as a smile lifted her raspberry lips.

"Ah, it's nothing. What're you doing out here?"

She smiled, showing her white teeth, but her hands intertwined, her fingers going in circles over each other. "I wanted to talk to you, since we didn't get a chance last night."

I couldn't explain why, but I liked her immediately. I was fine with her last night, but we'd spoken for only moments, so I didn't have time to form an opinion. Now my instincts were telling me she was a good person.

"Then let's talk," I said, scooting back to the ramparts and hopping on one of the merlons. "I'll admit, I'm curious to learn more about you. Sam is picky about who he trusts, so you must be very special."

Raven laughed, but it was heavy with insecurity. "I'm not special. Duran wanted nothing to do with me when we first met, but because of Magnus, he had no choice."

I patted the wall next to me. "I want to hear your version of the story. Tell me everything about you."

She nodded and came to rest beside me before opening up and speaking.

A couple hours later, the sun had gone down, and Raven came to the end of her story.

"And once I realized it was him, I just couldn't stop myself, and I kissed him. I'm sorry."

I burst out laughing, and for the first time in hours, I wasn't burdened by recent events. I could just laugh, and it was wonderous.

"You have a really nice laugh," Raven said, smiling. "But still I shouldn't have kissed your husband. It was wrong of me."

"Don't be. Morrigan knows, he wouldn't have kissed you first. I'm grateful actually."

She gave me a blank stare. "Why?"

"Because of Sam's past. I don't know everything. There are still parts of his life that he keeps to himself, but he's lived a rough life, and it's made him cold, hard to trust. I think my coming into his life helped, but I was worried our time apart would send him back into his shell. But clearly my fears were unfounded, so thank you, Raven."

"Even if I'm in love with him?"

I kicked out my feet and jumped down from the battlement, landing softly. "Is it love?"

She started to answer but paused, her fingers gripping the stone. "No. Well, maybe…no, it's not love, not yet, but I think it could be eventually. It certainly hasn't been an easy relationship between us, but even though we've only known each other a short while, I feel like I've known him my entire life."

"He has that effect. Really, I've only known him a few months, but I've seen so much more of his life than he could tell me. It's what immediately made me fall for him. I got to see the unfiltered version of Sam, who he really is rather than who he thinks he is.

"He's a hard man, but only on himself. He just needed someone to love who loved him in return."

I leaned back against the stone. "I have no issue with you being with him. Goddess knows I don't have a right to dictate who he loves. He cares for you; whether he'll admit it or not is a different matter. But I've seen the way he looks at you. It's similar to the way he looks at me."

Raven paused, her eyes hopeful. "Having been around Aliria, I was sure that you wouldn't mind, but I didn't want to get my hopes up."

I smiled at her, despite her bringing up my mother. I wouldn't worry about that now. "I'm fine with it, but if you're not completely sure about him, I won't let you anywhere near him. Do you understand?"

Raven nodded. "I am. I'm sure that I don't want to leave him. I don't want to go back to my old life. I want to stay here with him."

"And me?" I asked, picking up a small stone that had chipped form the wall. "It would eventually be a relationship with the three of us. Are you okay with that?"

"Um, we've only just met, but I can see us being really close friends…but romantically…just. Just give me some time on that, okay?"

I smiled at her, and she returned it. Her crimson eyes lit up and her nose crinkled as she gave me a big smile. "We certainly have time."

Raven jumped down after me, and standing next to her I realized something. Two somethings.

"You're taller than me," I grumbled. "And just look at your chest. That's not fair."

She glanced down at her perfect breasts and chuckled. "They're actually not as fun to have as you'd think. Especially with my hollow bones. They cause my back no end of strain."

I pursed my lips, not entirely convinced, but at seeing my sour expression Raven laughed, and I couldn't keep a smile off my face.

"C'mon. There's something you need to do," I said and offered her my hand.

She took my hand without question, but after walking back inside and down the castle's long stone hallways, she did get curious.

"So where are you taking me?"

"To see Sam."

"Oh."

We wound our way through the castle's three levels and stopped just outside Sam's room. I knocked, which felt silly, but I also didn't want to barge in and spring this on him.

He opened the door a moment later. He'd changed clothes. He wore a dull emerald tunic with three buttons at his chest and a pair of black trousers. His bright copper hair hung down to his collar, and he had a brush in hand. He scrunched his eyes together and scratched his clean-shaven face at the sight.

"Eris?" He looked up. "And Raven. This should be good. Well, come in, both of you."

He stepped aside, and I let Raven's hand drop, my heart beating faster as I picked at my nails, trying to work up the nerve for the conversation I'd been meaning to have since Sam returned.

"We need to talk," I said and went to sit on the bed.

Sam chuckled at that. "Feels like we've done nothing but talk since I got back, and all of it bad news. I'm guessing from your expression it's more of the same, so let me have it."

"I broke your trust."

His face darkened, and his half grin slipped into a grimace. "You did, but I also forgave you for it."

He couldn't stop the emotions that welled in his heart and slipped through our connection. He was conflicted by so many different emotions that I couldn't read them well; they flowed and mixed and churned chaotically inside his heart. *You say as much, but your heart can't lie to me. You haven't truly forgiven me.* I wanted nothing more than to fix what I'd broken, but there was nothing I could do.

I'd broken his trust, and I had to face the consequences of that.

"You said so, but you haven't not in your heart."

Sam went over to his nightstand and reached for his crystal decanter. He had it in hand when he looked at it and stopped himself.

He set it down and turned to me. "Maybe you're right, but you were right about everything else too. You were very clear about your preference for bringing others into our relationship from the beginning. I think Reina took advantage of you when you were weak after having been stabbed. That's not exactly your fault."

"I still broke your trust. I knew you wouldn't have approved, but I slept with her anyway. I'm sorry."

He ran his hands through his hair and tied it all back with precise, practiced motions. "You're right, I wouldn't have approved. Don't approve. But that's me putting my human ideals on you. You said it last night. You're not human, Eris. It's not fair of me to expect you to conform to a different species' ideals just because I can't be a little more open-minded."

I couldn't help it. I laughed, giggling with a wide smile on my face. It was in such conflict with the heavy atmosphere a second ago, but I couldn't help myself. Sam looked at me like I'd gone insane, but his frown faded, and his eyes lit up once more.

"What?" he asked incredulously.

"You've changed, my bonded. She's been a good influence for you. The you I met when I first came out of my prison would've never said those words. You'd have stormed off in rage and likely marched to the Darkwoods yourself and attacked Reina.

"I'll always love you no matter what, but I was right about Raven. She's good for you, for us."

He rubbed the back of his neck and looked up at Raven with warmth in his eyes. "She's all right, I guess."

Raven laughed. "You see what I had to put up with?"

I hopped off the bed and went over to Sam. He let me pull him down in a kiss, and his lips tasted of forgiveness. I'd hurt him; however much as he'd gotten over it to forgive me didn't change that I'd hurt the person I loved more than anyone else.

It wouldn't make up for what I did, but I had an idea that might help smooth things out.

"I love you, Sam. But I can't take back that I hurt you. And I'm truly sorry for that."

He smiled and nodded. "Still love you, though. That will never change."

"I know, but I think I have a way to not exactly make up for it, but for you to balance the scales. It's the only thing I can think of that might come close to making up for it."

He caught my meaning and looked over to Raven. His eyes went wide. "You can't mean what I think you mean—"

"Yep, consider it an order from your queen, my one and only knight."

I kissed him once more on the lips and turned, giving Raven a smile as I left.

Chapter 25 - Uncertainty

Sampson

"So," I said, stretching out the syllable as Eris shut the door behind her. "I'm not sure what to do here."

That brought a smile to Raven's lips. "Well, I think Eris wants us to fuck."

"No, I got that part loud and clear," I said as I walked over to the edge of my bed and sat, staring up at Raven.

"What? You don't want to?"

I let out a snort. "Not that simple. I mean, I like you and you're beautiful, but this isn't me…it wasn't supposed to be me."

Raven sauntered over, and I was all too aware how well her tight-fitting clothes accentuated the curve of her hips and pulled taut over her bust. She sat down next to me and set her hand next to mine, palm up. An invitation.

"Talk to me, D. Forget Eris for a moment and what we're supposed to be doing here, and just talk to me like we did back in Aldrust."

She wasn't wrong. I was always in my head, and despite that, she could get me to open up. I took her hand and ran my fingertips over her nails. "I wasn't supposed to fall in love. I worked for years, over a decade, putting walls up so people wouldn't get close to me, and so I couldn't get hurt if I lost them.

"But it didn't work. Maybe it never worked from the beginning. I found friends to care about, and then I found Eris. She was everything I didn't know I needed, and I found myself opening up to people again."

"And that's a bad thing?"

"Of course it is. I have people in my life that I care about, that I can't lose. It would break me. Eris isn't like me…you're not like me. You don't get a second chance at life like I do."

"So what?" she asked, her eyes darkened. "Loving or not loving us won't change the number of lives we get. We only have one, so why not make the most of it, so that even if we die, you don't regret what could've been."

Raven shifted on the bed, scooting closer to me before her hands shoved me back. She wrapped her leg around me and sat straddled atop me.

"A week ago, my world made sense. I hated it, hated every second of it, but I understood it. Then I was paired with you, and from the beginning I never knew how to act around you. You hated me for what I was, and I, too, understood that, because I hated what I was, what I'd given up for my revenge. And if we'd have left it that, my life wouldn't be so confusing right now, but you didn't. In the rare moments when you let your guard down and forgot that you were supposed to hate me, you showed me the real you underneath it all. I liked that man. He was funny, and kind in a world that could be so cruel.

"I like the you that you keep hidden away, and since we've been here, it's like night and day." She poked my chest hard. "This is the you that I like, the you that I want to get to know, so don't you dare go anywhere."

Raven leaned down, our faces an inch apart. Her long black hair fell across her cheeks to lie across my copper strands, and her breath brought sweetness to my nose. "Now, I'm going to kiss you, unless you stop me."

She started to move, edging her lips closer to mine. I brought my hand to clasp around her throat in pure reaction. Raven sucked in a breath. Her eyes dropped, holding sadness and longing in them.

No, don't look at me like that. I couldn't take it.

I eased my grip on her neck but didn't pull back. I slid my hand up to cup her cheek, my fingers resting along her jawline. With a push of my left hand, I sat up and pressed my forehead to hers, my fingers running over her cheek.

"I…I don't—"

420

"Kiss me, Sam."

There was no fight left in me, and my lips met hers as my arms slid around her.

Her mouth welcomed mine as she gripped the base of my neck and pulled me tight against her. I answered her embrace and opened my mouth, letting her warm tongue caress my teeth and tease my lips.

Raven was light as I took her in my arms, my hands resting comfortably on her shapely rear. My hands molded around her as firm muscle shifted when she wrapped her legs around my waist. She shimmied her hips roughly against the bulge in my trousers and broke the kiss, letting a moan escape as she ground her hips into me.

"Gods, it's been too long," she said breathlessly.

She leaned heavily on my shoulders and pushed me back to the bed just as she brought her lips against my cheek, pressing softly as she trailed toward my ear. Her tongue licked my lobe just before her mouth closed around it as she bit down, nibbling at my ear.

Her hot breath tickled my skin and only increased as she kept undulating her hips. "There'll be time for sweet and passionate later, but right now, I want you to fuck me. Rough, messy. Can you do that to me?" she purred, her voice dripped with lust.

I was so enraptured by her voice, by her hips, that if she'd asked me to murder someone I'd have done so gleefully.

I didn't speak, simply moved my hands from her ass to her lower back. In one single motion, I gripped her black shirt and removed it, tossing it aside.

Raven trailed a finger from my cheekbone to my chin, smiling as she propped herself back on her hands, giving me an unobstructed view. Her alabaster skin glistened with a light sheen of sweat that ebbed and flowed in the candlelight. I finally gave in and drank in the perfection of her full breasts. Her soft pink nipples stood pronounced, begging to be touched.

I caressed up her sternum and slid between the rise of her bust, my fingers assured as I slid over to her nipple. Her breast welcomed me, and I rolled my finger around the tip before squeezing hard.

Raven spasmed, releasing a heavy moan as her hand ran rough through my hair. With a flash of regret, I pulled my hand back and picked her up and turned over, lowering her to the bed. I leaned over her, placing a single kiss on each breast before I moved to her neck and pressed my lips to the base of her throat.

"How rough do you want it?"

"Hard, make it hurt."

"With pleasure."

Do not show me her memories.

"As you wish."

The Aspect took hold of my mind and guided my actions. My teeth poised at her flesh, I flicked out my tongue before tearing through and drinking a liquid sweeter than any wine. Her blood rushed hot into my mouth, and I swallowed a mouthful.

She groaned when my teeth broke through her skin, digging her nails into the meat of my bicep. To hurt and be hurt in return—I was more than fine with a little pain. Just as much of a masochist as she was.

I licked at her blood, my saliva closing her nascent wound and erasing the little ruby red drop that slid over her pale beauty to rest in the hollow of her collarbone. Her blood hit me harder than the best whisky, and the Aspect made its will known. It wanted more, and so did I.

"Give me your finger," I said.

Her arm rose languidly from the crimson sheets, and she smirked at me as she gave me a very specific finger.

I smiled. "In due time, Raven. But I need a claw."

Her hand twisted, elongated and a single black talon protruded from her index finger. "Better?"

"Perfect."

I took her hand in mine and wielded her claw like a scalpel. I brought it down between her breasts, eliciting a moan mixed with pain and pleasure. Blood welled from the cut, and I licked up her chest, closing the wound and swallowing every last drop of her wine.

"Oh, fuck. That's it, again. Harder."

I leaned over and kissed her, taking her lip between my teeth and biting, spilling her life afresh, over and over again. She raked her nails down my back, slicing shallow wounds across my shoulder blades, and I grunted in surprise, playing my tongue over hers.

After we broke away, she slid from under me and smirked at me. "I can't hold back any longer. I need you. Now." Raven unbuttoned her cotton pants and kicked them off in a frenzy.

She spread her legs for me, baring her soaking wet opening. She kept herself trimmed; only a thin tuft of black hair covered her otherwise pristine skin.

"What are you waiting for?" she said, pointing at my own trousers. "Off."

A laugh slipped through my teeth as I grinned at her. "Yes, ma'am."

My pants hit the ground, and Raven crooked a finger toward me, beckoning me to come to her. I did so willingly. I knelt over her, my girth pressed against her wetness, teasing the entrance. With a jerk, Raven wrapped her arms around my neck and thrust her hips toward me, sliding all the way to the base in one single, fluid motion.

She tensed and let slip a moan of delight as she clung to me for a split second. As she rode the initial high of pleasure, she looked at me with eyes so dripping with satisfaction, I nearly lost my composure and burst then and there.

Raven gripped her legs around my waist and twisted, throwing me to the mattress to sit atop me. She leaned down and pressed her lips to mine before she started working her hips vigorously.

With each heavy motion of her hips, she moaned into me, not letting her sounds escape our conjoined lips. She slid her hips up and down in delight. Finally, she rose as her hands went to my chest. She dug her fingernails in and gyrated her hips, swaying side to side as she built up her tempo.

Raven ground against me faster and faster. Her breasts bounced with each riveting roll of her hips. Her breathing deepened as sweat poured down her body. She worked back and forth in hypnotic rhythm as she built to her climax.

As she reached her peak, her thighs clutched tight against mine, and she screamed in ecstasy.

Her fingers stained red, Raven arched her back, and her midnight wings unfurled from her back, bathing us in stygian feathers as they drifted lackadaisically to the bed.

She collapsed on top of me, panting, trying to catch her breath.

Her hair stuck plastered to her porcelain skin in waves. I brushed it out of her face and down her wings. When her labored breathing finally calmed enough, she propped up on her forearm and gave me a lazy smile.

"Fuck," she breathed.

"That was the gist of it," I said, smiling.

Her lips found mine, and this time, it was a gentle kiss, bereft of anything but Raven's desire to be here with me, in this moment. I returned it, caressing her neck as I held her close.

"I think I enjoyed that more than I had a right to," I said, stroking her hair.

"I'm just glad you gave in to my little quirk," she replied, her voice lifting.

"That was mostly the Aspect's influence on me, I think…but I enjoyed it as well."

She took my chin in her hands. "Does that mean you'll do it again?"

"If that's what you want."

She smiled wide. "Oh, absolutely."

We stayed curled together for a while while we both enjoyed each other's company. But we had to get up eventually.

I went to move, but Raven stopped me, her hand locking around my wrist and guiding it to her breasts. My fingers uncurled as her bust filled my palm, her heart beating gently under her softness. I glanced at her, eyes narrowed. I didn't mind where my hand was at, but I was a little confused.

"I noticed you didn't get off," she said with a smirk.

I shrugged. "Wasn't focused on that, was entirely focused on you."

"Well, I can't have that, darling. That won't do at all."

Her eyes smoldered, and she drew me to her, my previous plans dashed as she enraptured me with her body once more.

***

By the time we both got out of the bath, we were both exhausted, and only marginally cleaner than when we entered.

I dried off with a towel, while scarcely taking my eyes off Raven. *Maybe I was wrong. I love Eris more than my own life, but there has to be something said about having both sides of the coin.* Eris was short, petite, and I loved it. But Raven was tall, nearly hourglass shaped with her full chest and thick hips.

Think I need a whiskey and confession after that.

I still wasn't sure how to feel about the situation, but when I stopped thinking for half a second and just enjoyed it, I had to admit how good it felt.

Once we were dry, we exited the steam-filled bath and back into my bedroom. One look at my bed, and I knew I needed to change the sheets. *We made a mess of things, didn't we?*

My saliva healed all of Raven's wounds, and a sip of a health potion had fixed me right up, but even with crimson sheets, I could still make out the bloodstains.

The door opened, and Eris walked in while both Raven and I had only towels on. Eris had given us both express permission to do it, but as I stared into her eyes, I couldn't stop the guilt that rose in me. Like I'd committed the worst crime possible.

Through our connection, Eris knew at once what emotions ran through me, and she padded across the stone and leapt into my arms.

"Hello, love," she said, placing a chaste kiss on my lips.

I easily supported her with one hand while I brushed her hair back with my free hand, and in that moment, I threw away every emotion I had for one simple fact.

I loved Eris, and she loved me. Nothing or no one in this world would ever change that.

"I love you, so very much."

"What about me?" Raven asked, coming over to us.

I smiled at her. "You're all right."

She laughed and punched me lightly in the chest. "Just all right."

"I think you're pretty great," Eris spoke up, winding her hand through Raven's while still holding mine.

"So—are we all okay with this?" I asked.

"With what?" Raven said, acting coy.

I held my hands up and circled my fingers. "With this, with us."

"I dunno ab—"

Eris grabbed Raven's arm and pulled her into a heavy kiss. Raven stiffened for a single split second, letting the towel separating them fall. Then Raven relaxed before returning it with equal passion. They both pulled away quickly, Raven's face as red as a tomato.

"That was...yeah, I'm okay with this. On one condition."

"What's that?"

She poked me, her eyes stern. "I get to call you Sam too. It's not fair that Eris is the only one allowed."

"I don't..." I began, then sighed. I just didn't care anymore. I couldn't run from Sampson Acre. Eris had been right all along. "Yeah, that's fine."

"Good, then I'm happy."

I shook my head with a smile on my face. "How did this become my life?"

"Because your wife is amazing," Raven said.

"That she is. Now let's get dressed and call a meeting, there's lots to discuss."

Chapter 26 - Reunion

Eris

After the three of us got dressed, Sam told us a little of what he needed to tell the guild.

He stood and walked to the door. "We've been here a lot longer than any one of us first thought. I was going to wait to tell the guild, but it's something I can't keep to myself. I'd want to know if it was me, so they deserve the truth. Then Raven and I are going to take the Heart back to Magnus and get some answers."

"I'm going with you."

"Like hell. I'm not letting you anywhere near Magnus."

Fire burned in my chest, hot enough to hurt. I loved Sam, knew he meant well, but this was my choice to make alone, not his. "I know you want to keep me safe, love. But I'm not as weak as I once was, and even if I was, this isn't a decision you can make for me. I'm going to see my mother, and you can either join me or get out of the way."

His eyes lit up in surprise at my tone, but he quickly composed himself and smiled. It was his lifted half smile that I loved so much. It told me that everything would work out, but behind the smile, the light in his eyes dimmed, and I knew he was terrified for my sake.

"I'll be fine, Sam. As long as we're together, nothing else matters."

He sighed. "I nearly lost you once already. I couldn't bear it if anything happened to you."

"Then we'll just have to keep each other safe," I said sharply and left the room, not giving him any time to argue with me.

Sam followed after me as I headed to the guildhall. He called a meeting while we walked. By the time we reached the double doors, Sam had finished speaking, and we went inside to wait for the rest of the Gloom Knights.

It took them over half an hour to arrive, and after forty-five minutes it was clear a few members wouldn't be joining us.

"Well, it appears Adam and Evelyn will not be joining us this morning," Wilson said.

"Can't even call them, names are grayed out," Gil replied, running his finger through thin air as he used his interface.

Everyone stared off into space as they doubled checked what Gil had said and a round of confused mutterings circled the room.

"Where do you think they went?" Makenna asked.

"I'll give you one guess," Sam said.

"Magnus? You think?"

"Only thing I can think of."

"Those idiots. They're going to get themselves killed if Magnus is a strong as you say he is."

"I don't know about that," Sam said, drumming his fingers along the edge of the table. "Magnus is, without a doubt, powerful beyond my understanding, but so are those two. Evelyn could rule this world through her strength alone, and Adam is beyond a genius. He and his guild built Machine City in just three years, after all."

"And how did that turn out for them?"

Sam rubbed at his chin. "Point taken, but you know what I'm getting at. Those two are stronger than anyone, and if anyone has a chance against Magnus, my money is on them."

"What about Aliria?" Makenna asked, shooting a glance my way. "She's an entomancer, like Eris, right?"

I couldn't hold the pain from my heart as I breathed out slowly. I reached for Sam's hand under the table for comfort. "Aliria is my mother."

Makenna furrowed her brow, narrowing her eyes. "I thought you said your mom was dead?"

"She was. I don't know how she is alive. It's impossible."

"Necromancy, perhaps?" Wilson offered.

"Doubtful. You didn't see it, Wilson," Sam began, running his thumb over mine. "There was nothing left but ash. Nothing left for any necromancer to use for resurrection, and even if there was, this happened before we arrived here—"

"Duran?" Wilson asked at his pause.

"Um, there's something else I have to tell you all, something Magnus told me. Something that's going to be difficult to understand."

"Well, let us have it, bud," Gil said.

So he did.

I didn't really understand the significance of his revelation; a thousand years had passed while I was stuck in the void, so I didn't get why they were upset out until Sam told us about losing their memories. I understood that well, since the Hive placed a high amount of reverence on memories and a person's story. It was why what happened to my mother was such an extreme punishment; her being erased from history meant her memories died along with her.

How are you alive, Mother? It's a wish borne from my darkest nightmares and my wildest dreams. I loved you so, and I hated you for what you became. I never understood that, and maybe now I can.

By the time everyone calmed down and accepted what Sam said, I came out of my thoughts and waited for what we were going to do.

Wilson pulled a flask from his vest pocket and took a small drink, running his fingers through his gray beard. "I—I don't know what this means for us, can't know if what you say is true, but I know you would never lie about something like this, so I believe *you* believe it's true. Whether Magnus was telling the truth is a different matter."

"I don't think we can take the chance that he isn't," Sam replied.

"I agree. And unfortunately, it does make sense. All the little details we skipped over in our rush to kill things in this world are starting to make a whole lot of sense now."

"So what do we do about it all?" Gil asked.

"We work with Magnus," Sam said. "Whatever's coming affects our entire world. This goes beyond any perceived retribution we owe him."

"Agreed. So, I guess we hand over the Heart and go from there."

"All right. Me, Eris, and Raven will get prepped and head out."

With that, the meeting adjourned, and Sam and I left to get ready. While the others looked like they wanted to head to the bar. My hunch was proven correct when Gil piped up. "Anyone else need a drink?"

"Save me one," Raven said as the others all voiced similar things.

Sam laughed and thumbed over at Raven. "Just watch your drinks around her, she's not above snatching them from you."

Raven laughed. "I would never do that to Gil!"

"You met him half a day ago!" Sam said, trying not to laugh.

"Yeah, and it took less than that to learn that he's a lot nicer than you! And besides, you make it so easy."

"I'll show you easy," he grumbled.

"You already did, four times."

At that, Sam couldn't stop from laughing, and Raven swiftly joined in.

I couldn't help but smile at their antics. *It's good to see both of them smiling. I was right. Raven is going to be good for him.*

I smiled sweetly at them as they composed themselves.

Sam's eyes lit up as he gazed at me. "And whatever we do, don't give any alcohol to Eris. She'll have her clothes off trying to seduce us both after one glass."

"That happened one time!"

That had been the wrong thing to say, as they both started laughing again.

Once they stopped, Sam and I made our way back to our room while Raven said she had to go pick up something.

"She's something else," Sam said as we both watched the sway of her hips as she ran down the hall.

"I really like her."

He turned to me. His eyes widened ever so slightly. "I didn't think you'd spent any time with her."

I nodded. "We talked."

"About?"

"That's between the two of us," I said and went inside our room.

We both changed into our armor quickly. I threw on my cloak and pulled it closed. Sam, meanwhile, changed into his new armor. It was pretty, as black as my eyes, with lovely splashes of green at his waist where a belt of some kind held his sword.

I walked over and ran my fingers over the sheath. "It's like a leaf. It's so pretty."

"Yeah, I found it fitting."

When Sam was finished, he went over to his nightstand and knelt, opening the bottom drawer. He paused when he opened his coin chest. "Huh, someone's been in here. The strand of hair I placed between the lids been moved."

"It was me," I said immediately.

He turned, smiled at me and shrugged. "Okay. Was just curious."

"I borrowed some money since I didn't want to ask the guild. I'm sorry."

Sam waved me off, grabbing several coin purses and stuffing them full. "Don't be. You're welcome to anything I own. And it's not like I don't have plenty of money."

"Thank you. I have noticed you're rather generous with your money."

"I'm not reckless with my money, but I usually overpay wherever I go."

"Why?" I asked, moving to lean against the bed. "It seems humans value gold more than anything else, why give it away so freely?"

He sighed. "Because I know what it's like to not have it. When we first arrived here, most of us took to adventuring, completing quests for rewards. It was fun, but the pay wasn't always consistent, and some months we struggled to make ends meet. It wasn't just that way for players, but NPCs too.

"So now that I have an abundance of money, I don't mind spreading a little around. I hope it helps people who might be going through what I went through once."

I couldn't help my heart as it swelled. "You really are a kind person. You just have different ways of showing it."

Before he could respond, Raven walked back in. She wore black leather armor that fit her incredibly well; it hugged her body, and I couldn't keep my eyes from her plunging neckline, as the leather left a good portion of the top part of her chest visible.

Sam looked up and tilted his head. "New gear?"

"Gil improved it for me. I wasn't just joking earlier. He really is a nice guy. I can see why you're friends."

"Yeah, he's the best."

Sam stood and stowed his money in his inventory. "All right, then, if everyone's dressed, let's get ready to go. We've got a busy day today."

The three of us packed in haste. I ran down to storage and grabbed everything I thought we would need, which wasn't much. Sam knew better than I about what he needed, but I followed Adam's guideline and just stuffed as much as I could into our three packs.

When everything was packed away, I hefted all three bulging bags in my arms and met Sam and Raven in the outer bailey. Sam took them from me, and they disappeared into his inventory.

"I'd step back if I were you," Sam said, backing away from Raven.

I did as he asked and took a few steps back in the dirt to stand beside him as we both stared at Raven.

In a magnificent display, Raven grew wings and folded them over herself, letting a rain of sleek black feathers obscure her from us. When she reappeared, it was as a huge black raven.

"Amazing," I gasped. "I've never seen a shapeshifter so large before."

"Thank you," she said, her voice projecting without a source.

I walked up to her and ran my hands gently through her soft, downy feathers. "You're so unbelievably beautiful," I said, turning my thoughts into words.

"All right, enough admiring the pretty bird. I'd like to put as many miles under us as we can today."

"Ass," Raven said, laughing. "Though you did call me pretty, so I guess I forgive you."

Sam climbed on first and helped me up. I nestled against his back and still kept my hands firmly on Raven.

She crouched and took to the skies with a burst of speed, and suddenly we were flying. The wind whipped furiously at my hair, and the chill in the air offset the beating rays of the sun as we soared over Lake Gloom.

Sam held me close while I leaned over and stared in wonder at the landscape rushing past in a blur as the grayish-green outskirts of Gloom-Harbor territory opened to the vast Rolling Hills. We flew for hours, and I eventually settled back into Sam's arms and just enjoyed the journey.

I cherished the simple alone time we shared while we flew.

As the sun dipped, Raven's speed slowed, and we began looking for a place to set up camp.

I set up the tent while Sam got the fire going and Raven prepared the food. While not as skilled as Sam was, Raven was still a hand in the kitchen, and her cooking was delicious.

Sam pulled out his flask and raised it to his lips, but he paused, and after a moment, he lowered his arm and handed it to Raven, who happily took a drink.

Once we'd eaten, we all crawled into our tent together and went to sleep. I don't think any of us were quite ready to spend the night together in *that* fashion, but it was nice cuddling up with both Sam and Raven.

In the morning we began after a light breakfast, and we made it to Castle Aliria before lunchtime. Raven landed on the tower, and as we disembarked, the faint clang of steel against steel could be heard. It blew away with the wind fast enough that I thought I'd imagined it.

I shook my head, and as Raven transformed back to human, the three of us made our way to the door.

A young woman with lovely light brown skin and auburn hair waited for us as the door opened.

"Welcome back, Duran," she said, a dark blush to her rich cheeks and a spark in her honey eyes.

"Good to see you again, Jasmine."

Jasmine peered around Sam and Raven to look at me. "Who's she?"

Sam laughed. "This is my wife, Eris."

I walked over and held out my hand. "Hello, it's nice to meet you."

Jasmine bowed slightly, brushing her radiant hair out of her face when she stood. "This way, Duran. Magnus has been waiting for you."

She turned on her heels and headed inside without another word. As Jasmine disappeared from view, Raven snickered. "Someone likes you."

"Someone is just a kid. Now let's not keep Magnus waiting. I'd rather him be in a good mood."

We hurried after Jasmine through a winding maze of identical corridors that started to make my head spin after a few minutes.

With each step, my heart beat a little faster. Heavy fear hooked deep into my stomach before rising to my throat. My mouth went dry, and my fingers trembled the closer we got. Sam noticed at once and took my hand in his. "It'll be all right, my love," he said. "We'll be right here the entire time."

I gulped and nodded as we reached our destination.

Jasmine opened the door and motioned us inside.

The throne room, for it could be nothing else, was long and wide. Along the walls were beautiful stained-glass windows that cast a rainbow of lights along the gray stone tile. In the back of the room rose a large black throne made of obsidian glass.

Sitting on the throne was a blond-haired man, who looked normal for a human. He had a kind face and deep tanned skin.

To his right was a woman who looked much like Jasmine, though older, with longer hair.

But my eyes swept to his left, and my world crumbled.

I forgot how to breathe as I stared unblinking at the woman whose name and face I couldn't have recalled before this very moment. A person who I'd thought lost to time. I could remember her actions, what she'd done, but I could never recall her face.

As I stared at her, the wall around what I'd forgotten about my mother fell away, and I knew beyond a shadow of a doubt that it was her. Her long blonde hair that tickled my nose when she held me as baby. Her gorgeous black and yellow eyes that always held the answer to whatever question I asked.

It was her.

"Momma?" I whispered.

She smiled at me, her eyes softened and held such warmth that I came undone. "Hello, my little fly. I've missed you."

My hand slipped from Sam's as tears fell freely down my face. "Momma!"

I raced across the floor and nearly collapsed into her chest, sobbing for everything I was worth.

Chapter 28 - Truth At the End of the World

Sampson

Aliria smiled down at her daughter and hugged her back, stroking her hair and whispering that everything would be okay. Her malice and hatred bled away as she consoled her daughter. So much so, she seemed like an entirely different person. She looked so like Eris in that moment, they could've been twins, rather than mother and daughter.

I left them to their reunion and approached Magnus. He smiled widely as he glanced over at them.

"It does the heart good to see that in this day and age. So many dark things abound that I don't get to witness this very often. But I digress. How was your trip? I only know pieces."

I told Magnus most of everything that had happened—the important bits that mattered, at any rate. He sat back in his chair and listened intently while I explained things. And when I was done telling him everything, he laughed.

"That was some adventure," he said, clapping. "I couldn't have imagined there was a curse on the heart itself, but I'm thrilled you persevered where others did not. I must admit, you didn't exactly inspire confidence at first, but you've exceeded my every expectation. Well done!"

"He's not bad," Aliria admitted, her arms around Eris.

"My bonded is amazing."

Aliria chuckled. "I'm beginning to agree with you, little fly. You picked a good one."

Magnus smiled. "That just leaves the completion of the quest. The Heart, if you will, Duran."

"Of course." I pulled the Heart from my inventory and handed it over, rightfully glad to be rid of the damn thing.

Magnus snapped his fingers, and the emerald appeared in his outstretched hand. He stared at it for a second before wincing. "Ow, that is a hefty curse. I can see why the quest gave so many of my men trouble, but at last it is completed. Thank you, Duran."

Quest: Steal Lachrymal's Heart
Type: Unique
Difficulty: S
Reward: 48000 Exp!

I waved away the notification and pulled up my Stats.

Exp: 6000/6000
Level Up! (x8)
Level: 68
100/6800
90 Stat Points Available!
1 Ability Point Available!

I whistled, long and slow. *That's quite a jump, though for how much I went through, it's a little light.* I had ninety stat points to allocate, and I knew almost exactly what I wanted to do with them. I added twenty-five to *Endurance*, maxing it out. Then I added the rest to *Durability, Battle Fatigue, Attack Speed,* and *Movement Speed*. When I was done, I was quite happy.

Character Name: Durandahl

Level: 68

Exp: 100/6800

Race: Hybrid (Hive)

Class: Hive Knight

Reputation: Wanted Criminal

Bounty: 1300 Gold

Stats (-)

Strength: 100 (Max)

Sub-Stats (-)

Attack Damage: 50

Constitution: 100 (Max)

Sub-Stats (-)

Health: 25

Health Regen: 25

Durability: 75

Endurance: 100 (Max)

Sub-Stats (-)

Battle Fatigue: 50

Battle Fatigue Regen: 10

Agility: 50 (75)

Sub-Stats (-)

Attack Speed: 25

Movement Speed: 20

Wisdom: 25 (35)

Sub-Stats (-)

Mana: 20

Luck: 0 (30)

Charisma: 0 (10)

__Proximity to Hive Queen less than 30 meters: +10 to all Main Stats__
__Arachne's Blessing: +15 to Strength and Agility__

I accepted the changes, and a rush of strength flooded through my veins. The penalty from being away from Eris was gone, and I now had the boost from being near her. When I was done with my stats, I stared back up at Magnus, not entirely sure what would happen next.

"What now?" I asked as Magnus stared at his prize.

"Now, we have one final order of business to handle," he said, stowing the Heart away. "Your reward. I promised you one, and I always keep my promises. So whatever you want—if it's within my power, I'll grant it."

I already knew what I wanted, knew it for a while. "I have two requests I would like to ask," I said holding up two fingers. "One, I would like to be a part of this going forward. Whatever is going on is obviously big, and I want to help."

"Done," Magnus said with a half-smile. "I was going to offer you a pace within my organization regardless. You've proven yourself a worthy and capable lieutenant.

"In fact, I have a gift for you. I think you'll like it."

Magnus held up his hand and scrolled through his interface before he flicked his hand out to me. a notification appeared in front of me.

__Ability Share: Will of the Immortal__
__Accept Y/N__

Yes.

Damn, he can share abilities just like Evelyn. Will of the Immortal—*it's a much better version of* Dance of the Immortal. *It gives me twenty seconds of complete time stop, and I can manipulate the time and space around me. I think that means I can bring people into the time stop with me if I'm close enough.*

"This is—"

"The highest tier of the Immortal ability. I'm sure you'll find it useful."

"I'll say."

I quickly replaced *Dance of the Immortal* with its superior counterpart.

Magnus smiled and inclined his head. "Now that concludes our first order of business, what is your second request?"

I glanced over at Raven, who kept her gaze firmly planted at her feet and refused to meet Magnus's eyes. *Ah, returned to your subservience again. I much prefer your true personality. Meek doesn't suit you.*

"Raven. I want her released from her contract."

Magnus frowned slightly, leaning back in his chair as his eye flicked from me to Raven and back again. He drummed his fingers on his stygian armrest. "You're asking a lot of me. I depend on Raven quite heavily…but I also asked much of you, and you delivered where many others have failed. You've proven yourself, and I do owe you. Very well. You shall have her contract. Is she going to remain bound to you?"

"That's not my decision to make," I replied.

Raven finally looked up from the ground and to me. She smiled. "I wish to remain his bonded."

"Excellent. Well, there you go!" Magnus said, standing from his throne. "I say a celebration is in order."

"That sounds lovely. I'm positively famished," Aliria said. "What about you?" she asked Eris.

"I'm perfectly fine with whatever."

"Darling, I'm going to take Eris and get her cleaned up and dressed properly. Why don't you and Duran have a drink in the dining hall in the meantime?"

"That's a lovely idea," he said, holding out his hand.

His ivory cane appeared out of thin air above his hand and dropped into his palm. With a flick of his wrist, it twirled around, and he leaned on it as the base struck the ground. I stared slack-jawed at his casual display of power.

"You said you weren't cheating."

"I told you once before, Duran. Cheating the system is impossible, and it's offensive to insinuate. Twist your thinking a bit. Perhaps the cane was always there, or would've been, given enough time," he said with a cheeky grin.

Magnus rubbed the carving embossed on the ivory with his thumb, drawing my attention. The hand holding the hourglass. *The hand that holds time in its palm.* Realization hit me like a sucker punch as all the pieces lined up. *I'm an idiot. It's been in front of me this entire time.*

"You're a time mage!" I nearly shouted, stunned.

Magnus stopped walking and turned back to me with amusement plain on his face. He rubbed his blond beard and chuckled. "I basically had to tell you, so you get no points for cleverness this time, Duran. But yes. Though I prefer chronomancer."

"How is that possible?" I asked.

He waved me to follow him as he left the throne room. "We have much to discuss about our future together, Duran. Let's at least do it over a drink."

I walked behind him as we headed to the dining hall. As we stepped inside, I found it had been changed a little.

Most of the long banquet tables had been removed for individual circular ones that littered the stone floor. Only one long table remained, and it was at the center of the room. Magnus's personal team of chefs worked like devils to get the room set up for us as we sat down at the table.

A swish of cloth behind me caused me to turn. Jasmine was beside me, leaning over, too close to me. "Can I get you an ale, Duran?" she asked sweetly, her earlier frosty attitude gone.

"Uh, water. Please."

"Of course." Her hand brushed mine as she left, and she spared me one last look before exiting to the kitchen.

"You're quite popular with the ladies, Duran," Magnus said with a laugh.

"I don't know why," I replied shaking my head. "I'm crass, easy to anger, and hyper-violent. I'm the furthest thing from a catch."

"You're also honest, dependable, and not hideous. Plus, Jasmine is young. She's spent her entire life here after her father was killed defending the castle. She doesn't know what love is and is misconstruing her infatuation."

I nodded. "Still, she's a lovely girl, but I've already got more than I can handle at the moment."

"Right. I was quite surprised you and Raven had gotten so close. Your first interactions were…hostile, to say the least."

"You could say she grew on me," I said, laughing as I ran my fingers over the smooth stained oak. "We actually get along really well, and after I let go of my anger, it was easy to become friends."

"More than friends, from where I'm sitting, but far be it for me to judge. I've had plenty of dalliances myself over the years. Aliria finds them healthy."

The door swung open, and Jasmine returned, followed by Magnolia. Jasmine set down my water and brought Magnus his wine. I thanked her and took a sip. The water was crystal clear. Condensation ran down the glass as

I drank. It was cool, probably the best tasting water I'd ever had, and all I could think about was the whiskey I wasn't having instead.

Huh, maybe I do have a problem. I drank the water and held the glass to the bridge of my nose, basking in the cold glass as water dripped into my eyebrows.

My headache went away as the chill soaked into my slick skin. I set the drink down as the main door opened and Aliria, Raven, and Eris walked in.

All three of them had discarded their casual clothes for much more formal attire. Aliria wore a black dress that revealed too much of her substantial cleavage. The dress was stunning and stopped just shy of her smooth knees.

Raven wore a simple red linen blouse that matched her eyes and a black skirt. Her hair fell down her back, and she looked stunning in the outfit. It fit her perfectly, but my eyes swept to Eris, and I couldn't take my eyes off her.

She wore black, like her mother, but it was a blouse, rather than a dress, that paired with a golden skirt that swished to her thighs. Her hair was tied back out of her face, and her smile lit up the entire room.

She was blissfully happy, and I loved how it made her glow in the firelight.

"Why, don't you all look lovely," Magnus said, taking a sip of his wine.

"Thank you, darling." Aliria took her seat by Magnus while Raven and Eris flanked either side of me.

Both of them rested their hands on my legs, and I gave them both a tentative squeeze. "You both look lovely."

They beamed at me.

Magnolia came around and brought them their drinks, while I stuck to water.

"All right, Magnus. Spill. How can you control time?"

446

"Oh, figured it out, did you?" Aliria asked.

"He had help," Magnus replied. "But I did tell you I'd answer your questions. To keep it simple, chronomancer is a legendary class, with only one person able to use it. Me. I've had it since the beginning. I was given greater power in this world, along with two others, to ensure we could maintain order. This was, of course, before the schism.

"Now I'm just trying to keep everything from falling apart."

Two others? Who—no, I've got a good hunch already, and there are more important questions I need answered now.

"You used time travel to bring Aliria back to life?" I asked.

"I did, though it cost me dearly to do it. Traveling that far back through time is something that I can only do once a lifetime. And since most of time has been erased, it's not something I can risk doing again.

"To be honest, most of my greater powers have been diminished. I've had to remove the spells and abilities that no longer work or are too dangerous to try to use."

"Is that how you can cast spells without using Script?" I asked, rubbing my chin.

He chuckled and took a sip of his wine. "In a manner of speaking. I'm still casting using Script circles or incantations, but one of my abilities allows me to manipulate time in my immediate vicinity. I simply condense the casting into nanoseconds. Before your eyes can even register the spell, it's complete."

I laughed. "Well, how do you explain the finger snaps and hand waving?"

He snorted as the glass of wine was at his lips, and he nearly did a spit take. Magnus quickly set his wine down and dabbed at his mouth with cloth. When he was finished, he smiled wide at me. "Consider it an idiosyncrasy of mine. It's easier to visualize a spell if I ground it with a physical motion, but it's not necessary."

I absorbed what he told me and leaned back. Everything he told me added up to what I'd seen him do, so I had no reason not to believe him. The logic fit.

"So what do we do about the system?"

"We wait. I have a few guests who should be arriving shortly, and we can procced once they arrive."

"In the meantime, I believe I made you a promise, Duran," Aliria said, speaking up over the rim of her wineglass.

Huh? Oh, right. She promised to get rid of the Aspect.

"Don't trust her, she speaks lies!"

Right, she promised to get rid of you.

"Don't do it."

Yeah, like I'm willing to trust you, either. You've only been playing nice because I've been feeding you blood. Don't think I've forgotten who got me into this mess in the first place, Aspect.

"You think you can get rid of it?"

"I know I can," she said as she drained her glass and stood. "Follow me."

All of us stood and returned to the throne room. Magnus took his place, and with a flourish, threw his cane in the air and it vanished. Raven and Eris stood next to Jasmine as Aliria walked over to me.

"Don't do this, knight…Sampson, don't let her destroy me!"

You brought this on yourself. You sought to control me, and you should have realized the foolishness of your plan. We could've been allies, but you turned against me first.

It bellowed in rage and sank its frigid claws into my heart. I dropped to my knees as pain tore apart my insides.

"Enough of that now, Aspect. Accept your death with dignity," Aliria said, placing her hand on my chest.

Immediately, the Aspect's presence lessened, allowing me to breathe again and the pain to subside. I looked up into Aliria's hornet-stripe eyes and shuddered at the insidious glee in them. "Unfortunately, there is only one way to get rid of the demon whispering in your ear. I must shatter your bonds."

"What!"

"Mother, no!" Eris shouted and ran over to me.

With a snap, Eris and Raven froze in place, living statues unable to move.

"The hell are you doing?" I went to move, but my legs wouldn't work. I couldn't move them.

"Aliria, stop this. You're going too far. Duran has proven himself; I don't want to lose a valuable asset."

Aliria turned and nodded. "I completely agree. Duran will be an excellent addition to our cause, but I want him under my bailiwick."

Magnus sighed, pinching the bridge of his nose. "Are you sure this is the right course of action?"

She smiled, a dark, dripping smile as her eyes glinted. She walked over to me and ran a single long finger over my cheek. "Don't look so grim. This is a good thing. I'm giving you power, and I'll even let my daughter have you. But you'll serve much better under my control. Eris is too young, inexperienced. I'll teach her the proper way to use the mantle of the Hive, but for now, you're far more useful under me."

"Magnus, stop this," I pleaded.

He shook his head, apologizing with his eyes. "I'll be sure to compensate you handsomely for this slight, Duran. It wasn't my intention, but Aliria could be right. This may be a boon to you."

Chitin slithered out of her fingertips and formed spikes at the ends of her fingers. With a press, she stuck them into my chest, and emerald mist drifted from her into my veins. It burned like acid as she pumped more and more of it into me; it traversed through me till it reached my heart and smothered itself over the Aspect's darkness.

It burned out the Aspect, and with a scream of agony, it fled. *"Farewell, knight. For what it's worth, I had fun."*

Something bubbled up through my lungs and into my throat. My stomach lurched, and I heaved obsidian smoke out onto the gray stone floor. It poured vile from the depths of my organs, as the wisps of hive magic sought out and forced every last shred of the Aspect from my body. I vomited until nothing came out but screams, and I fell to all fours, coughing until my throat burned, raw.

Alert! You are no longer soul bound to the Monarch of the Hive.
Alert! You are now soul bound to the Monarch of the Hive.
Alert! Scorpius's Blessing Unlocked!
+15 to Constitution and Agility
Unlocked (Hive Mind) Special: Scorpion Tail

"What…what did you do?"

"I made you mine, Duran. Now. Bow to your queen, knight!"

Her will pounded into my psyche and demanded to be obeyed. It was a command, one that I couldn't disobey.

I fell to one knee under the shattering command of her voice, and I lowered my head despite fighting with everything I had to stop it. She was too strong.

The cold stone sank through my thin cotton pants, but it wasn't what chilled me to the bone. I was powerless to go against Aliria; her mere voice struck me still and forced me to obey. Eris and Raven hung frozen in place. I couldn't help them, and they couldn't help me. I was truly alone against an enemy I couldn't even fight.

Aspect!

It bubbled from my chest, but gone was the frigid ice I'd grown accustomed to. Now a pleasant warmth spread through my body as a warm, gentle voice spoke in my ear.

"Hello, knight. How may I assist you?"

I need my chitin.

"Unfortunately, previous access to the Hive Mind has been severed. We can no longer use chitin molding. If you wish to use Chitin Molding, *you will need to access the* Hive Mind *Ability once more."*

Just fantastic. I'd been relying on the ability to mold my *Exoskeleton* to my whims. Now faced against Aliria, I'd grown complacent, too reliant on my abilities.

I've forgotten what made me strong when everything else fell apart. It's never been my class, my abilities. It's been the fact that I refused to give in and just die. I survived when Mom, Dad, and Micah were killed in front of me. I survived watching Sophia kill herself. I survived the guilt that ate at me for decades.

I'm a survivor.

And I'll survive you, bitch. I won't let you just take what you want from me.

I rose to meet Aliria's superior gaze with fire in mine.

"No."

Aliria stepped back. Her foot thumped against the stone behind her. "What? Do as you're told, knight. Bow!"

Her voice pounded through my psyche and demanded obedience, but I steeled myself, and it didn't have the impact she wanted. She had no power over me.

I stood and stared her down. "You are not my queen!"

Alert! Class Modification!

Class: Hive Knight (Errant)

The errant is a knight that has broken away from his monarch in order to go off on his own to right wrongs or to test and assert his own righteous ideals.

Alert! You are no longer Soul bound to the Monarch of the Hive.

Her command over me shattered, and I quickly equipped my sword. I took a single step forward as Aliria scowled.

"An Errant. I didn't think you had it in you. Why are you so bothersome?"

I drew my sword and levied the tip at her. "Just because you have power, doesn't give you the right to use people like objects. I am not yours to command and you will pay for what you've done."

For the first time, a single drop of fear rippled through her insectoid eyes, and I smiled. "Not so easy when your prey fights back, is it?"

I turned to Magnus, who'd gone back to rest on his throne. "Are you going to interfere?"

He shook his head and tilted his head to Aliria. "This was her gamble, and it backfired. I will not help either side. Settle your differences."

"I'm going to settle it with my sword through her throat."

Magnus sat back and placed his hands in his lap, fingers intertwined. "If you can."

He snapped his fingers, and Raven and Eris appeared next to his throne beside Jasmine and Magnolia.

I tuned them out; they were safe for now, and I had to focus on Aliria. Even as I was, I wouldn't be able to beat her easily. *But I'm not suffering under the penalty any longer. I'm at full strength.*

Before we fought, I equipped my shadowsteel armor and lowered into my stance.

Aliria stood, not moving, a half smile on her face.

I charged her.

My sword whipped toward her head, but movement came in from the left, and I stopped mid-swing as Jasmine stepped between us.

"Move, Jasmine!"

She shook her head. "I cannot."

"Why?"

Jasmine stepped toward me, her arms outstretched as liquid obsidian rushed over her. It crawled up her face as two points of ethereal green lit up the darkened stone.

"Because I cannot allow you to harm my queen."

CHAPTER 29 - DARKEST KNIGHT

What?

I stared at Jasmine as the quiet and shy girl I'd come to know transformed into an obsidian nightmare. Two short swords forged of chitin appeared in her outstretched hands. The glossy black chitin formed smooth over her skin, rounded, where mine was usually rough and jagged.

"Jasmine? You're a Hive Knight?"

"Did you think you were the only one?"

I held up my off hand, relaxing my posture. "Stop this. I don't want to hurt you."

She rushed forward so fast, I barely brought my sword up in time. Her twin blades arced towards my head, and only at the last second did I manage to put my sword between us.

I stagged under the strength of the blow and had to take a step back.

Jasmine chuckled through her dark helm. "As if you could. Now I'll ask you the same. Bow before your queen. I, too, wish not to spill your blood."

With a jerk, I forced her swords away and stepped back. *Shit. She's strong—and quick.* I grounded my stance and glared at her.

"Aliria is not and will never be my queen. I'll die before I ever bow to her!"

Her shoulders slumped as her head dropped. "So be it."

Before she'd even finished speaking, she charged me. I was ready for her incredible speed this time, but still she was faster than me.

I blocked her swing and struck with a side kick. The blow took her in the stomach, but she absorbed it easily because of her chitin and stumbled for only a second before she righted herself.

I'm a better fighter than her, but she has the advantage here.

The room was even ground for both of us, smooth stone and wide-open space gave us plenty of room to maneuver and would neither help nor hinder us. But I didn't want to fight her. She wasn't my enemy.

"Jasmine, please. We don't have to do this!"

"I'm afraid we do. If you will not serve and will not stand down, then I will do what I must to protect my queen. I'm sorry. I liked you, but none come before my queen."

Damn it! There was no getting through to her. *I'll have to subdue her first.* I glanced down at the poison running down my blade. Poison Blade *is really useless against another knight. I just need to get rid of it. It's not going to help now. What I need is more strength and speed.*

I just needed to buy time. I didn't want to unleash *Will of the Immortal.* Despite how powerful it was, it also had a stronger backlash, and I wasn't trying to kill her, I just wanted to take her out of the fight.

My inventory was filled with dozens of items, and I quickly grabbed two smoke bombs from my burglar's kit and tossed them in between us. They rolled across the slate and burst with two subtle explosions before they both billowed a ton of smoke that quickly filled the room and obscured both of us.

I knelt with my sword raised and hastily pulled up my interface.

Delete Ability: Poison Blade?
Y/N

Yes.

With it gone, I had two ability points, and I needed to make my choice quick. I flicked over to the ability list.

First Tier List
Aura of the Arachnid
Poison Blade

456

~~Exoskeleton~~

~~Chitin Shield~~

Hive Guard

Second Tier List

Chitin Armor

Chitin Sword

~~Arachne's Blessing~~

~~Scorpius's Blessing~~

Mantearia's Blessing (Locked)

Apocrita's Blessing (Locked)

Hive Mind (Passive)

Aura of the Arachnid. *That's the one that boosts my* Attack Damage, Movement Speed, *and* Verticality.

It was exactly what I needed at the moment, and I hastily selected it. *Chitin Armor* was also tempting, since I'd gotten used to having it, but it brought up a very interesting question that I needed answered.

If I could use Chitin Armor *through the Hive Mind, why would I ever take the Ability?*

"Because through the Hive Mind, you have a greater access to your full range of abilities, but at a greater cost. The corrupted Aspect took on much of the burden for you, and you paid in blood. But I am unable to do as it did. If you wish to use the Hive Mind, it will put a greater strain on your body and stamina."

So basically, it'll raise my Battle Fatigue much faster if I use it from the Hive Mind versus just acquiring the ability outright.

"Correct, knight."

I can deal with it. Besides, I can't use my new appendages without the Hive Mind. Makes it an easy choice. I selected *Hive Mind* and accepted my choices as wind whistled straight ahead of me.

Jasmine came crashing through the smoke, her bright green eyes trailing ethereally in her wake as her swords bore down on me. I rolled to the side as chitin struck stone where I'd been. She tore into the stone, sending chips flying to the air from the force of her blow.

She's really trying to kill me!

I had access to new abilities, but I didn't want to spam them; my fatigue might have been higher now, but I still had to be cautious of how I used my abilities. I activated *Aura of the Arachnid,* and a soft green glow bubbled over my skin before fading away.

A timer appeared in my vision, set at five minutes and dropping. Strength flowed through me, and my legs were lighter, surer of foot than before. Power breathed new life into my body, and I easily met Jasmine's next attack.

I ducked her duel slash, and as I rose, I wrapped my left hand around her wrists, clenching them to my side. With a whisper of thought, I summoned chitin to my hand and punched Jasmine as hard as I could. My fist struck her cheek, just above her chin. Her head snapped to the side under the force of the blow. Smooth chitin chipped from her face as I gouged deep furrows across her jawline.

She stumbled back as I disengaged, letting her hands drop as I whipped my sword toward her. Jasmine leaned off balance, throwing her entire body away from my swing as she fell back to the floor. Before she could hit the ground, four slender black limbs crawled from her spine and stuck to the stone as she rolled backward and came up in a high crouch.

Damn it. She's *quick on her feet too.* I didn't know how long Jasmine had been a Hive Knight, but it was clear she'd had a lot more practice than me.

I was a better swordsman, but she far outpaced me as a knight. *This isn't going to be easy.*

I don't have a choice. I need to end this now before one of us gets hurt.

With a grimace, I activated *Will of the Immortal.*

Time halted in its tracks. Jasmine stood still, her arms raised as she readied a slash. Raven and the others stood by the throne, looks of concern frozen on their faces. Only Magnus smiled, staring me down as he propped his leg on his knee.

"Now I understand the impulse, and I even empathize, but using *Will of the Immortal* is cheating, Duran. Fight her fair. I'll stop the rise in fatigue, but I won't reset the cooldown."

Magnus snapped his fingers, and the world returned to normal, and a timer appeared in the corner of my vision, counting down from ninety-six hours.

I glared at him, but taking my eyes off Jasmine had been a mistake. Her swords came for me, and I was too slow to dodge. They sank into my shadowsteel and scored a heavy gash in the metal from my chest to my waist.

As she pulled back, a soft tear came from my side. Jasmine had severed my sword sash. The green fabric fell lifelessly to the floor as my sheath clanged heavily on the gray stone.

Shit! I kicked the sheath away so it wouldn't trip me up and went on the offensive. Her duel swords made her dangerous, but she had very little defense save her armor.

All right, it's time to get serious. I activated *Chitin Shield* the same time as I called *Chitin Armor* from the *Hive Mind.*

Obsidian crawled over my skin like tar and bathed me in darkness as I raised my shield in front of me. I clutched my sword tightly and surged forward to meet Jasmine's next attack.

Both swords slammed against my shield, and I batted them aside as I thrust with my sword. It landed in the center of Jasmine's chest and stopped cold. Her chitin cracked under my blow, but I didn't manage to pierce through.

Jasmine grunted and sucked in a breath. At once, all four of her arachnid limbs struck from both sides. Two of them glanced off my shield, but the other two hit me in the ribs, slicing deep through both sets of armor. The only thing that saved me was the shadowsteel chainmail.

I jumped back as she retracted them, but her attack had been a feint. Jasmine shifted, throwing her hips as a large black tail made of chitin barreled into me. it struck hard enough that my chitin cracked and shattered as the blow lifted me off my feet and flung to the floor several feet away.

The air expelled from my lungs in a great gasp as I landed roughly on the floor and rolled, slamming my back on one of the stone pillars that held up the ceiling. I struggled to my feet as Jasmine came closer, and I saw what had hit me. A long, black tail trailed behind her like a length of thick rope. It coiled around her waist as the tip came into view. Her scorpion tail was capped with a massive stinger; poison welled at the zenith to slither down to the floor in heavy drips.

My back hit the column as I instinctively recoiled from it. *So that's what that blessing does. I need to figure how to fight with my own—and quickly—or she'll overwhelm me.*

I summoned my *Arachnid Limbs,* as I'd fought with them before. Warmth spread over my back as they formed. Jasmine struck once more with her tail, but I caught it with my spider legs. The tip of the stinger halted just shy of my face, and I heaved a sigh of relief as I lunged forward and slammed the side of my shield into her face. I expected it to strike home, but heavy resistance stopped it cold. She'd blocked my shield with her four limbs just as I'd blocked her tail. The tips of her legs peeled back to reveal sharp claws that quickly latched onto every side of my shield.

"A pity. You fought well, Duran."

She had me pinned, and I couldn't react fast enough as she brought her scorpion tail overhead and brought it down on my shield. It shattered through my chitin like glass and sent shards scattering across the stone as they fell, reflecting the light of the sun shining through the stained glass.

They clattered to the ground, and a sharp pain radiated from my left arm.

I looked over, and the pain only intensified.

Her scorpion tail broke through my chitin and tore through my forearm; the tip stuck out the other side.

I jerked my arm free, and blood rushed from the ragged wound. *Shit. Not good. I'm partially immune to the poison, but I can't deal with the side effects or a bleeding debuff right now.*

A terrible realization came over me, and I cursed as cold dread settled in my heart. *She's going to kill me if I don't stop her. I don't have a choice.*

I'm sorry.

I clenched my teeth and threw myself in a roll as she struck again. I came up and wielded my hand and a half sword in both hands. The timer for *Aura of the Arachnid* was running low, and I had two minutes to finish this.

It would be over in half that.

Jasmine struck again, but I'd seen her tricks. She was fast and unbelievably strong, far better than I was at handling the mantle of Hive Knight. But her combat skills were lacking. She relied too much on brute force. It left her vulnerable.

I stepped forward as she struck with her limbs. Instead of dodging, I turned my body as they glided past, barely licking at my chitin. As they struck air behind me, I used my own limbs to pin hers, and I struck.

I put my entire body behind my thrust and aimed for the spot on her chest that I'd hit earlier, where the chitin was weakest.

The blade hit dead center, and her armor couldn't withstand another strike. It buckled and caved under my steel, and it slid through her chest and stopped as the chitin of her back held.

I pulled my sword from her chest as the eldritch glow from her eyes dimmed. The smooth chitin peeled away, retreating under her skin. Blood welled at the corners of her mouth, and she collapsed. I caught Jasmine before she hit the stone floor and cradled her against my chest.

Without her armor, she seemed so frail as I held her. My own chitin faded as I canceled all of my abilities, and I sagged as my battle fatigue rose as I prematurely shut down *Aura of the Arachnid*.

My legs failed me, and my knees hit the stone hard as I held onto Jasmine. Her auburn hair covered her face and stuck to the blood that cover her cheek.

"Someone, help her!"

I pressed my hand to her wound as her blood painted my hands, staining them crimson. I looked up at Magnus and Aliria, who hadn't moved a muscle. "Magnus, help her! She's going to die!"

He shook his head, softly, just once. "She's already gone, Duran. I'm sorry."

"She's not, Jasmine's fine!"

I brushed the blood away from her mouth, only to smear even more blood across her tawny skin. Her head nestled in the crook of my arm, and her once-beautiful eyes of honey were nothing but glass.

He was right. Jasmine was gone.

"No, no, no." I glared up at Magnus. "Help her! You're a chronomancer, bring her back!"

"I can't."

What? No, that's fucking unacceptable! I laid Jasmine down as gently as possible and rose to face Magnus. I marched across the floor and ascended the steps of the obsidian throne, ignoring the concern across Eris's and Raven's faces. I grabbed Magnus by the collar of his black silk tunic, balling it in my fists and yanking him from his seat.

"Bring. Her. Back."

Magnus stared into my eyes, his too-light green burning a hole straight to my heart before he looked away. He swept his eyes to Jasmine's supine form, and he quickly brought his eyes back to mine. A tear fell down his cheek before he brushed it away with his thumb.

"I can't!" he seethed. Magnus brought his fingers to his eyes and wiped away any more tears before they could escape. "I can't bring her back. Not anymore."

"Damn you!" I threw him back and walked back over to Jasmine. Her blood pooled beneath her body. I crashed to the ground next to her and tried to fight the grief that rose in my heart. *Damn it!*

"Place your hand on her, knight."

I paused. *Why?*

"To reclaim her chitin. It will replace what you've lost and will be a great boon to you...it is also a way of honoring a knight who has fallen in battle. Her chitin will be carried on."

With only minor hesitation, I placed my hand on Jasmine's still-warm skin, and a heat crept into my palm as her chitin absorbed into my skin. Within a moment it was over, and as much as the Aspect had said it was a way of honoring her, it felt like desecration.

I'm sorry.

I opened my mouth to find the words, but whatever I'd been about to say was silenced by the soft vocals of a woman singing.

Magnolia knelt by her daughter, holding her head in her lap, singing softy while she ran her fingers through her hair as she cried and sang.

I couldn't understand the words, but I wasn't meant to; it was a lamentation for Jasmine and Magnolia alone.

Her words tempted my own grief, and I fought back my own tears and stood, turning back to the throne. "Please, Magnus, please bring Jasmine back."

"If it were within my power, I would have done so already. There is nothing anyone can do to help her any longer but lay her to rest."

My hope shattered, and I couldn't fight the tears any longer. They spilled freely down my cheeks. I couldn't take my eyes from the young woman I'd killed.

"Oh, Sam," Eris said, rushing over to me.

Her arm brushed mine, but I pulled away. I couldn't speak, couldn't have responded even if I wanted to. There was nothing I could say at that moment. I fell to my knees in front of Jasmine, trying to find the words, but none came.

"I—I'm…" I choked and cried.

Warm fingers took hold of mine, and I blinked away my tears to see Magnolia, smiling at me through her own tears. "It's okay."

"No, no, it's not. I…I killed her. Nothing is okay."

Magnolia squeezed my hand tight. "No, you didn't. She did," she said, before her gaze turned black as she tilted her head to Aliria. "You took advantage of my daughter's loneliness and twisted her to benefit your goals. All she ever wanted was a friend, and you used that against her!"

I wasn't any better. I brushed her aside when I could've so easily taken the time to get to know her. I'm sorry, Jasmine. I'd have been honored to be your friend. I reached over to the small pool of blood underneath her body and dipped my finger in it. I brushed it across my lips and closed my eyes.

Jasmine's memories flooded through me, and I made sure to burn every single detail into my mind, all the good and bad I experienced as the Mnemosyne showed bits of her life to me. Her senseless death could have been so easily avoided.

I won't forget you, Jasmine. I swear. It was a promise made to a dead girl. It didn't matter to her any longer, but it mattered to me. She deserved to be remembered by someone other than her mother.

I placed my hand over Magnolia's and looked into her eyes. "I swear I will remember her, always."

"Thank you, Duran. She liked you more than you know. Even after you left, she couldn't stop talking about you," she said, twisting the knife even deeper into my heart.

I let go of Magnolia's hand and stood. I turned to face Aliria, who held the same cold, impassive look as always, despite just watching her knight die right in front of her.

"Jasmine just died! Your knight. Say something!"

Aliria gave me a bitter smile. "She failed and lost to a knight who doesn't even know how to use his power properly. I'll find another."

I don't remember moving. One second I was by Jasmine's body, then the next my blade was a centimeter from Aliria's throat.

The only thing that spared her was Magnus.

"Let me go!"

Magnus shook his head in my periphery. "Your anger is understandable. Justifiable, even. But I can't let you harm Aliria."

"Argh!" I screamed wordlessly in her face, spittle flying to pepper her cheeks.

Magnus released me, and my shoulders hung heavy as I walked away from Aliria. I didn't know what to do with myself, stuck between wanting to avenge Jasmine and to just leave and go home, but I could do neither.

Magnolia lifted Jasmine in her arms and rose. She faced us, and with tears streaming down her face, she inclined her head in a shallow bow. "If you'll excuse me, I must go bury my daughter."

"Of course, Magnolia. Truly, I'm sorry for your loss," Magnus said, his voice weary.

"I'll help," I began and took a step.

"No…thank you, but this is something I must do myself," she said and carried Jasmine from the room, leaving behind a trail of too-bright blood and another ghost in my heart.

I stared at the pool of blood for a long moment before Raven and Eris walked over to me.

"There was nothing more you could've done, my bonded. You gave her every chance."

Bonded? Not so much now, my love. But the sentiment is still there.

"Doesn't make it hurt any less."

Raven ran her fingers over mine, not saying anything, but her crimson eyes held what she knew her words couldn't. We'd all experienced loss in our lives, and sometimes, a thousand words couldn't express what a simple touch and a look could.

"I love you both," I said.

No point in fighting how I feel, not anymore. I let go of them and stood in front of Magnus as he looked down from his throne. Sunlight streamed through the stained glass and covered us both in shimmering colors.

"Tell me why?" I said. "You brought Aliria back, and she was nothing but ash. Tell me why you couldn't do that with Jasmine?"

Magnus sighed. "I'll explain everything, I promise, but we're about to have company. It'll be easier to understand when they get here."

I threw my hands up, too impatient to wait. I wanted answers, I needed to understand why Jasmine had to die. And Magnus was the only one who could give them to me. "How long do I have to wait?"

He cocked his head to the side. "Not long. If you'll stop and listen, you can hear them."

What?

I paused, closing my mouth and doing as he suggested, listening. For a long moment, all there was was the steady breathing of the five of us and a bird singing softly outside. I was about to give up when Eris spoke.

"Metal, thuds. Someone's fighting in the hallways, getting closer."

It took a minute longer for me, but eventually I picked up what Eris heard, and she was right. There were definite sounds of fighting inching closer to us. *Who would be bold enough to attack—oh, of course it's them. Took them long enough. They even had a head start on us.*

I shook my head, too weary of everything that had happened. It was only a few minutes later when I realized I hadn't tended to my wounds, and I quickly pulled out a health potion and drank half of it.

The others bristled as the fight worked its way to just outside the door, but I stood calmly. A man screamed on the other side of the door, and there was a loud thump, then another. The doors buckled inward and slammed open as a badly bruised man in once-bright silver armor, now dented and stained red, came sailing into the throne room.

He landed with a thud and a let out a strangled, raspy groan as he stared up at us. "Intruders," he croaked before his eyes rolled back in his head and he slumped to the stone floor.

Two sets of brilliant golden eyes pierced the darkness. Sharp footsteps cracked as Evelyn and Adam strolled into the room.

Both of them were battered and bloody like I'd never seen them before. Evelyn's skintight leather armor was cut in numerous places, showing much of her pale skin as off-color blood dripped from the tears. Adam wore his medium plate armor, but while not as worn as Evelyn's, he had a fair number of welts and dents. Blood ran from a split lip and a cut on the side of his neck.

By the nine kings of hell, I've never even seen them bleed before.

They walked through the room in utter silence, and as they came closer, they both stared at me, nodded, and turned to Magnus, expressions like I'd never seen on their faces before. Confusion, rage and immeasurable relief all melded into shock as their mouths opened slightly.

"It really is you," Adam said. "After all this time."

Magnus lit up, so much warmth filled his eyes as the biggest smile broke across his face. "It's good to see you again, James. You as well, Jessica. I've missed you both terribly."

"Two hundred years," Evelyn seethed. "We spent two hundred years searching for you, Nicholas!"

"I know. And I'll explain everything, to all three of you."

Evelyn tiled her head. "Three of us?" she asked before turning to me. "You're including Sampson Acre?" She held up a hand as my mouth opened. "Don't misconstrue that, guild leader—I've grown quite fond of you these past few years, but you're not exactly one of us. This really isn't your concern."

"You know my full name?" I asked.

She nodded. "I'm the one who recruited you from that disgusting camp so long ago, after all."

"Jessica? Jessica Bell?"

"Indeed, and Adam is actually Jameson Bell."

I sighed into my palm. "All three of you have a lot of explaining to do."

CHAPTER 30 - BROKEN WORLD

Magnus, or Nicholas, whoever he really was, led all of us to his study. Once inside, we gathered around his map table, and he looked at each of us in turn.

"I know we have much to discuss, and bear with me, as it's a lot."

"Let's start at the beginning. How you three know each other?" I stared at both Adam and Evelyn, who'd drunk a health potion each and were back to their usual perfection. "I thought I knew you both, but I don't know you at all."

Evelyn smiled at me, brushing away a stray silver hair that fell in her face. "You knew part of us, the parts that we wanted to share. You, more than most, should know why we chose to do so."

I get it, I do, but I still can't help feeling a little betrayed. But that's wrong of me. "Okay, we're all entitled to secrets, but I mean, come on. You knew who Magnus was this whole time?"

"Not at all. We'd long since thought Nick died, since we couldn't find him after all these years since the schism happened. We assumed he'd been a casualty," Adam said.

I placed my hands on the wooden lip of the map table. "The schism, how did it happen?"

"An explosion in the bunker, we think. Something happened in the real world that took out several of our servers, leaving us with precious little data storage remaining. Which eventually led to the schism."

Adam slammed his fist down on the table. "You left out the most important detail, Nick. Tell him what you did."

Magnus sighed and looked over to Adam, his face pained. "After all that's happened, you're still angry?"

"It wasn't your call to make!"

"Then whose?" he fired back, his finger pointed at Adam. "It had to be us, and you weren't willing to make the call. I did what you couldn't."

"You killed thousands!"

"And saved thousands more."

"Hey!" I shouted, holding my hands up. "Both of you stop this and explain what's going on."

Magnus and Adam stopped and turned to me, anger on their faces. Adam motioned to Magnus. "Tell him."

He sighed. "Before the schism, there was a decision to make. A choice to leave things as they were and hope the A.I. could fix the issues, or to purge as much irrelevant data as possible to move what we could save to the non-damaged drives."

"You made the call to delete everything."

"Yes."

I pulled out the chair by the desk in the corner and sat back, trying to think. Eris and Raven had been quiet through the exchange, but when I moved, they came and sat back against the wall next to me while I drummed my fingers across the elegant cherry wood desk. *It was a hard call with no clear outcome on either side.*

"Could Ouroboros have fixed the system?"

Adam opened his mouth to respond but quickly closed it, his eyes shifting away. "Maybe. I don't know. But we had time to find out if she could—we didn't have to act immediately!"

"If we had waited for her to get finished with her analysis, we'd have lost even more drives to the corruption, and it would have cost hundreds of lives in the slim hopes that we might've been able to save everyone. It was a pipe dream, and you know it," Magnus said.

"You still—"

"James, he's right. Much as I didn't agree with how he went about it, he took decisive action, and much as you hate the cost, you can't deny he saved everyone he could," Evelyn said.

"You were just as furious as I was. Don't even deny it," Adam replied.

Evelyn leaned her hip against the table and crossed her arms. "I hated that he went around us without our consent and used your system access to do it. I hated the method, but I've always agreed with his results."

"Evelyn's right," I said, standing up. My fingers brushed against Raven and Eris as I passed, and I gave them both a reassuring smile. "Magnus did what he thought was best, and I can't say I wouldn't have made the same decision in his place. Risking the whole system in the off chance you can save everyone is a fool's gamble, and you know it."

"I thought after all you've lost, you'd agree that we have to save everyone."

"If we can. But not at the cost of everyone else. I've lost just as much as anyone else here, and not twenty minutes ago, I lost someone I would've liked to befriend. A girl who did nothing wrong but still died a needless death." I paced in a small circle, my footsteps clacking against the hardwood floor. "You can't save everyone. That's the lesson I've learned after all these years. Save who you can, when you can."

"Well said. Duran is right, especially now," Magnus said, coming over to clap me on the back. "This doesn't have to be a repeat of the past. We can work together this time."

Repeat? Ah, that's what this has been about since the beginning. "It's happening again, isn't it? That's what the void is doing creeping in from the Azure Depths," I said, placing my finger on the hyper realistic map. "The system is corrupted again."

"Yes. Our measures were only temporary, I'm afraid, and I don't know how bad the situation actually is this time."

"What happens if the system gets fully corrupted?"

"It's the end, of everything, of the entire Ouroboros Project."

"So we would all die, permanently."

"Exactly. There are no backups," Magnus said.

I pinched the bridge of my nose and heaved a sigh. *I need a drink.* I opened my inventory and pulled out my flask.

"Anyone need a drink? Just me. Okay." After a long pull, I capped the flask and passed it to Raven, because I knew she would want one. "All this time, and I still don't know what the Ouroboros Project's end goal was. Digital immortality is great and all, but this couldn't have been the entire goal, right?"

Adam shook his head. "It wasn't. This was supposed to be just temporary. Windigo Industries saw the writing on the wall when the first of the ghouls appeared. They started forming contingency plans in case the worst should happen."

"Windigo? Seriously? Those bastards are who're behind all this? So what, digital immortality was the best they could come up with?"

"Not at all," Evelyn interjected. "It was just one of the projects they had in the works."

"And how well did the others turn out?" Magnus asked her. "They built a damned spaceship in low orbit and ferried almost two thousand people off-world, and what happened to them, Adam, Evelyn?"

Both of them looked away, their faces set in stone.

Magnus slammed his fist on the wood. "Exactly. And how did our own end goal turn out? Twenty years. That was the promise we all received when we started working on the project. Twenty years, and our consciousness would be put inside clones of our bodies. That was our endgame, and what happened?"

He blew out a breath and combed through his hair.

"Raven, would you mind sharing?' he asked.

She froze mid-sip and pulled the flask from her lips. "No, ma—Magnus," she said and stood, handing him the metal flask.

Magnus drank deeply, nearly chugging the stiff whiskey I'd filled it with. He stopped and sat it on the table, spilling a few drops in the process. "Nine hundred and fifty-seven years. We've been here for nearly a thousand years and have no chance of ever going home again. If Earth even stands any longer. We're here, on Nexus, until the power runs out and ends it all.

"I don't know about the rest of you, but I know exactly which of the nine hells I'm headed to, and I'm not looking forward to it."

The air was heavy, the tension so thick I could have cut it with my knife.

"Look," I said, standing up from the chair. "This goes beyond any past grievances. We can't hold onto grudges when the literal end of everything is staring us in the face. I'm an outsider in all this, I'm not a scientist, computer whatever. I'm just a thug, but you three are the smartest, most powerful people in this world. If you can't come to an agreement, then we all die."

"Sampson has a point, brother. We have to do something. We can't repeat past mistakes and have us at odds with each other. We can find common ground."

Adam laughed, leaning over the table while his golden eyes stared down at the map, unblinking. "You're right about one thing, Jess. We can't repeat history, that's for damn sure." He looked up at Magnus, a decision made in his eyes. "We tried it your way last time, and all it bought was time. We do it my way this time."

Magnus's eyes narrowed. "I disagree."

The tension broke with the last syllable of his words. Evelyn smoothly drew two silver daggers the length of shortswords and shifted her weight to balance. Adam pulled two summoning crystals from his inventory and stood poised to throw them.

While on the other side of the study, Aliria pushed off the desk she stood against as chitin enveloped her, her hands elongating to wicked black blades.

Magnus stood impassively, but with his time magic, he didn't have to move a muscle.

I had a choice to make myself.

It wasn't the wrong choice, but as I drew my sword, I knew it wasn't right.

My blade raised, I stepped toward Evelyn. "Don't do this."

She lifted her lips in a smile. "You would raise your blade to me?"

"If you two are not willing to see reason. Unless you have a better plan than wait and see, I'm siding with the plan that has the best chance of all of us surviving."

"Even at the cost of thousands of lives?" Adam asked, his fingers twitching.

"I can't save everyone…but I can save Eris. I can save Raven, the two of you, and the Gloom Knights. The rest of the world be damned. I'll make that choice every time."

We stared into each other's eyes, just waiting for the pin to drop.

"All of you, stop this madness!" Eris shouted, breaking the tense silence.

I wasn't expecting her voice; she hadn't spoken since we entered the study.

Eris picked herself up from the dark floorboards and glared at all of us. "Look at where this has led! We're family, all of us! And you're about to slaughter each other? Over what? Because you can't agree on something?

"Children, all of you!"

There was a single split second where we could've continued as we were and went to war, but as I looked at each of the people I would give my life for, I lowered my sword and chuckled.

It started as a soft single chuckle, but it grew, and soon I was laughing so hard, it hurt to breathe. I had to lean on the table to keep from falling over, and when I got back up, everyone just stared at me.

"She's right! We're children. All it took was one confrontation, and over ten years of loyalty snapped like string. I was ready to fight you, Evelyn, knowing I'd lose. That says something about the severity of the situation, but come on! We can't do any better than try to kill each other over our differences?"

I eyed each of them and then walked out of the room.

"Where are you going?" Adam asked at my back.

"To the kitchen. I'm starving, and I think we could all use a drink. Come, don't come. I don't care. If you kill each other after I leave, that's on you. But I'm not going to fight my friends."

Eris and Raven followed me out, and I shut the wood door with a heavy thud.

Before I'd taken a step, Eris's heated hand intertwined with my fingers, and Raven looped her arm through mine. I ran my hand over Raven's smooth skin as I turned to Eris. "Thank you for that. I don't know what came over me."

"You were all scared, because I know I was. To face the end is a terrifying prospect, but it affords a measure of clarity once you've lived through it."

"This isn't just our end, it's the possible end for everyone, its big…and I don't know what to do, what I can do. I'm good at swinging a sword, but a sword can't fix what's coming. Maybe I should just let them handle it. I'm so far out of my depth I can't see the shore, and I think it's going to get worse before it gets better."

Raven tugged on my arm, pulling my attention to her. "Maybe you just do what you can, when you can. I don't think anyone is asking you to solve this yourself. Let those who know better handle the things you can't. You handle the things you can."

I smiled down at her. It was simple advice, but that's exactly what I needed in that moment, simple, to the point. I kissed the top of her head. "Thank you. that's exactly what I needed to hear."

"Good, I'm glad I could help. You can spoil me later," she said with a wink.

We walked the rest of the way in silence, our heads heavy with what we'd just been told, but I'd handled it better than the first time Magnus had shattered my world. *It's not like the signs weren't there from the beginning. I just didn't put them together, didn't want to think about how everything shifted in my world so easily.*

The only thing I can do is help where I can and do my best to protect those who matter more than anything else in my life.

When we got to the dining hall, we took a seat at the banquet table while Eris stared at the wide-open windows and wooden support beams along the walls that connected overhead. "It's a beautiful place," she said softly, clutching my hand as we all three sat side by side.

I laid my head down and rested my warm, almost feverish forehead against the cool smooth wood, waiting to find out if the others would join us.

It took a few minutes, but eventually the heavy wooden doors opened, and a parade of footsteps thumped across the stone floor towards us. After a few terse seconds, the chairs around the table scraped against the floor, and I finally looked up.

Magnus and Aliria sat across from us while Adam and Evelyn sat near the head of the table.

"Glad to see you all came to your senses," I said, leaning back.

"Well, given the stakes, tensions are going to run high all around. But as Eris said, we were behaving inappropriately."

"Yes. Thank you, little queen. I'd have hated to take your lover's head. I kind of like him."

I laughed and reached for my flask, only to find that I'd left in back in Magnus's study. *Oh, well.* "I'm glad too. It would be a pain to respawn and level up now."

"You wouldn't respawn. Not this time, Duran," Magnus said, laying his palms flat on the table. "It's why I couldn't bring Jasmine back and why I'm thankful no blood was shed between us. The system has worsened faster than before, and I'm afraid there are no more respawns for any of us."

I slumped over in my chair, deflating at his words. Silence filled the room, broken only by the subtle gusts of wind that howled through the open windows.

So this is it for all of us. We either fix what's wrong with the system or we die for real. Fuck, I'm not cut out for this.

Any thought of food soured in my mouth, and I fought the churning in my stomach and swallowed bile. *I've died before, but I've never had so much to lose as right now. I can't afford to die, not yet.*

"Okay," I said, raising my head. "How do we stop it?"

"We don't," Evelyn said, turning to me. "They do." She swept her hand past Magnus and Adam. "They helped build the damn thing. They're the only ones who can even hope to fix it."

"So what's the problem? Why can't you fix it?"

"It's not that simple," Adam said with a shake of his head. "I'm going to have to dig into the root directory to find out what exactly is going on, and that's complicated, to say the least."

"Do tell," I replied, drumming my fingers along the edge of the wood. "Seems there is a lot you still haven't told me."

He shook his head. "You know most of it..."

"But not all of it."

"Playing coy after all you've revealed to the boy? Don't get squeamish now. I've heard Magnus's side of the argument, but I'm so curious about yours," Aliria said, her arms crossed as she leaned to the side of her chair.

Adam sighed. "When the schism happened, Nick and I argued on the correct course of action, much like we're doing now. We just couldn't reach common ground, as he wanted the most extreme option." He looked from me to Magnus with fire in his eyes. "Nick went behind my back and used his admin access to override the system and force it to purge all non-essential data. He betrayed me."

"I'll say what I told you then, what I told you minutes ago. I did what had to be done. You were content to sit and watch while trying and failing to come up with an alternative. I took decisive action and saved everyone I could."

"It doesn't give you the right to play god!" Adam shouted, standing up so fast, his wooden chair clattered to the floor.

"Do you hear yourself, James? With the power we wield in this world, we're as close as we can be, you two especially. If not us, then who?" Magnus asked.

"This isn't what our power was meant for! We are supposed to be guardians, protectors, not executioners!"

"By the nine kings of hell! Can you two not fight for two seconds?" I asked.

They both turned to me as I ran my hand over my face, my jaw tight from clenching. "Adam, I understand your position, I do. But the perfect option doesn't always exist. We have to do what we can with what we have. And unless you have a definite plan to save everyone, it's just wishful thinking. Let's hear what Magnus has to say, because from where I'm sitting, he's the only one here with a plan already in mind."

He jabbed a finger at me. "This isn't your—"

"Let him be, brother. Guil—Sam is right. And he's earned his place here; even I can't deny that anymore."

Adam sat down in a huff, but when his eyes met mine, gone was the hostility. His eyes were back to the normal, back to the eyes of my friend. "You're right. Both of you. I just—the whole point of this entire project was to save as many people as we could."

"Which is exactly what I'm trying to do, James. You have to admit to yourself that what I'm doing is the best and only way we can save as many people as possible."

"I can't admit that, but I'll hear you out this time, at least," Adam said and knelt to pick up his fallen chair off the ground.

I stood up and leaned on the table, looking at Magnus. "I'm assuming that your plan is the same as before?"

"Essentially. Though we can't shrink the island, as it's the last landmass in this world, we delete everything we can, starting with the NPCs since they take up the most data besides players. We delete as much as we can to save as many people as possible."

"As long as everyone I care about is safe, I'll help in any way I can."

Magnus nodded; his lips pressed together as he folded his hands in his lap. "I'm glad to hear it, but we can't begin without James."

"You want my override code?"

"I need it."

I held my hands up. "What override code?"

Magnus stood from his chair as someone new entered the room, the clink of crystal on metal caused me to turn as Magnolia came in with drinks. But at a second glance, my eyebrows raised. I was wrong. I'd reflexively thought it was Magnolia, but it was actually Aliria. She carried a tray of drinks in both hands without so much as a wobble as she sauntered across the room. Her sharp heels cracked loudly against the stone.

"I've brought drinks for everyone, but don't get used to this," she said as she set the tray in the center of the table.

"Thank you, dear," Magnus said as he poured himself a glass of wine.

A crystal tumbler filled with amber called my name, and I snagged it from the silver tray before knocking it back. *Oh, that's delicious and just what I needed.* I grabbed the bottle and another glass and poured another for myself and handed a glass to Raven.

"Thank you, darling. I think we could all use a drink right now."

Eris declined a glass but held onto my fingers tightly as I leaned down and kissed her. She scrunched her face is disgust, but her eyes lit up with humor and warmth. "You taste like alcohol, love."

"Sor—" I began before Raven grabbed hold of my face and pulled me into a kiss of her own, her tongue dancing with mine.

"You're right," she said as she pulled away a second later. "He totally does." She laughed and kissed my cheek before laying her head on my shoulder.

It was for just a minute while everyone took a drink from the table, but I loved them both for being themselves in the face of such melancholy. *Times have never been as dark as these, and they're only going to get darker. I need to keep them close, to remind me of who I'm fighting for.*

Once we all had a bit of alcohol to ease the mood, we returned to the conversation at hand.

"This override code, what is it?" I asked.

"Nick went around me and used his access to initiate the purge. When it was over, I couldn't remove his access, but I had to make sure he didn't do something like it again, so I did the only thing I could and locked us both out of the system," Adam said, taking a sip of wine.

"But you left a way back in. An override."

He nodded. "But I can't give it to him, even if he's right. He's also not being completely honest. Even if it starts with NPCs, that's not where it will end. Because if it's not something we can fix, it'll eventually lead to him sacrificing players to save space like he did before. No one person should have the right to decide who lives and who dies."

Magnus sighed. "I wish you would see reason, James. But this isn't getting us anywhere."

He snapped his fingers, and Evelyn froze in place, her glass tumbler halfway to her pale lips.

"What are you doing?"

"Taking control of the situation," Magnus said as he rose from his chair. "You don't want to be responsible for the lives of everyone on Nexus. I get that, so once again, I'll do what you can't."

"Give me the override."

"Or what? You kill Jess? You wouldn't hurt either of us. I know that for a fact. I also know you can't hold her for long."

Magnus lifted his head and stared at Adam. I knew the look in his eyes well, and Adam was wrong; he'd kill Evelyn if that's what it took.

"I can either release her or kill her. And you can either save her or watch her die."

Adam rose from his seat, crystals in hand. "I'll stop you!"

"How? I'm your counter—you know you can't win against me." Magnus sighed; the lines on his face aged him ten years. "Don't make me do this, James. Give me the code!"

Adam raised his hand, his fingers twitched as he was about to throw his summon, but he stopped and lowered his hands. "Epsilon, forty-two, seven, three, nine, Delta."

"Thank you. Was that so hard?"

He scowled, his brows furrowed. "You're going to kill thousands, and you don't even care, do you?"

"Of course I do," he said, his hands clenched tight. Magnus picked up his nearly full wine glass and downed it in a single gulp. "But I do this for the good of the many, not the few."

Magnus snapped his fingers, and Lachrymal's Heart appeared, suspended in the air over the table. He reached out and touched a single finger to the brilliant emerald. "Epsilon, forty-two, seven, three, nine, Delta."

With those words, the Heart shuddered, and a chime rang through the dining room. A crack split the gemstone, which was followed by even more cracks as it shattered into a thousand pieces. They rained down to the table but disappeared before they touched the wood. We all stood and stared transfixed at where the Heart once resided.

In its place was a girl.

She had deeply tanned skin, a thin delicate face, and curly brown hair that stopped at her round chin. Her glazed eyes were green, the exact shade as Lachrymal's Heart. She wore a plain gray dress that stopped at her calves.

The girl hung in the air for a second before dropping to the table, folding her legs under her as she rested on her heels. After a time, she lifted her head and stared around the room, her jaw clenching and unclenching as she worked it around, trying to find a way to speak.

"Ah, there we go. I'm not used to this vessel yet," she said, her voice deeper than I was expecting from such a small woman.

She rose and climbed down off the table before walking over to Adam. "Master Bell, it has been too long," she said, bowing.

"Edna? Since when do you have an avatar?"

"I've had this form since the very beginning; there was just never a need to use it before. But it was the easiest option to converse with all of you."

"Who is she?" I asked as I got out my chair, letting go of Raven and Eris in the process.

Edna turned to me, a small, very sad smile on her face. "Hello again, Sampson Acre. My name is Edna, but you would know me better as Ouroboros. I am the governing A.I. for this world."

CHAPTER 31 - FALLEN

I marched around the banquet table and slapped Edna across the face.

She stumbled back from the force but remained standing, a small reddening welt rising where I'd struck her. Her green eyes wide, she raised a hand to her cheek, wincing as her fingers brushed her tanned skin.

"That hurt," she said, her mouth agape.

"You know what that's for."

Edna nodded, dropping her hand. "I assume that settles accounts with us."

I heaved a sigh, already tired of the headache that wasn't quite yet here, but I knew was coming. "Yeah, we're good now."

"Sam, what the hell? Why'd you slap my A.I.?" Adam asked, staring at me like I'd lost my mind.

"We had business to settle. It's settled. Let's move on."

I went back to my chair as Edna shook her head and stood by Adam as we all returned to our seats.

"Now that Edna is here, we can continue," Magnus said.

"I'm afraid you're mistaken, Mister Parks. You used a loophole in my programming last time to initiate the purge, and it has since been corrected. You will not be able to repeat the actions of the past."

Magnus sighed, tugging at the hairs on his chin. "Why must everything be so complicated?" he muttered before he looked up at Edna. "You refuse to help me?"

"I refuse to help you kill any more innocents."

"That's unfortunate."

"Shit!" Adam cursed as he turned to me. "Sam, take Eris and get away!"

What? I rose from my chair just as Magnus snapped his fingers, freezing me in place. Freezing all of us in place.

"Magnus, what the hell?" I asked, moving my neck to face him. "What are you doing?"

He looked up at me, his eyes haunted and pained; they must have weighed a thousand pounds for how heavy they looked in that moment. "Truly, I am sorry. You'll never understand how much I wish I didn't have to do this."

"Do what?"

"I was counting on us being able to resolve our differences and work together on this, but even with the override, I'm back to where I was before, but I still don't have full access. If Edna is unwilling or unable to assist me, then I must take alternate measures to achieve my goal. I'm sorry, Sam. But I need Eris."

"Why?" I shouted.

"Because I need access to Edna's root programming, but she's blocked my access and since she won't help, I need the codes."

"What does that have to do with Eris?"

Magnus laid his palms flat on the table, thumbs curled around the edge. "Eris is the last of the original NPCs created when this world was built. She's different than all of the others because she, and all the others of that time, were created by using a cloned version of Edna. Think of them like her children. As time went on, Edna started using the brain scans and personalities of the humans we introduced to create the NPCs. Eris is the only original left."

I struggled against my invisible prison but couldn't move anything but my neck. I jerked my head around the room before my eyes landed on Aliria. "Use Aliria instead!"

"Do you think I haven't considered that?" he shouted, slamming his fist on the table. "Why do you think I brought her back in the first place? She's incompatible now. My magic changed her code when it was introduced to her. I've already tried!"

"And you! Are you just going to stand there while he takes your daughter?"

Aliria couldn't meet my gaze, her eyes fell to the ground as she hung her head. "I do not wish to die again."

I turned to Magnus. "Can you get the code without harming Eris?"

After an eternity's pause, he shook his head. "It would destroy her. I'm sorry, Sam. I'd give anything not to take her from you. I know what she means to you, but it's the lives of all of us versus one girl. I will make that trade, so you don't have to.

"It'll be quick, painless, like falling asleep. It won't hurt her, I promise."

"I don't give a damn about your promises, they mean nothing! I won't let you fucking touch her!"

"You don't have a choice, I'm afraid."

"That's where you're wrong," I snarled, and activated *Aura of the Antimage*.

It dispersed off my skin and swirled around the table, shattering all of the magic that kept us frozen. As soon as I could move my body again, I pulled Eris to her feet and drew my sword.

Magnus stared at me in shock, his eyes wide, mouth agape. "Antimagic? But how?" He looked over at Evelyn and cursed. "Him? You chose him?"

"He's as worthy as any I've found these many years. You won't be able to hold us again."

Magnus sneered at her, kicking over his chair as he raised his hands, and ethereal green pentagrams appeared in his palm. As soon as they formed, they sputtered and died, fizzling out to nothing.

"Aliria," he barked.

She nodded and stepped onto the table, letting her chitin flow over her pale skin as two wicked swords appeared in her hands. "I'm afraid I must restrain you, my little fly."

Eris stared down her mother, her emotions so overwhelming that she was drowning in them. "You were going to let him kill me?"

"It's the only way for us to survive. I wish it weren't so, but it has to be this way."

I raised my sword, ready to charge her, but Adam grabbed my arm tight. "It's time to run, not time to fight. We need to get away before Nick's magic returns."

Adam tossed two crystals at the stone floor, and they shattered, reveling his lava golem and a handful of bane wolves. "They'll cover us, but we have to go now!"

"Do as he says, Sam," Evelyn said, drawing her twin blades. "Getting Eris to safety is the mission. We can fight later."

I nodded at them as Aliria cut one of Adam's bane wolves in half. Blood gushed from the split wolf before it dissolved in swirling shadow. The five of us took off towards the dining hall door as Adam's summons bought us a few moments.

"This house is a fucking maze, which way do we go?" I asked as the heavy wood door slammed shut behind me.

Raven stepped to the left and motions at us. "Follow me. I know the way."

She took off around the corner as we all jogged to catch up. I held Eris's hand in my left while Evelyn and Adam ran ahead of me.

"We cleared out most, if not all of Nicholas's guards on our way in," Evelyn said, turning to me as we ran. "We should have an easy way out if you can take Eris and fly out of here when we get outside."

As we ran by a door, it flew open, and a man in heavy plate mail jumped out with his sword raised. I twisted, bringing my sword up as his came down. I caught it on the guard and grunted as I tightened my grip.

I let go of Eris as I and the guard had our swords bound. "Protect her!"

Adam grabbed Eris as I fought with the guard. I stepped forward and threw my weight into my blade, maneuvering both to the left near the ground.

The guard's blue eyes lit up as he tried to compensate and bring his sword back, but I had my opening. I hooked the top of my foot around his heel and tugged, taking his leg out from under him. His head smacked hard against the doorjamb as he fell back. before he could rise, I thrust my sword through the gap in his helmet, puncturing his carotid.

His blood spilled around my sword as I pulled it free, his death rattle echoing in the empty room behind him.

Adam still held Eris as I turned and was about to join them when the clink of armor and voices sounded down the hallway behind me. "Go, take her! I'll cover us!"

"What about you?" he asked, his eyebrows raised, lips pursed.

"They don't want me!" I shouted. "I'll be fine."

"Sam," Eris said, tugging on Adam's iron grip.

"Go, love. I'll be right behind you," I said before turning away from her and walking around the corner.

Half a dozen men stood in the hallway, lambent torchlight reflected in their too bright armor. *Give me Chitin Armor, Aspect.*

"Of course, knight."

It slithered over my skin, and I gripped my sword tightly as I activated Spider Limbs and Scorpion Tail.

Chitin pooled heavily at my back, forming my new appendages as I met the first of the guards. The hallway was too narrow for them to surround me, and my jagged black scorpion tail made it dangerous for them to try.

A few paled at the sight. A demon made manifest in front of them.

I raised my sword as a tall guard came forward, a mace clutched in both hands. It was heavy as he swung; it displaced the air with a soft whistle as it barreled toward my head. With a thought, *Chitin Shield* formed to meet the challenge. As his mace rebounded off my shield, I whipped my sword in an arc, following the trajectory of the mace as it flew back. I angled my blade, and its edge parted the flesh at Mace's wrist, severing the fine tendons that let him control his weapon.

Mace dropped his mace and stumbled back, holding his dripping wrist. Blood welled through his fingers, and he groaned as his face scrunched in pain.

I lunged to end his life, but a second guard stepped forward and caught the tip of my blackened steel on the flat of his dagger, deflecting my strike. In his right hand was a short sword that came for my face as Dagger riposted.

Two of my limbs pulled me back as the blade licked the chitin by my cheek. I stepped back as my tail shot the tip of my stinger forward, its noxious poison trickling in a purple stream over the obsidian chitin. It punched through his steel chestplate hard enough that the tail lifted him into the air. Dagger choked as all the air was forced out of his lungs. He curled in on himself as he coughed, and blood splattered across the stone walls and floor.

I retracted my tail as Dagger slumped over, his lifeless head cracking hard against the ground.

"You son of a bitch!" another guard screamed as he leapt over the body of his comrade.

While he hung in midair, I stepped to him and brought the left side of my spider limbs up sharply to meet him. The man impaled himself on my appendages, two of them lodged in the upper part of his chest plate, but the third landed high, just under the man's eye as it pierced through his bone and into his brain.

Two of the other guards slunk around and attempted to flank me, but I attacked with the remaining three limbs and my tail. I punctured their armor with just as much ease as the others, and they both died quick—if not painless—deaths.

The final man was wiser than his dead friends and turned to run. His brains kicked in too late as I flung the suspended corpse of the guard at him. It hit his legs, and he hit the stone tile hard as the body pinned him to the ground.

I stepped over the dead as the man tried to crawl for his sword that had slid from his hands when he took the nosedive. I nudged it with my foot as his fingertips brushed the leather handle, sending it skittering down the hall.

The man looked up at me, his wide brown eyes panicked, shot through with fear.

"Mercy!" he pleaded.

"You'll find none here," I said as my sword ended his life.

I wiped the blood from my blade, staring at the scorpion tail as it drifted into the corner of my eye before curling around my waist. *For what Aliria tried to do, I have to admit they're damned impressive.*

No sounds crept toward me from either end of the hallway, so I hastily pulled up my interface.

Combat Results!
7 Killed (Human): 10500 Exp!
Total Exp Gained: 10500 Exp!
Exp: 6800/6800
Level Up!

Level: 69
3800/6900
10 Stat Points Available!

I paused at the notification, at the first life I'd taken today. *I'll make her pay for your death, Jasmine, I swear.*

With a thought, I closed the interface and let the *Chitin Armor* fade. My arachnid appendages wormed back under my skin, and I changed into my shadowsteel plate. *You gave this armor and sword to me, Magnus. I'm going to use them to destroy you both.*

Magnus would never lay his hands on Eris. I would die first.

I left the bloodied hallway and started working on finding my way back to the others. I encountered only minimal resistance as I wound through the sharp corridors. A few guards who engaged me met their end on my blade. I cut them down, not even bothering to use the chitin at my disposal.

With a flick of my wrist, I cast their blood off the edge of my blade as they dropped to the floor. Though the guards told me one thing, that I was going in the wrong direction. *Evelyn wouldn't leave even a single guard alive, so I need to pick a different route.*

I took a right at the next hallway I came to and picked up my speed.

It took another few minutes, but I eventually found my way to the stairs that led to the upper floors of the castle and the parapets. I took the stairs two at a time and burst through the doors as the sun hung low in the sky, burnt orange tinged the horizon as day began to fall to night.

The others gathered around Raven, who'd already shifted and had Eris sitting atop her, staring at me, eyes wide with concern. I smiled at her as I approached but shook my head when she attempted to climb off Raven.

"All right, let's get moving! What are standing around for?"

Evelyn walked across the ramparts to stand in front of me. She leaned up and flicked me on the nose. "Idiot," she said, but there was no heat in her voice. "Do you expect us all to fit on the giant chicken?"

"Ah," I so eloquently replied as I stared over at Raven. *Yeah, no way we all fit. Three is pushing it—four is out of the question.*

"Okay, Adam, take Eris and Raven and get out of here. Evelyn and I will work our way out."

"I'm not leaving you!" Eris shouted, hopping off Raven and sprinting the distance. "I won't leave you behind."

"We don't have time to argue about this. We'll be right behind you, I promise. Now go!"

Eris hung her head, her large obsidian eyes downcast as she reached out and brushed the tip of my hand. I pulled her in close and held her for a moment. "I love you, but Evelyn and I can take care of ourselves. We'll join you in a few hours, I promise."

Adam rushed between us and grabbed my shoulder. "As touching as this is, we're out of time. Larry just died, and that bitch took out my wolves like they were nothing. Nick is coming, we have to go!"

Eris and I broke apart, and I all but pushed her towards Raven. "Go!"

She didn't fight me and ran back to Raven, quickly climbing up her feathers.

"You too, Adam."

He shook his head. "I'm not leaving without Evelyn."

I threw my hands up. "Then both of you go, I'll stay."

"No!" the shouts of both Raven and Eris were deafening.

I was about to reply when Evelyn tensed. "Doesn't matter now. He's here."

The large doors burst open as Magnus strolled through with Aliria in tow. They were only a couple hundred feet away, and we were on the cusp of running out of time.

"Go, go, go!" I shouted and took off, but a firm hand grabbed mine and stopped me in my tracks.

Evelyn's golden eyes stared into mine as her hand wound around my wrist. "There's no more time. Make sure James leaves, do you understand, Sam?"

"What about you?"

"I'm going to buy you time to escape."

I shook my head violently. "Hell, no. I'm not leaving you here, Magnus will kill you!"

She gave me a small smile as she lifted onto her toes and pressed her lips to mine in a chaste kiss. "Yes, he will."

She stepped back, and my interface flared to life in front of me.

Ability Share: Return to Zero

Accept Y/N

Yes.

I waved away the screen as quickly as it appeared, not bothering to read what the ability did. "What's this?"

"A weapon. Use it when the time comes," she said as she pulled away from me. In her hands was the knife Thrayl had given me. She'd stolen it from my belt. "I'm taking your knife. You won't get it back."

She turned to face Magnus as he and Aliria drew near. My heart beat too loudly in my ears as my mouth ran dry. The last thing I wanted was to leave her alone, but I couldn't stay. I had to protect the others. I had to go.

"One last thing, Sam. Before we part," she said, raising the knife to her palm. "A gift, and a curse. Perhaps you'll use it better than we did."

Evelyn stuck the knife in her palm, wincing as she dug deep into her flesh. After only a second, she pulled something free from her hand. It was a small orange crystal, smooth like a cut gemstone. Her blood stuck the gem as a light pulsed within it.

"Catch!"

She tossed it back to me as she strolled toward Magnus. "It's been fun, Sam."

I caught the crystal in my right hand. As soon as it touched my hand, a searing pain flared to life as my skin bubbled and hissed. The gemstone burrowed into my palm. I clenched my teeth as I fought to keep from screaming and took off towards Raven.

Evelyn walked calmly towards Magnus, but as she turned away, she changed. The pale silver of her hair fell away to midnight as her hair changed colors. Her skin grew a few shades darker as she walked away from me. In a handful of seconds stood the girl who walked into my life all those many years ago and offered me a chance at salvation.

Evelyn was gone. In her place stood Jessica Bell.

As soon as Jessica got close, she activated *Aura of the Antimage*. It shot from her skin in a whirlwind towards Magnus, but I blinked, and he disappeared, reappearing in the same instant twenty feet away, out of range of her aura.

The wind picked up as I ran, but a single word carried.

"Move."

I turned back as Magnus spoke. Jessica shook her head, raising her swords.

Magnus spoke again, but it was lost to the breeze as she stood in his way, refusing to back down.

He shook with rage. The veins in Magnus's neck throbbed against his tan skin as he bellowed an unhinged scream.

Jessica fell.

She jerked, turning, her head tilted towards me. Her vacant eyes glassed as they stared through me. Jessica dropped to the ground and closed her eyes.

They would never open again.

I ran and climbed onto Raven as Adam stared at his sister, an all-too-familiar emotion clear in his eyes.

He twitched, two summoning crystals in his hands as hatred filled his face. I knew what he was about to do, and I understood. I understood. But I couldn't let him.

My sword cleared leather, and I bashed the emerald pommel into his temple.

Adam dropped unconscious, and I caught him on my shoulder as Eris took my hand. Raven didn't even wait for me to climb aboard as she took to the skies. We were high in the air in seconds, and only when I was sure Adam and I were secure did I look back.

Magnus and Aliria were small as they stood on the castle's tower, staring at us. He watched us leave for a few seconds before turning and walking away.

I pulled Eris close as we flew away from Castle Aliria as fast as Raven could. I didn't know what to say, what I could say. Evelyn was gone, but I didn't have time to mourn her. I would wait until we were safely back at the castle before I let myself grieve.

Evelyn and I had had a rocky relationship at best, but she was a comrade, a mentor, an infrequent lover at times, and my friend. But I never really knew her. The revelation that she wasn't who I thought she was was proof enough. Despite that though, in a dark part of my heart, I'd cared very deeply for her.

A single tear slipped down my cheek before I could stop it, and I brought my hand up to wipe it away.

What came up wasn't my hand. It was, but my skin was ghost white, the color bleached from my skin.

"What the hell?"

Eris turned at my voice, her compound eyes going wide as she looked up at me.

"Sam?"

"What?" I asked.

"We need to land," she said, loud enough for Raven to hear.

Raven swooped down to relatively open stretch of the Badlands. Sand swept up around us as she landed. Eris hopped off as I carried Adam and set him down gently.

"Hand me your pack," Eris said, holding her hand out.

I pulled it from my inventory as Raven shifted back to her human form and walked over, her eyes as wide as Eris's, and they never left mine.

"That is you, isn't it, Sam?"

Eris pulled out something and handed it to me. It was a mirror. I took it and held it up to my face. I couldn't hold back the gasp that slipped through my lips. *What the hell?*

I didn't look like myself any longer. I shared the same features that Evelyn had. My hair was a polished silver, my skin pale as a corpse, and my once-amber eyes were a brilliant gold, shining bright as I stared at myself.

"What the actual hell?"

Eris just stared at me, but Raven shrugged. "It's not a bad look."

I turned on her and pointed at my face. "This doesn't freak you out?"

Raven shook her head, kicking at a stray rock in the sand. "I served Magnus for years. You'd be surprised at how little fazes you after that."

I mean, that's fair, but this is…I don't even know.

Adam stirred on the ground, sitting up with a pained groan. He glanced around at the desert before his eyes landed on mine. He stared at me for what had to have been hours before he broke contact and dropped his head and slumped his shoulders.

"She's dead?"

"I…I'm sorry."

He was motionless for a long moment before he nodded. Adam stood, sand sticking to him and falling as he got to his feet. He looked at me and held his hand up before dropping it. "I'll explain…I'll…later…later."

Before I could ask what he meant, he pulled a scroll from his inventory and unfurled it. The Script circle flared to life, and Adam vanished as he teleported away.

I just stared at the spot where Adam had been for a long while after he left. I was so unsure about anything anymore, and Adam was literally the last person who could give me answers.

"Best to give him some space," a voice said beside me.

I looked down at Edna, who'd appeared at my side.

"Where were you during all that?" I asked, throwing my hands up.

"Around. There was nothing I could've done to physically help you. My interference is limited, as I explained to you when we first met. I can do little to directly help you, unfortunately. Though freeing me has given me back full access to the system once more."

"So, if you so chose, you could initiate a purge like Magnus wants?"

"I have the capability, yes, but it goes against my primary programming, which is why Magnus needs access to my source code to change my programming to his wishes."

I scratched at my silver stubble. "And he needs Eris to do that?"

She nodded. "Eris is a copy of my code, though scaled down and without any command functions, but our cores are virtually identical. With her, he'll be able to grant himself system admin access, and he can modify me at will."

Eris and Raven walked over. Raven dragged my discarded pack through the sand and used it as a makeshift stool while Eris wound her hand through mine and leaned heavily on me. I pulled her close and kissed the top of her head.

"So what do we do? How do we fight Magnus? Evelyn was the strongest fighter in the world, and even she couldn't stand against his chronomancy."

Edna shook her head. "Mistress Bell was designed to be the counter to Mister Parks. Which is why he was forced to such drastic measures. Mistress Bell knew exactly what she was doing."

"She still died," I spat. "I should've stayed and fought."

"And you'd have died right alongside Mistress Bell. Which was the last thing she wanted. She chose you as her successor. And I find I don't necessarily disagree with her choice. You'll do."

"I still don't know how I'm going to pull this off. Magnus is so far outside my league it's not even funny."

Edna shook her head and reached out a finger, tapping me on the chest. "I have a plan in the works, but it will take time to move everything into place. I will help you as much as I can, but Evelyn gave you the tools needed to succeed."

"What is that supposed to mean?"

"Pull up your character page."

I did as she asked and pulled it up. What stared back at me was unbelievable.

Character Name: Durandahl
Level: 69
Exp: 3800/6800
Race: Demigod
Class: Hive Knight (Errant)
Reputation: Wanted Criminal
Bounty: 1300 Gold
Stats (+)

What? What the—what! I closed the screen with shaky fingers, my head reeling. "Edna, what is this?

"What the hell does Demigod mean?"

Edna shrugged. "You must ask Master Bell that question. The shards go beyond my understanding."

She stared off into the distance, at a wyvern flying far off. "I must depart now. There is much that requires my attention."

"Wait!" I shouted and tried to grab her, but my hand passed through empty air as she disappeared as if she'd never been there in the first place.

"Dammit," I cursed and kicked a deep groove into the sand, sending grains scattering it a wide arc.

I plopped down next to Raven and leaned against her side as Eris came and sat in my lap.

"It'll be okay, love," Eris said, snuggling into my chest while Raven trailed her fingers through my hair, brushing against my scalp with her fingernails. It was divine, but I was drowning.

"I don't know how anything can ever be okay again. So much is happening that I don't understand, and I'm so far out of my depth it's scary."

"How do you think we feel?" Raven asked, twirling a lock of my hair around her finger. "I don't fully understand anything that's going on either, but I don't think we really have to understand it to do something about it. We protect each other to the end. That's what we do. Nothing else matters beyond that."

She's right. Without Adam to explain things to me, I'm just choking on what I don't know. He'll explain things in time, but he needs to grieve for Evelyn. We will all need to grieve for her. For everyone we've lost.

If we couldn't respawn anymore, that meant that those who had already died wouldn't be coming back. Alistair, Jasmine, Evelyn. I would never see them again.

Deal with it later. We need to get home.

I kissed Eris on the head and stood, giving Raven a kiss too.

"Thank you."

"Always," she replied, her crimson eyes alight as she smiled at me.

"All right. Let's go home."

CHAPTER 32 - COMING STORM

"Just sit still," Wilson scolded me for what had to have been the fourth time that hour.

"Sorry, shoulder's numb. It feels weird," I said, shifting in the leather chair. It clung to my exposed back and crinkled every time I moved.

"We're almost done, you big baby. Just a few more minutes," he said as he continuously hammered the needle gently into my skin, pausing only to dip it into the small jars of ink on the wooden table beside us.

I stared out the window of Wilson's room. It was much the same as mine, though not as spartan. Wilson had numerous canvas paintings hanging around the room. Some of us, some of scenery around the world, and more than a few of a woman I'd never seen before. She was young, striking, but not beautiful. She had the same gray eyes as Wilson.

His bed was carved form the same wood mine was, though he'd requested a queen, rather than a king, and his wasn't a poster bed.

The sun hung high in the sky, and I squirmed again in my seat after another few minutes of silence. *Why is it a sword wound bothers me less than a handful of tiny needle pricks?* "It's not that it hurts, jackass. It's just uncomfortable."

He scoffed and switched needles, changing to one dipped in a soft white ink. "Well, you're the one who insisted you had to have a tattoo. Now, seriously. Don't make me restrain you. I swear, I've tattooed eighteen-year-old kids who took it better than you."

I laughed, and his hard expression softened.

"I know you don't like sitting still, Dur—Sam. But if you keep fidgeting, you'll make me slip, and trust me, you don't want to have a permanent testament to your inability to sit in a chair for a few hours like a normal human, do you?"

I held up my right hand, still not used to the color. "You forget. I'm not human anymore."

Wilson sighed and put down the needle, dabbing at my bleeding flesh with a white cloth. He held it up, the blood a pale reddish orange. "How can I forget when your blood is this color? I just hope Adam comes back soon."

"It's only been a week since Evelyn died. We all know what he's going through. He just needs time to process."

He looked up at the picture of the woman on the wall and sighed.

"Yeah, I know." Wilson shook his head and picked up the needle again. "Though why you decided to get a row of jasmine as your first tattoo is something I don't get."

I titled to look at them. The outline of six jasmine flowers attached to a stemmed rose from my bicep to my shoulder, with a few petals falling away toward my chest. It was beautiful, even though it was only half finished.

"To remember her by. Jasmine deserves to be remembered by someone other than her mother, and I made a promise to never forget her."

"I understand that, I do," he said between hammering. "But why her? Why not get a tattoo to remember Evelyn, someone you've known for years rather than getting one for a girl you knew for a few days?"

I held my hand up again and turned my palm to face me. I ran my thumb over the rough calluses that had formed over nearly two decades. I stared at the silver-white scar on the center of my palm and closed my fist. "I don't need a tattoo to remember Evelyn. I remember her every time I wield a sword. She's with me every time I face an enemy, and she'll be with me when I run my sword through Magnus's chest."

"And how are we supposed to go about this?"

I shrugged my shoulders and winced when Wilson picked up a clean needle and jammed it an inch deep into my forearm.

"Ow!"

"Sit still," he warned me again as he pulled the bloody needle free.

"Okay, by the nine kings of hell, I got it," I said and proceeded to imitate a statue as he finished working on the tattoo, "but to answer your question, I haven't the slightest clue as to how I'm supposed to go about doing this."

He snorted. "Well, it's just our lives on the line, no big deal. Seriously, though. You'll figure it out. You always do."

"Only after you've told me how wrong I am at least a dozen times before I figure it out."

"Which is exactly why I know you'll figure it out. With me backing you, you can't possibly lose," he said and bumped my arm with his.

We didn't speak after that, and another hour and a half, and he'd finished his art.

"Some of my best work," he said and slapped my shoulder.

It stung, but I shook it off and stood from the leather chair. I looked at my ink and had to admit, it was spectacular. "Thank you, Wilson," I said, holding out my hand.

He came over and pulled me into a quick hug before he stepped back and brushed his hands over his well-tailored vest. "Think nothing of it."

He handed me a jar of ointment and told me to apply it several times a day for the next two weeks, and I promised him that I would.

I thanked him again and left his room, heading back to mine.

The silence of an empty room met me as I opened the door and stepped inside. *Raven and Eris must still be training.*

As proud as I was of both of them, it was practically all they'd been doing since we'd gotten back. They trained with Yumiko most days, but I'd seen Gil slinking in a couple times to help them work on their combat skills. Since without Evelyn, I was the best hand to hand fighter in the guild, I trained Raven and Eris on close quarters combat, but neither of them fought with a sword, so I left their weapons training to those much more qualified to teach them than I.

Sitting in that chair for nearly two hours had made me restless, but Wilson had advised against taking a bath right after, telling me to wait until at least the morning, but as long as I didn't get my shoulder wet, I didn't think it would be an issue.

I went to the bathroom and shut the door firmly behind me. I dropped out of my linen trousers, but before I went and got in the bath, I went to the mirror, and like I'd done every time I was in front of a reflective surface, I stared at myself. At my golden eyes and too-pale skin.

Still can't get used to them. I look alien, like I'm a different person. I chuckled. *I am a different person. I can't even deny that anymore. Over a decade of being Durandahl, and in less than two months it's all come crumbling down.*

As I stared into eyes that weren't quite mine, I sighed. *I don't know who I am anymore.*

I'd spent so much time burying Sampson Acre that I couldn't quite remember what it felt like being him again. *Maybe that's for the best. Sampson Acre ran from his problems, and Durandahl buried them under too much alcohol and violence. Maybe I don't have to be one or the other anymore.*

Maybe I can just be Sam. The good and the bad together.

As I walked away from the mirror, I glanced at the placid water and decided maybe for once, I would heed Wilson's advice.

I climbed back into my pants and exited the steam-filled bath. My open balcony caught my attention, and I habitually poured a drink from my decanter and walked outside to lean against the stone railing.

I can't believe what my stats are right now. It's ridiculous.

Character Name: Durandahl

Level: 69

Exp: 3800/6900

Race: Demigod

Class: Hive Knight (Errant)

Reputation: Wanted Criminal

Bounty: 1300 Gold

Stats (-)

Strength: 100 (Max)

Sub-Stats (-)

Attack Damage: 50

Constitution: 100 (Max)

Sub-Stats (-)

Health: 25

Health Regen: 25

Durability: 85

Endurance: 100 (Max)

Sub-Stats (-)

Battle Fatigue: 50

Battle Fatigue Regen: 10

Agility: 50 (90)

Sub-Stats (-)

Attack Speed: 25

Movement Speed: 20

Wisdom: 25 (35)

Sub-Stats (-)
Mana: 20
Luck: 0 (30)
Charisma: 0 (10)

Errant Knight: +10 to all Main Stats (+15 within 20 meters of Hive Monarch)

Arachne's Blessing: +15 to Strength and Agility

Scorpius's Blessing: +15 to Constitution and Agility

I closed my interface and marveled at the view that I never got tired of looking at. It was hot, August was in full swing, and it let itself be known as sweat formed almost instantly as I stared over my castle's walls and out into the wide, green hills. The drink was cold in my hand, courtesy of the frost stones I'd dropped in there, but as I went to take a sip, I paused.

The familiar scent of whiskey burned deliciously in my nose, and my mouth watered as condensation dripped cool over my fingers. I wanted to drink it, wanted it very much. And that was the problem.

Magnus was right.

I pitched the entire glass over the edge in disgust and turned to go back inside as the glass shattered far below me.

I threw on a clean blue shirt and was about to go train with the girls. I opened the door and nearly walked into Adam as his fist raised to knock.

He froze, a half smile on his pale face as his dull golden eyes lit up with humor. "Well, we couldn't have timed that better if we tried."

"Adam!" I clapped him on the shoulders and gave him a huge bear hug.

"Okay, okay. I missed you too, buddy. Put me down!"

I released him and invited him in. He chuckled as he walked in and glanced around the room. "You know, you haven't changed the room at all since the last time I was in here, three years ago."

I shrugged and sat back on my bed. "What can I say, if it isn't broken, why fix it?"

"Fair enough," he said as the humor dropped from his eyes. *Damn, guess neither of us could keep it up for long.* "Where've you been? We were worried about you."

"Uh," he said and tugged on his ear, not looking at me. "I went to bury Jess."

"You went back to Magnus?"

Adam nodded. "Had to. I couldn't leave her there."

"What do you mean? Her body should've disappeared."

He shook his head and sighed. "The bodies of guardians don't fade, so hers stayed, as will mine and Nick's when the time comes."

"Where is she?"

"Machine City. Our old home. She liked it there, and no one will disturb her."

Adam stared out the window, his mind miles away. I went over to my nightstand and poured him a glass of whiskey. I handed it to him and poured one for myself.

"To Jessica," I said, raising my glass.

"To Jess."

We drank, and I sighed as the fire burned down my throat. It was delicious.

He handed me the glass, and I sat them back where they belonged. "I hate to ask while you're grieving, Adam, but we need to talk."

Adam sighed and nodded. "Yeah," he said, motioning me to follow as he walked out to the balcony. "I'm sure you have a lot of questions, and I'll do my best to answer them."

"Okay...by the nine kings of hell, where do I start?" I threw my hands up and once again caught sight of my skin. "Let's start with whatever the hell that crystal was Evelyn gave me?"

"I'll tell you what I know, but it's not much," he said, leaning on the railing. "They're called Shards of Divinity. Fragments of creation. Where they come from, what they can do, I don't know. But from what I've seen, they defy reality, or maybe they transcend it. I didn't get a chance to study them much before we entered the Ouroboros Project. Though I think I can say one thing for certain: I'm sure you've seen your character page, at what's written there.

"They're god-makers."

"Gods?"

He nodded. "And not like the ones we programmed to help watch over Nexus. Actual divinity."

"How did you get them?" I asked, my hands shaking.

"That's a very long story for another time. But I do know that Jess chose you to be her Shardbearer. She liked you, even if she didn't always show it."

I paused, letting my mind absorb what Adam had told me. It was insane, but with what I'd seen these past few weeks, anything was possible. *I never considered myself overly religious. Sure, I believed, but Earth's god abandoned us, left us to die by the hands of those monsters. But creating gods? That's crazy.*

"How would one go about creating a god?"

"Your guess is as good as mine," he said, shrugging. "The shards, they're drawn to each other, I assume the more you have, the stronger you become, but that's just a theory. There was no change when we combined our shards.

"Speaking of change, I know the whole pale skin, golden eyes look probably isn't your thing, so if you want to go back to your old appearance, all you have to do is concentrate on how you want yourself to look in your head and focus on it. Should do the trick."

I closed my eyes and let the warm breeze wick the sweat from my brow as I focused on who I wanted to look like, my old self, before I was given the mantle of Hive Knight, before the Aspect took control of my body and forced my body to change to its whims. I wanted to look like the old me.

After a solid minute of focus, a tug pulled at my chest, and a warmth spread throughout my body. When I opened my eyes, my regular tanned skin was back.

"There you go. Took you less than time than it took Jess and I the first time we tried it. We spent like an hour back to back trying…" He faded out and lapsed into silence.

"We'll pay Magnus back for what he did. He won't win." I patted Adam on the back, but I knew that nothing would help ease the hurt in his heart. I'd gone through it too many times myself, and nothing ever really helped.

"I appreciate it, Sam. But I thought you agreed with Magnus?"

"I did. Still do, I guess. But I won't let him kill Eris."

He turned and looked at me, his eyes so filled with sorrow that it hurt. "Even if it means sacrificing everyone else?"

I shook my head. That was the wrong way to look at it. "You said it yourself—we'll find another way."

Adam didn't answer right away. Instead, he stared out over the castle for a long moment. "I said that then too, the first time, that we'd find another way, and I ran out of time. If I'd just said yes to Nick, then Jess would still be alive."

"And Eris would be dead. So would I, and Raven too, probably. Jessica knew what she was doing, knew that she would die, and she still stood in the way so that we could get away. I wish more than anything she were still here, but I don't think there was a way for us all to escape."

"I know, but it doesn't make it hurt any less. I've got to go, Sam. We'll talk later about what to do...just not now, okay?"

"Yeah, take all the time you need."

He didn't respond, just walked out of the room without another word. I watched him leave and turned back to lean on the balcony, trying to figure out what to do and failing. *I hope Edna will have a plan, because I don't know how we're going to get out of this one.*

I didn't have a clue, and I really wanted another drink. I shook my head. *Let's go see what the girls are up to.*

***

I awoke with a groan at the shrill tone blaring in my ears, signaling an incoming call. My interface popped into existence without my command, and a single name appeared in front of me.

Miguel.

I hit decline and rolled over, Raven's pale back and backside pressed against me as I snuggled closer to her. On the other side me, Eris acted as the big spoon for both of us, and her scorching arms clung around my waist as her hot breath tickled my back.

Last night was...interesting. Yeah, that's one word for it.

Both Raven and Eris weren't quite ready to share a bed with me together, and to be honest with myself, I didn't know if I was ready for it either, but they'd subverted my expectations by taking turns while the other watched.

514

Once the initial awkwardness faded, it'd actually been fun but left me more exhausted than if I'd fought a hundred men.

Both of them know how to take it out of me, that's for sure. Though as they sandwiched me between them in their sleep, I argued that it wasn't the worst thing in the world.

I was about to wrap my arm around Raven and go back to sleep when my interface chimed again. It was Miguel again. *I swear to the gods if someone isn't dead, I'll kill him.*

I hit accept. "This better not be about that job, Miguel."

"Long live the Shadow King."

I blew out a breath. *Shit.* "I'll be there in a few hours."

The call went dead.

I groaned and sat up. Eris clung to me and partially came with me before I turned and laid her head on my chest. She mumbled something in her sleep and scooted over, draping her naked body over me and snuggled closer to me.

"C'mon, love, time to get up."

Light chuckling whispered next to my ear, and I turned as Raven leaned in, pressing her lips to mine in a good morning kiss, her ample bust teasing my arm as her pink nipples awoke from the cold.

"Good morning, darling," she said as she pulled back and looked down at Eris. "She's too cute when she's sleeping."

"That she is." *I told Miguel a few hours. A minute or two won't hurt anything.* Raven scooted closer to me, her thighs holding my calf hostage as she kissed the side of my neck.

"Who called?"

"Miguel, a distributer of sorts. I thought he was calling about a job he keeps bugging me about, but its bad business. We really need to get going."

"Get going as in right now or…can it wait a few minutes?" she purred in my ear.

I wound my hand over her cheek and brought her in close for a kiss. Her mouth parted, and her tongue met mine in a gentle embrace as her nails dug into my back. I took her lip between my teeth and bit down, drawing a single bead of blood that swirled iron-red over her lips.

"Harder," she moaned.

I bit down just a little harder, savoring her blood as it washed over my tongue. Raven's hand trailed over my chest and down my obliques as she slowly wrapped her hands around my length.

Before she could do anything with her hand, something poked my side, and I turned over to find Eris awake, sitting on her knees with one arm folded under her chest, the brown of her nipples barely covered, while her right hand jabbed into my side.

"No fair. You two started without me," she said, frowning, almost pouting.

Raven peered around me, took one look at Eris's pout, and burst out laughing. A full-bellied laugh that had her nearly rolling on the bed, shaking.

I tried to hold it in, but Raven set me off and I joined her in laughter.

All the while, Eris stared at us with the same expression on her face, which just set us off again when we stood up.

When I came to the second time, I pulled Eris in for a kiss because her face got so red, I thought she'd burst. Her frosty eyes quickly thawed after our lips touched. "Good morning, love."

"Good morning, my bonded," she said and looked around me to Raven. "Good morning, dear."

"Same to you, sunflower," Raven said to Eris, then turned to me. "So, I'm guessing we're not going to pick up where we left off?"

"'Fraid not. We've got places to be, loves. Let's get ready."

We dressed and left the castle in under an hour. I wasn't sure what to expect with Miguel, but he'd given the code that was designated critical emergency, so it had to be big.

It took just under four hours to fly to the outskirts of Arroyo and walk into town. It was quiet this afternoon, no ships docked at port, so most of the town was void of life. Our walk to the Gray Cask was uneventful. The worn stone building was quiet as we approached, and when we stepped down the steps into the bar itself, we were met with absolute silence.

The Cask was never closed, never this empty. It unnerved me so much that I immediately drew my sword and stepped in. The multitude of wooden tables were empty, their chairs on top of them. The bartender was nowhere to found, and only one occupant sat silent at the bar, nursing a bottle of brandy.

Miguel's fancy black shirt and pants were wrinkled, his oil-slick hair disheveled, and his rich brown skin was pallid, like he'd had hadn't slept.

He took a sip of his drink and waved me down. "Put your sword away, Duran. No one's here."

"The Cask never closes."

"It does today, kiddo. Maybe never to open again."

I took another look around, and my instincts told me that Miguel was telling me the truth, so I sheathed my sword and stepped fully into the bar. Eris and Raven fell in behind me, and Miguel looked from me to them and dismissed them, turning to face me.

"Take whatever you want from the bar, my treat."

"I'm good—"

"Thank you, Miguel. Sam speaks highly of you," Raven said as she meandered behind the bar and grabbed a bottle of top shelf whiskey.

He let out a bark of laughter. "You're a terrible liar, but I appreciate the sentiment," he said, brushing his fingers through his hair. "Sam, huh? You look like a Sam."

I shrugged. "What's this about?"

"It's bad. I got the most recent batch of mushrooms, the Gloom, from your mage and started selling them. Things were going well; people couldn't get enough of them, and we raked in a mountain of gold."

"So what's the issue?"

"We fucked up, both of us." Miguel threw his hands up. "From what your mage told me, he didn't have time to test the mushrooms, and I didn't vet them before I started selling them."

"Oh shit, don't tell me—"

"They're not poisonous or anything, but they are incredibly addictive, and people can easily overdose from them."

"So were the Gloom Shrooms, what's the difference?"

"The Gloom never killed one of the Compass Kings' sons."

"Godsdamn it, who?"

Miguel sighed and downed his brandy while I waited for an answer. "Fabian Clark."

"Gerrard Clark's only son. Fuck."

"Right," he said, pouring him another drink. "No one cares when it's a nobody, but soon as someone important dies, everyone is up in arms."

I sighed and absentmindedly reached for the bottle of whiskey next to Raven. She moved it just as my fingers brushed it, and my hand closed around empty air. She smiled at me and placed her hand over mine. "You told me you're trying to quit."

"Thanks," I said and went back to the task at hand. "Okay, so what's the backlash? We can handle the vengeance of one king."

Miguel stood up suddenly, his wooden barstool tipping back and clacking against the uneven stone floor. "You don't get it. It's not just one king. It's all of them, and they brought in Kincaid, too."

My blood ran cold. "By the nine kings of hell."

"You understand now?"

"We can't take on the Merchants Guild."

"We flew in their faces too long; you know as well as I how swift and terrible their retribution will be."

"How bad is the fallout?"

Miguel paused, throwing his empty tumbler at the rack of liquor behind the bar. Glass crashed and spilled amber over the wood to drip to the stone.

"Bad. Hasn't gone out yet, but it's only a matter of days. Merchants Guild put a bounty on the Gloom Knights."

"How much."

"Quarter million per head."

My heart dropped. *We're so, so screwed.*

Footsteps clacked sharply on the stone outside, and there was a brief knock at the door.

"And a hundred thousand for mine." Miguel nodded to me and snagged the bottle of whiskey on the counter, tipping it back. "While this is the main reason why I called you here, we have another matter to discuss," he said as he shuffled over to the door.

I threw my hands up. "If this is about that job, I think we have too many things going on to worry about that right now," I replied as the door opened.

"Not even for a friend?" a rich, feminine voice asked.

I turned as she strolled into the Cask.

She was tall, just under six feet, with refined features and beautiful pale skin without a single freckle to mar her ivory perfection. Her flowing scarlet hair shimmered like flames alight as she walked in. Her emerald eyes lit up in delight as she smiled at me with her ruby lips.

"I know you," I said. "At the Auction House. Morgan, right?"

She just kept up her smile before looking past me. "I'm glad to see your bonded was returned safe and sound."

I glanced over at Eris, but she wasn't looking at me; her eyes were transfixed on Morgan. She rose from her seat in an instant and dropped to her knee, bowing her head low. I tapped her on the shoulder.

"What are you doing?"

"What are *you* doing? Bow!"

Morgan chuckled and went to Eris, kneeling and taking her chin in hand. "Raise your head, child. And don't fault your bond mate. He doesn't have your lovely eyes."

She rose and glanced at me. "I should formally introduce myself. My name is Morrigan."

"The Morrigan? Goddess of demi-humans?"

"I like Morgan better, but yes."

I snorted. "What even is my life anymore?" I looked back at Miguel, whose eyes were probably as wide as mine, and raised an eyebrow.

"Don't look at me, kiddo. I didn't know."

Whatever. "Okay," I said and turned to face Morgan. "What does a goddess need from me?"

Morgan stared me down for a moment before she shook her head slightly and bared her teeth in a ferocious smile.

"The gods and I have a request to make of you."

End of Book Two

AUTHOR'S NOTE

Thank you for reading my book!

Let me thank you for getting this far. It truly means the world to me that you have not only picked up and read the first book, but the sequel as well (unless you're one of those weirdos who read books out of order). If you enjoyed what you read (or hated), please leave me a review. They are the lifeblood of an author and are just as important as you picking up the book in the first place. I'm grateful regardless, but taking two minutes to leave a small written review or even just a rating since Amazon allows those now, which takes only seconds, means everything to us.

Also, if you read this far, then you probably have a few questions about the supernatural aspect of this novel. Have no fear, all will be explained in due time, but I would like to formally welcome you to my universe, my Shardverse.

Thank you for giving my work a chance —Grayson

ABOUT THE AUTHOR

Grayson Sinclair loves books, has loved them since he was a child. Reading has always been a passion of his, even when he really should have been focused on other things, like school. The worlds in books were always more magical and exciting than anything real life could offer, and he hopes a few of you will get lost in his worlds for a short time.

His website is Graysinclair.com, or you can find him on Facebook, Twitter, and Reddit.

While you wait for the next book in the Trinity of the Hive series, why don't you check out the short story by Grayson set in the same universe? **Swords of Legend: In Remembrance**.

ABOUT THE PUBLISHER

Starlit Publishing is wholly owned and operated by Tao Wong. It is a science fiction and fantasy publisher focused on the LitRPG & cultivation genres. Their focus is on promoting new, upcoming authors in the genre whose writing challenges the existing stereotypes while giving a rip-roaring good read.

For more information on Starlit Publishing, visit their website!

You can also join Starlit Publishing's mailing list to learn of new, exciting authors and book releases, including **Grayson Sinclair's next book**!

For more great information about LitRPG series, check out the Facebook groups:
- GameLit Society
- LitRPG Books

THE LITRPG GUILDMASTERS

Who we are: The LitRPG Guildmasters is a group of dedicated LitRPG and Gamelit authors trying to spread the word of our favorite genres. By working together and introducing new people to amazing books we hope to expand the genres that we love. Sign up to our Newsletter to get a **free book** and follow us on Facebook to keep up to date on our latest work. If you love LitRPG check out the LitRPG Guild Website, our Discord server, and the LitRPG Adventurers Guild Facebook Group.

LitRPG Guildmasters Titles:

Altered Realms: Ascension by B.F. Rockriver

Brightblade by Jez Cajiao

Ethria: The Pioneer by Aaron Holloway

Grim Beginnings: The Ashen Plane by Maxwell Farmer

Primeverse by R.K. Billiau

Shattered Sword by TJ Reynolds

Tower of Gates: Hack by Paul Bellow

Cipher's Quest by Tim Kaiver

Watcher's Test by Sean Oswald

Star Divers by Stephen Landry

Fragment of Divinity by Jamey Sultan

Hive Knight by Grayson Sinclair

Condition Evolution by Kevin Sinclair

To learn more about LitRPG, talk to authors including myself, and just have an awesome time, please join the LitRPG Group!

Made in the USA
Middletown, DE
02 November 2021